# CHRISTMAS
## Family Rescue

## LAURA SCOTT
## MAGGIE K. BLACK

## MILLS & BOON

CHRISTMAS FAMILY RESCUE © 2024 by Harlequin Books S.A.

SOLDIER'S CHRISTMAS SECRETS
© 2019 by Laura Iding
Australian Copyright 2019
New Zealand Copyright 2019

First Published 2019
First Australian Paperback Edition 2024
ISBN 978 1 038 93694 3

CHRISTMAS WITNESS CONSPIRACY
© 2020 by Mags Storey
Australian Copyright 2020
New Zealand Copyright 2020

First Published 2020
First Australian Paperback Edition 2024
ISBN 978 1 038 93694 3

This is a work of fiction. Names, characters, places, and incidents are either the
product of the author's imagination or are used fictitiously, and any resemblance
to actual persons, living or dead, business establishments, events, or locales is
entirely coincidental.

MIX
Paper | Supporting
responsible forestry
FSC® C001695

Published by
Mills & Boon
An imprint of Harlequin Enterprises (Australia) Pty Limited
(ABN 47 001 180 918), a subsidiary of HarperCollins
Publishers Australia Pty Limited (ABN 36 009 913 517)
Level 19, 201 Elizabeth Street
SYDNEY NSW 2000
AUSTRALIA

® and ™ (apart from those relating to FSC®) are trademarks of Harlequin
Enterprises (Australia) Pty Limited or its corporate affiliates. Trademarks indicated
with ® are registered in Australia, New Zealand and in other countries.
Contact admin_legal@Harlequin.ca for details.

Printed and bound in Australia by McPherson's Printing Group

# CONTENTS

# Soldier's Christmas Secrets

## *Laura Scott*

**Laura Scott** is a nurse by day and an author by night. She has always loved romance and read faith-based books by Grace Livingston Hill in her teenage years. She's thrilled to have published over twenty-five books for Love Inspired Suspense. She has two adult children and lives in Milwaukee, Wisconsin, with her husband of over thirty years.  Please visit Laura at laurascottbooks.com, as she loves to hear from her readers.

## Books by Laura Scott

### *Justice Seekers*
*Soldier's Christmas Secrets*

### *Callahan Confidential*
*Shielding His Christmas Witness*
*The Only Witness*
*Christmas Amnesia*
*Shattered Lullaby*
*Primary Suspect*
*Protecting His Secret Son*

### *True Blue K-9 Unit*
*Blind Trust*

### *Military K-9 Unit*
*Battle Tested*
*Military K-9 Unit Christmas*
"Yuletide Target"

Visit the Author Profile page at millsandboon.com.au for more titles.

Be strong and of a good courage, fear not, nor be afraid of them: for the Lord thy God, he it is that doth go with thee; he will not fail thee, nor forsake thee.
*–Deuteronomy* 31:6

This book is dedicated to Michael Christman, a man who has bravely faced cancer only to come out stronger within his faith. This book is for you.

# ONE

Hawk Jacobson parked his SUV and moved silently through the dark, cold December night, automatically raking his gaze over the area searching for a possible threat. As a private investigator, he didn't have set hours, and tonight he was returning home later than usual.

After entering his house, he didn't bother turning his lights on as he made his way through the interior. Hawk paused near the side window, the one overlooking Jillian's home. Dark windows outlined by bright Christmas lights indicated his neighbor, Jillian Wade, and her young daughter, Lizzy, had retired for the night.

Just as he was about to step back from the window, he saw two men, dressed in black from head to toe, ski masks covering their faces and guns held at the ready in their hands, moving silently through the night and heading straight for Jillian's house. *No!* Hawk sprang into action. Armed with a knife and a gun, yet hoping not to use either, he silently let himself out of his house. Picking the second man who was still standing on the driveway as his target, he stealthily approached from behind. With surprise on his side, he took him down, hitting him in the back of the head and rendering him unconscious. With one hostile out of commission, he went searching for the other.

The front door of Jillian's house was ajar, and he hated knowing the guy had breached her personal space. Years of military training enabled Hawk to move silently down the hall. The gunman was hovering between the two bedroom doorways, as if unsure which one to try first. Indecision was his enemy. Hawk grabbed him from behind, covered the guy's mouth and took him roughly to the ground and held his gun at his temple.

"Who sent you?" Hawk asked in a harsh whisper. "Why are you here?"

The man's eyes, which Hawk could see from the round openings of the ski mask, showed no emotion. The hostile didn't make a sound, apparently too well-trained to talk. Hawk was about to knock the guy unconscious when a slight movement caught his eye. The door to the second bedroom was open a crack and he saw Lizzy's frightened face peering out at him.

He froze, wishing more than anything that the little girl didn't look so terrified. Was she afraid of the gun? Probably, but he couldn't risk hiding it from her. "It's okay," he called softly. "It's me. Hawk."

She quickly closed the door. With a frustrated sigh, Hawk pressed on the man's twin carotid arteries to put him to sleep, making sure he was unconscious but not dead. He took a moment to lift the ski mask, but the man's face wasn't familiar. Hawk didn't recognize him. Leaving him be, Hawk rose to his feet and lightly rapped on Jillian's door. "Jillian? It's Hawk. I'm coming in."

"Hawk?" Jillian's voice was sleepy. "What are you doing here?"

Entering her room felt wrong, but there wasn't a moment to waste. The two hostiles wouldn't stay unconscious forever. "I stopped two guys from trying to kill you. Get up. We need to leave."

"What are you talking about?" She sounded grumpy. "What two men? I can't leave. Lizzy's asleep."

"No, she's not. I just saw her. One man is on the driveway near the front door, the other is just outside your room. Hurry. I'll get Lizzy while you throw some stuff together. But don't pack like this is a vacation, we're traveling light."

"But…"

Hawk was done talking. He turned and made his way to Lizzy's room, stepping carefully over the body on the floor. He pressed again on the guy's neck to give them more time, then reached for the door of the second bedroom and opened it. "Lizzy? It's Hawk. I know you're scared, but you and your mom need to come with me, okay?"

Lizzy didn't answer. Not that he really expected her to. He stood for a moment, sweeping his gaze over the area. Lizzy's bed was empty. There was a small desk, a dollhouse, a closet and dresser. She must be hiding in fear, likely in the closet or under the bed.

The bed. He dropped to his hands and knees, pressed his cheek to the floor. "Lizzy, your mom is waiting for us. We need to go."

A muffled sob was the only sound she uttered.

His heart squeezed painfully in his chest, but he forced himself to ignore it. There was no time to waste. He reached under the twin bed, found her arm and tugged. She resisted, but the little girl was no match for him. He gently pulled her out and gathered her stiff body into his arms. She clutched a tattered brown teddy bear against her pink fleece footie pajamas, like a shield.

"I'm sorry, Lizzy. But we have to go." He carried her to the next room, where a grim-faced Jillian was dressed in jeans and a sweatshirt, tossing items into an overnight duffel bag.

"Lizzy." She held out her arms for her daughter and Lizzy practically jumped to get away from him, grabbing onto her mother and clinging like a baby monkey.

He told himself not to take it personally as he slung the duffel over his shoulder and cupped Jillian's elbow in his hand. "Grab coats for you and Lizzy. We'll take my car."

"I'm not sure—" She stopped abruptly when she saw the man lying in the hallway. "Who? What? Oh my—" She looked as if she might scream, so he cut her off.

"Later. We need to be quiet in case there are others nearby." Hawk steered her around the body. The man groaned, indicating they were running out of time.

In the kitchen, Jillian snagged her purse from the counter. They paused long enough to grab winter gear, especially for Lizzy. There hadn't been time to change her out of her pajamas, but that didn't stop Jillian from putting winter boots on her daughter. Hawk waited impatiently, desperate to get them out of the house.

Outside, the second man remained unmoving. Hawk's SUV was in the driveway, where he'd left it. But Jillian dug in her heels, resisting him much like her daughter.

"Wait. Where are we going? Shouldn't we call the police? I don't understand…"

"Not now," he said forcefully. "We'll talk later."

"Fine, but I'm not going without Lizzy's car seat."

Giving in was easier than arguing. "Give me your keys, then get into the SUV."

Thankfully she did as she was told. He grabbed the child seat out of Jillian's rusted sedan and hurried over to his vehicle. Within minutes he had the car seat strapped in and Lizzy plunked inside. The little girl's crying shredded him.

After sliding in behind the wheel, he wasted no time in backing out of the driveway. Keeping an eye on Jillian's house in the rearview mirror as he drove away, he caught a fleeting glimpse of a black-clad man staggering out through the front door, holding the ski mask in his hand.

Fearing more hostiles on the way, Hawk hit the gas, speeding as fast as he dared through the slick, snow-covered streets of their Brookland, Wisconsin, neighborhood, until he reached Highway 18. Then he headed west toward the interstate.

"I don't understand," Jillian said. "What's going on? Who were those men?"

He glanced over at her. "I don't know. But they were armed and dangerous."

"Why did they come after me?" Jillian's voice sounded shaky and confused. He had to give her credit for not falling apart. She lifted a hand to her long, dark-red hair, a gold wedding band on the third finger of her left hand glinting in the moonlight.

"Could they have been looking for your husband?"

"My husband is dead," she said in a flat tone.

"Lizzy's father?"

She glared at him with clear exasperation. "Weren't you listening? My husband, Lizzy's father, is dead. James was killed in Afghanistan a few years ago."

Hawk went perfectly still, his gaze locked on the highway stretching out before him. He wanted to tell Jillian that he was really James—and that he wasn't dead. That he didn't die in Afghanistan but almost had from a small plane crash that had killed his three teammates and their pilot, deep in the Appalachian Mountains. That despite the fact that he looked completely different thanks to the horrible facial fractures and scars he now wore on his face, he was right here, next to her. But the words remained locked in his throat.

Two hostiles. Professional hit men. No way they had shown up just to take out Jillian or Lizzy.

They'd come for him.

To finish the job of killing him.

Jillian gripped the armrest with such force her fingertips went numb. Two men wearing ski masks and carrying guns had come to her house! She couldn't comprehend what was happening—it was all so surreal. If she hadn't seen them for herself, one lying in the hallway and the other on the snow-covered ground, she would have thought Hawk had lost his mind.

Lizzy's crying increased in volume.

"It's okay, Lizzy." She reached back to stroke her daughter's knee. The four-year-old was obviously terrified. "We're fine, see? Everything is just fine. Mr. Hawk has come to save us, isn't that nice? We're going to be all right."

It took a while, but her daughter's sobs slowly quieted. As Jillian had hoped, the little girl began to nod off, still clutching the teddy bear close. Car rides had that effect on her.

Jillian glanced at Hawk. Her strong, silent, scarred yet kind neighbor who didn't say much but was always there to lend a hand. At times it was as if he knew what she needed done before she did. She would come home from work to find her lawn had been mowed or a broken shutter repaired. Just that morning he'd gotten up early to shovel her driveway so that it was clear before she needed to head to work, the last day of school before Christmas break. It was odd yet sweet. Hawk wasn't one for small talk, either. He would simply lift a hand to acknowledge her, and that was all.

Frankly they'd spoken more tonight than they had in the five months she'd known him.

She was grateful he was there to help her now. She noticed Hawk kept his eyes on the road and made several turns, getting off the interstate, taking side streets and then getting back on. He was obviously taking care to be sure they weren't followed.

Not once since he'd moved in next door had he ever made her feel uncomfortable. He'd never indicated he was interested in anything other than being neighborly. Maybe because he assumed she was married.

Her gaze dropped to the gold wedding band her deceased husband had given to her five years ago. She'd taken the diamond engagement ring off but not the plain band. She wasn't sure why. James had been the love of her life, but barely a year after they'd married he was deployed to Afghanistan. Two months after he'd gotten there, he'd been sent off on some secret mission that he couldn't talk about. One that had ultimately killed him.

James had never known about Lizzy. She hadn't known about her pregnancy until after he'd died. She'd never understood why God had taken James from her so quickly, and she had stopped attending church after his death for several months. When she'd moved here to be closer to her mother, she'd found her faith and comfort in the church again.

"Jillian?"

"Huh?" She pulled away from her sorrowful thoughts. "I'm sorry, what did you say?"

"I have a cabin in the north woods. I'd like to take you and Lizzy there until we can figure out what's going on."

"A cabin?" She wasn't sure why the news surprised her. In the months she'd known Hawk, he'd been home at odd hours. Sometimes leaving before she did, and at other times, remaining at home as she left for school. In fact she'd often wondered exactly what he did for work but hadn't wanted to pry. From the scar on his face, she thought he might be on disability or something. He knew she was a second grade school teacher at Brookland Elementary, but only because she'd offered the information.

"I don't want you to feel uncomfortable with me," he went on. "There are two bedrooms, a small kitchen and bathroom with indoor plumbing. It will be safer there than at a motel."

"Safer how? I still can't figure out why those two men came to find me in the first place. I'm a teacher. Why would anyone want to hurt me?"

"I know. I'm sorry."

She let out a sigh. None of this was his fault. "Your cabin sounds fine. But shouldn't we call the police?"

"Not yet."

She frowned. "Why not?"

"By the time the police arrive, the two gunmen will be long gone. I only temporarily incapacitated them, I didn't kill them.

There's no real proof of what happened—it would be our word against no one. I need to do a little digging before we call the authorities."

She wasn't sure she understood his rationale, but the idea that the gunmen might already be gone bothered her. She wished she'd thought to take a picture with her cell phone, especially of the guy lying on the floor outside her bedroom.

Silence stretched between them. Now that Lizzy was asleep, her thoughts raced. One gunman had gotten all the way inside her house. How was it that she hadn't heard anything? She was normally an extremely light sleeper.

And how had Hawk gotten there in time to prevent the gunmen from hurting her? The fact that he'd taken out two gunmen without making a sound should have scared her to death.

But she felt safe. Ironic, since she didn't even know Hawk's last name or what he did for a living.

"Hawk—is that your real name?"

"Yes." He cleared his throat. "Hawk Jacobson."

She nodded, rolling the name around in her mind. "I want to thank you. For coming over to save us."

He was silent for a long moment. "I'm just glad I was able to get to you and Lizzy in time."

"Me, too." She shivered and rubbed her hands together. "How far is the cabin?"

"Thirty minutes." He glanced at her, his gaze impossible to read in the darkness. "Try to get some rest."

She shook her head, knowing sleep would be impossible. "Do you think this could be related to one of my students? Like maybe one of the kids' parents is into something illegal? I just can't figure out what else it could be."

"Anything is possible." Hawk's voice was husky and a bit hoarse, something she hadn't noticed before now. As if he might have a sore throat. "When we get to the cabin you can make a list of possible suspects."

"They're students, not suspects." The words were sharp and

she winced, knowing she was taking her frustration out on Hawk. "Besides, I think the police should be the one to search for the men responsible."

Another brief pause before Hawk spoke. "I'm a private investigator and I have friends who are cops in the Milwaukee Police Department. I need you to trust my judgment on this. Give me a little time to figure out what's going on."

Hawk Jacobson. Private Investigator. Friends who were cops. That was a whole lot more than she'd known about him an hour ago.

"Okay," she reluctantly agreed.

The rest of the car ride was silent. Hawk exited the freeway and took a curvy highway heading northwest. Then he pulled off on the side of the road and shut down the vehicle.

"I need to go in on foot, make sure the place is safe," he told her. He took a gun out of his side holster and held it out to her. "Stay here. If anyone approaches, I want you to shoot first and ask questions later."

She recoiled from the weapon as if it were a venomous snake. "I'm not touching that thing." She glanced at Lizzy. "We're better off without it."

Hawk's lips tightened, giving her the impression he wasn't happy. But he so rarely revealed any emotion that she thought she may have misinterpreted it. He gently placed the weapon in her lap. "You'll use it if your life or Lizzy's is threatened."

Without waiting for her to respond, he slipped out of the car and shut the door behind him.

She watched him round the front of the SUV and head into the woods. One minute he was there, the next he was gone, somehow without leaving obvious boot prints in the snow behind. The man moved with incredible silence, making her wonder where he'd learned such a skill.

The service? Had Hawk spent time in the military the way James had? Yet if that was the case, why was he working as a private investigator? Why not join a police force?

She shook her head. This insatiable curiosity about her neighbor wasn't healthy. Hawk's personal decisions were not any of her business. She wasn't interested in anything beyond friendship.

Ignoring the gun in her lap, she twisted the wedding band on her finger, thinking about James. How much she missed him. How he was everything she could have asked for in a husband and how he would have been an amazing father to Lizzy.

Then she thought about Hawk. Who was here, now. Who had not only helped her with house maintenance without being asked but was determined to keep her and Lizzy safe.

She slipped the ring off, and then, besieged by a rush of guilt, pushed it back on. Staring out through the windshield, she wondered how long it would take Hawk to check out the cabin. This sitting in the darkness, waiting, was getting on her nerves.

She heard a noise and froze. Then she did something she never thought she'd do. She picked up the gun. It felt heavy and cold in her hand and she had to wrap both her hands around the handle to keep it steady.

Another rustle and she instinctively knew the sound wasn't from Hawk returning. The man was too quiet to cause this much noise. She tightened her grip on the gun, sweeping her gaze from the windshield to the passenger-side window, searching for anything amiss.

Two deer walked out from the woods. They stopped, looked at her with glassy eyes and then gracefully leaped and ran across the street right in front of the SUV.

She let out her breath in a whoosh. Deer. A doe and her fawn. Not men wearing ski masks.

Yet she didn't release her grip on the gun.

Five minutes later, she noticed a dark shadow stepping out of the woods. She tightened her grip on the weapon but within a few seconds recognized the shadow as Hawk. The moonlight on his face made it easy to see his scar.

He quietly approached the car, nodding an acknowledgement

when he caught her looking at him. He came around and slid into the driver's seat.

"It's clear."

She held out the weapon. "Take this. I don't want it."

He took the gun and pushed it back into its holster. He drove a quarter mile down the road and turned into a gravel driveway.

The cabin was about a hundred yards in, nicely surrounded by trees. He pulled to a stop and then climbed out. "Do you want me to carry Lizzy?"

"I'll get her. She might cry if she wakes up to a stranger."

He nodded, grabbed the duffel and went over to hold the door. A dusting of snow clung to her boots, so she kicked the lower doorjamb to clear them before going inside. Lizzy snuggled against her chest as Jillian carried her across the living room. She hesitated, glancing at Hawk questioningly.

"There are twin beds in this room." He opened the door to the right of what looked to be a bathroom. "The other room is off the kitchen."

"Thanks." She went inside and gently set Lizzy on the twin bed closest to the door. After removing her winter coat and boots, she tucked her daughter into the sleeping bag on top of the bed. She straightened and turned to find Hawk standing close.

Too close.

In the darkness she couldn't see his face very clearly, but she had often wondered about the deep scar he carried along his left cheek. Catching a whiff of his aftershave, she found her pulse kicking up and her knees going weak.

It was the same brand James used to buy.

"Excuse me." Moving abruptly, she ducked around him and left the bedroom. Her heart was pounding erratically and for a moment she feared she was losing her mind.

In that brief instant, she'd thought the man standing beside her was James. Same height, same weight, same aftershave.

Impossible. James was dead. This was nothing more than her

overactive imagination playing tricks on her. Hormones reacting to a familiar scent.

She wasn't interested in a relationship with Hawk.

Yet for the moment, her life and Lizzy's depended on him. On his strength and ability to keep them both safe from harm.

# TWO

Battling guilt, Hawk silently followed Jillian into the living room and began making a fire in the wood-burning stove to heat up the cabin. He hadn't meant to frighten her, but given the way she'd bolted out of the room, he knew he must have. He'd worked hard over the past several months to remain nonthreatening. To provide help without getting too close.

But discovering Lizzy was his daughter had changed things. He'd wanted to peer down at her tiny face while she slept. He'd wanted the right to bend down to kiss her forehead and whisper good-night.

Unfortunately, his life, the life he should have had, remained far out of reach. Maybe forever.

Not that it should matter. There were more important things to worry about at the moment. Like who'd sent professional assassins to Jillian's home. To kidnap them? Or kill them? Kidnapping he could understand, because it would be a way to use Jillian and Lizzy as leverage against him. But killing them made no sense.

It occurred to him that if his real identity had been uncovered, then the assassins would have come directly to his house, not Jillian's. Which meant his current identity was safe.

For now.

Yet he knew his recent probing into Rick Barton's past had not gone unnoticed. Senator Barton was a powerful man in Washington, DC, but very few knew the truth about how Barton had climbed the ranks. Hawk must have gotten close enough to discover certain information about Barton to trip someone's suspicions.

Almost two years had passed since he'd begun to remember his past, yet it also felt as if it had only happened yesterday. His memory had more holes in it than Swiss cheese. He hadn't even remembered Jillian right away. Memories and images had come to him in bits and pieces.

He was the only special ops soldier who knew the truth about what happened in Afghanistan, and even then, he didn't have a good memory to guide him. The other members of his team who'd been with him that fateful day were gone. Powerful men had tried to silence him once. They wouldn't hesitate to do it again. It was up to him to expose the truth.

Too bad he had no idea whom he could trust.

When he finished with the fire, he stood. "I'll make coffee."

Hawk went into the kitchen and opened the cabinet that housed the coffee maker. He filled the carafe with water and added scoops of coffee from the can he kept in the freezer. As the coffee dripped, he did a quick mental inventory of his house back in Brookland. He had no doubt that at some point the professional hit men would go back to the scene of their failure, eventually identifying him as the one who'd helped Jillian and Lizzy escape.

They wouldn't find anything personal at his place. He didn't have a home office, preferring, instead, to work in the small space he rented in the strip mall not far from where he lived. The only information he kept at his office was related to his clients. All of his personal paperwork, most of which had been expertly forged two years ago, was kept in a safe deposit box at the bank.

For years, he'd thought his secret was safe. Until now. How long before the hit men put two and two together to figure out that Hawk Jacobson was really James Wade?

Based on the extensive governmental resources he believed Barton had at his disposal? Not long.

Feeling grim, he realized they'd be forced to move locations first thing in the morning. And go where? He had no clue.

"I can't drink coffee this late," Jillian said. He glanced over to find her standing on the other side of the room, her arms crossed over her chest as if she didn't dare get too close. "But I think we need to call the police. Now. Tonight."

He didn't answer, mostly because he wasn't sure what to say. He wanted, needed to tell her the truth, but this didn't seem like the proper time or place.

She wouldn't appreciate his view that going to the authorities could very well be like stepping on a rotten log, allowing professional hit men to pour out like termites.

"Calling the police is what normal people do," Jillian insisted. "Just because you happen to be a private investigator, it doesn't mean we shouldn't let the authorities know that two men came into my house with weapons with the intent to kill me."

"Actually, we don't really know what they intended to do."

She scowled. "I'm pretty sure they didn't intend to play nice with their guns."

It was a good point. He decided to probe further. "Does the name Senator Barton mean anything to you?"

She blinked in confusion. "Senator Rick Barton? Not really. I mean, I know he sits on a committee related to the Department of Defense, but I can't even tell you what state he's from or what he looks like."

"He sits on the Armed Services Committee," Hawk corrected. "He's a senator from Virginia and happens to be good friends with Todd Hayes, the current Secretary of Defense." He waited for some sort of recognition to dawn in her eyes, but she only shrugged.

"Yeah, okay. That sounds right. I'm not totally up on all the players in our government, but whatever. I don't see what either of those guys has to do with your decision to postpone calling the police."

"Powerful people in high places can convince the cops to turn a blind eye to what might be happening under their nose." He hesitated, the holes in his memory making it difficult to say anything with certainty. All he remembered was seeing Major Rick Barton deep in the hills where he wasn't supposed to be. He sensed there was more but couldn't bring the fragments of his memory together into a full picture.

Now she looked annoyed. "Oh, come on—" She abruptly cut off what she was about to say when Lizzy began to cry.

"Mommy! Mommy! Bad mans are coming to get me!"

Jillian spun on her heel and charged into the bedroom. Hawk stayed where he was, unwilling to add to Lizzy's frightened state. He knew she'd watched him holding a gun on one of the intruders and was reliving that scary moment in her nightmares.

He poured himself a cup of coffee and sat down at the kitchen table. He needed to think. To understand what was going on so he could plan his next steps. A good soldier always had at least one backup plan.

Several things bothered him. Why had Barton decided to send hit men after Jillian tonight? The fact that James Wade had married her five years ago wasn't a secret. The army knew about Jillian, they'd provided her benefits while he was overseas, and he assumed they'd provided death benefits after he'd been pronounced dead, despite how they'd obviously never found his body.

So why now?

And why not wait until the dead of night rather than 10:30 p.m.? The two guys had been professionals, but they were clearly not prepared to face an opponent like Hawk—someone with equal or better training than they had. Whoever provided the intel must have mentioned they were facing a grade school teacher and a four-year-old child. Not a soldier.

The burn of anger at the thought of those two men getting their hands on Jillian and Lizzy was difficult to ignore. But anger, much like indecision, was the enemy.

He took a deep breath and let it out, slowly. He toyed with the idea of calling Mike Callahan, a former private investigator he'd once worked with. Mike had recently gotten married and had taken a position with the sheriff's department. Mike owed him a favor, and Hawk could easily collect. Not that he'd really have to use the favor as leverage. Hawk knew that Mike, or any of the Callahan siblings, would help him out, no questions asked. That was the type of family they were. The Callahans had welcomed him into their home and made him feel like he was one of them.

Still, he preferred to work alone. At least for now. But he wouldn't risk any harm coming to Jillian or Lizzy.

What he really wanted to do was to stash Jillian and Lizzy someplace safe while he continued working the case. Should he send her to stay with the Callahans? They were about the only people he trusted. Yet at the same time, he didn't dare let Jillian and Lizzy out of his sight.

Not when he knew that he was the only reason they were in danger.

He scrubbed his hands over his face, fighting a wave of exhaustion. Jillian deserved to know the truth about his real identity. Yet he worried how she'd react. Five months ago, when he'd found her, he had moved in next door as a way to help her out. He'd noticed the plain gold wedding ring on her finger without the diamond engagement ring he'd given her. That, along with her little girl, had convinced him she'd moved on with another man. He couldn't blame her since he was legally dead.

But he'd been wrong.

He had a daughter. The news was stunning and he realized he should have figured it out sooner. He wanted to talk to Jillian but feared she'd be upset with him when she learned the truth. And worst of all, she might feel as if she needed to stay with him to honor their five-year-old wedding vows despite the horrible scars that grooved his face.

She was the beauty and he was the beast. With a face that scared Lizzy. He hated knowing his own daughter was frightened of him. Yet he couldn't change who he was. Who he'd become.

When it was clear Jillian wasn't returning to the kitchen to pick up the conversation where they'd left it off, he dumped the dregs of his coffee in the sink and made his way into his room.

Tomorrow morning, he'd have several decisions to make. They'd need a new place to go and they needed to air the truth.

If she was angry with him, then fine. He'd take her anger over her pity any day of the week.

Jillian fell asleep comforting Lizzy, only to wake up at dawn with a crick in her neck.

Stretching with a muffled groan, she eased out from Lizzy's bed. She tiptoed out of the room to use the bathroom and then headed into the kitchen, shivering a bit in the cool air.

There was no sign of Hawk. Clearly, he hadn't followed through on her request to call the police.

Even now his reluctance made no sense. But enough was enough. Better late than never, right? She went over to her purse and dug out her cell phone.

One bar, indicating the battery was nearly dead. Great. She didn't have a charger and, from what she could tell, there wasn't one around here, either. The place was comfortable but rustic.

She stared at the screen, wondering who would respond if she called 911. Surely not anyone from the Brookland Police Department, which was where the crime had taken place.

"What are you doing?"

Hawk's hoarse voice was so unexpected she let out a yelp and almost dropped the phone.

"You shouldn't sneak up on me like that." She knew she sounded cranky, but seriously, the man needed to wear a cowbell around his neck.

"Don't call the police yet. Not until we talk."

Now he was reading her mind? Ugh. She turned the phone off to preserve what was left of her battery and tucked it into the pocket of her sweatshirt. "Talking isn't exactly your strength," she felt compelled to point out.

The right corner of his mouth kicked up in what may have been the hint of a smile. The first she'd ever seen from him. "Maybe not, but you'll want to hear my story."

His story? The one behind his scar? He was right about that, since she'd been wondering about his story for the past five months.

"Sounds like we'll need coffee." She moved into the kitchen and made a fresh pot of coffee. While she did that Hawk opened a cupboard and pulled out a box of instant oatmeal packets.

"This is about all I have on hand for breakfast," he said, his voice full of apology. "Or we can stop for breakfast when we leave."

"Leave?" Once again he knocked her off-balance. "Why are we leaving so soon?"

He didn't answer right away, a trait that annoyed her.

"Well?" She pulled two mugs out of the cabinet and set them beside the coffeepot. "I thought you said we were safe here."

He filled a teapot with water and put it on the stove. "We are, but it's only a matter of time before they track us here."

Her stomach clenched. "They? Who?"

"The men who came for you last night. They'll find out my name and will search for my license plate number and for any other properties that I might own. That will lead them here, to this cabin."

His words sent a chill down her spine. "Okay, now you're scaring me."

"I know. I'm sorry, but we'll stay one step ahead of them."

She poured two mugs of coffee and, since there wasn't any milk, made do with adding sugar to hers before handing him the one that was black. Their fingers brushed and she was startled by the tingle of awareness she felt. What was wrong with her? This was the wrong time, wrong place and definitely the wrong man!

"You said we need to talk."

He nodded before taking a sip from his mug. "It's a long story, goes back a couple of years."

"Okay." She took a seat at the table. "I'm listening."

"I used to be in the military," he said, his blue gaze centered on hers.

"I thought so," she said with a nod. "Just like James." At his silent stare, she added, "My husband."

"Yeah. Well." Hawk looked away, clearly uncomfortable. "I—I did a lot of work that was considered classified."

Just like James, but this time she didn't voice the comparison out loud.

"I was on a team with three other guys," he went on and suddenly a bad feeling came over her.

"You were with James, weren't you? Is that what you've been trying to tell me? That you knew my husband?" She knew her voice was getting louder but couldn't stop it. "All this time, you knew James but never said anything?"

"Jilly, please, just listen for a minute," he begged.

She sucked in a harsh breath. "What did you call me?"

Hawk winced and blanched. "I—uh, I'm sorry. I didn't mean to be so familiar…"

"No." She rose to her feet and took a step back from him, her mind whirling. He'd called her Jilly, just like James used to.

Then she remembered that brief moment in the bedroom when she'd thought Hawk was actually James. She stared at him, her thoughts spinning out of control.

"Jillian, I'm sorry to tell you like this. But I was sent on a secret mission, and me and my team saw something we shouldn't have. We were flown home to be debriefed by the Pentagon, only there was a storm that took us further west. We ended up landing in Columbus, Ohio, and they stuck us in a small prop plane. We crashed in the Appalachian Mountains. Everyone died in the crash except for me. And I—" his voice trailed off for a long moment before he continued "—I was badly injured. I had no memory, no ability to walk, my face was damaged beyond recognition and I still don't know how I managed to survive."

"You—you're James?" The blood drained from her face and she collapsed in the chair she'd just vacated. "I don't understand."

"I'm Hawk," he corrected. "I didn't even remember my name for a full year. I only remember watching hawks flying over my head for days on end, so that's the name I went with. I picked Jacobson because I had some dim memory of my father being named Jacob."

Her heart squeezed in her chest at what he'd gone through. Then she realized what he'd said. "But you did eventually realize you were James, right? And chose not to come home to me. To us."

"That's not entirely true. I didn't remember you right away, and when I did, there were only bits and pieces. I stayed away because after the crash I saw men combing the woods, searching for me." Hawk's expression went cold. "They were not there to rescue me but to kill me. They had guns, Jilly. And if the older couple who'd found me hadn't sheltered me from those men, I wouldn't be here now."

"But what about five months ago?" she persisted. "You moved in next door to me on purpose, didn't you?"

"Yes." The teakettle whistled and he quickly removed it from the burner. "I came to Milwaukee because I knew you had family here and wouldn't have stayed at Fort Bragg. Even then, it took me a while to find you in Brookland. Once I did, I couldn't stay away. I needed to make sure you were safe."

She couldn't argue that he had saved them.

"I want you to know I won't hold you to anything," Hawk continued. "James as you knew him is gone. Hawk was the lone survivor of that plane crash. Where we go from here is totally up to you."

"Where we go from here?" The realization of what he was saying sank deep.

Hawk was James. He was her *husband*. Lizzy's *father*.

And she had absolutely no idea where to go from here.

# THREE

Hawk busied himself with making a bowl of instant oatmeal for Jillian. The truth hung between them like a dark storm cloud, threatening to burst, bringing snow and ice pelting down. Telling her the story wasn't as difficult as he'd anticipated, but he wasn't sure the truth had fully sunk in yet.

He'd been honest with her when he'd claimed James was dead. That year he spent hiding in the mountains, recuperating from his injuries, had changed him. James had died in the plane crash, leaving a man called Hawk behind.

That he'd survived when the rest of his team had died haunted him still. The Callahans would claim God had a plan, but he didn't believe it. Not the way he used to. He'd lost his entire life that day.

Even now, sometimes he awoke from a nightmare, hearing his team's screams as the plane plummeted down into the mountainside. Only to realize it was his throat that was sore from screaming.

His time on the mountain was a blur. He'd lost track of the days that had passed, the hours that had gone by while he watched a pair of hawks flying high in the sky. He'd dragged himself down the mountain, inch by painful inch, with no particular destination in mind. Thankfully, he'd eventually come across a cabin tucked into the woods. It was actually the garden offering fresh vegetables that had caught his eye. He'd been helping himself to fresh tomatoes and cucumbers when Jolene and Ken Thornhill had found him.

Ken had carried a shotgun, but one look at Hawk's scars had him putting the weapon away. Hawk had convinced them not to call the authorities, and the couple, being mountain people and distrustful of the cops anyway, had readily agreed. The Thornhills helped get him back on his feet. Their home remedies worked just as well as any hospital-based therapy.

Except for the scar.

And when the men with guns had come looking for him, they'd hidden him in their root cellar until they were gone. Hawk was convinced the men were soldiers sent by Barton to find him and silence him for good. Especially since the plane had gone down after conveniently springing a fuel leak.

He owed the Thornhills his life. But they hadn't wanted any form of payment. He'd sent them cash when he'd managed to work enough to get some, but the money had come back to him as undeliverable.

Shaking himself from thoughts of the past, he carried the bowl of oatmeal to the table and set it in front of Jillian. She hadn't said anything for the past several minutes and, even now, avoided looking directly at him.

"Eat," he encouraged softly. "You'll need to keep up your strength."

She obediently picked up the spoon and took a small bite. Lizzy chose that moment to come out of the bedroom rubbing her sleepy eyes, looking adorable in her pink footie pajamas.

"I hav'ta go potty."

"Sure. This way, sweetie." Jillian jumped up from the table and crossed over to their daughter, steering her into the bathroom.

Hawk put the kettle back on to boil, hoping Lizzy liked oatmeal. He had no idea what his daughter liked to eat or her favorite things to do. He'd noticed a dollhouse in the corner of her bedroom and now wished he'd thought to bring some of the dolls along for her to play with.

At least she had her teddy bear. The one she'd clutched protectively as he'd pulled her from beneath the bed.

He glanced at his watch, estimating how much time they had before they needed to hit the road. Less than an hour. Doable, but only if Jillian and Lizzy finished their breakfast ASAP.

The teakettle whistled as Jillian and Lizzy emerged from the bathroom. Lizzy clapped her hands over her ears.

"Too loud!"

Hawk winced, nodded and moved the kettle, adding hot water to two more bowls of oatmeal. Then he carried them to the kitchen table, setting one down near Jillian's bowl and taking his to the other side.

Jillian lifted Lizzy onto her lap. It pained him to know Lizzy wouldn't want to sit with him. As he watched, Jillian bowed her head and softly thanked God for the food she was about to eat. He was reminded of how the Callahans always prayed out loud before meals, but he'd never joined in.

No one spoke for several long moments as they ate. And it was Lizzy who eventually broke the silence.

"Can we go home, Mommy?"

The question hit him in the face like a blow. He looked at Jillian, unsure if he should speak up or not.

"Not today, sweetie." Jillian hitched the little girl higher on her lap. "Finish up your oatmeal like a good girl."

"We can try to find a place that's kid-friendly," he offered. "I know a place that rents individual cabins. It's not too far away and has a playground I'm sure Lizzy would love."

Jillian shrugged. "Whatever you think is best. We'll make the most of wherever we end up, won't we Lizzy-girl?"

Lizzy nodded her head, her drooping pigtails bobbing up and down. His daughter's hair was dark, like his, without any sign of Jillian's reddish glints. But the rest of her features were mirror images of her mother's. She'd be just as beautiful as Jillian someday.

He finished his meal before they did and carried his dishes to the sink. "We'll need to leave soon."

"Okay." Jillian's voice sounded resigned.

There was no point in saying anything further; moving again was necessary in order to keep them alive. And while he still felt terrible knowing that he'd brought danger to their doorstep, the only thing he could do now was to stay ahead of the danger curve.

He took his turn in the bathroom, spending less than ten minutes. He heard Jillian and Lizzy's voices in their bedroom and hoped they were getting their things together.

Thankfully, Jillian had done the dishes, so there was nothing more that needed his attention. He pulled on his leather coat, grabbed his keys and waited, gazing out through the large picture window of the living room.

A movement outside caught his attention. He froze, his gaze tracking the shifting of leaves and the sudden uprising of a bird from the bushes.

Too late! They'd found the cabin.

He hurried into the bedroom as Jillian was trying to coax the teddy bear from Lizzy's grip. "We need to go. Get your coats, leave the duffel behind. We're heading out the back."

"The back?" The confusion in Jillian's green gaze morphed into fear. She instantly yanked the bear away, shoved Lizzy's coat on, then hers, before lifting Lizzy into her arms. She returned the teddy bear hoping the stuffed animal would help keep Lizzy calm. Her voice dropped to a whisper. "They're here?"

He nodded, gently pulling her toward him. Ushering her into his bedroom and to the back doorway he had built in there just for this type of thing, he considered their options. First, they needed to get out of the cabin and deeper into the woods without leaving a blatant footprint trail behind. Using the SUV was out of the question; the hostiles were too close. He'd have to make do with the snowmobile he had hidden in the woods toward the back of his property.

Outside, the December air was crisp and cool despite the sunshine. Keeping Jillian in front of him, he covered their backs as he guided them into the woods. He could tell Jillian was trying to move silently, but to his ears it sounded as if they were a stampede of elephants announcing their location to anyone within a fifty-mile radius. He worried, too, about leaving footprints in the snow. The snow wasn't deep and there were spots where there were leafy areas to step on as a way to mitigate the risk.

Thankfully, Lizzy didn't say anything but kept her head tucked against her mother's shoulder, still gripping the tattered teddy bear. He wished the little girl trusted him enough to allow him to carry her, knowing they'd be able to move more quickly. But he didn't want to risk her tears.

Knowing the woods helped. Prior to renting the house next to Jillian's he'd spent a lot of time up here. The place had reminded him of the Thornhill cabin in the mountains.

The cluster of bushes he'd been aiming for was straight ahead. He picked up his pace, moving ahead. Jillian did her best to keep up, but her foot got caught on a branch. He managed to catch her before she hit the ground.

He gently set her on her feet and gestured toward the cluster of bushes. She nodded her understanding and headed in that direction. Hawk continued sweeping his gaze over the area, looking for signs the hostiles were near, surprised that they hadn't covered the back side of the cabin but had chosen to come in from the front and the west.

Although he knew there very well could be more.

When they reached the cluster of bushes, he carved out a small space with his hands and drew Jillian down. "Stay here, I'll be back soon."

She clutched at his arm. "Don't leave us," she begged.

It wasn't by choice but out of necessity. He leaned down so

his mouth was near her ear. "I have a snowmobile nearby. I promise I'll be quick."

Tears welled in her eyes, but she gave a jerky nod, showing she understood. He drew out his gun and handed it to her. This time she didn't protest but clutched it with both hands while keeping one arm around Lizzy, holding her close.

He hesitated. There was so much he wanted to say, but there wasn't time. He needed to move, to draw the hostiles away from Jillian and Lizzy.

He'd willingly sacrifice himself to keep them alive and safe.

This was so much worse than waiting in the car. Since they were surrounded by snow-covered trees and bushes, any sense of being safe was eroded by the cold breeze that made her shiver. Her fingers were beginning to go numb, but she didn't dare let go of the gun.

She silently prayed that God would watch over them. Keeping an internal monologue in her head helped keep her fear in check. Hawk would return for them. He had a snowmobile nearby and would be here soon. He wouldn't let the men combing the woods reach her and Lizzy.

Hawk was James, except he wasn't. Her husband had never moved so stealthily. Her husband had smiled and laughed often, and while he may not have been verbose, he certainly had spoken more than Hawk did.

Nevertheless, he was her husband. She was still married to the man. Wasn't she? Maybe not, since James had been declared dead. But he wasn't dead, not really. He was just—different. Thinking about it made her head hurt. It was all so confusing.

*Come on, Hawk, where are you?*

"Mommy?" Lizzy lifted her head.

"Shh," she whispered.

Lizzy wiggled a little and Jillian feared her daughter wasn't going to stay silent much longer. Hoping and praying Hawk would return soon, she kept her mouth right near her daughter's ear.

"Be quiet for just a little while longer."

Lizzy nodded her head and leaned against her, rubbing her cheek against the teddy bear's head.

Jillian let out a sigh of relief. So far, so good.

A twig snapped. The sound sent a stab of terror deep into her stomach. She went still, her breath locked in her throat and her heart thundering in her chest. She pressed Lizzy's face against her chest, hoping the little girl wouldn't do or say something to give them away.

Since rediscovering the church after moving to Wisconsin, she'd leaned on God often and didn't hesitate to do that again, now.

*Please keep us safe, Lord! Please!*

The sound of rustling leaves seemed close. She imagined one of the black ski-masked men making his way toward their hiding spot. How much longer? She dreaded every passing second, fearing the worst.

Then abruptly there was an *oomph* sound and a muffled thud. Still, she didn't move, didn't so much as blink. She wanted desperately to believe Hawk had taken care of the guy, but for all she knew, he'd fallen flat on his face the way she nearly had a few minutes ago.

Another ten seconds passed. She strained to listen but heard nothing.

Suddenly Hawk loomed in front of them, a streak of dirt covering his scar. He gave a nod and held out his hand. She shakily put her hand in his, allowing him to pull her and Lizzy to her feet.

She wanted to ask what was going on, but as if he sensed her intent, he lifted a finger to his lips. She nodded in understanding.

They weren't safe yet. And it struck her then that they may never be safe again.

From this moment on, safety could very well be nothing more than an illusion.

Hawk gently but firmly pulled her in a different direction. She couldn't tell if they were going closer toward the cabin or farther away. It wasn't easy to navigate while carrying Lizzy, because she couldn't see her feet. Twice she felt a branch of some sort pressing against her shin, making her lift her foot higher to get over it.

They moved through the dense woods in what felt like slow motion. But soon enough, Hawk tugged on her arm, indicating they could stop here.

She glanced around, thinking she'd find the snowmobile he'd mentioned. When she didn't see it, her hopes plummeted. Had someone stolen it? Or had the ski-mask guys found it before Hawk had?

Hawk stepped over to a bush and began moving snow-laden branches. Her eyes widened in surprise when she saw the camouflage-green snowmobile hidden behind the shrubbery.

It took Hawk a while to get the thing uncovered. It soon became clear that the bush hadn't been a bush at all but dozens of loose branches placed strategically around the machine.

He swung his leg over the seat and gestured for her to get on in front of him. She hesitated, worried about Lizzy.

"Keep her in front of you," he whispered.

She nodded and did as he asked. The seat seemed far too small for the three of them but her protest was swallowed by the roar of the engine.

She felt Lizzy shuddering against her, guessing that the little girl hated the loud sound. Hawk hit the gas and the machine moved forward, the twin skis gliding over the snow, fallen branches and leaves. She let out a screech as he went even faster, tearing a path through the woods.

Stealth was not an option now. The way they roared through the woods broadcasted their location to anyone still searching for them. Clutching Hawk's knee with one arm, while clinging to Lizzy with the other, she grew convinced that he was the only one capable of getting them out of there.

But where would they go? It wasn't as if you could drive a snowmobile down the center of a plowed road. Or could you? Maybe. Yet as fast as they were moving, she knew the machine carrying them didn't have the necessary speed to outrun a car.

Bare branches slapped her in the face, making her eyes sting with tears. She curled her body around Lizzy's, protecting the little girl the only way she could.

The trees thinned and she wondered if they were getting close to the road or to the end of Hawk's property. She felt certain they'd escaped, until she heard the loud echo of gunfire above the drone of the engine.

No! Jillian gasped, horrified that the ski-masked men were still out there, shooting at them.

"Keep your head down," he ordered.

Doing anything else was impossible anyway, but what about Hawk? He was the most exposed, and if something happened to him…there was no hope for her and Lizzy to survive.

She prayed again as Hawk continued driving. The woods seemed to go on forever, thinning out a bit, then growing thicker again. She had no idea how much land Hawk owned, or if they were out on someone else's property by now.

Did it matter if they were? It gave her a measure of hope that the owners might call the police.

The gunfire had stopped, but she couldn't relax. Not with Hawk still driving like a maniac.

Then he abruptly pulled over and stopped the machine. Silence reigned except for the ringing in her ears.

"Take Lizzy and stand over there for a minute," Hawk said, urging her off the snowmobile and pointing at a pine tree.

She wanted to protest but knew it was useless. She awkwardly climbed off the machine, feeling Lizzy's weight slipping down.

Hawk jumped back on the snowmobile and rode it about

eighty yards away before abandoning it. Then he pulled several items out of a storage area behind the seat, before hurrying toward her. He was careful to step only on the tracks made by the sled.

She was impressed by his actions, knowing the machine would draw the men in the woods away from them. She hitched Lizzy in her arms.

"I'll take her." Hawk didn't wait for permission but took Lizzy from her, after storing what looked like duct tape and twine in his jacket pocket. "This way."

Lizzy didn't cry, too frightened to do anything but hang on. They once again moved through the woods, faster now that Jillian wasn't impeded by her daughter's weight.

Hawk stopped in front of a large tree. "We're going up."

Her jaw dropped. "Up? The tree?"

He nodded, pulling another length of twine out of his jacket pocket. "I'll carry you while you hold Lizzy."

She shook her head, thinking he was crazy. No way could Hawk carry both of them all the way up a tree. And what would they do when they got up there? Swing from the branches like Tarzan and Jane? She'd fall on her face for sure.

"Like this." He placed Lizzy back in her arms. "You're going to put your arms around my neck and lock your legs around my waist, keeping Lizzy tucked between us."

"She'll fall," she protested.

"She won't. She'll hang on to you. Trust me."

She did trust Hawk. Had trusted him to get them out of danger twice now. Knew that God was somehow guiding him.

"Hold tight, Lizzy." The little girl nodded and wrapped her tiny arms snugly around her neck. Then Jillian faced Hawk's back and locked her arms around his chest. When she lifted her legs around his waist, pressing Lizzy securely between them, he began to climb, using the rope around the tree for leverage.

How he made it up the tree was a mystery. The muscles of his chest and shoulders bunched beneath her arms with the strain, but he didn't make a sound as he went vertical.

She wasn't sure what she expected, but the flat platform about two-thirds of the way up the tree was a surprise. Especially when she saw that there were three full sides to the thing that protected them from view. Hawk managed to get up and over the edge of the platform, landing on his hands and knees.

"You can get off now," he whispered.

It was scary being up so high, but she unlocked her legs first, then slid to the side so she was sitting on the platform next to him. Holding Lizzy close, she edged closer to the trunk of the tree, seeking some sense of stability.

"We made it," she whispered in awe.

Hawk nodded. "We still need to be quiet, okay?" He didn't wait for a response but pulled out his gun and flattened himself against the platform. He inched to the edge, peering down to see what was going on down below.

She lifted her hand to push her hair out of her face, frowning when she saw blood. For a moment she didn't understand, but then she noticed several more drops of blood staining the platform.

He'd been shot!

# FOUR

"Hawk! You're hurt!" Jillian whispered in a low, urgent tone.

"It's nothing. Keep Lizzy quiet, okay?" Ignoring the pain in his shoulder, Hawk looked carefully over the edge of the deer blind, searching for hostiles. He had two guns and a knife but didn't want to use them unless there was absolutely no other option. He'd taken one man temporarily out of commission, but there were three more, and he couldn't bear the thought of Jillian and Lizzy witnessing him killing a man.

Yet he'd do whatever was necessary to keep them safe.

They were in danger because of him. Because he'd poked the sleeping bear by probing for information on Senator Barton. It was the only thing that made sense.

Pushing the thought away, he kept his gaze focused on the wooded area below while internally planning their next move. He needed to call Mike Callahan for help, but he wasn't thrilled with the idea of putting his buddy in danger.

Jillian did her best to soothe Lizzy, urging the little girl to stay quiet. Lizzy's hiccuping sobs were muffled against Jillian's chest and he hated knowing his daughter was so frightened.

Peering through the trees, he could see the dark shape of the snowmobile where he'd left it, eighty yards from where they were hiding.

Time to implement the next phase of his plan.

"Stay up here with Lizzy," he whispered to Jillian.

"Where are you going?" There was thinly veiled panic in her voice.

He wasn't sure how to answer her without causing her to become even more afraid. He trusted his ability to take out the three men but hated leaving her here, alone. Pulling out his phone, he found Mike Callahan's number and showed it to her. "If I'm not back in an hour, call Mike. He's a cop and will keep you and Lizzy safe."

"Why can't we call him now?" Jillian argued. "Then you can stay here with us."

"He's at least forty-five minutes away, maybe more." He thrust the phone at her. "Please, Jilly. I'm asking you to trust me on this."

She held his gaze for a long moment, before reluctantly nodding. He wanted nothing more than to pull her close in a reassuring hug but needed to get moving.

Soundlessly, he climbed down the tree, ignoring his injured shoulder, and moved quickly without the added burden of having to carry Jillian and Lizzy. On the ground, he took a moment to get his bearings.

He found a branch and used it to help wipe away his footprints from the base of the tree. Then he took a roundabout and silent path toward the snowmobile.

Hawk halted behind a tree when he caught sight of one hostile positioned twenty yards in front of him. Hawk could only see his back, it was clear the man's attention was focused on the snowmobile.

His mistake. Hawk managed to sneak up on him from behind, taking him down without making much of a sound despite the ache in his shoulder. Hawk knocked him unconscious, then bound and gagged him using the duct tape in his pocket.

Another one down, two more to go.

Hawk moved silently away, estimating that another assailant would be at the three o'clock position. Hiding behind a tree, he searched for a sign and then found him.

The second guy didn't go down as quietly as the first one. Could be because Hawk was feeling the effect of blood loss, but he refused to acknowledge weakness. When he had the second man unconscious and tied up securely, as well, he looked for the next one.

Keenly aware of the minutes ticking by on his allotted hour, he hoped Jillian wouldn't place the call to Mike before he'd had the chance to take the last attacker out of commission.

Hawk knew that taking down the last man would be the most difficult. The hostile must know that his cohorts were compromised and would have no reason to stay at his point location.

Ducking behind a thorny bush, Hawk wiped snow away to uncover a large rock. He tossed it high in the air, then crouched down and watched carefully for signs of movement when it landed with a dull thud.

For several long seconds there was nothing, but finally, the slightest movement from the twelve o'clock position caught his eye. Target in sight, Hawk moved in.

Another movement had him dropping to the ground. The sound of gunfire echoed loudly through the woods, narrowly missing him. Gut instinct had Hawk rolling to the side and returning fire at the spot where he'd seen the muzzle flash.

Then there was nothing but silence.

Because he'd hit his target? He wasn't sure.

He waited another five minutes before edging along the ground toward the nine o'clock position. The man was lying there, dead from a gunshot wound to his chest.

Hawk sighed and rose to his feet, staggering a bit. Four men taken down total, one dead. A wave of despair hit him hard. He hated knowing that he'd killed a man even though it was in self-defense.

After a long moment, he pulled off the man's ski mask, realizing this guy was the same one who'd been in Jillian's house. Searching for ID proved fruitless, but he did find a set of car keys. Hawk tucked them away. Returning to the snowmobile, he fired it up and rode back to the tree with the deer blind.

"Jillian? You and Lizzy okay?"

"Yes," came the faint response. "Just cold."

"I know. Did you call Mike?"

"Not yet."

"Good." He gathered every ounce of strength and determination, knowing he'd need it get up the tree and back down with Lizzy and Jillian. It was much harder this time: his left arm was weak and he didn't have the same surge of adrenaline roaring through his veins. But he managed, and soon the three of them were back on solid ground.

"Now what?" Jillian asked, her body shivering with cold.

He indicated the snowmobile. "Now we find the vehicle belonging to the men who came to find us."

She looked as if she wanted to argue, but he gestured for her to get on the snowmobile first with Lizzy. He slid in behind them and reached out to grab the handlebars.

The trip to the highway didn't take long, and he quickly found the black SUV, a newer make and model compared to his own.

"We need Lizzy's car seat," Jillian protested as he ushered them inside.

"I know." Hawk didn't want to stay at the cabin for much longer, fearing more men were on the way, but the cabin was only a half mile up the road. Getting the car seat didn't take much time, and soon they were back on the highway.

He cranked the heat for Jillian and Lizzy while considering their next move. They'd been found at the cabin far too quickly. He never should have gone there in the first place.

The weight of Jillian's and Lizzy's safety was incredibly heavy on his shoulders.

He couldn't afford to make another mistake.

\* \* \*

Jillian gratefully absorbed the warm air blasting from the vents of the SUV. She'd prayed the entire time they'd been up in the tree stand, and God had answered by not only keeping them safe but providing a method of escape.

Between Hawk's ingenuity and God's support, they'd made it out the woods alive. Yet it was difficult to relax. She felt certain the danger was far from over.

She wrestled with the fact that Hawk was really James. She'd lived next door to him for five months— how could she not have figured it out? This all seemed like some sort of twisted movie plot rather than something that happened in real life.

She glanced over at him, searching his profile for signs of the man she'd once married.

Now that she knew the truth, it was easy to spot the similarities and differences. His intense blue eyes were the same, but the prominent cheekbones were gone, and she felt bad about the deep scar grooving his face. Hawk was leaner and more muscular than she remembered, and his voice, which always sounded hoarse now, made her wonder if there had been some sort of internal damage to his vocal cords as a result of the plane crash.

Hawk didn't laugh the way James had, or talk as much. He was serious and to the point.

She turned away, mourning the loss all over again. Maybe Hawk was right to claim James had died in the Appalachian Mountains. The man sitting beside her, the one who'd climbed up and down a tree with her and Lizzy on his back, seemed very different than the man she'd married.

And for the life of her, she couldn't look at him and think *James*. He was Hawk.

"You'll need to stop at a drugstore. I need bandages and other supplies to take care of your wound."

He gave a small nod. "Later. Right now I need to figure out a place to go where we'll be safe."

"You mentioned a place with individual cabins and a playground for Lizzy," she reminded.

He hesitated and shrugged. "Yeah, that's where we're headed. But it's just five days before Christmas and I'm not sure they have openings."

"I can't imagine individual cabins being a hot place to spend Christmas."

He glanced at her in surprise. "It is for me."

"Because you're a single guy without a family." The minute the words were out of her mouth, she wished them back. "I mean, until now."

Hawk didn't respond and she knew that she'd stuck her foot in her mouth, big-time. Yet it was hardly her fault. She'd only known he was James for a few hours.

Terrifying hours that they'd spent hiding from armed men wearing ski masks.

The silence grew uncomfortable. More proof that they were virtual strangers rather than husband and wife.

"How do you know about this place with cabins and a playground anyway?"

"Used it last summer when a friend of mine needed to hide out for a while."

"Mike Callahan? That friend?"

He nodded.

More silence, and it occurred to her that attempting to have a conversation with Hawk was harder work than panning for gold. Not that she'd ever tried panning for gold.

"I'm sorry," she finally said.

He frowned. "For what?"

She let out a sigh. "For insinuating that you don't have a family. It's just—difficult to wrap my mind around all of this."

"Understandable. And as I said before, it doesn't have to change anything between us."

*But it did,* she thought. Knowing Hawk was James changed *everything.*

She found herself thinking about the future more than ever. How her relationship with Hawk would move forward after the danger was over.

"Mommy, I'm hungry," Lizzy said plaintively.

Glancing at the clock, she was surprised to see it was approaching eleven o'clock in the morning. Considering they'd been up by six and running for their lives since seven, she couldn't blame Lizzy for wanting to eat.

"We'll stop at a restaurant soon," Hawk surprised her by saying. "There's one not too far away. And there's a drugstore nearby, too."

She was glad to hear they'd soon have the supplies they needed to tend to his wound.

"Can I have chicken strips?" Lizzy asked.

Jillian smiled. "Sure."

"Okay." Lizzy was satisfied with that response.

"I take it those are her favorites?" Hawk asked.

"Yes. With lots of ketchup." She was saddened by the fact that Hawk didn't know these small details about his daughter. Her favorite foods, favorite books, her friends at day care.

Five months that they could have spent getting reunited had been wasted. In fact, she doubted that Hawk would have come clean at all if it hadn't been for her need to be rescued.

"You have no idea who they were?" She glanced over her shoulder at Lizzy to make sure she wasn't listening. Amazingly, despite running for their lives, riding a snowmobile and going up into a tree, Lizzy still had her ragged teddy bear. Her cheek was resting on the teddy bear's head, her eyes drooping with sleepiness.

"No. Other than I assume they were sent by either Barton or Hayes."

"But why come to my house?" Jillian asked.

Hawk glanced at her. "It's no secret we were once married. The only thing I can figure out is that they intended to kidnap you and Lizzy in order to get me to come out of hiding."

Chills rippled down her spine at his theory. "But that doesn't make any sense. It wouldn't have worked. I didn't even know you were alive until this morning."

"They didn't know that," Hawk reasoned. "I have to assume that my prying into Senator Barton's past triggered several alarms. They'd never found my body after the plane crash but probably chalked that up to me crawling off somewhere to die."

"Maybe." She wasn't convinced.

"It's possible they now believe we've been in touch with each other over the years."

Ridiculous, since there had been no contact since the day she'd been informed that James had died.

"That was the worst day of my life," she said in a low voice.

"What was?"

She struggled to ward off tears. "Finding out you were dead on the same day I discovered I was pregnant."

Hawk's grip on the steering wheel tightened to the point his knuckles went white. A thick, heavy silence hung between them for several miles. "I'm sorry you had to go through that," he finally managed.

She sniffled and swiped at her face. Why she was getting all emotional over this, she had no idea. She felt guilty for making him feel bad. "It was hardly your fault. It was just—rotten timing."

"Yeah." There was a pause, then he asked, "Who came to see you?"

She shook her head helplessly. "I can't remember his name now but probably have it at home somewhere. I think he left his card. Master Sergeant Somebody-or-other."

"I'm surprised you kept it all these years."

"I kept a lot of things over the years." There was no reason to feel defensive, and she tried to tone it down. "I have several pictures of us together. I show them to Lizzy so she'll remember you."

"That's, uh, nice." Hawk's tone held uncertainty and she realized she'd done it again. Lizzy didn't have to remember her father from a photo.

He was here now. He looked different, yes, but he was still her father. And they needed to find a time to tell the little girl that Hawk was her daddy.

Which also meant that in the eyes of God, they were still married.

All at once, it all seemed overwhelming. She'd made a life for herself and Lizzy, and now things would never be the same. Hawk deserved to spend time with his daughter, she wouldn't keep that from him.

And what about the two of them? What had he said earlier? That he wouldn't hold her to anything? What did that even mean? She'd loved James with her whole heart.

But there was no denying Hawk was mostly a stranger.

She'd never been with another man, not even on a date. At first it had been because of Lizzy. Being a single mother, even with her mother's support, had been difficult.

Four months after Lizzy's first birthday, her mother had suffered a stroke and died. Leaving Jillian and Lizzy alone, again.

"I'm sorry," Hawk said, reaching over to put his hand on her knee. "I'm sure it was difficult raising Lizzy by yourself."

She stared at his broad, calloused hand, wishing she dared take it in hers. She hated this awkwardness between them. "I have a box of your things saved in the basement, too." She hoped changing the subject might ease the tension. "In case Lizzy wanted them someday."

Hawk's brow furrowed in a frown. "What kind of things?"

She shrugged. "Little things, the pocket watch you got from your dad, the birthday card you gave me just before you left for deployment." She tried to think back to what she'd tucked away for their daughter. "Oh, and I recently pulled out that packet of information you sent from overseas."

His hand tightened on her knee. "What packet?"

"The brown envelope. You sent it from Afghanistan."

"What was inside?" There was a new sense of urgency in his tone.

"I don't know. You said it was nothing important. That I shouldn't bother opening it and to put it away until you came home."

"And you're certain I sent it to you from Afghanistan?"

"I'm certain that's what you told me when you called." She grew frustrated with his persistence. "Don't you remember sending it to me? Or calling to let me know to expect it?"

"No. I don't." Hawk's clipped tone made her stomach clench. "There are still holes in my memory and I don't recall sending you anything from overseas."

Her stomach clenched with fear. "You think someone else sent it to me?"

He shook his head. "No, I'm sure it was me. I only wish I could remember what it was."

The knots in her stomach tightened. "You should know that I made a call to Fort Bragg during my lunch hour, to let them know I had some stuff of yours they may need. It was probably a lame thing to do, but I was cleaning out the basement and thought maybe the information in the envelope might be important."

"When?" his tone was sharp.

"Earlier this week." She thought back. "Monday or Tuesday. I remember thinking no one would get back to me until after the holidays."

"Did you talk to anyone in particular?"

She shrugged. "The woman who answered the phone said she'd let her superior know. I can't remember her name." She abruptly realized the timing was too much of a coincidence. "You think those men came because of the envelope?"

Hawk glanced over at her. "There's only one way to find out. Once I have you and Lizzy stashed someplace safe, I'll head back to check it out."

Jillian gaped at him. "No! It's too dangerous."

Hawk didn't say anything but she recognized the stubborn glint in his steel blue eyes.

She forced herself to relax. The envelope could be nothing. She'd gotten it over four years ago.

Yet even as Hawk pulled into the parking lot of a drugstore, she couldn't help but hope and pray the brown envelope held the key to getting them all out of danger.

# FIVE

Hawk couldn't shake the fact that two men in masks had come to Jillian's home three days after her phone call to Fort Bragg. He realized that his initial assumption had changed. It wasn't his probing into Barton's past that had caused the attack, but Jillian finding the envelope he'd apparently sent more than four years ago.

He absolutely needed to get his hands on the contents of that envelope. But not until he'd made sure Jillian and Lizzy were safe.

He was surprised at how seriously Jillian took the task of caring for his wound. She was a woman on a first aid mission. After purchasing supplies she deemed appropriate, they sat in the front seat of the SUV. She used wipes to wash the front and back of his shoulder, then added antibiotic ointment before placing gauze over the through-and-through bullet wounds.

"We need to get you to a hospital right away." Jillian pinned him with a stern glare. "This will get infected."

"Soon." He knew she was right, but there wasn't time. Not to mention that bullet wounds were an automatic report to the cops, and he wasn't letting that happen. He made a mental note to ask Mitch Callahan if his ER nurse wife, Dana, could get him antibiotics. Enough to hold him over until Jillian and Lizzy were safe.

"I'm hungry," Lizzy said again. "And so is Teddy."

Jillian finished taping the gauze down before turning to her daughter. "I know. The restaurant is right across the street, see?"

Lizzy leaned forward in her car seat. Hawk pulled his T-shirt back on, then shrugged into his leather jacket, hoping the bullet holes marring the smooth leather weren't too obvious. "We'll be there in less than five minutes."

Jillian sat back in her seat and pulled on the seat belt. She placed the garbage from the supplies she'd used neatly in a bag. She was tougher than he remembered, more resilient and independent. It felt weird to have her taking care of him after being alone for so long.

Even with the Callahans, he'd maintained a level of privacy. There were six Callahans in total, and all of them had names starting with the letter M, thanks to a quirk of their parents. Marc was an FBI agent, Miles a homicide detective, Mitch an arson investigator, Matthew a K-9 cop and Maddy an assistant district attorney, while Mike, who was a deputy sheriff now, used to be a private investigator like him. Hawk was closest to Mike but had helped some of the other siblings from time to time over the last couple of years.

Now it was his turn. He decided that after they ate lunch, he'd make the call to Mike asking for as many of the Callahans as were available to meet him at the cabin motel.

The restaurant loomed before him. He passed all the close parking spots to choose one that was behind the building, far enough away that it couldn't be seen from the road.

Satisfied for the moment, he took a few minutes to search for a GPS tracking device. Logically, he felt four armed men with guns wouldn't want a GPS device on their vehicle, but he needed to make sure. Thankfully, he was familiar with this particular SUV make and model, so he knew what he was looking for. He didn't find any type of tracking device, which made him let out a sigh of relief. Still, he'd need a different car and knew the request wouldn't be a surprise to the Callahans.

They'd had a lot of practice hiding from bad guys with guns and had a well-oiled routine.

Jillian took Lizzy out of the car seat and he stepped forward, intending to take the girl from her arms. But then he hesitated, remembering how scared Lizzy was of him and his scarred face.

"Will you let Hawk carry you?" Jillian asked their daughter as if reading his thoughts. "My arms are getting tired."

Lizzy hunched her shoulders, dipping her head shyly, and nodded. Hawk smiled, hoping his expression wasn't too frightening as he gently pulled Lizzy from Jillian's arms.

Lizzy didn't exactly lean against him for support, but she didn't seem upset by being close to him, either. She still had the teddy bear and he was secretly surprised the stuffed animal had made it this far.

He renewed his silent promise to keep Lizzy and Jillian safe from harm.

"You have an ouchie." Lizzy's soft fingers lightly touched his deeply grooved cheek. "Does it hurt?"

It took a minute for him to respond. "No, it doesn't hurt."

"Did your mommy kiss it and make it better?"

This time a genuine smile bloomed on his face. "No, my mommy wasn't there when it happened."

Lizzy studied him intently. "Maybe my mommy could kiss it and make it better."

Jillian let out a choked sound that could have been a horrified gasp or a cough, he wasn't sure which.

"It's okay, Lizzy," he reassured her, wishing he'd gone to see a plastic surgeon to have the scar fixed. Not that he was convinced he'd look all that much better afterward, but it may be enough to be more appealing for his daughter. And, for that matter, to Jillian. "I promise it doesn't hurt."

"Table for three, please," Jillian said to the restaurant hostess.

"Right this way."

Within minutes they were seated at a corner booth that over-looked the main highway. Hawk sat with his back to the wall, facing the door. He mentally mapped out an escape plan as Jillian and Lizzy discussed what they wanted from the menu.

"Would you like to start with something to drink?" Their server, a plump woman whose name tag read Patty, smiled brightly. She had freckles and shockingly red hair that seemed too harsh to be natural. She waited, holding her pen and pad at the ready.

"Coffee for me," Hawk said.

"Me, too," Jillian added. "And chocolate milk for Lizzy, please."

"Coming right up." Patty quickly returned with a pot of coffee for the adults. The chocolate milk arrived a few minutes later.

They ordered their meals. Burger medium rare for Hawk, turkey club for Jillian and chicken strips with French fries for Lizzy. While they waited for their food to arrive, he pulled out his phone and called Mike.

"Hawk? What's wrong?" The alarm in Mike's tone made him smile.

"I need a favor."

"It must be bad if you're calling in a favor." Mike Callahan knew him too well.

"It is." Hawk watched as Lizzy colored on a paper place mat, with crayons provided by the restaurant to keep children busy. "Meet me at the cabin motel you used last summer with the usual."

Mike let out a low whistle at his request. "The usual being a vehicle, computer and disposable phones."

Hawk rotated his injured shoulder. "Yeah. Also, check with Mitch, see if Dana can get any antibiotics."

"You're wounded?" Mike sounded truly alarmed, as if Hawk being hurt was inconceivable. "What happened? Why didn't you call sooner?"

The corner of Hawk's mouth quirked in a smile. It was nice knowing you had a Callahan covering your back. "Long story. I'll fill you in later."

"Okay, give me an hour, maybe a little longer to get the antibiotics. I don't think Dana can just get them from the hospital without obtaining a prescription."

Hawk's smile faded at the implication. "I don't want her to get in trouble."

"Trust me, Mitch won't let that happen. But we all owe you, Hawk. We'll do our best to get what you need."

"Thank you." Hawk knew it was more than owing a favor. The Callahans cared about him and wanted to help. It made him realize how much he'd missed being part of a team. Being the lone survivor of the plane crash intended to kill him, he had forged ahead alone. The Thornhills had helped but then hadn't wanted anything more to do with him. Which in hindsight was smart on their part. He'd brought danger to them once, and it was clear they didn't want any further contact that would put them in jeopardy.

He glanced at Jillian, thinking about how he'd lived next door to her for the past five months. Friendly and helpful, yet keeping his distance.

Now he wanted more.

He disconnected from the line and then turned off the phone. He made a mental note to destroy it when they left the restaurant.

Ten minutes later, their meals arrived. Jillian cut up Lizzy's chicken strips and then once again bowed her head to pray. Lizzy was watching him curiously, so he mirrored Jillian's actions, bowing his head and clasping his hands in front of him while she said a whispered prayer.

"Dear Lord, we thank You for keeping us safe in Your care. Please continue to provide us the strength and wisdom we need to seek justice." She paused, then added, "And thank You for this food, too. Amen."

"Amen," Lizzy quipped.

Hawk cleared his throat. "Amen."

Jillian glanced at him in surprise, a pleased expression on her face. "Thanks, Hawk."

He had no idea what she was thanking him for but nodded. "Let's eat. We need to hit the road soon."

She frowned but began to eat her club sandwich. After a few minutes, she asked, "You spoke with Mike?"

"He'll meet us with everything we need." Hawk didn't want to say too much in front of Lizzy. "And he'll stay with you while I go back to your place."

"No. I don't want you to go alone." The stubborn glint was back in her green gaze.

Hawk didn't respond because he wasn't sure how many of the Callahans would be free to come to his aid. If only two brothers were able to come, then he absolutely wanted them both to stay with Jillian and Lizzy. He needed them well protected. If a third was able to come, then he might be able to take someone along for backup.

He desperately needed to get his hands on that envelope. The one he didn't remember sending from Afghanistan. The one Jillian had recently called Fort Bragg about. Hawk had a feeling deep in his gut the contents of the envelope would help him get to the bottom of this mess.

He only hoped and prayed there was evidence in there linking Rick Barton to something illegal.

Because it was clear he couldn't depend on his moldy Swiss-cheese memories.

Jillian was relieved that Hawk had called Mike Callahan for assistance. Not because she didn't trust him, but because she was afraid his wound would soon impact his ability to keep them safe.

Had James ever been as stubborn as Hawk was? Her memories of James were fond and loving, focused on the good times they'd spent together far more than on the bad. They'd met at the restaurant where she'd worked while finishing up her teaching degree. They were only married for a year before James had been deployed and had dated for six months before that. Eighteen months total, another reason that it wasn't easy to mesh the current reality of Hawk with her fading memories of James.

Their marriage hadn't been perfect, no marriage was. Still, she'd mourned a long time for what she'd lost.

Yet James, er, Hawk was sitting beside her.

Lizzy played with her French fries, as if they were tiny dolls who were living in a home together. A tall French fry was telling the smaller one to go clean up her room. "No. Don't want to," Lizzy said in a high, fake voice. "I wanna go outside and play."

"You must clean your room!" The stern taller fry was obviously the mother talking to her child. Jillian's lips curved in a smile.

"Guess there's no daddy French fry," Hawk said in a low voice.

Jillian glanced at him in surprise but then realized that Hawk's keen sense of perception never missed a thing. "Not yet, but that will change once we're able to tell her."

"Tell me what?" Lizzy asked. She popped both the tall French fry and the smaller one into her mouth.

Hawk froze and Jillian could tell their daughter's innocent question, one she had no intention of answering, had shocked him more than any gunshot ever could.

"We wanted to tell you that we're going to another cabin, but this one has a playground." Jillian injected enthusiasm in her tone. "Won't that be fun?"

Lizzy nodded, but her tiny brow puckered in a frown. "Will the bad men find us there?"

A look of horror crossed Hawk's features and then quickly vanished. He reached over and covered her tiny hand with his. "Lizzy, I'm doing everything possible to make sure they'll never find us again."

Lizzy held his gaze for a long, poignant moment. "Okay."

Jillian gave her daughter a quick hug. "Are you finished? We need to leave."

Lizzy bobbed her head up and down. "'Cept, I hav'ta go to the bathroom."

Jillian sensed Hawk's impatience but he didn't say anything. He wasn't used to traveling with young children. So far, Lizzy had taken everything in stride, but it was only a matter of time until she grew cranky. Hawk hadn't seen anything like one of Lizzy's temper tantrums.

It was another ten minutes before she had Lizzy tucked into her car seat and they were back on the road. Hawk didn't say much as he drove, making her wonder what was going through his mind.

James hadn't been afraid to open up to her about his thoughts and feelings. There was a time they'd shared everything.

Yet she also knew that even if her husband hadn't been in a plane crash and left for dead, he probably would have come home from Afghanistan a changed man. In her time at Fort Bragg, other army wives had vented their frustration over the changes in their spouses when they'd come back from being deployed. The moodiness, the quietness, the nightmares.

It was shocking to think that this new version of James, the man she now called Hawk, may have been the same, whether he'd been involved in the plane crash or not.

"What?" Hawk asked, breaking the silence.

She blushed, realizing she'd been staring at him. "Nothing really, just wondering what you were thinking."

He gave a curt nod. "That I should have had plastic surgery to minimize the scar."

She was taken aback by his response. "What? No! I mean, why? That sounds pretty drastic."

Hawk's gaze cut to the rearview mirror to look back at Lizzy before returning to her. "I'm too scary. I don't think telling her the truth now is a good idea."

It was her turn to glance back at their daughter. "She's not afraid of you, Hawk. At least, not anymore."

Hawk's mouth tightened in a grimace. "I'm not sure I believe that. I hate the idea she might be frightened of me."

She lightly touched his forearm. "You need to understand that the day care centers spend a lot of time on their 'Stranger Danger' safety campaign. It's never been about you and your scar but about strangers in general." Jillian knew that her own attitude toward Hawk over these past months hadn't helped. Sure, she'd been grateful for his help and generous support, but she'd never gone out of her way to befriend him, either.

Because of the scar? She didn't want to think so. Hawk was handsome in spite of the scar and she was certain women had let him know how attractive he was during the time they'd been apart.

Hawk dropped his gaze to her left hand. The wedding band she wore felt as if it were burning into her skin.

"It's the same one you gave me," she admitted softly. "I put the diamond away after you…after I got the news, but kept wearing the band."

"Why?"

She hesitated and then told him the truth. "I wanted to save the diamond for Lizzy."

"I meant, why wear the wedding band." Hawk's gravelly voice sent shivers of awareness down her spine.

That was a more complicated answer. "I guess deep down, I still felt married. I wasn't interested in anyone else and wearing the wedding ring kept men away."

There was another long silence. "When I first found you, I thought you'd moved on with someone else. I didn't realize Lizzy was my…" He didn't finish but shrugged and tipped his head back toward their daughter. "I want you to know I wouldn't have blamed you if you had, Jilly. Moved on, I mean."

"Well." She tried to smile. "I guess it's a good thing I didn't."

He looked surprised by her response but didn't say anything more.

Fifteen minutes later, Hawk pulled onto a poorly plowed road, the SUV bouncing from side to side as he navigated between rows of trees. The area was not unlike the wooded landscape surrounding Hawk's cabin. When Hawk brought the vehicle to a stop, Jillian hoped and prayed that this time they wouldn't be forced to flee on foot.

"Stay inside," he said as he pushed open the door on his side. "This won't take long."

She nodded and tried to relax back against the seat. But her nerves were still on edge, and she found herself scanning their surroundings the way Hawk might.

The playground was due west, several yards to her left. The snow wasn't terribly deep and she thought Lizzy might still be able to enjoy the swing set.

Apparently, Hawk need not have worried about there not being a cabin available this close to the holiday, because he returned a short time later with two keys. "I picked the largest one, across from the playground. Hope that's okay."

"Sounds good to me."

"There are three bedrooms," he added. "One room has twin beds."

The SUV bounced again as he drove toward the large cabin across from the playground. She carried Lizzy inside while Hawk unlatched the car seat and brought that in with them.

"We're not keeping the car?" she guessed.

"No." He frowned as he took note of Lizzy's footie pajamas. "I should have asked Mike to bring clothes and stuff for Lizzy. I'll pick some things up on my way back from your place."

"Yeah, well, about that." She cleared her throat as Lizzy ran into the living room. "I forgot to tell you something important."

His gaze narrowed. "Like what?"

"Mommy! I wanna watch TV!"

"I'll be right back." Jillian went into the living room, found the remote and searched for a cartoon channel. When Lizzy was satisfied, she returned to the kitchen. Hawk didn't move, his arms crossed over his chest, his expression forbidding.

She held up a hand as if to ward off an argument. "I forgot to mention the envelope isn't at home."

"Where is it?"

She grimaced. "I left it on my desk at school. The last day before the holiday break is so chaotic—we had a party, then did a Christmas program for the parents. I completely forgot about it."

"At school." Hawk's shoulders relaxed. "Okay, you can tell me where your classroom is and I'll find it."

It was her turn to cross her arms over her chest. "It's better if I go with you."

"No."

The single word made her cheeks flush with anger. "Yes. The place is closed for the holiday break. And you won't know which key to use. Besides, with me being there, we'll be in and out in a heartbeat."

Hawk held her gaze for several long moments, clearly not happy. He turned away without saying a word.

She told herself she didn't care if he was upset with her. The school was locked down and so was her classroom. Sending Hawk in alone seemed wrong. That was her space.

They needed to work together on this, but it was clear Hawk would rather operate alone.

Did that extend to his personal life, too? He claimed he hadn't told her the truth about who he was because he thought she'd moved on, but she wasn't buying it. There had been many opportunities for him to have casually asked questions about her life, about Lizzy, but he hadn't.

She sensed Hawk would rather live alone in a house than be a part of the family with her and Lizzy.

And that knowledge cut deep.

# SIX

Hawk stood at the window overlooking the playground, clenching his jaw so tight he feared he'd crack a few molars. He couldn't remember ever being this angry with Jillian before. Why in the world would she place herself in danger? She needed to be safe. If anything happened to Jillian, who would take care of Lizzy?

A cold fist squeezed his heart. He was the only one who should be facing danger. Not Jillian. She and Lizzy were innocent.

He tried to relax his jaw to think about the situation logically.

Sneaking into Brookland Elementary might not be the highest risk situation they'd face. Not as bad as being trailed through the woods by four armed men. But her assistance wasn't necessary.

He much preferred going alone.

Several moments later, Jillian left the kitchen, and her muted voice talking to Lizzy reached him from the living room. He wanted to join them but forced himself to stay where he was. He also wanted to call Mike to get an ETA, but he'd crushed his cell phone and Jillian's with the heel of his boot and dumped them in the trash outside the family restaurant while Jillian and Lizzy were in the restroom.

Normally he prided himself on being patient. It was the hallmark of a good special ops soldier. Blowing out a heavy sigh, he began to formulate a strategy for once the Callahans arrived. He needed more information on Barton but didn't want to place Mike or his brothers in the senator's crosshairs. But he also needed to get into the elementary school for the envelope that may hold the evidence he needed to fill some of the holes in his memory.

His body tensed when he saw a black SUV pulling up. Upon recognizing Mike's familiar face behind the wheel, he went out to meet him.

"Hey," Mike acknowledged as he slid out from behind the wheel and tossed the keys toward him. Hawk caught them in the air. "This is your new ride. Noah is on the way, and Matt said he and Duchess would be able to help out, too."

"Thanks." Hawk was humbled by the response. Noah Sinclair was married to Maddy, the only female of the Callahan siblings. Noah was a cop. So was Matt Callahan, and Duchess was Matt's K-9 partner, a large black-and-tan German shepherd.

"Oh, and Dana was able to get the antibiotics you requested," Mike continued. "She hit up one of her ER physician friends who agreed to write the prescription as long as you come in to be seen in the next few days."

That wasn't going to happen until they managed to get to the bottom of this mess, but he let it go. The throbbing in his wounded shoulder had become more intense over the past hour, and he hoped the antibiotics would help control the potential infection brewing there.

Mike thrust a bag at him. "Take the antibiotics, make sure you drink a lot of fluids, then get the phones activated so we have a way to contact you. I need you to fill me in."

Hawk nodded and carried the supplies inside. He downed the antibiotic and went to work on the phones, then turned his attention to the computer. Mike joined him at the table at the same time Jillian came over to see what they were doing.

"Hi. I'm Jillian Wade," she introduced herself to Mike.

"Mike Callahan." Mike rose to his feet and offered his hand.

Hawk had to stop himself from jumping up and stepping between them. A ridiculous response, as Mike was happily married to Shayla and a doting father to their son, Brodie.

He really needed to get a grip. Jillian didn't belong to him anymore. James was dead. He was Hawk now.

"Nice to meet you," Jillian said warmly. "Glad you're here to help. We can use it."

"Yeah, so, how do you know Hawk, anyway?" Mike's curious gaze annoyed him.

"We're next-door neighbors." Jillian gestured toward Hawk. "And when two armed men showed up at my house with guns, Hawk saved our lives."

"Our lives?" Mike questioned.

"Me and my daughter, Lizzy," Jillian said, jerking her thumb toward the living room, from where the sound of cartoons could be heard. "She's four."

"I have a four-year-old son, too." Mike beamed. "Brodie is a great kid."

Hawk was getting tired of the small talk. He didn't do chit-chat and didn't see the point. "Can we get back on task here? Talk about the men with guns?"

Mike's expression turned serious. "What do you know about them?"

"Only that they're professionals," Hawk admitted. "Likely with military training, but not Special Forces."

"Why not Special Forces?" Jillian asked.

Hawk shifted in his seat, uncomfortable talking with her about this. If he had his way, he'd shield her and Lizzy from all the bad things that happened in life. "Because I was able to take them both out without a problem. They made mistakes and I capitalized on them."

Jillian held his gaze for a long moment. "Could be you're just a better Special Forces guy than they were. You did that with the four men who tracked us to the cabin, too."

"Four men?" Mike whistled under his breath. "Who did you anger?"

"Fair question." Hawk gestured toward the computer, where he'd brought up the image of the man he suspected was behind all of this. "What do you know about Senator Barton?"

Mike squinted at the screen. "Not much, but I'm willing to dig into his background for you."

"Maybe later." Hawk couldn't help wanting to protect one of the few friends he had.

"Why don't you start at the beginning?" Jillian suggested. "Telling Mike half a story isn't going to help. He needs to hear everything, going back to your deployment in Afghanistan, through the plane crash and the recent events."

She was right. Hawk glanced at his watch. It was after one in the afternoon, and he knew they shouldn't use the key to enter the elementary school until after dusk had fallen.

As briefly as possible, he told Mike about his deployment as a special ops soldier, how his team had died in the Appalachian Mountains and his subsequent memory loss and survival against the odds. Mike listened intently, without interruption. When Hawk got to the part about Jillian being his wife and the information he'd sent, Mike's gaze widened in surprise, at the relationship as much as at the information.

"So Jillian calls Fort Bragg about this envelope and within days a two-man team breaks into her house." Mike let out a snort of derision. "That's no coincidence."

"Agreed. And the two-man team turned into a four-man team at the cabin." Hawk gently massaged his injured shoulder. "I was able to take them down, but only put one of them out of commission permanently."

Mike grimaced, understanding how difficult their escape had been. "Impressive that you were able to get away safely, although maybe I should ask Dana to come out here to look at your shoulder."

"It's fine."

Mike rolled his eyes and glanced back at the face on the computer screen. "And you think this is all related to Senator Rick Barton?"

Hawk nodded. "I know he was a major in the army while I was overseas. Heck, he bragged about his military background while running for office last year. I have a snippet of memory of him standing and talking to someone else while deep in the Afghan mountains. But other than a sense of horror and wrong-doing, I have no idea what that bit of memory means. I have to think he was in a place he wouldn't normally be. From what I remember of Afghanistan, officers didn't go into the mountains on their own. Not without a special ops team."

Mike pursed his lips thoughtfully. "Yeah, I get that. Officers are usually calling the shots, directing the team about what to do... Not off somewhere on their own."

"Exactly," Hawk said. "And I also discovered that Todd Hayes, who's the current secretary of defense, was stationed in Afghanistan as well. The two of them being overseas and now in Washington seems too much of a coincidence."

"Agreed. Seems logical to get the envelope first and see if there's something inside that will provide a clue." Mike shrugged. "I propose that once Matt and Noah get here, you and I hit the road, leaving the two of them and Duchess to watch over Jillian and Lizzy."

"No, I'm going with you," Jillian said before Hawk could respond. "I have a key to the school and my classroom. I know where I left the folder and this will all go more smoothly if you take me along."

To his credit, Mike didn't respond but glanced at Hawk. "Your call."

"No, it's my call," Jillian interjected, a sharp edge to her tone.

"I'm serious about this. If we get caught, I have a good reason to be in the school, you don't."

Hawk tried to come up with logical response that would convince her to stay behind, but he sensed it was useless.

Jillian would continue to insist on going along, and he didn't have a good way to stop her, short of physically restraining her.

"Fine," he finally agreed. "You can come with us, but you need to promise to follow orders without question." He narrowed his eyes. "Your life and ours will depend on that."

Jillian didn't hesitate. "I promise. And thank you."

"Don't thank me." Hawk couldn't hide the frustration in his tone. "The only other option is to tie you to the chair and take the keys from you by force."

She simply raised a brow. "You would never hurt me."

No, he wouldn't. She was his weakness, which was exactly why he didn't want her accompanying him. If more armed men showed up and used Jillian or Lizzy as leverage, he'd fold like a lawn chair.

Mike hid a grin and Hawk knew that his buddy was enjoying this, far too much.

It wasn't that long ago that the situation was reversed. Mike was protecting his wife, Shayla, and his son, Brodie. Shayla had been stubborn back then, too.

They'd managed to survive, breaking open the case surrounding Mike's father's murder without anyone getting seriously injured.

Hawk could only hope and pray that this situation would turn out the same way.

He couldn't imagine a future without Jillian and Lizzy in it.

Jillian did her best not to let Hawk know how much his attitude toward her coming along to get the envelope stung, but it wasn't easy.

"Mommy! I don't wanna wear my pajamas anymore."

She went into the living room to find Lizzy unzipping her

footie pajamas. "Honey, we don't have anything else for you to wear, so you need to keep your pajamas on."

Lizzy's lower lip trembled. "I wanna wear my pink leggings."

They were her favorite, Jillian knew, but there was nothing she could do to fix it.

"We can stop to pick up some stuff for her on our way back," Hawk offered. "I don't blame her for wanting something else to wear."

"Pink leggings," Lizzy repeated, gazing up at Hawk as if he'd given her the world instead of a change of clothes. "With a flowery skirt on top."

"Pink leggings and flowery skirt," Hawk repeated. "Got it."

"Maybe something Christmassy, too," Jillian suggested.

Lizzy nodded and excitedly hopped from one foot to the other. "I wanna look like an angel, like in the Christmas program."

"I'll do my best," Jillian promised. It made her feel better to have another reason to go with Hawk to Brookland Elementary. She doubted Hawk had a clue how to shop for a four-year-old.

"Maybe we should leave early, stop at the store along the way," Hawk suggested.

"Fine with me." She knew her voice was cool but didn't care.

Moments later the sound of an approaching car had both Hawk and Mike heading over to the door. She stayed by Lizzy, only relaxing once the two men put their respective weapons away and greeted the newcomers.

"Come on Lizzy." She took her daughter by the hand. "Do you want to meet the doggie?"

"Yes!" Lizzy ran into the kitchen but stopped abruptly when she realized Duchess was at eye level. "Big doggie."

"Duchess, friend." A man who looked similar to Mike placed his hand on Lizzy's head. "Friend," he repeated.

"Scary big doggie," Lizzy said, huddling close to Jillian's legs.

"She's very friendly, Lizzy," he said with a smile. "Hold out your hand and let Duchess give it a little sniff."

Lizzy held out her hand, and Duchess lowered her nose and took in the little girl's scent. Then Duchess licked Lizzy's fingers, making her laugh. Lizzy stroked the dog's fur and Duchess licked her again.

Lizzy ran back into the living room with Duchess on her heels. Jillian was reassured by how well Duchess interacted with her daughter and knew Lizzy would be unrelenting in her demand for a puppy of her own, after this.

Hawk introduced her to Noah and Matt, then got down to business. "I need you two to stay here with Lizzy while we head back to Brookland," he instructed. "Shouldn't take us longer than two hours to get there, find the envelope, stop to pick up a few things and get back."

Noah and Matt nodded in agreement. Matt asked, "Anything we can do while we're here?"

Jillian saw the indecision in Hawk's blue eyes.

"We need to dig into Senator Barton's background," Mike said when Hawk remained silent.

"It may be too dangerous. I'll do it when I get back," Hawk quickly interjected.

"We have time," Noah said. "May as well be productive."

"Don't worry, Hawk." Mike clapped him on his injured shoulder, making Hawk wince. "We can handle the heat."

The last bit of anger Jillian had been clinging to instantly evaporated. Hawk wasn't just being overly protective of her but of his friends, as well. He didn't want any of the Callahans or their brother-in-law to be in danger from investigating the senator.

The time he'd spent surviving on his own in the Appalachian Mountains must have really changed him.

"The computer can't be traced to us," Matt added. "We'll be fine. As long as Lizzy accepts us being here with her."

"Duchess has already won her over," Jillian said with a smile. "I think she'll be fine."

"We'll bring dinner back with us," Mike said, glancing

around the kitchen. "That way we can continue working without interruption."

Hawk appeared to be resigned to the arrangements. "Let's go, then. We have a lot to do."

Before they got into Mike's SUV, Mike and Hawk smeared mud over the front and back license plates. She assumed that was to make it difficult for anyone to trace the vehicle to them.

The ride to Brookland seemed to take forever. Jillian rode up front as Hawk drove, but the two men kept up a stream of conversation that centered around Mike's new job, the rest of the Callahans and other things she didn't know anything about.

When they passed a store that carried both children's clothes and toys, Jillian tapped Hawk's arm. "Let's stop there, first."

"Sure." He pulled into the parking lot and found a parking space. They were all out in the open so there was no way to hide their vehicle.

Inside the store, Jillian quickly headed for the children's clothing section. It didn't take long to pull out two outfits for Lizzy, the pink leggings with a flowery skirt that she'd requested and a green-and-red one with a Santa elf on the front. She hoped the elf would be okay in lieu of an angel.

"Size 4T," Hawk murmured, peering at the tag. "What does that mean?"

"Four Toddler," Jillian and Mike replied at the same time.

Hawk still looked confused but let it go. A toy display was strategically placed near the children's clothing. Hawk picked up a box containing a doll wearing a puffy gold dress and held it out to her. "Do you think Lizzy would like this?"

She was touched by his question. "She'd love it."

"Good." He tucked the doll dressed in gold into the cart beside the two outfits. "Do you need anything, Jillian?"

Her cheeks went warm and she quickly shook her head. "Maybe some groceries for breakfast and lunch."

They bought the basics, which Jillian sensed was more than Hawk had anticipated, then headed over to the shortest checkout lane. Hawk insisted on paying with cash, and soon they were back on the road. Dusk was falling early as it was the shortest day of the year.

Jillian provided directions to Brookland Elementary. Hawk pulled into a parking spot near the front door and shut down the engine.

"Ready?" he asked.

She nodded and pulled the keys out of her coat pocket. As she approached the door, she sucked in a harsh breath.

The door wasn't locked, the mechanism clearly having been broken.

"Get behind me," Hawk said in a low tone as he pulled out his gun. "Mike, cover from behind."

"On it."

They carefully entered the building. Jillian was glad to see that the main school corridor looked the same as it had when she'd left the previous day, which seemed like a week ago rather than just over twenty-four hours.

But when they approached her classroom, they found the door handle was broken there, too. And when she pushed open the door, she saw the classroom was a disaster.

Desks were turned over, their contents spilling over the floor.

"They found the folder before we did," Hawk said in a resigned tone.

Jillian stepped closer to her desk. Every drawer had been opened, and the three-ring binder containing her lesson plans that she'd left on her desk was lying on the floor.

She picked it up, flipping to the back pocket.

The brown envelope was still there, tucked inside. The assailants who'd ransacked the place had missed it! She took it out and handed it to Hawk. He looked at her name written in his handwriting from over four years ago, and then opened it up.

"Photos," he said, an edge of excitement in his voice. "We have what we need, let's go."

Jillian was happy to leave, although she felt she needed to report the school break-in to the police.

As they headed outside and climbed back in the SUV, the sound of gunfire rang out.

Hawk hit the gas and drove like a maniac out of the parking lot.

They'd been found!

# SEVEN

The back wheels of the SUV fishtailed as Hawk took a hard left out of the parking lot in a desperate attempt to ditch the gunmen. He couldn't afford to assume there was only one gunman: there may very well be another one stationed along the single road leading away from the school.

"Get down." He pushed Jillian's head toward her lap. He needed to get away. Instincts had him making a quick right, then right again, then left.

Jillian was murmuring something that sounded like a prayer. Hawk continued to make random turns, doing his best to get far away from the school without being tailed. As he drove, he was grateful for Mike's idea of putting mud over the license plates.

Mike had opened one of the back windows and was peering behind them, with his gun held ready.

"See anyone following us?" Hawk asked.

"Negative."

It was good news, but he couldn't afford to assume they were safe. Not yet.

Maybe not ever.

Five tense minutes passed. Hawk concentrated on putting distance between them and the school while Mike kept his gaze on their tail. The interior of the SUV grew cold, but Hawk ignored the discomfort.

After a total of fifteen minutes passed, Mike sat back in his seat and rolled up the window. "We're clear."

Hawk nodded but continued to keep one eye on the rearview mirror just in case. He couldn't afford to be caught off guard again.

Jillian sat up, pushing her red hair out of her face. "God has been watching over us," she said softly.

"Amen," Mike agreed.

Hawk wasn't sure how to respond. Despite the holes in his memory, he could remember a moment he'd sat in church with Jillian, but it had been so long ago. Before his deployment to Afghanistan. Before he'd caught a glimpse of Rick Barton in the Afghan mountains.

Before their plane had crashed into the Appalachian Mountains, killing everyone on board except for him.

Knowing that Jillian and Mike had maintained their faith made him wonder if he'd given up too soon.

Was it possible that God had been watching over him for the past five years?

He shrugged the thought aside and focused on getting back to the cabin motel without taking a direct route. In fact, he'd gone further east than he'd intended, so he took a left and headed north for a bit, before turning again to head west.

"Don't forget we need to bring dinner back," Mike spoke up from the back seat.

Hawk nodded. "Let me know what you want."

"Jillian, what do you think? We need something that Lizzy will like, too," Mike said.

Hawk mentally kicked himself for momentarily forgetting about Lizzy. Being a father, Mike had automatically remembered they were feeding a child. Hawk needed to remember he had a daughter. He cleared his throat, awkwardly. "Whatever Lizzy and Jillian want is fine with me."

"How about pizza?" Jillian offered. "We can get a small cheese pizza for me and Lizzy, and a large loaded with everything for you guys."

"Works for me," Mike said. "Okay with you, Hawk?"

"Sure." Hawk wasn't concerned about food, although the antibiotic was making his stomach feel queasy. He was preoccupied with how the gunmen had gone to the school to find the envelope, which meant they'd traced Jillian's call. Had they gone to the school prior to sneaking into her house? It made sense, but while he felt certain that had been the sequence of events, there was no way to know for sure.

At least they still had the envelope. He'd only taken a quick glance at the two photos inside and had been disappointed not to see Rick Barton's familiar face. He'd have to take a closer look to see if he recognized who the guy was and whether there was something incriminating in them.

There must be, or the senator wouldn't have sent men wearing ski masks with guns to get it.

"There's a pizza place up ahead," Mike said, tapping him on the shoulder. "We're only about ten minutes from the cabin motel, so it's a good place to stop."

Hawk grunted in agreement. The next exit was three miles away, and he took the exit, keeping a wary eye on the road behind them.

As darkness had fallen, it became increasingly difficult to keep track of a tail. Headlights came and went, some round, some square, but it was almost impossible to tell makes or models of the vehicles they belonged to.

No cars followed him off the interstate. He dug in his pocket for money to pay for the pizza, but Mike waved him off. "Stay here, I'll get them."

The door shut behind Mike, leaving him with Jillian. He glanced at her, trying to think of something to say.

She lifted a weary hand. "Don't say it. I already know you were right. I shouldn't have insisted on coming along."

"That wasn't what I was going to say," he protested. "It's true I hate putting you in danger, but I have to admit that if you hadn't been there, we may not have found the envelope."

There was a brief silence before she asked, "Do you think they wrecked my house, too?"

Although he wanted to protect her, he couldn't bring himself to lie. "Yes, I believe they searched your house, too. Why stop at the school and not go all the way? It's probably the first thing they did after we left."

Jillian looked as if she might cry but then surprised him by muttering, "Those rotten jerks."

"Yeah." He wished he had the right to pull her into his arms to offer comfort. Regardless of the fact that the gunmen had followed the envelope to Jillian's home and school, it was only because he'd sent it to her.

Why would he do such a thing? It went against his nature to put his wife in danger. Although he hadn't known about Lizzy, but still...

Then again, he hadn't anticipated being in a plane crash, either. It must have been right after he'd seen Barton in the mountains that he'd sent her the photos. Right after they'd been told they were being put on a plane to Washington, DC, to be debriefed.

And it had sat dormant all this time. Until Jillian had decided to clean out the box of his stuff.

"I hope the photos are helpful," Jillian said, breaking into his thoughts.

"Me, too." He thought about pulling them out now but caught sight of Mike heading toward the SUV carrying two large boxes of pizza.

"That didn't take long," Jillian said, glancing back at Mike as he slid in behind Hawk.

"Nope." Mike grinned and patted the boxes. "I got two large pizzas, one with half cheese and half with the works. I figure the guys will be hungry."

"Good plan," Jillian agreed.

Hawk started the SUV and drove out of the parking lot. Instead of heading immediately west, he took the ramp going on the opposite direction. He sensed Jillian eyeing him curiously, but she didn't say anything.

After five miles, he got off the interstate and took a highway headed south. He knew from previous trips that the highway would eventually take them to the cabin motel. It was longer, but worth the effort to make sure they weren't followed.

"Must be the scenic route," Mike commented from the back seat.

"Yep." The tantalizing scent of pizza sauce and cheese made his mouth water. "Won't take much longer."

"Hey, I've got the food back here, I won't starve," Mike joked.

"Save some for Lizzy," Jillian admonished him.

Their banter was an effort to lighten the somber mood. Hawk appreciated it but couldn't shake the memory of the close call. He needed to find a way to stay one step ahead of these guys, since the senator had more money and resources than they did.

When they reached the cabin motel, the pizza was greeted with enthusiasm. Jillian took the bag of clothes they'd bought for Lizzy and quickly took her daughter into the bedroom to change. It wouldn't be long before she'd need to put her jammies on again, but that didn't seem to matter. When Lizzy came out wearing the pink leggings and holding the doll in her arms, his heart thumped crazily in his chest.

"Thank you, Mr. Hawk." From the way she said that, he knew she must have been prompted by Jillian.

"You're very welcome," he managed in his usual hoarse voice. He longed to take his daughter in his arms but knew it was too soon.

At least she wasn't crying at the mere sight of him.

"Are you hungry?" Jillian asked, putting a pillow on the kitchen chair so Lizzy could reach the table.

"Yes," Lizzy agreed, holding the doll in one hand while trying to climb into the chair with the other.

"Let's put Belle over here, shall we?" Jillian suggested. "We don't want her to get messy."

"Okay." Lizzy was content to have her doll placed in the living room.

"Let's say grace," Mike suggested.

Hawk wasn't surprised and took note of how Jillian eagerly participated in the brief prayer.

As the others dug into the pizza, he took a moment to pull the two photos out of the brown envelope. The top one was a clear view of a soldier meeting with a man who looked to be an insurgent, based on how he was dressed and the AK-47 he cradled in his arms.

The second photo was even more interesting. It was a close-up photo of an open box of guns. Hawk shifted his gaze from one photo to the next. The box was on the ground near the two men, the American soldier and the unknown rebel.

He sat back in his chair for a long moment, the implication reeling in his mind. Was it possible he'd witnessed a gun sale between one of the men he'd fought alongside and the enemy?

And if so, how did Senator Barton fit into the puzzle? He had to assume this was the reason he and his team had been targeted.

Because they'd seen too much.

Safe in the cabin, Jillian tried to put those moments that they'd been under fire out of her mind. Focusing on Lizzy helped and she silently promised herself that next time, she'd listen to Hawk.

If she and Hawk hadn't escaped today, what would have happened to Lizzy? With no surviving relatives, their daughter would no doubt end up in the foster care system.

She was thankful that God had kept them safe, but she also knew that her insistence on going along with Hawk and Mike could have ended far differently.

Her stomach unknotted enough that she was able to eat two slices of pizza. Watching Hawk, she noticed that he'd pulled out the photos from the envelope and was studying them carefully. Before she could ask him about them, Mike did.

"Something interesting?" Mike asked.

Hawk nodded. "Yeah. I think I know why I've been targeted."

"Why is that?" Noah asked.

Hawk slid the photos across the table toward the others. "Take a look, tell me what you see."

Jillian leaned over to see for herself, but the glare on the photo made it difficult to see the details.

"Mommy, I'm done," Lizzy announced.

"Okay." She stood and went over to get a wet napkin to wipe off the tomato sauce and cheese from her daughter's hands and face, before setting her down. "Don't forget Belle."

"I won't." Lizzy scampered over to pick up her doll and began to play in the living room.

"One of our guys sold guns to an insurgent?" Noah asked, his tone reflecting his horror.

"That's what I see," Hawk agreed, his expression grim. "Who is this guy? Other than being an American soldier?"

Jillian could barely comprehend what they were saying. "You mean, one of our men sold the enemy guns for money?"

"That dirtbag" Mike said harshly. "To put American guns in the hands of the insurgents is beyond awful. How many of our men and women died being shot by American guns wielded by the enemy?"

"Too many," Matt said quietly. "No wonder Senator Barton has sent armed men after you."

"Yeah, except there's no way to prove Barton was involved," Hawk said.

Jillian's stomach knotted up all over again. Holding onto the photos felt like holding onto a stick of dynamite. The whole thing could blow up in their faces at any time.

"Maybe we should send it to the newspapers," Mike suggested. "Going public may be the best way to protect you and your family."

Hawk grimaced. "My word and a grainy picture of a guy I can't identify? That won't get me very far." He paused, then added, "Besides, even if I could prove this soldier is linked to Barton, the situation could be taken out of context and turned the other way. Barton could claim the guy was an insurgent informant who returned the box of stolen guns to the US."

There was a long moment of silence as they imagined how that scenario would play out.

"What if we can find other evidence?" Noah suggested. "Something that would link Barton to the guns?"

"You mean like serial numbers?" Hawk shook his head. "Too many years have passed to track them down."

"Are we sure Senator Barton is involved?" She asked. "It's a serious allegation against a powerful man."

There was a long moment before Hawk spoke up. "I believe Senator Barton is involved, because I have a clear memory of seeing him in the Afghan mountains." He pointed to the photo on the table. "Just like this."

"But that guy isn't Barton," Noah said, stating the obvious.

"I know." Hawk's expression went hard. "But don't you see? Whoever this guy in the photo is, he must have friends in high places. They rigged my team's plane to crash in the mountains."

"True," Mike said, trying to appease Hawk. "So let's say Barton is involved. Maybe it's about money and power. Could be Barton has always aspired to be elected into office. What if we tried to trace the money?" Mike gestured toward the computer. "Digging into his campaign funds may reveal something interesting."

"Again, this was all five years ago." Hawk abruptly stood, revealing his frustration. "Anything that far back will be well covered up by now."

"We don't know that until we look," Mike said.

Hawk shook his head. "It's impossible. My family won't be safe until we can find proof that links Barton to the guns."

"Hawk," Mike began, but it was too late. Hawk strode out of the kitchen, walked through the living room and disappeared into one of the bedrooms.

Leaving a tense silence in his wake.

The Callahans looked at each other, then at her. "Don't worry," Mike said in an attempt to be helpful. "We'll figure this out."

Jillian tried to summon a smile, but inside she felt an overwhelming sense of dread. Until now, Hawk had been her pillar of strength.

His lack of faith was like taking a sledgehammer to the foundation of her fragile home.

"Excuse me," she managed as she rose to her feet. She followed Hawk's path through the living room, making sure Lizzy was okay, before she lightly rapped on the bedroom door.

There was no answer, but that didn't stop her from opening the door a bit. "Hawk?"

She could see his dark silhouette standing in front of the window, the moonlight reflecting over the lingering patches of snow. She pushed the door open further and went inside.

Jillian was torn between offering comfort and demanding he find a way to keep Lizzy safe.

"I'm sorry." His hoarse voice was low and rough. "I never should have survived that mountain crash. And I never, ever should have mailed those photos to you."

"Hawk, please. It hurts me when you say things like that." She tentatively approached, resting her hand on his back. His muscles went tense beneath her touch, and she feared he'd pull away from her. "I'm glad you survived the crash. And I'm grateful to have you here with me now."

For a long moment he didn't move, but then he slowly turned to face her.

She stared up at him, searching his expression in the moonlight. Then she lifted her hand and cupped his scarred cheek. He flinched and tried to move away, but she held firm. "Please don't lose faith," she whispered.

"Jilly…" Her name was little more than a sigh. He slowly placed his hands on her waist and drew her close. She slipped her hand around his neck and pulled his head down so she could kiss him.

His mouth on hers was familiar yet different. The chemistry between them had always sizzled, but there was also a newness to the embrace. And when they finally came up for air, she felt more confused than ever, unable to fully mesh the Hawk she was with now to the man she'd once married.

# EIGHT

Hawk had no idea how it happened. One minute he was beating himself up inside for being so stupid as to bring danger to the two people he loved most in the world, and the next he was kissing Jilly as if he'd never stop.

"I—um," he fumbled for what to say, sensing an apology would not be welcome. He may have holes in his memory surrounding the past, but right here, right now, was crystal clear in his mind.

Jilly had kissed him. She'd put her hand on his scarred cheek, refusing to let him pull away, and had kissed him. He found it hard to imagine she wasn't repulsed by his scarred face.

He'd held his wife in his arms for the first time in five years, and now that he had, he realized how much he didn't want to let her go.

Yet even while he silently rejoiced over their kiss and embrace, he warned himself not to read too much into what had transpired between them. They were on the run and in danger. Emotions were always heightened in times of stress.

James was gone, and only Hawk remained. He refused to hold Jillian to vows they'd exchanged what seemed like a lifetime ago.

Even as all these thoughts tumbled through his mind, he couldn't imagine his life without Jillian and Lizzy.

His wife and daughter.

"Hawk, I know you've been through a lot, but you can't give up. I need you to be strong." She paused and added, "Lizzy and I both need you to stay strong and focused. There has to be something we can do to reveal the truth about what happened five years ago."

"I'm not giving up," he assured her, regretting his moment of weakness. He'd stared at the photos, willing his memory to return, but the gaps had stubbornly remained. He remembered Jilly, the brief moment he'd seen Barton in the mountains, but not the identity of the soldier in the photo. He shook off the depressing thoughts. "I promise I won't rest until you and Lizzy are safe."

"I believe you. And remember, we're in this together," she said, reaching for his hand.

It was on the tip of his tongue to point out that her only job was to keep Lizzy safe, but he didn't want to ruin the moment. Instead he gave her hand a squeeze before letting go and moving back toward the living room.

"Mommy, look! Belle is on TV!" Lizzy pointed excitedly at the television screen as she clutched her doll to her chest. "Isn't she beautiful?"

"Not as pretty as you," Jilly said with a smile, dropping a kiss on top of their daughter's head.

Hawk was secretly pleased his gift had made Lizzy happy. Sure, one doll couldn't make up for missing the past four years of her life, but it was a start to forging a relationship of some sort with his daughter.

"I found it on the kids' channel," Mike offered. "Figured she'd love seeing it."

"Thank you, Mike." The way Jilly smiled at Mike made Hawk grind his teeth together to keep him from saying something stupid. Mike was hardly a threat; the guy was head over heels in love with his wife. There was no reason for Hawk to act like a jealous fool.

"Mr. Hawk, will you watch Belle with me?" Lizzy asked, looking up at him with a shy smile.

Hawk's heart melted and he knew he'd do anything to keep his daughter happy. "Sure, for a few minutes."

He dropped down beside her on the sofa, watching Lizzy more than the cartoon on the television. Her joy made him smile. Lizzy clapped her hands, dragging his attention to the television. He had no idea there was a whole movie about the doll he'd picked up on impulse at the store, but apparently his instinct had been right on.

It took him a minute to realize the movie Lizzy was watching was *Beauty and the Beast*. Belle was Beauty, and the interaction between Belle and the Beast reminded him too much of his new relationship with Jilly.

Only he knew his physical handicap wouldn't change after a kiss and declaration of love.

"Hawk, do you have a minute?" Mike called from the kitchen.

With reluctance, he left his daughter's side and crossed over to join them.

"Remember Ryker Tillman?"

Hawk nodded. He'd met the soldier six months ago, when they'd all worked together with Mike and the rest of the Callahans to uncover the truth about an organization known as the Dark Knights, who were responsible for former Milwaukee Police Chief Max Callahan's murder. "What about him?"

"I just spoke to Ryker. He's busy now, but he agreed to head up here tomorrow to help us identify this guy." Mike tapped the photo. "Maybe once we know who this guy is, we'll be able to find the link to Barton."

The possibility sparked a glimmer of hope. "That would be great."

"Listen, we need to hit the road," Matt said. "But we'll return in the morning."

Hawk wanted to protest but understood the Callahans and Noah all had wives and kids waiting at home. "Thanks."

The men pulled on their jackets and headed outside.

Hawk walked with them, watching as they split up. Mike headed toward the SUV that Hawk had stolen from the masked men. They'd run the plate but it was only registered to a corporation, not an individual. The corp was called Maxwell, Inc. and didn't sound familiar. The plan was to abandon it near the lakefront, in the complete opposite direction from where the cabin motels were located.

Matt and Noah would follow in the vehicle they had arrived in, picking up Mike and taking him home.

When they were gone, Hawk made a final sweep of the area outside the cabin, familiarizing himself with the terrain, before going back inside.

In the living room, he could hear Jillian telling Lizzy to get ready for bed now that the movie was over.

He sat in front of the computer, staring morosely at the picture of Senator Rick Barton on the screen.

Was Jillian right? What if Barton wasn't involved? Was Hawk being foolish to trust a five-year-old memory fragment? After everything he'd been through, there was no doubt his mind could easily play tricks on him.

He pulled up the search function with a renewed sense of steely determination. The memory was real. Jillian had proved real, and so was what he'd seen that day in Afghanistan. He couldn't believe otherwise.

Which meant there had to be proof somewhere of Barton being involved in dirty dealings.

He just had to find it.

Jillian tossed and turned on her twin bed next to Lizzy's, the memory of Hawk's kiss making it impossible to sleep.

When he'd pulled away, she'd thought for sure he was going

to apologize for kissing her despite the fact that *she* was the one who'd kissed *him*.

Kissed Hawk, not James. Weird how the two men had become separate in her mind. It wasn't the scar that grooved his cheek that made him different, but more the man he'd become.

Maybe because her memories of James were pre-Lizzy, pre-deployment. The reality of Hawk helping her escape the gunmen in her home, in the woods outside his cabin, and again outside the elementary school, was very different.

Caring for Hawk felt like a betrayal to James. Those years after she'd been told James had died, she'd mourned what they'd lost. The chance to be a family.

Yet now that Hawk was here, alive and well, she still hadn't told Lizzy he was her father.

She must have fallen asleep at some point, because the enticing scent of fresh brewed coffee woke her up the following morning.

Peering over at the bed on the other side of the wall, she could see Lizzy was still asleep. Moving as silently as possible, Jillian slid out of bed and made her way to the door. She opened it just enough to slip through, then closed it behind her.

Hawk was in the kitchen, his dark hair damp from a recent washing. She put a hand to her tousled auburn hair and wished she'd taken the time to find the brush she'd purchased for Lizzy.

"Good morning," she greeted him as she came into the kitchen. "I hope you didn't shower with that wounded shoulder."

Hawk glanced at her, his blue eyes intense. "Morning. And no, I didn't. Are you hungry? I was about to make eggs but wasn't sure how you and Lizzy preferred to have them cooked."

She was surprised he didn't remember she liked her eggs over easy while he always made his own sunny-side up. "Lizzy likes them scrambled."

"And you?"

"Over easy." She crossed over to the coffeepot and filled a

mug. He pushed the carton of milk toward her and then opened the cupboard to pull down a small container of sugar.

"Thanks." She added the milk and sugar to her coffee and then took a seat at the table, putting distance between them.

The urge to walk into his arms and greet him with a good-morning kiss was strong. She had to remind herself that they weren't living together like husband and wife but as two people hiding from gunmen.

"Did you sleep okay last night?" It was an inane question to break the silence.

"Caught a few hours on the sofa." He broke two eggs in a bowl and whisked them with milk. "Pored over everything I could find online about Barton but still came up empty-handed."

She sipped her coffee, secretly doubting the clarity around Hawk's memory of seeing Barton in the Afghan mountains. The soldier in the photo was clearly not the senator, and she doubted that someone like Barton would be involved in selling American guns to the enemy.

"Mommy? I hav'ta go to the bathroom."

"Coming." Jillian put her coffee aside and went over to help her daughter get out of her footie pajamas. She took advantage of the opportunity to shower and to wash Lizzy up, too. When they were finished in the bathroom, Lizzy demanded to wear her Christmas outfit.

"Are you hungry?" Jillian tucked a strand of her wet hair behind her ear. "Mr. Hawk is making scrambled eggs for breakfast."

"Yum." Lizzy skipped as they entered the kitchen. "Did you add cheese?"

Hawk looked crestfallen at the plain eggs. "I'm sorry, but we don't have any cheese."

"That's okay. Lizzy likes scrambled eggs even without cheese," Jillian quickly interjected.

"Cheese makes them taste better," Lizzy pointed out.

"Next time." Hawk set the plate of scrambled eggs in front

of their daughter and then a second plate with two eggs over easy in front of her.

Jillian waited until he joined them with his own eggs, also over easy. She put out a hand, inviting him to take it, at the same time reaching for Lizzy's. "Shall we pray?"

Hawk hesitated, then nodded. His hand was warm around hers but she refused to let that distract her. "Dear Lord, we thank You for keeping us safe and for this food we are about to eat. Please guide us on Your chosen path, amen."

"Amen," Lizzy mimicked.

"Amen," Hawk added in his hoarse voice.

She was pleased he'd joined in the prayer and stared for a moment at their joined hands, before forcing herself to let him go. James used to attend church with her, but it seemed as if Hawk had forgotten that part of his life.

She hoped and prayed Hawk would find his way back to his faith.

"The guys will be here in a couple of hours," Hawk said, breaking the silence.

Jillian glanced through the windows at the overcast sky. "That's fine. I'm hoping Lizzy can use the playground before it rains or snows."

"The temperature is above freezing, so it shouldn't snow."

"It would be nice to have a white Christmas," she said. Then she realized that what she should be praying for was to be safe at home, with the bad guys behind bars by Christmas.

A seemingly impossible task.

"I wanna swing!" Lizzy had glommed onto the comment about the playground. "And go down the slide!"

"We'll check it out after breakfast," Jillian promised.

"I'll tag along," Hawk said.

She was surprised by his offer. "I'm sure we're safe here if you have other things to do."

Hawk rubbed at his sore shoulder for a moment. "I don't have anything else to do until the guys get here."

"You've been taking your antibiotic, right?" she asked, noticing the gesture. "Maybe I should take a look at your wounds."

"The wounds are fine. The antibiotics are working, and the skin around the wound is red but not obviously infected. At least, not yet."

She feared it was only a matter of time but said nothing. Hawk would keep pressing forward until he was physically incapable of doing anything more. Wasn't that how he'd gotten himself out of the Appalachian Mountains? She could only imagine how difficult it had been for him to drag himself from the plane wreck, hiding while men combed the area for him, and then still managing to find relative safety.

It was humbling to realize the man she'd married had an underlying will of steel.

Upon finishing breakfast, Jillian began cleaning up and washing the dishes. Hawk joined her at the sink, pitching in to help.

"I can do this," she offered.

"I know. So can I."

She smiled and shook her head at his stubbornness. With the two of them working together, the task didn't take long, and soon they were bundled up in their outdoor gear and crossing the clearing toward the playground.

"I want Mr. Hawk to push me," Lizzy said after Jillian lifted her into the swing. "I wanna go really high!"

Hawk looked pleased with the request and eagerly stepped forward. Jillian moved back to give them room.

Hawk was tentative at first, pushing Lizzy carefully as if she were a fragile doll that might break. But Lizzy pumped her legs and cried, "Higher! I wanna go higher!"

He glanced at Jillian as if needing approval, before pushing Lizzy high in the air. The little girl squealed with glee and a wide smile softened Hawk's face.

"You should have figured she's a thrill seeker like her father," Jillian pointed out.

"Thrill seeker? I was never like that," he protested.

She arched a brow. "Have you forgotten that death trap of a motorcycle you used to ride before we got married?"

"Motorcycle? I drove a motorcycle?" He looked genuinely confused and she realized he hadn't remembered that part of their life. Those carefree days before he was sent overseas.

"Never mind." She waved a hand, wishing she'd never brought it up. "It doesn't matter."

When Lizzy got bored with the playground they headed back inside. She'd just found another movie on the kids' channel for Lizzy to watch when two SUVs pulled up in front of the cabin.

She recognized Mike Callahan, Matt Callahan and his K-9 Duchess, but the other man who emerged from the second SUV was a stranger.

Hawk opened the door and gestured for them to come inside.

"Hawk, you remember Ryker Tillman," Mike said, gesturing to the dark-haired stranger who wore his hair military short.

"Glad you could make it." Hawk held out his hand.

"You don't remember me, do you?" Ryker asked. "From years ago, not just the couple of months ago when we worked together to help Mike."

Hawk narrowed his gaze, staring at the guy intently. "You were in my special ops platoon. But not on my team."

Ryker smiled. "Is that a memory or a calculated guess?"

Hawk grimaced. "The latter, I'm afraid. My memory is still in bits and pieces."

"It's okay," Ryker assured him. "It was a long time ago. I'm just glad you're alive and well."

"Thanks. Oh, and this is Jillian."

"Ma'am," Ryker said with a nod.

"Please call me Jillian." She felt out of place amongst the group, so she went to the sink to boil some eggs, thinking it might be a good idea to have egg salad sandwiches for lunch. Not that there was enough food to feed all of them, but it gave her something to do.

"Ryker, I—um, need you to check out this photo for me." Hawk went over to pull the two photographs out of the brown envelope.

"Yeah, Mike texted a picture of them to me, but the image was too grainy to make out the guy's features." Ryker took the photographs from Hawk's hands and peered down at them for a long moment.

Jillian put the eggs in a pan of water and set them on the stove. After turning the electric burner on, she searched for the pan cover.

"I'm pretty sure this is Master Sergeant Colin Yonkers," Ryker said finally.

The pan cover slipped from Jillian's fingers, hitting the floor with a loud clang. The four men in the kitchen turned to stare at her in surprise.

"What's wrong?" Hawk sensed her distress. "Do you recognize the name?"

Jillian's mouth went dry and she reached a shaky hand toward the photograph. "I need to see that."

Ryker handed it over and she peered at the face of the American soldier standing next to the insurgent, who was holding some sort of assault rifle.

There was no mistake.

"It's him," she whispered. How could she have missed it the first time she'd looked at the photo?

"Who?" Hawk slipped his arm around her waist as if sensing she might fall.

She raised her gaze to his. "The man who came to tell me you were dead. Master Sergeant Colin Yonkers. I'm pretty sure I still have his card in the box of your things I kept in the basement."

Mike let out a low whistle. "That's an interesting twist."

Jillian stared at the photograph, double-checking to make sure it wasn't her own mind playing tricks on her.

But that day was clearly etched in her memory. This soldier

in the photograph was the same man who'd come to tell her James had died in the line of duty.

But it was all a lie.

This man was the criminal responsible for the plane crash that had nearly killed Hawk.

The man who had taken away her husband.

# NINE

Hawk tightened his grip around Jillian's waist. Her face was pale and her fingers trembled with fear or anger or both.

He could relate.

"Easy," he cautioned. His concern for Jillian momentarily displaced his anger over knowing that Yonkers had betrayed their country. Betrayed Hawk's team.

Had Yonkers been one of the soldiers who'd combed the wooded Appalachian mountainside for him? Hawk wished he could remember.

"I can't believe it," Jillian whispered. "The same man who sold guns to the enemy came to tell me you were dead."

"I know." He ached to pull her close and to kiss her but didn't want to make her uncomfortable in front of their audience.

"I remember Yonkers," Ryker spoke up.

Hawk turned to look at his fellow soldier. The one he hadn't remembered serving in Afghanistan with him. "What do you remember?"

Ryker hesitated a moment, glancing at Mike and Matt before continuing. "I remember he was trained as a special ops soldier, the way you and I were. I was assigned to the Charlie team, but you were in the Bravo team."

Bravo sounded right, although Hawk wished he could re-member the names and faces of his teammates, the ones who had died in the plane crash, more clearly. "And where was Yon-kers assigned?"

"Alpha team." Ryker shrugged and spread his hands. "We were all sent in different directions, to infiltrate the insurgents."

Hawk remembered that much, as well. "So the entire Alpha team could have been involved in the arms dealing. Who was their commanding officer?"

Again, Ryker looked puzzled. "All special ops teams re-ported up to the same commanding officer, Colonel McCann, now known as General McCann."

The name triggered something in Hawk's fragmented mem-ory. "Major Rick Barton reported to the colonel, didn't he?"

Jillian sucked in a harsh breath.

"Yes, along with Major Todd Hayes," Ryker admitted. "But there were others, as well. It wasn't as if Yonkers was the cap-tain in charge of Alpha, the way you were in charge of Bravo."

He'd been in charge of the Bravo team? Hawk hadn't remem-bered that, either. Maybe his mind had shut out all things mili-tary while he was in survival mode on the mountain. Memories that were too painful to deal with.

Or maybe he simply didn't remember as much as he'd origi-nally thought. The memory fragment of Rick Barton could be nothing more than his imagination.

A cold tightness squeezed his chest. Did he have this all wrong? He'd been so focused on Barton—had he been chas-ing the wrong man?

None of it made any sense.

"We'll investigate Yonkers, see if we can find out what he's been up to these past five years," Mike said.

Hawk nodded. "He must have friends in high places to send highly trained men with guns after us."

"Understood," Mike agreed.

"Could be he's part of a mercenary group," Ryker offered. "A lot of soldiers joined them after leaving the army."

Mercenaries were known to take dangerous jobs for high pay. It was a possibility he hadn't considered. "You're right. It's an angle we need to explore."

Jillian pulled away from Hawk, quickly rinsed the pan cover she'd dropped and placed it over the eggs on the stove.

Hawk wished he knew what she was thinking.

Mike, Matt and Ryker took seats at the kitchen table. Hawk glanced at Jillian before joining them. She stood with her back to them, staring down at the pot of eggs, waiting for them to boil.

Mike took over the computer, using it with an ease Hawk envied. He could do the basics required to run his private investigator business but knew he lacked the skills Mike possessed. Pursuing a job as a private investigator allowed him the flexibility he needed to dig into Barton's past. With a faked background, he knew he'd never have made it into the police academy, and becoming a PI was the next best thing.

The pages on the screen flipped from one subject to the next as Mike started with some of the well-known mercenary groups.

"Here!" Excitement punctuated Mike's tone. He turned the screen so Hawk could see it better. "Check this out."

"The Blake-Moore group?" Hawk shrugged. "I've never heard of them."

"Maybe not, but Yonkers's name is listed as a member. And look, the two founders are Kevin Blake and Harper Moore. They were soldiers, too. Does either of them look familiar to you?" Mike asked.

Hawk stared at the two photographs on the screen, trying to fit them into the empty puzzle-piece slots of his memory. "I don't think so. But Ryker would know better than I would."

Ryker slowly shook his head. "Sorry, but I can't place them, either. Could be they were over there, but I don't recognize them."

"It's a good find," Mike insisted. "I think it's possible the men who came after you and Jillian were members of this mercenary group."

"Because I have the photograph that implicates Yonkers?" Hawk tried to understand how this fitted. "Seems extreme. Why would Blake-Moore risk it? I ended up killing one of their men fighting back in self-defense."

"Maybe Blake or Moore were in on the arms deal?" Matt suggested. "If that was the case, they all have a lot to lose."

Hawk warmed to the idea. He wished he could place these two men who'd formed their own mercenary group. He tapped the screen. "Who hires these mercenary groups?"

Ryker, Matt and Mike all exchanged a knowing look.

"Anyone can hire them," Ryker finally said. "Private companies, for example, might need to hire protection for bigwigs traveling to dangerous areas of the continent."

"What about the US government?" Hawk pressed.

There was another moment of silence before Ryker nodded. "Yeah, I've heard that the government hires private groups like this, too. It's sometimes easier to use hired guns than to justify sending military troops."

That made sense to Hawk. "So guys like Barton and Hayes could have hired Yonkers and others to come after me."

"Anything is possible," Mike admitted. "But I'm not sure it's the likely scenario. Private groups like Blake-Moore don't have the same government oversight that the military has. Could be that Yonkers and whoever was working with him started something while deployed in Afghanistan and carried it over to the private sector."

"Yeah," Ryker chimed in. He spread his hands. "After all, who would know?"

"The weapons have to come from somewhere," Hawk pointed out.

"True. Maybe they still have an inside source within the army." Matt reached down to pat Duchess, who'd come in from the living room. "Regardless, it's a place to start."

The task of investigating a private mercenary group was daunting. Hawk had no idea where to start.

"I still have the letters you sent me," Jillian said, breaking the silence.

Hawk glanced at her with a frown. "Letters?"

"Yes." She turned to face him. "The ones you sent from Afghanistan. I'm certain you mentioned some of the guys by name."

For a moment he felt a surge of excitement and then remembered the damage done in her classroom. "I'm sure they already searched your house, Jilly," he gently pointed out. "The same way they searched your classroom."

"Yes, but they missed the envelope in my classroom. Maybe they missed the letters, as well?" Jillian had taken the eggs off the stove and was running them under cold water. "When I was going through your things, I took the letters and put them in Lizzy's room. They may not have found them there."

Hawk considered the possibility. As much as he wanted to know what was in the letters he'd sent his wife, he wasn't convinced they would be helpful. "Not sure it's worth the risk. If I was Yonkers and had mercenaries to do my bidding, I'd have someone staked out at your place. The same way they were staked out at the school."

"Would be nice to know what information may be in the letters," Mike pointed out. "Who knows, maybe you mention either Kevin Blake or Harper Moore by name."

"It would be a good link to have," Ryker agreed. "Something to go along with the photographs."

"I can show you where the letters are," Jillian offered.

"No. You're not going along this time," Hawk said firmly. "Remember last time?"

Jillian stared at him for a long moment. He tried not to fidget in his seat. It was almost impossible for him to deny Jillian anything, but he knew forcing her to stay safe with Lizzy was the right thing to do.

She broke away from his gaze and left the kitchen without saying a word.

Taking a big chunk of his heart with her.

Jillian plopped on the sofa next to Lizzy, fighting the urge to cry.

She wasn't sure why she was so upset. After experiencing the gunfire at the school, she'd decided her role was to stay with Lizzy, to keep her safe.

But she wanted Hawk to be safe, too.

The thought of losing him made her sick to her stomach.

She couldn't lose him. Not after finding him after all these years.

"Mommy, will you play dolls with me?" Lizzy asked.

She forced a smile. "Sure."

Lizzy took a throw blanket from the sofa and made a tent over the coffee table. "This will be Belle's house."

"I see," Jillian commented. Her daughter was creative when it came to playing, and Jillian remembered how she and James had once talked about having a large family.

At the time, she hadn't wanted Lizzy to be an only child like her. James had agreed.

Did Hawk even remember that conversation? She doubted it.

Jillian closed her eyes for a moment, reaching out in prayer. God would watch over them.

Hadn't He watched over James during the past five years?

The murmur of male voices piqued her interest, but she forced herself to play with Lizzy. Caring for her daughter was the most important thing right now.

She never should have mentioned the letters.

Lizzy played with Belle, making the doll dance under the tent as if the area were a ballroom. Jillian used a stubby stick from the wood sitting in front of the fireplace and used it as the Beast.

When Hawk had chosen Belle as a gift for Lizzy, had he envisioned himself as the Beast? She hoped not. The scar didn't matter, it was the man inside that was attractive to her.

They played for a while before Hawk interrupted them. "Jilly? The guys are going to head out to get sandwiches for lunch. What would you and Lizzy like?"

"I was going to make egg salad sandwiches for the group," she protested.

"No! I want a grilled cheese," Lizzy announced.

"We can save the eggs for breakfast. Is that okay with you, Jillian?" Hawk asked.

She shrugged. "Sure, why not?"

"What would you like to eat?"

"Turkey with cheese, lettuce and tomato," she responded. "When are you leaving?"

"Not until later this evening. Maybe nine or ten tonight."

She nodded, understanding the need to go in while it was dark.

Hawk went back into the kitchen to relay their order but then returned shortly thereafter. "Will you please tell me exactly where you put the letters?"

She didn't answer right away, listening as Lizzy sang the opening song to *Beauty and the Beast*. "In Lizzy's closet," she finally told him. "There's a small lace-covered jewelry box that I found at a secondhand store. There's a velvet shelf inside that lifts out. The area underneath is meant for larger jewelry but I used that as a place to store the letters."

"Is that where you put your diamond engagement ring?" he asked.

"Yes." She lifted her gaze to his. "There's also one of our wedding photos in there. Those were the keepsakes I was saving for Lizzy."

"Thank you." Hawk tucked a strand of her hair behind her ear. "I appreciate that you tried to keep me in our daughter's heart."

Suddenly it was all too much. "Don't go. Stay here with us. I'm sure the others can find the letters without your help."

The words had barely left her mouth when Hawk shook his head. "I can't do that. This is my problem. It's bad enough I'm exposing my friends to danger. I need to be the one to take the biggest risk."

He was right. Logically, she understood, but her heart rejected everything about Hawk being in the center of danger.

"How's your shoulder?"

"Fine." His gaze skidded from hers in a way that convinced her he was stretching the truth.

"I want to see it." This time, she wasn't taking no for an answer. If the wounds were dramatically worse, then she'd insist he allow one of the others to go inside Lizzy's room to get the letters.

Hawk let out a sigh and nodded. "Fine. But I'm telling you it looks okay. At least the front does. It's hard to see the entry wound in the back."

"I'll be the judge of that." She gestured for him to sit at the other end of the sofa.

He slipped his arm out of the T-shirt and showed her his shoulder. The dressings covering the front and the back looked fresh from the morning. She peeked beneath the gauze, not liking the redness that puckered the edges of his skin. To her eyes, the front wound looked worse than the back.

"I'm not sure how much longer you can let this go with just oral antibiotics." She set the old dressings aside and left to get fresh gauze. The packets were in the bathroom and she returned and quickly redressed them.

"They're working fine." Hawk winced as he put his arm through his shirtsleeve. "I've suffered worse."

She knew he meant after the plane crash. The strength of will he'd used to survive in the mountains amazed her. She wanted to throw herself into his arms, but the low rumble of a car engine indicated the guys were back with the promised food.

The rest of the day passed by with excruciating slowness. Lizzy was pretty good at keeping herself occupied, but by the time they were finished with dinner, even her daughter's mood had turned cranky.

"Bath time," Jillian announced, eager to get her daughter down for the night.

"Okay!" Lizzy happened to like baths and eagerly ran toward the bathroom.

"Jilly." Hawk caught her hand before she could follow their daughter. "We're heading out. Keep your disposable phone handy, okay? Matt and Duchess are going to stay here with you while the rest of us head into town."

"I know." She was glad to have Duchess around, since the dog kept Lizzy entertained. "Hawk, promise me you'll be careful."

His blue eyes bored into hers. "I promise."

She gave him a quick hug and a kiss, then pulled away to follow Lizzy, feeling the intensity of Hawk's gaze on her back as she went.

The only thing she could do now was to wait. And pray.

*Dear Lord, keep Hawk and the others safe in Your care!*

Hawk hated leaving Jilly and Lizzy at the cabin but reminded himself they would be safe with Matt and Duchess watching over them.

He desperately needed some sort of break in the case. Having the photo of Yonkers with the insurgent was a start, but he needed more.

It was a lot of hope to pin on a handful of old love letters.

The trip to Brookland seemed to take longer than it had the previous day. Hawk didn't want to believe it was because Jillian and Lizzy weren't with him, but he couldn't deny the keen sense of loss.

How had he become so dependent on them? For the past five

months he'd been content to live nearby, offering nothing more than a helping hand.

Now he wanted more. Maybe even a chance at a future.

An impossible dream if he couldn't figure out who was behind the recent attacks.

"I think I need to pay Yonkers a visit," Ryker said, breaking the silence. "Maybe I can infiltrate the Blake-Moore organization."

"Not yet," Hawk protested. He didn't like the idea of any of his friends being in danger. "We don't even know if they're involved. This could be something Yonkers did on his own."

"Then maybe we should kidnap him and bring him to the cabin for questioning," Ryker pointed out. "It's a way to get to the heart of the issue. Your wife and daughter deserve to be safe."

Hawk was touched by Ryker's offer but wasn't convinced. "Hold that thought for now. We'll go that route if we have to."

"The address you gave me is on the next block," Mike said from the driver's seat. "Where do you want me to park?"

"Here is fine." Hawk zipped up his leather jacket and pulled on his gloves. Jilly's keys were in his pocket, but he suspected he'd find the door already open, the way the school's had been.

"We'll give you ten minutes," Ryker said. "If you're not back by then, we're coming in after you."

"Got it." Hawk silently acknowledged he'd missed working with a team. Being with Ryker and the Callahans reminded him of the men he'd served with on the Bravo team.

He straightened. Bravo team! He had a clear memory of standing outside their camp with the men of his team. He wished more memories would fall into place. The sooner the better.

Hawk slipped out of the car and into the darkness. The earlier sunshine had melted much of the snow, making it easy to avoid leaving tracks as he approached Jilly's.

As expected, the door was ajar. The interior had been ransacked the same way her classroom had been, only worse. The

Christmas tree was on its side, the ornaments broken into dozens of pieces. He clenched his jaw, furious at how they'd ruined Jillian's home. Holding his temper in check, he carefully made his way to the upstairs bedrooms.

Lizzy's room had been searched but not messed up like the living room. Inside the closet, he found the lacy jewelry box. He checked to make sure the engagement ring and the letters were inside.

They were. With a sense of relief, Hawk tucked the box beneath his arm and moved back across the room.

A creak on the staircase on the other side of the door made him freeze in his tracks.

*Someone was out there!*

# TEN

As much as he didn't want to let go of the jewelry box with the letters, Hawk carefully set it down on the floor so he would have both hands free. He didn't move for ten full minutes, waiting for the hostile on the stairs to reveal himself. He didn't so much as blink, keeping all five of his senses laser sharp. When he heard the slightest brush of fabric against the wall, he knew his patience had been rewarded.

Yet he continued to wait. When he heard another sound, closer this time, he mentally judged the distance between himself and the doorway to Lizzy's room.

Not yet, he warned himself, despite the fact that every muscle in his body was tense with the need to move.

Another sound and the barest movement of the door.

*Now!*

Hawk lashed out with his booted foot, kicking the door into the intruder. There was a muffled thump, but then the door flew open, nearly hitting him in the face.

The intruder came straight for Hawk like a mini bulldozer. Hawk used the guy's momentum to spin him around, slamming him into the wall. Hawk's momentary satisfaction evaporated when the guy continued to fight, hitting and kicking with all his might, refusing to go down easy.

Hawk took several blows, including one directly in his injured shoulder, which caused a red haze of pain to cloud his vision. Gritting his teeth and ignoring the pain, he wrapped his fingers around the guy's neck, wrestling him to the floor. He continued to hold pressure against his carotid arteries, until the hostile's strength faded. When he felt the man's body go limp, he eased upright and took a moment to draw in a ragged breath.

His shoulder throbbed and he could feel the dampness of fresh blood oozing from the through-and-through bullet wounds. He sighed. Man, he was getting too old for this. He found some of Lizzy's hair ribbons and used them to bind the attacker's wrists, then took off the guy's boots so he could use the shoelaces to tie up his ankles. Once he had the intruder trussed up like a Christmas turkey, Hawk pulled off the ski mask and waited for him to regain consciousness.

This ridiculous game of hide-and-seek had gone on long enough. He wanted answers.

And this time, he wasn't leaving until he had them.

Knowing Mike and Ryker would be waiting, Hawk called Mike's phone. "I've got a hostile tied up here, will be out soon."

"Did you find the letters?" Mike asked.

"Yes." Hawk disconnected the call because the guy on the floor began to move. When the hostile realized he was tied up, he stopped his struggles and looked up at Hawk.

"Who sent you?"

The assailant didn't answer. Hawk felt his body tense with frustration. He leaned over, getting in the guy's face.

"Who sent you?" he repeated, his low, gravelly voice harsh with anger.

Again, the man didn't respond.

Hawk pulled out his gun and put the barrel against the perp's temple. "Give me one good reason not to kill you right here, right now."

There was another pause, but the frightened look in the guy's widened eyes gave Hawk hope that he'd start talking.

"I'm following orders," the intruder finally said.

"Whose orders?" Hawk pressed the barrel of the gun more firmly against his temple. "Who from the Blake-Moore group is giving the orders?"

The surprise in the guy's eyes confirmed Hawk was on the right track. "If I talk they'll kill me."

"I'll kill you if you don't." Hawk hoped and prayed the guy wouldn't call his bluff. "Which one? Kevin Blake or Harper Moore?"

"Moore," the man finally admitted.

The answer surprised him. "Why?"

The intruder shook his head. "I don't know. I just do what I'm told."

"Tell me your name. And if you were you one of the men up at the cabin." Hawk pressed.

The guy's gaze skittered from his in a way that confirmed Hawk's suspicions.

"I guess I should have killed you then." Hawk stared down at the guy. "Why did you go after Jillian Wade?"

"We weren't supposed to hurt her. We only wanted the photographs."

Hawk nodded. So far this guy was confirming their suspicions, but he needed more. "Who hired the Blake-Moore group to come after me?"

The intruder shook his head. "I don't know. I told you, my job is to follow orders."

"What's your name?" Hawk wasn't sure why he cared so much about who this guy was, but he wanted to verify he was former army, too. He didn't think a private mercenary group would hire anyone but former military, but maybe former law enforcement?

"Ben Dugan."

"Okay, Dugan. Tell me about the weapons being sold in Afghanistan."

Dugan frowned. "I don't know anything about that."

Hawk wasn't sure he believed him. A noise at the doorway had him spinning around with his weapon ready. But it was only Tillman who'd come to offer assistance.

Hawk turned back to his hostage. "You said you only wanted the photographs. You didn't know what was on them?"

"No. I don't have any idea what you're talking about."

"We can make him talk," Ryker drawled.

"I'm not sure he knows anything," Hawk answered.

There was a long silence as Hawk considered his options. It wouldn't necessarily surprise him that the boss of the operation had withheld key information from his men. Yet he knew Dugan had every reason to lie.

"Fine. Don't tell me about the gun sales. We'll figure out the rest on our own." Hawk glanced at Ryker, who shrugged and nodded.

"What should we do with him?" Ryker asked.

Hawk gestured toward the door. "We'll leave, then call the police. They can arrest him for trespassing and vandalism."

"No! Wait! Don't! They'll kill me!"

After tucking the frilly jewelry box beneath his arm, Hawk hesitated, staring down at the mercenary. "And if I don't turn you in to the authorities, you'll just come after me again. I can't risk it."

"I have money saved up, they pay us well." Dugan's tone was pleading. "Let me go and I'll disappear."

He wasn't sure he believed him, but at the same time, he didn't want any more blood on his hands. The one mercenary he'd killed in self-defense was more than enough.

"I'll take care of him for you," Ryker offered. "I'll haul his butt into town and dump him on the cops' doorstep."

Hawk appreciated it but shook his head. "It's not worth it."

"We can't just leave him here," Ryker pointed out.

"Sure we can. We'll give him fifteen minutes before calling the cops. That seems fair enough." Hawk headed toward Ryker, then glanced over his shoulder. "And Dugan?" Hawk waited until the guy looked him in the eye. "If I see you again, I will kill you."

Dugan didn't answer, but Hawk didn't care. Getting out of his binds wouldn't be easy, but it was possible. Hawk followed Ryker as they stealthily made their way through Jilly's house and out the back door, making sure to take care in case Dugan hadn't been alone.

But they didn't see anyone else when they met up with Mike at the SUV.

Ryker jumped into the back, leaving Hawk to ride shotgun. He settled into the seat and glanced at his friend. "In twelve minutes, we're going to call the police and report the intruder and subsequent vandalism," Hawk told him.

Mike lifted a brow at the strange request but didn't ask anything further. "What did you find out?"

"His name is Ben Dugan and he works for the Blake-Moore group, as we suspected. He claims his orders came directly from Harper Moore and that the intent was only to get the photographs from Jillian without hurting her or Lizzy."

Mike let out a snort. "Yeah, right."

Hawk gingerly rotated his injured shoulder, understanding where Mike was coming from. The bullet hadn't been a warning but an attempt to silence him for good. And it galled him to know that his body had protected Jillian and Lizzy. If the bullet had been lower…he shook his head, unable to finish the thought.

"You and Ryker left him tied up?" Mike asked, breaking the silence.

"Yeah. Gave him fifteen minutes to get away before calling the cops."

"Why?" Mike asked, his expression mirroring his confusion. "Don't you want him arrested?"

"I do but he claims the mercenaries will kill him if he gets caught by the cops. Figured we'd give him a chance to escape."

Mike glanced at the rearview mirror, exchanging a look with Ryker. Hawk knew they were curious about his motives, but he didn't care. Hawk closed his eyes, trying to relax despite feeling every blow Dugan had landed.

The wound in his shoulder would need medical attention, soon. Hawk fought off the sense of overwhelming despair. He'd gotten the letters and a small amount of information, but still nothing solid to go on.

He needed to find a way to keep Jillian and Lizzy safe from the mercenaries who stalked him. No easy task, considering the wealth and power these men had to get what they wanted.

Remembering how Jillian had prayed made him wonder if that would help. Was God really up there, looking out for him? He felt as if it was worth a try.

He sent up a silent prayer, asking for the strength and wisdom to keep his wife and daughter safe from harm.

Relishing the sense of peace that washed over him.

Jillian couldn't relax while Hawk, Mike and Ryker were gone. Oh, she appreciated Matt's being here with Duchess to watch over them, but it wasn't the same as having Hawk protect her and Lizzy.

Strange how much she'd come to lean on Hawk over these past few days. To the point she didn't feel safe or at ease without him at her side.

Matt's phone rang. Jillian leaped up from the sofa, her stomach knotting with worry. She trusted in Hawk's abilities and was grateful he wasn't alone, but she feared the call was bad news.

"Yeah, I'm looking him up now," Matt said as he tapped the computer keyboard.

Jillian came up to stand beside him, anxious to know what was going on.

"I found Benjamin Dugan, and he's former army and was stationed in Afghanistan the same time you were."

"Is Hawk okay?" she whispered.

Matt nodded, then put his hand over the phone. "Yeah, they're all on their way back. This is Ryker on the phone. They were able to get a name from one of the mercenaries."

Relieved to know Hawk was okay, Jillian sank into the kitchen chair beside Matt and kept her gaze on the army soldier on the screen.

"He was Team Alpha, too," Matt continued. He put the phone on speaker so he could work as he talked. "I have a photo here of him with Yonkers. Guess that explains why he joined the Blake-Moore group."

"We need to know who gave the Alpha team their orders," Ryker said. "I think it's clear that the Alpha team has turned mercenary. But we need a connection to someone higher up on the food chain."

"Agreed." Matt continued searching the images, moving so fast on the screen she couldn't keep up. "I'll dig around a bit more. Just get here as soon as you can."

"Did you find the letters?" Jillian asked before Ryker could end the call.

"Yeah, Hawk found them."

"Were any of the names in the letters familiar?" She wanted to believe the letters were useful, that this little excursion hadn't been for nothing.

"I can't answer that yet, it's too dark to read them. We'll take a closer look when we get there."

Jillian sensed there was something Ryker wasn't telling her but decided to let it go. Matt had told her Hawk was okay, so she did her best to be patient.

"No reason for you to wait up," Matt said, scratching Duchess behind the ears.

She gave him a blank stare. "I couldn't sleep even if I wanted to."

Matt sighed and nodded. Sitting there with nothing constructive to do was excruciating. She wanted to help with the investigation. Doing what, she had no clue.

She tried to remember the contents of Hawk's—James's—love letters, but couldn't remember anything other than how much he'd missed her.

And she'd missed him, too. Especially the morning when she'd found out she was pregnant. Then the fateful knock had come on her door just hours later, revealing a man wearing a full-dress blue uniform.

She'd known James was dead the moment she saw the man standing there. She'd been sick to her stomach, either from the devastating news or the effects of her pregnancy. Or both.

Except James hadn't been dead. He'd been in a plane crash and left for dead, surviving against all odds.

She was so lost in the memories, that she didn't hear the SUV drive up until she heard voices coming from outside. When Hawk stepped through the doorway, she lunged up from her seat and threw herself into his arms.

He caught her against his chest and held her close for several long moments. It wasn't until one of the guys loudly cleared his throat that she realized they were blocking the doorway.

"Sorry," she murmured, stepping back from Hawk's embrace. She frowned when she noticed fresh blood stains on his shirt. "You're hurt!"

"It's nothing." Hawk moved into the kitchen so that Ryker and Mike could come in out of the cold. "The wound opened up a bit, that's all."

She sent a steely glare toward Ryker, who couldn't look her in the eye. "You said he was fine."

"I am. Leave him alone, Jilly," Hawk said gently. "We got what we went for and more."

The jewelry box looked incongruous in Hawk's rough hands. He held it out toward her, but she shook her head.

"You should look at them. The names will mean more to you than to me."

Hawk nodded and carefully set the box on the table. He went over to wash his hands at the sink before returning to open the jewelry box. When Jillian saw her engagement ring, tears pricked her eyes.

She'd taken the diamond ring off on the one-year anniversary of James's death. So long ago, yet at the same time, it seemed like yesterday.

Hawk caught her gaze for a moment before lifting out the top part of the jewelry box to reveal the letters tucked beneath. He pulled them out and set them on the table.

The ribbon she'd used to tie them together was pink, old and frayed. She'd chosen the color for Lizzy. It was still her daughter's favorite color.

Hawk put the letters in order, the most recent on top, as she took the seat next to him. He carefully opened the last letter he'd ever written to her and began to read.

Seeing his tight, messy scrawl brought fond memories to the surface. She remembered how much she looked forward to hearing from James, hanging on every word he'd written. Reading them over and over until the paper grew worn and thin.

A burst of anger at what they'd lost, at what had been taken from them, sent her stumbling to her feet. She went into the living room and collapsed on the sofa, burying her face in her hands as she tried to hold herself together.

She knew she should be grateful for finding Hawk after all these years. To know he was alive and had found his way home to her.

But the acute sense of loss wouldn't go away. How different would her life and Lizzy's be if James hadn't seen something he shouldn't have?

Useless to play the what-if game.

"Jilly." Hawk's low voice caused her to lift her head from her hands. The cushion shifted as he sat beside her. "We're going to be all right. I promise to keep you safe."

He misunderstood what was behind her emotional breakdown. "I'm so angry at the men who did this to you," she finally managed. "To us."

"Anger won't help us figure out the person responsible for all of this," he pointed out in a reasonable tone that made her want to shove him off the sofa.

"Maybe not, but I can't help it. They tried to kill you. Took you away from me, from Lizzy. It's not right! They had no right to do that to us!"

"Easy." Hawk's tone was soothing as he put his arm around her shoulders. "We'll get to the bottom of this. The men responsible will go to jail for a very long time."

At the moment it wasn't much comfort. Leaning against Hawk, she tried to rein in her temper.

He was right. Getting angry wouldn't help them understand who was responsible.

She lifted her head and looked at him. "Did the letters help?"

There was a moment's hesitation before he nodded. "I mentioned Colin Yonkers several times. He was part of the Alpha team, and from what I can tell—we were once friends."

Friends? She stared into Hawk's blue eyes and saw the regret. This news, along with his concussion, could explain his repressed memories. She couldn't imagine finding out your friend was selling guns to the enemy.

And worse? Knowing the same friend tried to kill you to keep the secret from seeing the light of day.

# ELEVEN

Hawk didn't want to tell Jillian how difficult it had been for him to read the letters he'd written to her so many years ago. Most of the time it was as if they were written by a stranger. More proof that he was a different man back then, as revealed by letters full of love, hope and faith. Until the day he'd lost his entire team in a plane crash, which had left a hard, cracked, scarred shell of a man behind.

His stomach knotted with the realization that the love he'd once shared with Jillian was gone forever. That simple, pure love was something they could never get back.

He told himself to focus on the fact that he was here with Jillian and Lizzy now. The way she leaned on him, and had gotten so upset with Yonkers on his behalf, was sweet.

The letters hadn't revealed as much as he'd hoped. Although, in addition to several mentions of Yonkers, there was also one brief reference to Major Rick Barton. The phrasing gave him the impression that the Bravo team had reported up through Barton.

Was that reporting relationship the reason he still had that snippet of memory about the guy? And if so, had Yonkers's Alpha team reported up to Barton as well?

What did it all mean?

"Hawk?" Jillian's soft voice drew him from his swirling thoughts.

"What is it?" He kept his arm around her shoulders, holding her close.

"I'm glad you're here with me. With us."

Her words were a soothing balm against the jagged edges of his heart. He ached to kiss her, but the guys were still in the kitchen, so he refrained from giving in to temptation.

"When this is over..." Jillian began, but he silenced her with a finger over her lips.

"Don't, Jilly." He couldn't help remembering those letters. The words of love James had written. "I don't want you to make any rash promises. We'll just take things one step at a time, okay? Ensuring your safety and Lizzy's is my one and only priority."

"Hawk..." she tried again, but he shook his head and gently pulled away from her.

"The man you once loved is gone, Jilly. Reading those letters proves it. I'm not that guy anymore. James is gone, forever. And no amount of hoping and praying will bring him back."

Jilly jumped to her feet, temper sparking in her green gaze. "Hawk and James are more alike than you realize. They share a brain and a heart. Don't you see? That's all that matters."

He sighed, knowing she was missing the point. But then she continued, "Of course you're different now. Any soldier who serves overseas in combat comes home a changed man. You know that as well as I do. I'm not the same woman I was when we first married, either. Being a mother changed me. Honestly, Hawk, if you would put your future in God's hands, you'd find out exactly what God has in store for us."

Her words resonated deep within. He remembered the faith he'd displayed in his letters. Was Jillian right about rediscovering his faith? Was that part of the heart and brain he shared with James? He remembered how his earlier prayer had brought a sense of peace.

"Okay, you're right," he finally said. "We've both changed, and focusing on the past isn't helpful. We'll move forward from here, together."

"I'd like that," Jillian agreed.

He held up a hand. "But keeping you and Lizzy safe is still the main priority."

"Your safety, too," Jillian added.

His gaze held hers for a long moment. It humbled him to know she cared about him.

About Hawk. The man he'd become.

"Hawk? You need to see this." Mike Callahan's voice interrupted his thoughts.

"Be right there." He wanted to reach out to Jillian but tucked his hands in the front pockets of his jeans. "Get some rest. I'm not sure how long the guys will stay, but you need sleep."

She hesitated before nodding. "Good night, Hawk."

"Good night."

He watched her enter the bedroom she shared with Lizzy. He felt as if the earth had shifted slightly to the left and he was having trouble regaining his footing. The idea that she saw parts of James within him was disconcerting.

"Hawk?" Mike repeated.

He returned to the kitchen to see what the guys had found.

"Check this out." Mike tapped a photo on the computer screen. "We did a search on Barton and found this."

A chill snaked down Hawk's spine. "Colin Yonkers."

"Yep. That's a picture of your old buddy Yonkers shaking hands and looking all chummy with Senator Rick Barton."

"When was that taken?"

"Two years ago," Ryker spoke up. "So far we haven't found anything more recent."

A handshake at some charity function from two years ago wasn't the link he was hoping to find, but it was a start.

"Listen, Hawk, I need to hit the road, I promised Lacy I'd be back tonight. She has her hands full with Rory and being pregnant." Matt Callahan stood near the door, with Duchess at his side. "I took some time off work. So I can return tomorrow, if that helps."

Hawk realized the hour was half past midnight. "Yeah, sure. Why don't all of you get out of here? You have families to take care of."

"I don't," Ryker said dryly. "Maybe we should call Duncan O'Hare—he doesn't have a family, either."

Hawk reluctantly grinned. Once he'd felt just like Tillman and O'Hare, alone in a world where Callahans were falling in love like apples dropping from trees. "No sense in dragging Duncan into this. And you still have a life, don't you?"

Ryker shrugged. "Not really. Been feeling at loose ends."

"You're welcome to bunk here. There's a third bedroom no one is using. But don't feel obligated to stick around. You can always return in the morning with the others."

Ryker shrugged. "No sense in driving back and forth. After being in Afghanistan, I've learned to sleep anywhere."

Hawk was touched by the offer and wondered if Ryker was doing this because of his own experiences in Afghanistan. Ryker had mentioned being on Team Charlie, and Hawk was curious about what Ryker had gone through back then.

Not that Ryker's secrets were any of his business.

"Not sure what more we can do until the morning anyway," Mike said, rising to his feet and stretching his cramped muscles. "Even if we find more photos of Yonkers and Senator Barton together, it won't mean anything. We need to talk directly with Yonkers."

"Or with someone else from Alpha," Ryker added. "Dugan didn't know anything, but someone else will. Yonkers didn't pull this off on his own. I'll see if I can find anyone that might be in the area."

"Thanks again," Hawk said as the Callahans made their way outside.

"We've got your back," Mike said, clapping him on his un-injured shoulder. "The same way you had ours."

Hawk nodded. He hadn't thought twice about helping Mike and the other Callahan siblings when they'd run into trouble over the past couple of years. It had honestly never occurred to him that he'd one day need their help in return.

Yet here he was, needing everything they had to offer and grateful for it. Nothing was more important than keeping Jillian and Lizzy safe.

When their taillights faded out of sight, he went back inside. Ryker had taken the seat behind the computer. Hawk rubbed his throbbing shoulder—he knew he couldn't put off cleaning the wound any longer. So far, the antibiotics Dana had obtained for him were keeping the infection at bay. But he was feeling chilled and hoped he wasn't running a fever.

"You should get some rest," Ryker said as if reading his thoughts. "I'll work here for a bit longer and then hit the sack."

"Okay, thanks." Hawk wasn't about to argue. He headed into the bathroom and shucked out of his T-shirt. Fresh blood oozed from the saturated gauze over the wound. Gritting his teeth, he removed the old dressing and then used soap and water to clean the wound as best he could.

Unfortunately, he couldn't reach the entry wound in the back of his shoulder very easily. He slapped water over his shoulder, making a mess. The exit wound in the front was worse, but he knew that either one of them could be a source of infection. The ibuprofen would help, but not for long.

They needed to find a way to get to the bottom of this mess. Before he ended up in the hospital.

Reminding himself to drink more fluids, Hawk finished re-dressing his wounds and returned to the kitchen to chug down a full glass of water with the ibuprofen.

Antibiotics, fluids, ibuprofen and rest. That was all he could do for the moment.

But when he stretched out on his bed, his mind wouldn't shut down. He kept thinking about the letters he'd written to Jillian so many years ago.

She'd told him that Hawk and James were entwined together, and maybe she was right. His basic personality couldn't have changed that much.

But when he read those letters, he'd felt as if he were eavesdropping on a conversation between Jillian and someone else. A relationship that made him jealous.

He knew that his experience in the Appalachian Mountains had changed him. Jillian could say that a part of James was still with him, but how did she know for sure? Especially when he couldn't be certain?

The thought scared him. Far more than four hostiles coming after him.

Because he knew that if he gave his heart to Jillian and she decided that she didn't love Hawk the way she once had loved James, he would never recover.

He couldn't lose Jillian twice in one lifetime. That was too much to ask of any man.

Which meant he needed to keep a bit of distance between them, until she honestly accepted him for who he was.

Hawk Jacobson, not James Wade.

Jillian woke early in the morning. The darkness lingering beyond the windows proved that dawn hadn't yet broken over the horizon. The air was chilly, but aside from that, the atmosphere was so nice and peaceful she decided to stay snuggled under the covers. There was no reason to be up this soon. Besides, she wasn't sure how many of the guys had stayed overnight in the cabin. It would perhaps be better to wait before finding out.

And she really didn't want to wake Lizzy up yet. Her daughter had dealt with all of this running for safety like a champ, but Jillian had no idea how much longer Lizzy would tolerate being in the cabin without her friends at day care or any of her things to play with.

Her thoughts circled around to last night's conversation with Hawk. Deep down, she was troubled by the way he felt so completely severed from James. It just didn't make any sense. She believed that, at the core, Hawk and James were the same man.

Granted, a terrible tragedy could change a person's outlook on life, altering how they saw the world, but it couldn't change who you were deep within.

Or could it?

She didn't want to entertain the notion that he might be right. Not after how Hawk had acted around her since the night he'd caught those men sneaking into her home. She'd witnessed Hawk's actions firsthand over these past few days and knew that he hadn't changed much from the man she'd fallen in love with. A little, sure. But not a lot.

After all, she'd changed, too. Hawk didn't seem to appreciate the ways she was different. Was that because he didn't remember their lives before his deployment as clearly as she did?

Those days were gone, but that didn't mean they couldn't experience them again in the future. Even if they decided to give their relationship a try, especially since Hawk deserved to be in close contact with Lizzy, she wasn't sure that he'd understand her need to maintain her financial independence. She was on Christmas break now but planned to be back in her classroom at Brookland Elementary when school resumed after the New Year.

James had told her he preferred her to stay home once they had a family. He'd been a latchkey kid and hadn't liked it, so he'd wanted something different, something better, for his own children.

Yet upon learning of James's death, she'd faced the cold, hard reality that she needed to be able to support herself and Lizzy. Thankfully, she'd finished her teaching degree and was able to find a job, but it hadn't been easy.

Now that Hawk was back in her life, she understood he may

be able to provide for her and Lizzy financially, but she wasn't about to give up her hard-earned independence.

Nope. Giving up her teaching job wasn't going to work for her. She liked spending time with her students. They certainly kept her on her toes. Even more important, she enjoyed her admittedly minor role in shaping their future. Any one of these children she taught had a chance to do something amazing with their lives.

Especially Lizzy.

She thought about what to make for breakfast and wished she hadn't made the hard-boiled eggs yesterday. She didn't mind having them for breakfast, but Lizzy wasn't a fan. There might be pancake batter, which would work, but she couldn't remember if there was any syrup.

Realizing she couldn't stay here any longer, she slid out of bed and padded across the room, hoping not to wake Lizzy.

When she opened the door she was surprised to find Hawk and Ryker seated at the kitchen table. The scent of coffee was welcome, so she slid through the doorway, softly closing the door behind her.

After quickly using the bathroom, Jillian entered the kitchen and helped herself to a mug of coffee.

"Good morning." Hawk's greeting was sweet. The man she'd met a few days ago had never indulged in small talk.

"Morning," she returned, adding milk to her mug. "What's going on?"

The two men exchanged a glance that made her put her mug down on the counter. Something was obviously up and she sensed she wouldn't like it.

"We found Yonkers," Hawk finally admitted. "And we're thinking of going after him."

Yup, she didn't like it. Not one bit. "Why? Isn't this a job for the police? Can't you call in the authorities and make them take care of him?"

"Based on what proof?" Ryker asked reasonably. "A grainy five-year-old photo? It's not enough."

She opened her mouth to argue, but Hawk held up his hand. "Jilly, hold off a minute. We just want to talk to Colin Yonkers, nothing more."

"He has a sister in the area," Ryker continued. "We're going to head over there as soon as the Callahans return."

She still didn't like it. "His sister is innocent. Why drag her into this?"

"So are you and Lizzy," Hawk countered. "And again, we're not going to hurt her or drag her into anything. We just need to talk to her brother."

She crossed her arms over her chest, feeling helpless. She didn't want to be left with one of the Callahans as a babysitter again. The time she'd spent yesterday, waiting for Hawk to return, had been interminable.

The sense of dread wouldn't go away. It made her think that if Hawk left her again today, he wouldn't return.

# TWELVE

The hurt, disappointment and despair in Jillian's green eyes made him feel like a jerk. He understood where she was coming from, but it wasn't as if he and Ryker were going to hurt Yonkers's sister, Olivia Habush.

Hawk chose to believe that finding Olivia lived in Madison, less than an hour from their cabin motel, was an indication they were on the right track. That this next step was meant to be. Maybe even a sign that God was showing them the way.

He'd begun to realize the importance of having faith and believing that God was watching over them.

Additionally, there was a remote possibility that Yonkers was staying with his sister, or someplace close by, not caring that his actions could place Olivia in danger. Or maybe too arrogant to believe he'd be discovered.

"Please don't do this," Jillian said in a husky whisper. "I can't bear the thought of putting more innocent lives at risk. There has to be another way."

Hawk didn't want to upset Jillian but knew they were running out of time. *He* was running out of time. His shoulder wound was worse today. Not only was it throbbing like crazy, but the edges of the wound were red and puffy. He knew there was an infection brewing deep within.

It wouldn't be long before he'd be too sick to keep Jillian and Lizzy safe.

"I promise we won't hurt her," Ryker spoke up. "That's not the kind of soldiers we are. We were trained to keep innocents safe from harm, and that includes Yonkers's little sister."

Jillian's pleading gaze drilled into Hawk's as if Ryker hadn't spoken. "It's not just that. I'm afraid of losing you, too, Hawk. You and the others helping us."

He didn't think it would help to point out that he would do whatever it took, even putting his own life on the line, to save her life and Lizzy's. "I know. But once we talk with Yonkers, we'll have what we need to put this issue to rest once and for all. This will all be over soon. Just another twenty-four to forty-eight hours."

Jillian pressed her lips together in a tight line. "Forty-eight hours brings us to Christmas Eve. Is this how you want to spend your first Christmas with your daughter? On the run from the bad guys? Doesn't Lizzy deserve something better?"

Ryker shifted uncomfortably in his seat as the disagreement turned personal. He abruptly stood and made his way to the door. "I'll—uh, leave you two alone for a bit. I need to check the perimeter, anyway."

Before Hawk could say anything, Ryker disappeared outside, closing the door firmly behind him. Hawk couldn't blame the guy for ditching them. This was between him and Jillian.

He rose to his feet and stepped closer to his wife, wishing he dared to pull her into his arms. But her defensive stance warned him off.

"I need you to trust me on this, Jillian," he finally said. "I need more information before bringing my case forward to the authorities."

"Need or want?" Her tone was full of challenge.

"Both," he admitted. "I told you before, it's not easy to hide from men in power. If Senator Barton spins some tale that makes it look like I'm the bad guy, I'll be tossed in jail or killed. They've already tried to silence me once. No reason to think they won't do it again."

"But you know more now," she persisted. "You've put some of the puzzle pieces together. Can't Mike or Matt Callahan help protect you? They're cops, aren't they?"

Hawk suppressed a sigh. It wasn't that long ago that Mike was in trouble himself, and being a cop hadn't saved him. In fact, each of the Callahan siblings had overcome adversity over the past couple of years. Unfortunately, he knew only too well that there was a dark side to law enforcement and within the government.

No one was immune to greed.

And the photo of Yonkers selling weapons to the enemy proved it.

"Soon," he promised. "When we have more than an old photo and my fragmented memories to go on, we'll turn everything over to the police. Or maybe the FBI." The idea of going to the federal government had been nagging at him for a while now. The locals didn't have jurisdiction over crimes committed overseas. But the Bureau of Alcohol, Tobacco, Firearms and Explosives did, as well as the Federal Bureau of Investigation.

Maybe he should contact both agencies, just to cover his bases.

"Mommy, I'm hungry."

Lizzy's plaintive tone diverted his attention to his daughter. She looked adorable, with her pink cheeks and hair messy from sleep.

"Let's use the bathroom first, okay?" Jillian left the kitchen to take care of Lizzy.

While they were in the bathroom, he rummaged for something to make for breakfast. There was more oatmeal, and the hard-boiled eggs Jillian had made yesterday. Worked for him, but he suspected Ryker may want something more substantial.

They could stop by a grocery store on their way to Madison. He quickly made two bowls of oatmeal and peeled two hard-boiled eggs.

Ryker returned as Jillian and Lizzy were eating. Hawk told him they'd stop for something to eat along the way, and Ryker nodded in agreement.

"Everything okay?" Ryker asked in a low tone.

"For now." Hawk knew things wouldn't be okay until the danger was over. "Find anything outside?"

Ryker shook his head. "It's all clear. But I have news. I called Mike and Matt and they're going to be here within the hour."

"Good." Hawk liked the idea of Matt Callahan and Duchess watching over Jillian and Lizzy.

"Listen, I think we should convince Mike to stay here, too," Ryker added. "We've been here for two days now, and that's a long time to stay in one place."

Hawk understood Ryker's reasoning. Staying in one place for too long would eventually expose them to danger. Sure, they'd used disposable phones and a satellite computer, but a senator wielding enormous power could infiltrate any precautions.

"We'll check out other places to stay while we drive," he agreed.

"As soon as the Callahans arrive, we need to hit the road," Ryker said.

Hawk glanced over at Jillian, who was wiping oatmeal off Lizzy's face and hands. "Yeah, I hear you," she said without looking him in the eye.

"Let's get you changed," she told Lizzy, taking her into the bedroom.

Hawk hated the tension widening the gulf between them. But not enough to change his mind about what he and Ryker needed to do.

They had to find Colin Yonkers. No matter what it took.

\* \* \*

Jillian wanted to scream in frustration when Hawk and Ryker left the cabin, leaving Mike and Matt Callahan to babysit.

Lizzy was thrilled to see Duchess, the only bright spot of the day.

Ignoring the men hovering in the kitchen, she played Go Fish with Lizzy. The way Mike and Matt exchanged glances she could tell they knew she was upset, but they had no idea how to deal with it. She understood that Hawk's plan wasn't their fault, but they hadn't even tried to talk him out of going to see Colin Yonkers's sister.

As an only child she could only imagine what it was like to have siblings, but she highly doubted that any sister would turn on her brother.

This was nothing more than a fool's errand. One she hoped and prayed didn't turn deadly.

Thirty minutes later, Jillian's anger and frustration faded. She had never been good at holding a grudge. And when she had Lizzy settled on the sofa watching a Disney movie, she returned to the kitchen.

"What can I do to help?"

Mike raised his eyebrows as Matt hid a smile. "You're helping by letting us stay here."

"That's not enough. I'm too restless to sit around like this. There has to be something I can do to assist with the investigation. I may not be a computer whiz, but I can still help with whatever you're searching for."

Again the men exchanged a look that made her grind her teeth with annoyance.

"Why not?" Mike finally said, turning the computer toward her. "We've been searching for photos of Senator Barton and Colin Yonkers. So far, we've only found one of them together."

She remembered seeing the picture last evening. "Did you find a picture of Colin's sister, Olivia?"

"Yes." Matt took over the computer keyboard so he could

bring up the picture they'd found on a social media site. "Don't worry about Olivia. Ryker and Hawk won't hurt her."

She truly wanted to believe that. Scrolling through the photographs, she stumbled across one that brought her up short.

"Wait a minute. Who is this guy?" She pointed to a man sitting next to Olivia with his arm around her shoulders.

"Probably her husband," Mike offered. He leaned close to see the image more clearly. "Her last name is Habush, so it stands to reason she's married."

Jillian stared at the image for a long time. Something about the guy nagged at her. He looked familiar. But where would she have seen him?

"I can find his first name easily enough." Matt once again took over the keyboard while Jillian searched her memory. It was there, just out of reach. She'd seen that man before.

"His name is Timothy Habush," Matt announced. "Seems they have a son, Aaron."

The memory clicked into place.

"That's it! He came to Brookland Elementary, claimed he had a son named Aaron going into second grade. Asked the principal if he could watch my class for a while." Jillian couldn't believe she hadn't remembered sooner. "But according to this social media page, his son is only three years old. He lied." The sick feeling in her stomach intensified. "He's a part of this. Maybe he was one of the soldiers in the Alpha team. We need to call Hawk and Ryker to warn them." She fumbled for her disposable phone, but Mike already had his cell in his hand.

"Hawk? Where are you?" Mike demanded.

Jillian held her breath, wishing he'd place the call on speaker.

"Good, stay put. We're coming out to meet you. We have new information that will impact your visit to Yonkers's sister." There was a pause as Mike listened. "I know you don't want them in danger, but this is important. Just stay where you are, we'll meet up with you soon."

"Where are they?" She pounced on Mike the moment he

disconnected from the call. "Did they already meet up with Olivia Habush?"

Mike held up his hands. "No, they actually just finished breakfast and were about to head out when I caught them. Apparently they were planning their strategy over steak and eggs."

Jillian felt dizzy with relief. "Good. That's good. Let's go."

"Hold on, Jillian." Matt placed a hand on her arm to stop her. "There's no reason for all of us to go."

"I'm not staying here alone." Jillian narrowed her gaze. "We're all going, understand?"

"She's right," Mike interjected. "I don't want to leave her without a vehicle. Besides, we may need a different strategy altogether. Let's just head to the restaurant and figure out where to go from there."

Jillian didn't waste time. She had Lizzy bundled up for the trip, her Belle doll and teddy bear along for comfort.

As Mike drove, she replayed the day she'd met Timothy Habush at the elementary school.

Why had he come to her classroom? To scope out where she taught? Had he been one of the ski-masked men who'd come to her house that day?

She pressed a hand to her racing heart. It was a good thing she'd insisted on helping, or Hawk and Ryker may have walked into a deadly trap.

Sitting at the family restaurant, waiting for Jillian, Lizzy, Mike and Matt to arrive, chafed at Hawk's nerves. Logically he knew Mike wouldn't have called if it wasn't urgent, but he still resented the Callahans for dragging Jillian and Lizzy along.

They were so close to finding out the truth. Madison was just fifteen minutes away. They could be in and out with a location for Colin Yonkers before anyone was the wiser.

"Here they are now," Ryker commented.

"About time." Hawk knew he sounded grumpy. "This better be good."

He and Ryker had asked for a table large enough to seat all of them comfortably, including a booster seat for Lizzy. When everyone was settled and had fresh coffee, Hawk pinned Mike with a glare.

"What's going on?"

"Olivia's husband Timothy Habush came to visit my school last week," Jillian said. "The day after I made the call to Fort Bragg."

"What? Are you sure?" Hawk couldn't believe what Jillian was telling him.

"I'm sure. We found his picture on social media." Jillian took a sip of her coffee. "He claimed he had a son named Aaron going into second grade and asked to watch my class for a few minutes. But he lied. His son is three, not seven."

"So he's a part of this." Hawk was dumbfounded. This was an unexpected twist. One, he realized grimly, he should have anticipated.

"Tim Habush," Ryker repeated, his forehead wrinkled in a frown. "I can't place the name."

"Me, either, but that doesn't mean he wasn't part of Team Alpha." Hawk thought about it for a moment. "Or maybe a different team."

"What do you mean?" Ryker asked.

He shrugged. "Think about it. Yonkers wasn't in charge of the Alpha team, but he could have just as easily been coordinating the gun sales with another team. Not Bravo, because I was in charge there and we were friends, but another one."

"I brought the computer." Mike pulled it out and set it on the table. "We can try to poke into Habush's background."

"Not here," Hawk said quickly, glancing around the restaurant. At ten in the morning, it wasn't jam-packed, but he still felt as if they were too exposed, too noticeable. "There's a motel across the street. Let's move there."

"Fine with me," Ryker said, pulling cash out of his pocket and tossing it on the table. "Let's go."

"I want pancakes," Lizzy announced.

Hawk glanced at her in surprise. For a moment he'd forgotten she was sitting beside him. "Sure thing. We'll order you some pancakes to go."

The order didn't take long, and soon they were back outside and across the street at the Family Inn Motel. They rented a room and crowded into it.

Jillian set Lizzy up on the bed with her pancakes and cartoons. When Jillian returned to sit beside him, he put his arm around her shoulders and gave her a quick hug.

"Nice work recognizing Habush. It's another angle to investigate."

"Makes me wonder if there are two teams after us." She frowned. "Maybe Habush is the guy who tossed the classroom looking for the photos, while others came to my house."

Hawk shrugged. "Anything is possible, but I think they're all one and the same."

"Found him," Ryker announced. "Hawk was right. Habush was the team leader for Delta. In fact, I think Duncan O'Hare might have been on Team Delta, too."

Hawk leaned over to see the computer screen for himself. "Does Habush work for Blake-Moore, as well?" He knew Duncan O'Hare didn't, because he was also a Milwaukee cop, like Matt Callahan.

"You got it." Ryker tapped the screen. "All roads lead to Blake-Moore. I still think I could infiltrate the company. Or we could ask Duncan for help."

It wasn't a bad plan, but Hawk knew there wasn't enough time. His shoulder felt as if it were on fire. "We can still go to the Habush home and convince Olivia to talk."

"And if her husband is there? Along with Yonkers? Then what?" Jillian clearly didn't like the idea.

"We can do a little recon, first," Ryker said in a placating tone. "We don't even know if anyone is home."

"I like that idea." Hawk wanted, needed to keep moving.

"We'll check things out and then let you know what we find."
He looked at the Callahans. "I need you to stay here."

"I'm coming with you," Mike said quickly. "Matt and Duchess can keep an eye on Jillian and Lizzy."

"I agree." Jillian's comment surprised him. "I'd rather there were three of you in case you run into trouble."

"We're only checking things out," Hawk reminded her.

"Yes, but no one knows we're here," she argued. "We just arrived ten minutes ago. Please take Mike with you."

"Hey, what am I? Chopped liver?" Matt asked. "Don't forget, I am a cop."

Hawk put his hand on Matt's shoulder. "I'm trusting you and Duchess to keep the two most important people in my life safe from harm."

All hint of humor fled from Matt's gaze. "I know. We'll be fine."

Hawk rose to his feet and gestured toward the door. "Time to go."

Mike and Ryker followed him out into the cold winter air. The sky overhead was cloudy, but not enough to indicate snow was on the way.

He let Ryker drive. Ryker drove past the Habush home, but there were no lights on and no vehicles in the driveway, leading him to believe no one was home.

"We need to get closer." He leaned forward, trying to get a glimpse of the back of the house as Ryker made a circle around the block. "Drop me off here."

"Why don't you let me go?" Mike offered.

"This is my problem." Hawk pushed open the passenger-side door before Mike or Ryker could argue further.

The cold air made him shiver, or maybe it was the fever he was fighting off. Using evergreens for cover, he inched past the house and into the backyard of the Habush home.

He froze when he noticed the back door of the home was hanging ajar. Not good, considering it was late December.

Moving silently, he approached the house. When he was close enough to a window, he peered inside.

A kitchen chair was lying on the floor, amid broken tableware.

Had the place been ransacked, like Jillian's home had been?

And if so, why? What in the world was going on?

# THIRTEEN

Jillian found it impossible to sit still, but every time she tried to pace Duchess would wind between her legs, to the point she kept tripping over the beautiful German shepherd.

"Here, Duchess." Lizzy patted the bed. The K-9 gracefully jumped up and snuggled in next to her.

Worrying about Hawk was useless. He had plenty of support between Ryker and Mike, not to mention being a highly trained special ops soldier. He was much stronger and more dangerous than anyone she'd ever met. Yet earlier this morning she'd noticed his face looked pale and drawn, and she'd caught him massaging his injured shoulder whenever he thought no one was looking.

How much longer before he'd agree to go to the hospital for treatment? She feared that delaying medical care would end up causing more damage to the injured muscles in the long run.

But Hawk was stubborn. More so than James had been.

She prayed for Hawk's, Mike's and Ryker's safety, and for Olivia's, too. She trusted the men not to do anything rash, but it was still difficult for her to believe that questioning Yonkers's younger sister was their only option. She couldn't help thinking of Olivia and her three-year-old son, Aaron.

Not so different from her and Lizzy.

"Mommy, look! *The Grinch Who Stole Christmas* is on!"

She turned in time to see the green-faced Grinch scowling from the television screen. "That's great, Lizzy."

"That's Rory's favorite show," Matt spoke up. "He would watch it every day if we let him."

She was curious about the Callahan family who were apparently the only friends, beside Ryker Tillman and Duncan O'Hare, that Hawk had. "How old is Rory?" she asked.

"Three and a half," Matt answered. "He'll be four in February."

"Lizzy will be five in March." She sat down beside Matt. "I can't believe she'll start kindergarten next year. She's ready, but I'm not."

"I know, they grow up fast." Matt scratched Duchess behind the ears. There was a moment of silence before he continued, "I want you to know Hawk has been very supportive of the entire Callahan family over the past couple of years. We'll have his back on this until we get to the bottom of whatever is going on. We all owe him a huge debt of gratitude."

"Thanks. That means a lot to me." She stared down at her hands. When Hawk had brought the jewelry box to the cabin motel, she'd slipped the diamond ring back on the fourth finger of her left hand along with the plain gold band. She'd thought he'd say something, but he hadn't. Or if he had noticed the rings, he didn't let on. Finally she lifted her gaze to Matt's. "Hawk is different from the man I married."

Matt frowned. "Because of his scar?"

"No, I don't care about that." She waved an impatient hand. "The scar only adds to the air of mystery around him. Do you know he lived next door to me for five months and I never once suspected that he was James?"

Matt lifted a brow in surprise. "Why do you think that is?"

"Well, for one thing, it never occurred to me that my husband wasn't actually dead. But I think it's even more than that.

Hawk is more intense. Less talkative." She couldn't seem to put her feelings into words. "I can't explain it, but he's different. In so many little ways."

"I can understand that, but deep down, he's the same man with the same values." Matt shrugged. "It's not that different for me. Rory is my son in every way, except biologically. He is actually my wife Lacy's nephew. Lacy's sister was murdered, so she was forced to go on the run with Rory to keep him safe. Once we found out who killed her, we were able to formally adopt Rory. He was about nine months old. But even without the paperwork, I always felt as if he was my own flesh and blood. Lacy is pregnant, and I can't imagine loving the new baby any differently from Rory."

"Wow, I had no idea." She glanced at Lizzy, realizing her daughter's situation was almost the exact opposite. Hawk was biologically Lizzy's father but hadn't been a part of her life over the past four years.

Until now.

Once the danger was over, she and Hawk needed to talk about the future. The idea of going back to living in separate houses, even if they were right next door to each other, wasn't good enough.

She wanted more. She wanted it all.

The engagement ring glittered on her left hand next to the gold wedding band. She wanted a family.

Hawk pushed the door of the Habush home open while remaining plastered against the side of the house, his Glock held ready.

He had no idea what he might find upon going inside.

It was likely no one was in there, but he refused to make rash assumptions. He was beginning to think Jillian had pegged it correctly when she suggested there was more than one team after them.

Why else would one team turn on the other?

The back door opened into the kitchen. He silently entered the house, avoiding the broken bits scattered across the floor. Keeping his back to the wall, he ventured further inside.

He frowned when he found the living room apparently untouched. Nothing seemed to have been disturbed.

The place hadn't been ransacked, after all. Clearly something had gone down in the kitchen, though.

And where were Olivia and Aaron Habush?

After clearing the living room, Hawk made his way down the hallway to the bedrooms. Those rooms hadn't been disturbed, either, although they appeared more lived in. There was a master bedroom and a kid's room, judging by the train motif. Clothes were strewn about in the child's bedroom, giving Hawk the impression they'd left in a hurry.

Why? And what had happened in the kitchen?

He poked his head one last time in the master bedroom, searching for a clue behind what had transpired here. There was a framed photograph on the bedside table. He crossed over to pick it up, to examine it more closely.

The photo was a family picture of Tim, Olivia and Aaron Habush.

There was something about Habush that nagged at him. But when he tried to think back to his time in Afghanistan, he couldn't place the guy. Either because of the holes in his memory or because he hadn't interacted with him very much. The fact that Habush was the leader of the Delta team made him fear it was his memory.

Which brought him back to the possibility that his brief memory around Senator Rick Barton wasn't accurate, either. Every last bit of circumstantial evidence they had all pointed to the Blake-Moore mercenary group.

After replacing the photo where he'd found it, Hawk moved back to the kitchen. He stared at the scene for several long moments, trying to imagine what had transpired.

Remnants of breakfast food were on the table, bits of scrambled eggs and bacon. He crossed over and felt the coffeepot: it was still slightly warm. Glancing back at the table, he noted one of the chairs had a booster seat, no doubt used by the little boy, Aaron. The broken dishes were on the floor near the overturned chair, which was right next to Aaron's booster seat. Seemed logical that Olivia might have been the one sitting beside her son.

Only two plates and one broken coffee cup. Did that mean Tim hadn't been here before they left? That he'd burst into the kitchen to grab his wife because he was in a hurry to leave? So much so that he hadn't bothered to make sure the door was closed and locked behind him?

Had Olivia resisted for some reason? Maybe leaving the back door open as a warning sign that something bad had happened?

There was a scrap of paper on the floor, half buried by a broken piece of a plate. Hawk picked it up. It was a receipt for gas purchased last week.

The location of the gas station was near Brookland Elementary. He clenched his jaw, even though the receipt didn't tell him anything new. Jillian had already identified Tim as being at the school the day after she'd called Fort Bragg about the envelope Hawk had sent her.

But it gave him an idea. He opened kitchen cabinets and drawers until he found one full of paperwork. When he rifled through them, he found more credit card receipts.

Scanning the purchases, he felt adrenaline surge through his bloodstream. There were several charges for gas, and he found one that had been made near the area of his cabin.

Tim Habush was part of the team in coming after them at the cabin—that much was clear. And likely in on the gunrunning, as well. But that didn't explain why he'd taken his wife and son and bolted out of their home.

He took every single receipt he could find, stuffing them deep into his pockets so he could review them more closely later. At least the gas receipt put Tim Habush near his cabin and provided a connection to Yonkers.

Still, it wasn't enough, and as Hawk slipped back out of the house and back toward the SUV where Mike and Ryker waited, he wondered why these guys were always a step ahead of him.

When he stepped outside, he came up short when he sensed someone nearby. He lifted his Glock, then slowly lowered it when he recognized Ryker.

"You were gone for a long time," Ryker said. "I've been covering the back, and Mike is out front."

Hawk should have expected his buddies wouldn't simply sit and wait. "Thanks, but there isn't anyone inside."

Ryker nodded. "What did you find?"

Tillman's keen perception made him smile. "Let's get back to the motel where we left Matt and Jilly. I'll show you what I have."

Ryker didn't argue. "Stay here. I'll get Mike."

When Ryker moved to the front of the house, Hawk looked down at the ground, looking for tell-tale signs of a struggle, mentally kicking himself for not checking sooner. Still, he could see where he'd come in but couldn't tell between Ryker's boot prints and several others.

He was losing his touch. Sure, maybe it was the infection developing in his shoulder, but the moment he'd noticed the back door was open, he should have scouted the ground for clues.

His gaze narrowed on several broken tips of a bush beside the house. There was a hint of blue thread on the tip, maybe from denim jeans.

It was looking more and more like Olivia and Aaron were hauled out of here against their will. He just wished he understood why.

"Hawk? You okay?"

Hawk turned to face Ryker and Mike who had both been inside the house. "Yeah, I'm fine. Let's get out of here."

The trip back to the motel didn't take long. Jillian ran to him as he entered the room.

"Hawk! Is everything all right?"

He knew she was mostly concerned about Olivia and her son. "The house was empty," he quickly informed her. "But it looks as if they left in a hurry. And maybe not of their own volition."

Jillian paled. "What do you mean?"

Hawk described the scene in the kitchen as he pulled crumpled receipts from his pockets and dumped them on the small table. "I can't explain why Olivia's husband or her brother would drag her out of there like that. It doesn't make any sense."

"What's all this?" Matt began straightening the receipts.

"Found one for a gas station near Brookland Elementary on the same day Jillian saw Tim Habush checking out the second-grade classroom. And then another one for gas several days later, only this time it was a station not far from my cabin. So I grabbed all of them to see what else we can link together with what has been happening."

They spread the receipts out and began reviewing them. Hawk found a third receipt for a fast-food restaurant near Jillian's house. The date stamp was for Friday, the same day her home had been breached by two masked men.

He thought it was possible Tim Habush and Colin Yonkers had been staked out nearby, watching Jillian's house until it was time to make their move.

"Wait a minute, do you notice that none of these receipts are for anything past Saturday?" Jillian spoke up.

"I have two from Friday," Hawk said, lifting them up for her to see. "This is three total, all near places you and I have been."

"But none are more recent." Jillian scowled. "It's almost as if Tim Habush hasn't been home since Friday."

At that moment it clicked. The reason Tim Habush's photo had nagged at him back at the house.

It was the man he'd unmasked at Jillian's house. The same one he'd recognized outside his cabin.

Tim Habush was dead.

Hawk had shot him in self-defense.

\* \* \*

Jillian caught the flash of horror in Hawk's gaze and instinctively knew what he was thinking.

"He was one of them, wasn't he?" she asked softly. "Up at the cabin."

Hawk slowly nodded. "He's dead. He shot at me, so I returned fire."

Jillian's heart ached for Hawk. A woman she didn't know was a widow, her son fatherless. She felt bad for Olivia and Aaron Habush, yet knew Hawk hadn't wanted to hurt anyone. The way he'd left the men alive at her house proved it.

But that hadn't prevented him from doing whatever was necessary to save her and Lizzy.

Hawk abruptly stood, pushing away from the table. The space inside the room was cramped and she could tell he wanted to get out.

"We need to head back to the cabin motel." He avoided looking at anyone directly. "We'll stay one more night, then find somewhere else to go."

"Why not just stay here?" Ryker asked.

"Um, there aren't enough rooms open," Mike spoke up. "No connecting rooms for sure. When I paid for this room, the manager told me that there was only one other vacant room on the other side of the building. I guess it must be too close to the holiday."

"We need to make sure the cabin is wiped down anyway," Hawk said, hovering near the door. "And my antibiotics are still there, along with my supplies."

"You're feeling worse, aren't you?" Jillian stepped forward and placed her hand on Hawk's forehead. His skin was hot to the touch. Cold fingers of fear squeezed her heart. If anything happened to Hawk...

"I'm okay, but I need those antibiotics." Hawk pulled away from her touch and opened the door to the motel room. "Let's go."

Jillian wanted to argue but concentrated on bundling Lizzy

into her winter coat as the men quickly filed out of the room. She was troubled by Hawk's illness and tried to think of a compromise.

Originally she hadn't wanted to be left with the Callahans while he worked the case. But that was before she'd gotten to know them. Mike and Matthew were both decent men, as was Ryker Tillman. She needed to convince Hawk to turn everything over to the authorities and assure him that the Callahans could keep her safe while he received treatment for his injury at the hospital.

Even if they didn't get to the bottom of this right away, they could start up again after the holidays. And once Hawk was feeling better.

Hawk came back to the room, looking impatient as he waited for her.

"We're ready." She carried Lizzy to the door.

"I'll take her," Hawk offered. Lizzy didn't mind when Hawk gently pulled her away. "We'll go to the cabin for a few hours, but Mike and Matt are going to search for a new place for us to stay. They promise to find something kid-friendly."

"Okay." She liked the way Hawk held Lizzy against his chest, clutching her teddy bear with her small head tucked beneath his chin.

The trip back to the cabin motel didn't take long. She was all too aware that the first thing Hawk did was to find the bottle of antibiotics. He downed the pills, chasing them with a large glass of water. Then he added a couple of ibuprofens and took those, too.

While he cleaned the place up, no doubt getting rid of any and all evidence of their staying there, she went into the bedroom to pack up Lizzy's things.

A strange thumping noise coming from outside made her frown. What in the world? It almost sounded like...

A helicopter?

For a moment she was paralyzed with fear, then found the strength to take immediate action.

"Come with me, Lizzy." She held Lizzy close and rushed into the kitchen. The thump, thump, thumping noise grew louder.

"Hawk! A helicopter!"

Hawk joined her a split second later, glancing around the room. "Where's Ryker?"

She shook her head helplessly. "I don't know. I don't think he came inside with us."

Hawk grabbed the car keys off the table and crossed over to the door. "We have to get out of here. Hurry!"

"We can't outdrive a helicopter," she protested. It took her a moment to pull on her winter coat and Lizzy's too, before following him outside.

The chopper was coming in from the north, fast and low, looking like a dark menacing bird of prey about to pounce.

"Hurry!" Hawk shouted, staying behind her as they made their way toward the SUV.

But even as he spoke, four men, dressed completely in black and with rifles slung over their shoulders, emerged from the helicopter. They rappelled down until they were on the ground and quickly came toward them.

Jillian froze, holding Lizzy tightly against her chest as the little girl sobbed with fright.

They were surrounded!

# FOURTEEN

Ryker had been right. They never should have come back to the cabin motel. As Hawk turned to face the men, all four strategically standing in a semicircle around them, with the SUV at their backs, Hawk pushed Jillian and Lizzy protectively behind him. Then he raised his hands up in a gesture of surrender.

The only possible source of rescue would be from Ryker. Hawk didn't have a clue where he was but knew the soldier would have heard the chopper. He hoped and prayed Ryker was hiding in the woods, getting ready to make his move at a strategic time.

"You want me? Fine." Hawk hoped these men couldn't hear the hint of desperation in his tone. Lizzy's crying wrenched at his heart, but he did his best to ignore it. "You've got me. Now let the woman and child go. They don't know anything, I'm the one you came for."

The four armed men didn't say anything but stood in place as if waiting for something.

Or someone.

The SUV was only about thirty feet away. Thirty feet that may as well have been thirty miles.

He never should have come back here. If Jillian and Lizzy

died today, it would be his fault. He could hear Jillian trying to reassure Lizzy, even though the situation was bad. Worse than bad.

He sent up a desperate prayer that God would keep his wife and daughter safe from harm.

"Let them go," Hawk repeated. "I'll come with you without a struggle once they're safe in the SUV and have driven far from here."

Still no response from the four men. Clearly they were waiting for their next order. From whom, he didn't know.

Yonkers? Or higher brass within the Blake-Moore group?

He scanned their faces. At least they weren't wearing ski masks this time. Hawk tried to search his fragmented memory for recognition. It was highly likely that one or more of them had served with him in Afghanistan.

But he couldn't place a single one. They were strangers to him. Strangers that wouldn't hesitate to put a bullet through his heart.

"I'm not leaving without you," Jillian whispered.

He ignored her because it wasn't her decision. Hawk tried to come up with an escape plan. With Ryker's help, he thought they might be able to take out all four of them, giving Jillian and Lizzy the chance to get away unharmed. The only problem was that his and Ryker's chances of surviving such a rash attempt were slim to none.

Didn't matter. Nothing was more important than keeping Jillian and Lizzy safe. And he sensed Ryker would feel the same way.

He remembered what Ryker had said about not hurting Olivia and Aaron because that was not the kind of soldiers they were. They were wired to protect the innocent. Especially women and children.

He could trust Ryker to keep Jillian and Lizzy safe.

The sound of movement coming through the trees snagged his attention. He tensed, ready to make his move.

When a familiar figure came through the trees, surprisingly alone, Hawk knew he shouldn't have been surprised.

Senator Rick Barton.

His memory hadn't been wrong. He had seen Major Rick Barton in the Afghan mountains five years ago.

Realizing the senator was the one behind all of this made Hawk sick to his stomach. He should have sent all of his evidence to the FBI or the CIA.

Now it was too late.

"Hello, James."

Hawk didn't answer, partially because there was a lump in his throat the size of Mount Rushmore.

"I know you may find this difficult to believe but I'm here to help," the senator continued. "You've stumbled into a bit of a mess, wouldn't you agree?"

Hawk stared at Barton without responding. He wasn't buying the oh-so-innocent act. Senators didn't come after a soldier with a chopper full of armed men.

Not unless the mission was to silence a threat.

"We don't have a lot of time, James." The senator's easygoing tone now held a hard edge. "So let me sum things up for you. I know you witnessed a gun deal five years ago outside of Kabul between Colin Yonkers, an American soldier, and the insurgents. I know that the plane carrying the Bravo team was sabotaged and crashed in the Appalachian Mountains. I know your body was never found and I always suspected you'd turn up one day. And finally I know you have proof of the gun deal." Barton paused for a moment, then spread his hands wide. "That covers just about everything, doesn't it?"

A strained silence hung between them for a long moment. Hawk knew that a prolonged silence often made others want to talk to fill in the gap, but Rick Barton had been trained the same way he had been.

No one spoke or moved a fraction of an inch.

"Not even close." Hawk finally said in a harsh tone. "You

forgot to mention how you sent armed men in ski masks to my wife's house. How you ordered her home to be ransacked along with her classroom in an effort to find the proof I currently have in my possession. How you also sent four men after us at my cabin, but only three survived." Hawk took a moment to meet the gazes of each of the four men. "I guess that soldier didn't mean much to you, as I see you've replaced him easily enough. Tell me, are they all willing to die for you the way Tim Habush did?"

"Those weren't my soldiers," Barton protested. "I'm telling you, I'm not the one out to hurt you. If you'll just come with me to Washington, DC, then we can straighten this out."

Yeah, right, Hawk thought snidely. He knew if he went with the senator there was no way he'd actually make it to Washington, DC alive. More likely they'd shove him out of the chopper to his death where it would take weeks, maybe even months, before his body was found.

But if he could buy some time for Ryker to get Jillian and Lizzy to safety, it might be worth it. He wished he knew exactly where Ryker was. And he wished he'd never allowed Mike and Matt Callahan to go out ahead of them to find a new place to stay.

His mistakes might result in the deaths of his wife and daughter. And that couldn't be tolerated.

"Here are my terms. I'll go with you back to DC, if you'll let Jillian and Lizzy go."

"No." Jillian spoke out loud for the first time since the armed men had all but surrounded them. "We're not leaving without you, Hawk."

"Hawk?" Like a rattlesnake finding a mouse in the grass, the senator pounced on his new name. "Is that the name you're going by these days? No wonder it was so difficult to find you."

The new name had helped keep him under the radar. If he hadn't sent Jillian those stupid photographs all those years ago, they wouldn't have found him now. Hawk couldn't stand knowing that this mess was his fault.

As he stared Rick Barton down, he tried to plan his next move. Because he wasn't going to let Jillian and Lizzy suffer because of his choices.

"Let Jillian and Lizzy go," he repeated. "Once they're far enough away that they can't be seen, I'll go with you to DC. That's my offer. Take it or leave it."

The senator's smile was humorless. "You seem to think you're in a position to negotiate, James. But you're not."

Hawk's muscles tensed. He hoped and prayed Ryker was nearby, l-istening to the conversation, ready to jump in to help get Jillian and Lizzy to safety as needed. The moment the senator flinched, he'd make his move.

"But since I'm not the one behind all of this, I'm happy to oblige," Barton said as if he were giving Hawk a medal instead of a death sentence. "Maybe then you'll realize that my only concern is getting to the bottom of the gun dealing in Afghanistan. So sure, go ahead." Barton waved a dismissive hand. "The woman and child are free to go."

"No," Jillian protested, her voice loud enough to be heard over Lizzy's crying. "I'm not leaving you."

"Yes, you are." He turned to give her a steely glare. "Hurry. I need you and Lizzy to be safe."

Her eyes pleaded with his, but he refused to budge. Finally she nodded and hitched Lizzy higher in her arms.

"Reach out to the Callahans," he murmured in a low voice, hoping the armed men wouldn't hear beyond Lizzy's sobs. "They'll help you."

Jillian gave a slight nod to indicate she got the message. She took several steps backward, until she was near the SUV. After securing Lizzy in her car seat, she walked around and slid in behind the wheel. The entire process seemed interminably slow, but Jillian finally had the car in gear and began rumbling down the driveway.

He watched, memorizing the way she looked, hoping it wouldn't be the last time he'd see her, before he turned to face Barton.

The moment Jillian and Lizzy were no longer in danger, Hawk sensed the tension between the gunmen relaxed. Maybe Lizzy's crying had gotten on their nerves, too. Either way, they no long perceived him as a threat.

That was their mistake.

"Ready?" the senator asked.

Hawk didn't move. "Not until she's out of sight." He didn't dare rake a gaze around the area to find Ryker's position. The guy was either out there ready to help, or he wasn't.

Hawk hoped and prayed it wasn't the latter.

Jillian couldn't believe Hawk had stayed behind with the senator. She should have known he was right all along. Men in power could do whatever they wanted.

Even sending four armed men rappelling down from a helicopter to capture them.

While she'd been partially hidden behind Hawk, she'd dialed 911 from the phone in her pocket. At least, she hoped she had. It wasn't an easy thing to do when you couldn't see the numbers.

But the 911 response wouldn't be quick enough. Not considering they were way out here in the middle of nowhere. By the time the sheriff's deputies arrived, Barton and his armed men would be long gone.

Taking Hawk with them.

She considered calling again but didn't think that would create a faster response. However, remembering the phone gave her an idea. She slowed the SUV, twisted in her seat and used the disposable phone she'd been given to snap a quick picture of Hawk standing with his spine ramrod straight and staring at Barton while surrounded by four armed men. If anything happened to him, she wanted proof of what had gone down here.

Leaving Hawk at Barton's mercy caused tears to well in her

eyes, blurring her vision. She swiped them away, knowing she needed to drive safe for Lizzy's sake.

But fearing the worst made her heart ache. She couldn't lose Hawk now that she'd found him. She just couldn't!

*Please, Lord. Please keep Hawk safe in Your care!*

In an attempt to stall for time, she kept her speed slow. Using her phone, she called Mike Callahan, leaving a message when he didn't pick up. Keeping the phone close, she turned her attention back to the rural highway.

Mike returned her call within two minutes. "What's going on?"

"Senator Barton dropped four armed men from a helicopter to surround us. Hawk convinced them to let me and Lizzy drive away in the SUV, but he's back there alone with them. The senator is planning to take Hawk to DC, but I don't believe he'll make it there alive." The words tumbled out in a rush, as fear stabbed deep. "We need to do something."

"Where's Ryker?"

Good question. "I don't know. He wasn't in the cabin when the chopper arrived, so I have to assume he's hiding in the woods somewhere, waiting for the opportunity to help."

"Good. At least Hawk isn't alone."

She wanted to fast-pitch the phone through the windshield. "Didn't you hear me? There are four armed men with the senator! That's five against two!"

"I heard you, Jillian, but you have to have faith in Hawk and Ryker's abilities. They are both highly trained soldiers. And I need you to calm down and be patient. Matt and I will meet you at the gas station just outside Paloma. It's the closest town to the east."

She didn't want to be calm. She wanted them to rush over to help rescue Hawk. She heard Lizzy sniffling in the back seat and managed to pull herself together. "Okay, fine. I'll meet you at the gas station in Paloma."

She disconnected from the call and took several deep breaths in an attempt to calm her racing heart. She unflexed her fingers from their death-like grip on the steering wheel and tried to think rationally.

Mike was probably right about Hawk's and Ryker's skills. At some point during the standoff, she'd hoped Ryker would rush in, guns blazing, to take out the threat. But obviously that would be too dangerous. Not just for her and Lizzy, but for Hawk and Ryker, too.

Maybe now that she and Lizzy were out of the way, they'd find a way to escape. She thought about how Ryker might wait until they were all hiking through the woods back to the chopper. She'd watched Hawk in action enough to know that a surprise attack from an unknown assailant would be their best chance for escape.

Who was she kidding? She wasn't a trained soldier and really had no idea how or when Ryker should make his move.

All she could do was to continue driving Lizzy safely out of harm's way.

And pray.

Hawk waited a full five minutes after Jillian and Lizzy left before he gestured toward the chopper. "Okay, they're safe. Let's go."

Senator Barton looked relieved to have Hawk's cooperation. But that didn't prevent him from instructing one of the armed guards to pat Hawk down.

Hawk tried not to wince as he held his arms out to the side. The bullet wound was throbbing again. He didn't say a word when the gunman relieved Hawk of his weapon and tucked it away.

If Ryker was listening, Hawk hoped he'd take up a position somewhere along the path to the chopper. It wouldn't be easy to take out all four men, but he'd been in worse situations.

It was easier to think clearly now that Jillian and Lizzy were safe. He was confident the Callahans would protect his wife and daughter.

No point in thinking past the next step. If he didn't return to them, so be it. At this point he was putting his faith in his skills, in Ryker and, most important of all, in God.

He moved toward the opening in the woods exactly where Barton had come out just, what, twenty minutes ago? He could see by the broken branches that the senator had lost his warrior edge.

Which was good. Because Hawk needed to be able to escape from him before they reached the chopper.

"Wait," Barton called before they entered the woods. "Nate and Jackson, you stay in the rear. Wes and Tom, you're behind me. Keep Hawk in the middle just in case he decides to get cute."

Hawk was fairly certain that whatever moves he made to escape weren't going to be considered cute. But he didn't respond as Barton went first, followed closely by Wes and Tom.

They only took about ten steps when Ryker made his move. Hawk was ready. The moment he heard the scuffle behind him, he lashed out at the guy in front of him, hitting him hard on the back of his head while grabbing his weapon.

The man—Wes?—let out a cry before crumpling to the ground. Tom quickly turned to shoot, but Hawk fired first. Tom went down, dropping his weapon. He wasn't dead but curled in a ball, holding a hand to his injured thigh. After double-checking to make sure Wes was still unconscious, Hawk grabbed Tom's weapon and rushed after Barton.

"Stop or I'll shoot," Hawk demanded. He didn't have to look behind him. He was certain Ryker had done his job with the last two men.

Barton went pale as he lifted his hands in the air. "James, listen to me. You're making a big mistake. I'm trying to help you! There was no reason for you to kill anyone!"

"If you wanted to help me, you shouldn't have come in with a chopper and armed guards," Hawk countered. "So don't bother feeding me that line. I don't believe you. Now we're going to head back to the clearing, nice and slow."

Barton didn't move, and Hawk could tell the senator was weighing his options.

"Now!" Hawk let his impatience show. Maybe because all this fighting had reopened his shoulder wound for what felt like the tenth time. At this rate it would never heal. "Move it."

"Have it your way." Senator Barton took a few steps toward Hawk, clearly not willing to get too close.

Hawk moved to the side and gestured with the weapon for Barton to walk past him. After a few steps, Hawk saw that Ryker had tied Wes, who was groaning as he regained consciousness, and Nate to different trees. Ryker had also tied the two injured men together, as well. He'd taken possession of the weapons, holding one ready, two others looped over each shoulder.

"I have your Glock," Ryker told him.

Hawk gave him a nod. "Thanks." His gratitude was more for coming to the rescue so than for reclaiming his weapon, and Ryker knew it.

Words weren't necessary.

"You're making a big mistake," Barton said again. "You can't seriously think you're going to get away with killing a senator."

"I'm not going to kill you," Hawk replied in an even tone. "I'm going to make you talk."

"I have been talking! I've told you I'm not the one who is out to hurt you! I want to help! You won't believe me!"

"Keep walking." Hawk stumbled a bit and caught the look of concern Ryker shot in his direction. He wasn't done yet.

They needed information from Barton.

The wail of sirens cutting through the silence made Hawk frown. He hadn't expected such a quick response to the gunfire, considering how far out in the country they were.

"Change of plan," Hawk told Ryker. "Let's get the senator and his men back to his chopper."

"Roger that," Ryker agreed.

"Police sirens," Barton said in what seemed to be relieved surprise. "Good. That's a relief. It means help is on the way."

*Good? Relief? Help is on the way?* Hawk exchanged a glance with Ryker. Why was the senator glad to hear the police were on their way?

Was it possible that Hawk had it wrong? That the senator really wasn't out to hurt him?

Or was he planning to turn this entire incident back onto Hawk and Ryker?

As the sirens grew louder, Hawk grimly realized they'd soon find out.

# FIFTEEN

From her position at the gas station, Jillian could hear the police sirens. Her 911 call had worked! She clenched the steering wheel tightly, hoping and praying Hawk and Ryker were all right.

Moments later, two sheriff's department vehicles drove past. On the heels of that, Mike and Matt Callahan arrived to park beside her. Mike lowered his driver's-side window, and she did the same with the passenger side.

"We're going back to the cabin motel," she announced, leaning over so he could hear her. "The police are headed there, too."

Mike and Matt exchanged a long look that she easily interpreted as not being in favor of her plan.

Too bad. She wasn't taking no for an answer.

"I'm going." She abruptly threw the SUV into Reverse and began backing up away from the parking space.

Mike quickly backed up, too, cutting her off. "Hold on," he shouted. His voice came loudly through their respective open windows. "Let's just wait for a minute, okay? I can't take you anywhere near the line of fire. We need to wait until the sheriff's deputies have the scene under control."

"I don't want to wait." Her voice sounded petulant even to her own ears, so she tried to search for a reasonable alternative. "I promise we'll stay out of danger, but I need to make sure Hawk is okay. Ryker, too. I can't just sit here without knowing."

"Jillian, you're going to get me in trouble with Hawk," Mike said with a heavy sigh.

"I don't care." She wasn't budging on this.

"Okay, you can follow us," Mike said. "We'll go in first. But I'm warning you, I'm going to stop far away from any hint of danger."

"I understand." She couldn't argue, especially since she had Lizzy in the back seat. Even being a little closer would be better than sitting way back here. "Thanks, Mike."

"Yeah." He didn't look happy but continued backing up and then heading out of the gas station first, leaving her to follow.

Jillian raised the window. As she drove, she stayed close to Mike's rear bumper. Seeing Duchess in the K-9 crate area of the SUV was oddly reassuring. It made her realize that they basically were adding three more cops to the attempt to rescue Hawk.

If they weren't too late.

As she followed Mike back up the long, winding road leading to the cabin motel, she watched the sky, hoping, praying she hadn't somehow missed the helicopter taking off. She imagined that if that happened, Hawk would be in the back like some sort of prisoner.

The brake lights flashed on Mike's SUV, causing her to slow to a stop. He slid out from behind the wheel, as did Matt. Matt walked around to let Duchess out. Mike stepped toward her vehicle, holding his hands up as an indication she needed to wait.

She nodded, knowing he and Matt were right to be the ones to go in to find out what was happening. Three cops, she reminded herself. If there was a way to rescue Hawk, she believed the Callahans could do it.

"Mommy? Where are we?"

She twisted in her seat to look back at her daughter. "We're back at the cabin motel. Mr. Mike and Mr. Matt are going to find Daddy."

The word slipped out before she realized what she'd said. Lizzy scrunched up her forehead as if confused. "Daddy?" she echoed.

Jillian regretted she hadn't had this discussion with her daughter sooner. Especially considering the very real possibility that Hawk may not survive whatever was going on in the clearing.

"Yes, Lizzy. Mr. Hawk is your daddy. He was gone for a long time, but now he's back. And he loves you very much."

"Is going to live with us like a family?" Lizzy asked.

That gave her pause. She cleared her throat. "I don't know, we'll have to wait and see."

Lizzy frowned, not liking that answer, but Jillian wouldn't lie to her.

As much as she'd come to care for Hawk, depending on him to keep them safe from harm, she hadn't dwelled too much on their future.

The idea of living with Hawk as husband and wife, as a family, made her aware of the way she'd responded to his kiss. The attraction was still there, at least on her part.

But things were so different now. It simply wasn't realistic to believe they could just pick up where they'd left off five years ago.

And what did Hawk want to do once the danger was over? She had no idea.

She stared at the diamond engagement ring. Had she put it on prematurely? They needed time to talk. To get to know each other. To find out all the ways they'd both changed.

Before they could even consider what their future might hold.

Hawk gestured to Ryker that Wes and Nate should be placed into the helicopter. "Tie them inside, then get the two injured men, as well. I want them all out of here before the cops arrive."

Ryker nodded and quickly went to work. Hawk wasn't sure what his buddy thought about Senator Barton's response to having heard the police sirens. The senator's reaction continued to nag at him.

"Tell me about Yonkers." Hawk drilled Barton with a steely glare, the tip of his weapon never wavering from the man's chest.

Barton nodded. "I asked you to keep an eye on Yonkers for me. I'd heard some chatter about the guy leaving camp alone and didn't like it. Rumor had it he was up to no good. So I ordered you to keep an eye on him."

Hawk mulled over the senator's claim. "Where were we when we had this conversation?"

"In the mountains." Barton frowned at him. "It's not as if I could have that conversation with you in camp."

Was that the memory that had haunted Hawk all these years? Was that the reason he'd suspected Barton was involved in something illegal? Because they'd had a secret meeting where he'd been ordered to spy on one of his fellow soldiers?

On his friend?

Ryker hauled the first injured soldier into the chopper and went back for the second as if oblivious to the conversation.

But Hawk suspected the former special ops soldier was listening to every word.

"So how is it that you know that the Bravo team's plane was sabotaged?" The sirens were louder now, and Hawk knew they were running out of time. "If you knew we were in danger, why didn't you stop it?"

"I didn't think you were in danger once we had your team stateside," Barton explained. "Yonkers was still in Afghanistan, so I figured it was safe. It wasn't until I heard about the plane going down over the Appalachian Mountains that I realized how badly I'd misjudged the level of corruption. I'm sorry about that."

Sorry? He was sorry that Hawk had lost his entire team?

That he'd barely escaped with his own life? That he'd lost four years of being with his wife and daughter?

*Sorry* didn't begin to cover it.

Ryker tossed the second soldier into the chopper. "The police are getting close," he warned.

"So why not simply arrest Yonkers and be done with it?" Hawk asked. He was torn by indecision. He knew his memory wasn't exactly reliable, but it was difficult for him to buy into the senator's story. Barton wasn't telling the entire truth, although there could be bits and pieces of his story that were correct. But why would Barton have come here with the intent of dragging him back to DC with the help of four armed guards? Who did crazy stuff like that?

"Because Yonkers didn't have the power to bring down your team's plane." Barton finally responded to Hawk's question. "A stunt like that took someone higher up on the command chain than Yonkers. And frankly, I don't know who I can trust." Barton spread his hands wide. "For a while, I suspected you were involved, James. That you had decided to join forces with Yonkers."

"That's ridiculous." Hawk didn't hesitate to protest. "I would never sell out my country for money."

Barton nodded slowly. "I believe you."

"Did you hire the Blake-Moore group?" Hawk asked.

Barton frowned. "No. Who are they?"

"A mercenary group formed by two ex-soldiers. Yonkers works for them." Hawk watched Barton's face carefully for a reaction.

"I don't know anything about them." Barton's expression turned grim. "But maybe I should."

Barton was either an award-winning actor or telling the truth. Hawk couldn't decide which. He glanced at Ryker as if seeking advice. Ryker tipped his head toward the chopper and he understood the soldier's unspoken directive.

"Get out of here," Hawk told the senator.

Before Barton could make a move to get into the helicopter, two deputies burst through the path from the woods. "Police! Drop your weapon!"

Suddenly weary, his shoulder hurting to the point his vision was getting blurry, Hawk slowly did as he was told. He tossed the gun in his hand along with the two AK-47s on the ground and then held his hands out from his sides, palms up. His injury hurt too much to lift them up over his head.

"It's okay, Officers," Barton called out. "I'm Senator Rick Barton. Everything is fine here."

Huh? Hawk wondered if he was becoming delusional from the infection brewing in his shoulder.

The deputies glanced at each other but didn't lower their weapons. "Who called 911?"

Hawk realized it must have been Jillian. Either during their standoff or right after she'd left with Lizzy.

"Not me," he managed to say. "The senator took us by surprise, arriving in a helicopter." He decided to stick to the truth.

"Well, someone did." The deputy wasn't inclined to believe his meager attempt to explain what was happening here. Hawk wasn't entirely sure what was going on, himself. Why was Barton sticking up for them? "And here you are, pointing a weapon at a senator," the deputy said.

"He wasn't pointing a weapon at me. I told you, this is nothing more than a misunderstanding." Barton's voice had taken an authoritative tone.

"That's for someone else to determine," the deputy responded. "For now, we'll take both of these guys into custody."

Ryker hadn't moved from his stance in front of the open chopper door. Hawk wondered if he thought that being there would help hide the fact that there were two bound and two wounded soldiers inside.

"Deputies, if you'll allow me to call Special Agent in Charge Dennis Ludwig at the FBI, I'm sure we can get this cleared up without an issue." Barton reached into his pocket and pulled out a phone.

The deputies looked stunned as they listened to the senator request to speak directly with SAC Ludwig. After a brief interaction, Barton held the cell phone out toward the deputies. "For you."

The deputy closest to Hawk stepped forward and gingerly took the senator's cell phone. The one-sided conversation was brief. "Yes, sir. I understand, sir. Thank you, sir." The deputy handed the phone back to the senator. "We'll be on our way, now."

"Thank you for your dedicated service to our community." Barton slipped the phone back into his pocket.

The two deputies turned and retraced their steps through the woods, leaving Hawk speechless.

"Why?" Hawk forced the question past his tight throat.

"I tried to tell you. I'm on your side." Barton glanced back at the helicopter. "Obviously, I handled this wrong, and two good men were injured because of it." He swung back to face Hawk. "I'll take responsibility for this mess, but not for sabotaging your plane."

Hawk wasn't sure how to respond.

"Call me on my personal cell when you feel safe." Barton rattled off his number, then abruptly turned and jumped into the back of the chopper.

Taken by surprise, Ryker quickly stepped out of the way.

"Hope to hear from you soon," Barton shouted before giving the pilot the signal. The rotor blades on the top of the chopper began to spin.

Ryker instinctively lowered his head, the same way Hawk did. They retreated to the back of the clearing, watching in stunned surprise as the helicopter rose off the ground.

The whirling blades made too much noise for them to talk, so they simply waited until the pilot banked the chopper and flew out of sight.

"What just happened?" Hawk finally asked, breaking the silence.

"No clue." Ryker hesitated, then turned back toward the now clearly visible path through the woods. "If Barton's not the one who hired Blake-Moore, then who is? It has to be someone who knew about the gun deal in Afghanistan."

"I have no idea." Hawk didn't like this recent turn of events. It was difficult to wrap his mind around what Barton had said. That the senator had actually prevented him and Ryker from being arrested.

Still, something wasn't right. Even if Barton was one of the good guys, he had a funny way of showing it. He remembered how both Todd Hayes, the current secretary of defense, and Colonel McCann—now known as General McCann—whom Barton and Hayes had reported to, had also served overseas. It could be one of them, or someone else.

Hawk still had no idea whom he could trust.

Jillian waited in the SUV with Lizzy for what seemed like an eternity. What was taking them so long? Finally, Mike came back to talk to her.

"The police are securing the scene. Follow me, I'm going to drive up closer so we're not blocking the driveway."

"Okay." Anxious to do something, anything, she gladly followed Mike to the area in front of the cabin motel. There were two sheriff's vehicles, but even as she arrived, two of the deputies were returning from a path in the woods.

Jillian frowned, wondering why they didn't have Barton in custody. And where were Hawk and Ryker?

"What's going on?" A deputy standing near his vehicle asked.

"We've been instructed by the FBI to clear the area," one of the deputies from the woods replied.

"What do the Feds have to do with this?"

"No idea. But we're out of here."

"Wait, what are you talking about? What happened back there?" Mike protested.

"Listen, this is above our pay grade. You want to argue with a senator and the FBI? Have at it." The deputy didn't so much as give Mike a second glance.

None of this was making any sense. Jillian stayed inside the SUV with Lizzy, watching in confusion as the sheriff's deputies returned to their respective vehicles.

A loud thumping sound had her tightening her grip on the steering wheel. The helicopter! No! Wait! She wanted to scream at the top of her lungs. Had Barton convinced the cops to back off? Was the senator right now taking off with Hawk bound and gagged in the chopper? And what about Ryker? Had he tried to help rescue Hawk? Or was he still hiding somewhere in the woods?

The sound of the helicopter leaving didn't seem to bother the deputies. They didn't waste a second in getting into their respective vehicles and driving back down the winding driveway leading to the highway, giving her the sense that they wanted to distance themselves from whatever had gone down.

Unable to sit still a moment longer, Jillian pushed open her door and jumped out. Her gaze cut to Mike. "What was that about?" She had to shout in order to be heard above the helicopter. "Where's Hawk? And Ryker?"

Mike and Matt exchanged an uneasy glance. "No idea, but sit tight. We'll check it out."

"Maybe one of us should stay back?" Matt suggested.

"No. Both of you go and find them. Hurry!" Jillian felt sick to her stomach, fearing the worst. "Please?"

Mike headed toward the woods, while Matt followed more slowly with Duchess at his side.

She stood, her arms crossed protectively over her chest, staring at the helicopter that moved swiftly across the horizon. Her stomach was in knots at the thought that Senator Barton had Hawk as his prisoner.

She never should have agreed to leave. If not for Lizzy, she wouldn't have. But Hawk had been right to remind her that Lizzy's safety had to be her top priority.

There was a rustling sound from behind her. She frowned, wondering if a deer or some other animal had come out of hiding, or if Ryker had decided to make his presence known.

She turned, her eyes widening in surprise when she saw a man standing there, holding a gun pointed directly at her.

Jillian froze, her heart thumping wildly in her chest.

Not Ryker. A stranger. But not a total stranger—there was something familiar about his facial features.

"Well, if it isn't Mrs. James Wade." The man was dressed all in black, which reminded her of the men who'd chased them through the woods at Hawk's cabin.

"Who are you?" She demanded.

"You don't recognize me? I suppose I should be grateful for that." He took a step toward her and then gestured toward the SUV with the nose of his gun. "Get in."

His facial features suddenly clicked in her mind. She remembered him as the man who'd told her James was dead as well as seeing his face on the computer screen.

Colin Yonkers, the former special ops soldier turned mercenary.

"Now!"

She didn't want to get into the car, but the bite in his tone wasn't easy to ignore. She looked helplessly through the window at Lizzy, wondering if this was how it would end.

No, she refused to give up. Jillian opened the driver's-side door, silently praying for God to provide her the strength and wisdom she needed to save her daughter.

# SIXTEEN

Hawk led the way back through the woods toward the cabin motel, stopping abruptly when he came face-to-face with Mike and Matt Callahan.

"What happened?" Mike demanded.

Hawk glanced at Ryker, who shrugged. "Barton covered for us with the deputies and left. Where is Jillian and Lizzy?"

"Waiting in the clearing," Matt answered.

Hawk scowled. "I trusted you to keep them safe."

"She insisted," Mike said wryly. "It was all I could do to make her stay in the SUV with your daughter."

Duchess wheeled around then, growling low in her throat. Matt instantly removed the K-9's leash so as not to hamper the dog's ability to move. "What is it, girl?"

Hawk didn't like the way Duchess was acting, especially when the K-9 instantly turned around and disappeared back the way they'd come. Pushing past Matt, Hawk ran after Duchess.

His vision was growing blurry, but he forced himself to keep going. Something was wrong. Very wrong. The K-9 had picked up on it.

Hawk burst through the trees into the clearing. His gaze

landed on Jillian standing near the driver's-side door of the SUV. There was a man dressed in black standing behind her.

He came to an abrupt halt roughly twenty feet from them when he realized the guy was holding a gun. Duchess stood right in front of Jillian and the gunman, continuing to growl low in her throat.

"Duchess, heel," Matt commanded.

It took a moment for the K-9 to abandon her post. She trotted to Matt's side and sat, ears perked forward as she continued to stare at the gunman.

"Stay back, or I'll kill her," the gunman threatened.

Hawk took a deep breath and let it out, slowly. He recognized the gunman as his old buddy, Colin Yonkers.

For a moment he wondered if the guy was here alone or if other mercenaries were right now hiding in the woods.

"Well, if it isn't my old friend James Wade," Yonkers drawled in a snide tone. "I couldn't believe it when we found out you were still alive."

"I'm sure." Hawk tried to think of a way to get Yonkers away from Jillian. He felt a flash of anger toward Senator Barton. The guy knew Yonkers was guilty but hadn't had him arrested.

And now the former soldier was holding a gun on his wife. Hawk needed to find a way to keep Yonkers focused on him, rather than on Jillian and Lizzy.

From where he stood, he was close enough to the SUV to hear Lizzy crying from inside the SUV.

"It's me you want, Yonkers," Hawk called out, holding his hands up in a gesture of surrender. "Let the woman go. I'm the one you want. It's been that way since Afghanistan, hasn't it?"

"You've been a problem from the very beginning, James," Colin said in a conversational tone. "But it ends here. I want all three of you to drop your weapons. Now!"

Three? Hawk did his best not to react to the realization that one of them hadn't stumbled forward into the clearing, and was still in hiding.

Had to be Ryker.

"Okay, fine." Hawk carefully took the strap of the AK-47, which he'd picked up from the ground after the senator had flown off in his chopper, from around his body and tossed the gun to his left side. The motion sent a shaft of pain up his arm, but he ignored it.

He needed every ounce of his strength and will to get them out of this mess.

*Please, Lord, I need You now more than ever. Grant me the strength to protect Jillian, Lizzy and the Callahans.*

"The others, too," Yonkers insisted.

Hawk didn't dare look back at Matt and Mike. He kept his gaze focused on the hostile in front of him. He heard the sound of two thuds indicating the Callahan brothers had tossed their weapons aside.

He knew Ryker was armed, but that wouldn't help unless he could figure out how to get Jillian far enough away from Yonkers for Ryker to get a clean shot.

"Take me," Hawk repeated. "She doesn't know anything."

"I'm not so sure about that," Yonkers replied, obviously stalling for time as he planned his next move. Hawk had the impression that the guy had hoped to have Jillian and Lizzy in his custody as hostages before Hawk returned. And that he hadn't realized the Callahans were at the scene as well.

Two small facts in their favor.

"Where's your sister, Olivia?" Hawk asked.

His attempt to divert Colin's attention worked. The former soldier frowned. "What do you mean? Olivia is fine."

"Not so much," Hawk countered. "I was at her place, and she's missing. So is her son, Aaron."

Yonkers looked confused for a moment, then gave his head a little shake. "You're lying. She's fine. I stashed her someplace safe."

"Does your sister know her husband is dead?" Hawk was

hoping, praying, that Ryker would get in position, soon. "That I killed him at the cabin?"

The flash of guilt in Yonkers's eyes confirmed that he'd told his sister the truth. Had Olivia blamed Colin for her husband's death? "Shut up!"

Hawk ignored the directive. "You can't kill us all," he pointed out. "You may as well take me and let the others go. Too many dead bodies and the authorities will get suspicious."

"Not if I make it look like an accident," Yonkers countered. "It worked for the plane crash in the mountains."

Hawk wasn't surprised to hear Yonkers knew all about the plane crash over the Appalachian Mountains. Yet Barton seemed to think that the sabotage was someone higher up in the arms-running organization. Like maybe the owners of the mercenary group.

"What, you're planning to stuff all of us in the SUV?" Hawk was determined to keep Yonkers talking. He imagined Ryker was hiding in the woods, planning his next move. "Doubt that will work."

"No, I think the cabin will be better. A Christmas tree fire that got out of control, killing every one of you." Yonkers gestured with his gun. "You three go inside first, with the dog. One wrong move and I won't hesitate to put a bullet into Mrs. Wade's pretty little head."

Hawk didn't want to go inside the cabin, leaving Jillian and Lizzy with the mercenary. But what choice did he have?

Jillian stared at him with wide, frightened eyes. He could tell she was worried about Lizzy. He wanted to reassure her that they'd find a way out of this mess, but he knew that Ryker wouldn't make his move unless Jillian was out of harm's way.

"We aren't the only ones who know about the gun sales to the insurgents," Hawk said. "We already sent the proof to the authorities." It was a desperate bluff and he knew it. Yet there was always the possibility Yonkers might buy his story.

"If you had, this place would be crawling with Feds. Besides, I was hiding in the woods when the locals left. Now get into the cabin, or she dies." Yonkers lifted his gun closer to the back of Jillian's head.

Feeling as if he were letting her down in the worst way possible, he took a step toward the cabin, his brain frantically searching for a way out.

"Your plan won't work," Jillian abruptly said, breaking her silence. "We don't have a Christmas tree. Killing us in the cabin will never look like an accident."

"A faulty heater, then." Yonkers wasn't daunted by Jillian's comment. "I'll figure out something, now get moving!"

Hawk took another step, when a slight movement in the trees behind Yonkers caught his eye.

Finally! Ryker was in position.

It was now or never. They couldn't risk being held up in the cabin. The close quarters would only work against them.

He looked directly at Jillian, imploring her to understand what he needed her to do. She returned his stare for a long second. Then she deliberately closed both of her eyes and opened them again. Good. That meant she was in sync with his plan. She had no doubt figured out that Ryker was still out there and could help them. She was willing to do whatever was necessary.

He looked down at the ground, then back up at her. He did it twice and she blinked again, acknowledging the plan.

Time stopped as if the universe was holding its breath, waiting for what would come next.

"Now!" Hawk shouted as he dove to the ground. Duchess let out a series of loud barks, distracting Yonkers.

Jillian hit the ground at the same time Hawk shouted. A sharp crack of gunfire echoed through the clearing.

Yonkers dropped forward, hitting the ground right behind Jillian, the impact from Ryker's well-placed bullet taking him out. Hawk shoved himself upright and ran over to Jillian. After taking a moment to kick Yonkers's gun out of the way, he turned to attend to his wife.

"Are you okay?" He patted her arms and legs, searching for any sign of an injury.

"Fine," she managed. She threw herself into Hawk's embrace as Matt and Mike rushed forward. Duchess stood guard over Yonkers, as if determined to make sure the guy didn't get back up.

He didn't.

"Lizzy," Jillian said in a choked voice. "I don't want her to see Yonkers."

Hawk looked up at Matt, who quickly went around to the other side of the SUV. Matt opened the back passenger door, then deftly unbuckled Lizzy from her car seat. He hauled her into his arms, cradling her close, staying on the opposite side of the SUV from where Yonkers was lying on the ground.

"It's okay, everything is fine," Matt crooned. Duchess came over to his side, apparently understanding that Yonkers was no longer a threat.

Duchess nudged Lizzy's foot with her nose and Lizzy turned her tear-streaked face toward the K-9. "Duchess," she said, holding out her tiny hand toward the animal.

The diversion worked. Hawk helped Jillian to her feet and together gave the mercenary a wide berth as they went over to where Matt waited with Lizzy.

Ryker had come out of the woods and was talking to Mike, no doubt getting the other side of the story that he'd missed while hiding.

"You're sure there isn't anyone lurking around?" Hawk asked.

"I didn't find anyone. That's what took me so long to get around to a spot behind Yonkers. I had to move slowly, to be sure I didn't stumble onto any unpleasant surprises."

Hawk nodded. "Nice timing." Hawk didn't look away from his buddy when Jillian took Lizzy into her arms. "That's twice you bailed me out in a matter of hours."

Under different circumstances, he knew Ryker might have

made a smart comeback. But his buddy eyed Jillian and Lizzy, and simply nodded.

"Yes, thank you, Ryker." Jillian's smile was wobbly and she looked as if she might cry. Hawk knew they needed to call this in, and to turn over the evidence they had about the arms dealing to the FBI. He felt certain that with Yonkers gone, the rest of the operation would fall apart.

The danger was finally over.

Jillian collapsed on the sofa inside the cabin, cradling Lizzy close. Her entire body trembled, and even though logically she knew the danger was over, she couldn't seem to stop shaking. It was as if Yonkers still held the gun on her.

If not for God watching over them, she knew this situation would have ended badly. Yonkers had made it clear that he would find a way to kill them all in order to protect his secret.

So many deaths, all to cover up the sale of American guns to the insurgents.

She hoped and prayed Lizzy hadn't seen too much from her car seat. Of if she had, that her daughter was too young to understand.

Duchess followed her to the sofa, as if instinctively knowing that Jillian and Lizzy needed her. Lizzy put a hand on Duchess's silky fur and murmured, "Nice doggie."

"We're safe now, Lizzy," she assured her daughter.

Lizzy nodded and cuddled her teddy bear close.

Hawk stood there watching them for a moment, then pulled out his phone. "I need to call Barton. He needs to help us mitigate the damage from taking down Yonkers. I'm sure it won't be long before the sheriff's deputies return. I'm surprised the owner of this place hasn't called them already."

"Agreed." Ryker lifted a brow. "You better sit down to make the call, Hawk. You're not looking so good."

That caught Jillian's attention. She sent a sharp gaze toward

Hawk in time to see him sway a bit before dropping into the closest kitchen chair.

She wondered when he'd taken his last dose of antibiotic. It wasn't easy to shift her daughter off her lap and onto the sofa. Duchess lightly jumped up next to Lizzy, curling up beside the little girl.

Jillian pushed off the sofa and headed toward Hawk. "Where are your antibiotics?"

Hawk shook his head and then turned his attention to his call. "Barton? It's Hawk. Yonkers is dead. He threatened to kill Jillian, so we took him out of commission." Hawk fell silent for a moment. "Yeah, get here as soon as you can. Bring the Feds."

Jillian put her hand on Hawk's arm, gasping at the heat emanating from his skin. He was running a fever. Taking more oral antibiotics weren't going to help.

He needed to get to the hospital.

"Ryker, will you please stay here with Mike?" Jillian asked. "Matt, I'd like you and Duchess to come with me and Lizzy while we take Hawk to the closest hospital. He's burning up with a fever and I'm sure his gunshot wound is infected."

"Not yet," Hawk protested. "I need to wait for Senator Barton."

"Why?" Jillian demanded. "Ryker and Mike can fill Barton in on the details. You can't wait much longer."

Hawk remained stubbornly silent. She sent Ryker an imploring look. "Talk to him, will you?"

Ryker let out a sigh. "Hawk, listen to your wife. We have this under control."

"What about the Blake-Moore group?" Hawk asked, enunciating the words carefully as if he were having trouble speaking. "They're still out there, somewhere."

Jillian felt a chill snake down her back. "I thought Ryker checked the area for them?"

"Not here," Ryker quickly spoke up. "He just means that the organization is still in business."

It occurred to her then that they still hadn't figured out who had hired the Blake-Moore group. Although, at the moment, she didn't care. Hawk had begun to shiver, despite the burning heat radiating from his skin. "We need to go now. Or call an ambulance." She glared at him. "Your choice."

"No ambulance." The words were a bit slurred and that was enough to scare her almost as much as being held at gunpoint.

Maybe more. Hawk had been so strong, so invincible since the moment he'd saved her from the masked gunmen at her house, that it hurt to see him like this.

"Matt, I need your help." She tried to help Hawk stagger to his feet, but he was far too heavy.

Thankfully, Ryker and Mike stepped up to help. With a man on either side of Hawk, they hauled him to his feet. Jillian went over to the sofa to get Lizzy.

"No! Don't wanna ride in the car!" Lizzy kicked out her feet. "I'm hungry!"

"I know." Jillian felt bad she'd forgotten about providing food for her daughter. So much had happened in what seemed like such a short time. "We'll take some crackers with us in the car. We need to take Daddy to the hospital, okay?"

"Will these work?" Matt pulled a box of saltine crackers from the cupboard.

"Yes, thanks." She wrestled Lizzy back into her coat. "We'll ride with Duchess. Won't that be fun?"

Bringing up the dog worked. Lizzy took the proffered cracker and began to eat as Jillian carried her out to the car. She was horrified at how weak Hawk was in his efforts to get into the vehicle.

"Should I call an ambulance?" She glanced at Matt, indecision crowding her eyes.

"By the time they get here, you could be more than halfway to the hospital." Matt opened the back of the SUV for Duchess. "I say we just go. I'll drive."

She didn't argue, knowing it was best to have her hands free to keep Lizzy happy with crackers. Besides, she was worried about Hawk. They'd put him in the back next to Lizzy.

Matt didn't waste any time in barreling out of the long, winding driveway to the highway. Traffic was light, but since it this late in December, dusk was already beginning to fall although it was barely three thirty in the afternoon.

Twisting in her seat, Jillian looked back at Hawk. He was slumped in the corner, with his eyes closed. Lizzy was munching another cracker, seemingly in a better mood.

"Hurry, Matt," she whispered. "I'm worried about him."

"I know." Matt pressed his foot harder on the accelerator.

The ride seemed to take forever, but it was surprisingly only fifteen minutes before Matt gestured to the blue H sign, indicating the hospital was up ahead. "We're close now."

"Good." Jillian handed Lizzy another cracker, then leaned back to pat Hawk's knee. "Hawk? Can you hear me? We're almost at the hospital."

Hawk's eyelashes fluttered but he didn't respond. A cold fist of fear clutched her heart.

What if they were too late? What if the infection in Hawk's bloodstream was too far gone?

She couldn't bear the thought of losing Hawk. She needed him. Lizzy needed him.

When Matt pulled up to the front of the entrance marked Emergency, she jumped out and ran inside. "Help! We need help!"

Two staff members wearing scrubs followed her outside. Matt had opened the back door and was trying to support Hawk's weight.

"Get a gurney!"

One of the staff members spun around to head back inside. Jillian hovered near the nurse.

"He suffered a gunshot wound in his left shoulder a few days ago. I'm afraid it's infected."

The nurse barely glanced at her. "He's going into septic shock. We need to get him inside, stat!"

Septic shock? Jillian couldn't believe how Hawk had gotten so sick, so fast. She moved out of the way to make room for the stretcher. With Matt's help, the two hospital staff members were able to get Hawk on the gurney. After securing the straps around his torso, they quickly ran with him inside the emergency department.

Jillian watched them go, then slumped against the SUV and buried her face in her hands.

*Dear Lord, please heal Hawk's infection. Don't take him from me to bring him home to You. Not yet. Please? Amen.*

# SEVENTEEN

The bright overhead lights hurt his eyes and the muted sounds of voices were unintelligible. For a moment he wondered if he were being held prisoner in Afghanistan, because he couldn't understand what the people around him were saying. But then slowly, fragments of conversation began to make sense.

"Give another liter fluid bolus. Has the antibiotic run in yet?"

"Yes, it's in. Second fluid bolus is infusing now. Check out his labs, looks as if he's still a bit acidotic."

"Repeat his basic chem and have it run stat."

"Okay. Should I call upstairs for a bed?"

"No, we need to arrange a transfer to Trinity Medical Center. That bullet wound in his shoulder will need surgical intervention."

"I'll get the Access Center on the phone."

Some of it was gibberish, but Hawk began to realize that he was in the hospital getting treatment for his infected shoulder. And that they were planning to transfer him back to Milwaukee's Trinity Medical Center.

Except he wasn't going anywhere. Not until he knew where his family was.

"Jillian." The word was little more than a dry croak.

"Just relax, Mr. Jacobson, you're doing fine." A hand rested lightly on his right shoulder.

"Jillian." He repeated her name with more force, determined to get an answer. Where were Jillian and Lizzy? He didn't like being separated from them. As much as he trusted Ryker and the Callahans, he couldn't relax until he knew where Jillian and Lizzy were.

Bits and pieces of the most recent events were coming back to him. Primarily Senator Barton taking off in his helicopter, and Yonkers holding Jillian at gunpoint. They way they'd managed to get away from him.

Logically he knew the danger was over.

But he sensed there was more. He kept coming back to the way Barton believed someone higher up was pulling the strings. Who had hired the Blake-Moore group? Someone within the government? Was that higher up? He wondered about General McCann and Major Todd Hayes.

One of them or someone else, but likely the same man who'd sabotaged the plane that killed his teammates.

The nurse moved away and he quickly reached out with his strong hand, grabbing onto her forearm with a firm grip. Whatever they'd given him so far, it seemed to have done the trick. He could feel his strength returning by the minute. "Where's Jillian?"

"Easy now, you're going to dislodge the IV we placed." Her voice was soothing while she tried to wrestle her wrist from his grasp. "Maybe we need to give you something to help the pain and reduce your anxiety."

He instantly let her go. "No. I don't want narcotics or any sedatives. I'll be fine once you tell me exactly where my wife and daughter are."

"I think they're in the waiting room," someone spoke up.

Hawk squinted against the harsh lights, trying to put a face with the voice. "I need to see them. I'm not leaving until I see them."

"I'll see what I can do," the voice promised.

Hawk relaxed and tried to take stock of his situation. His left shoulder still throbbed, but not nearly as badly as before. He didn't feel feverish, either, and assumed the antibiotic they'd spoken about had already begun to fight against the infection. He felt stronger and thought that he could likely get out of there under his own power, if needed.

He didn't remember much of the trip to the hospital. Last thing he remembered, he'd been freezing cold and shivering, his brain feeling as if it were muffled by cotton. Then suddenly he'd awoken here under the bright lights, surrounded by medical personnel.

"Hawk?" Jillian's voice was full of trepidation. He turned his head and tried to see her more clearly. If only they'd shut that stupid light off. It was making his head hurt.

"I'm fine." He managed to drum up a weak smile. He held out his hand, grateful when she clasped it tightly. "Lizzy?"

"She's okay. I left her with Ryker because I wasn't sure how bad you'd look." Jillian stepped closer and he took note of the worried furrows in her brow. "You scared me. I've never seen you so sick."

"No reason to be afraid, Jilly. I've suffered far worse than this." Although he had to admit modern medicine did wonders for helping a guy get over a raging infection. "They want to transfer me to Trinity, but I need to get out of here."

"That's not a good idea," Jillian protested. "You seem better, but you don't realize how bad you were just a couple of short hours ago. Now that we're all safe, I'd rather you get the treatment you need."

The immediate danger was over, but Hawk knew that he wouldn't rest until he'd spoken personally with the FBI about what he knew and what he'd theorized.

"Did Barton show up?"

"I don't know, but Ryker took Matt back to the cabin and just returned a few minutes ago." Jillian glanced around as if

she were uncomfortable talking to Hawk in the middle of the
emergency department. "They told me I could only stay a few
minutes. And I need to get back to Lizzy. Please listen to the
doctor."

He didn't want her to leave. He didn't like having her and
Lizzy out of his sight. But he nodded. "Stay in the waiting room
for a little while yet, okay?"

"We will." She surprised him by leaning down to press a kiss
on his cheek. "I'm glad you're better, Hawk."

"Me, too." He ached to kiss her properly, but she was already moving away. A glance up at the IV pole confirmed the
fluid the nurse had hung was only a fourth of the way infused.

He decided to wait until the full liter was finished, before
getting out of there. The cops would be there soon as gunshot
wounds were an automatic report to the police. Even though
it had happened days ago, Hawk didn't want to deal with the
local law enforcement agencies.

He'd need Barton and his FBI buddy to avoid ending up in
jail.

His condition must have stabilized because the bevy of hospital staff around his bedside dwindled and the bright lights
were dimmed to a tolerable level. The doctor returned and informed him that Trinity Medical Center was willing to accept
him as a transfer and that an ambulance would be there shortly.

It was on the tip of his tongue to refuse the transfer, but then
he realized this was his ticket out of there. "I can't afford an
ambulance ride. My wife will drive me."

The physician frowned, not liking that answer. "You can't
go in a personal vehicle with an IV running."

"Take it out." Hawk kept his tone reasonable. "I'm not riding
in an ambulance all the way to Milwaukee. That's a ridiculous
waste of money when I have access to a vehicle and someone
to drive me."

The doctor reluctantly nodded as if the financial aspect of

Hawk's argument made sense. "Fine. But I think someone from the sheriff's department will be here to talk to you first."

Yeah, that wasn't happening. Hawk waited for the doctor to move away, then yanked out the IV, pressing the edge of the sheet over the bleeding wound until it stopped. He swung upright and managed to get off the gurney. Thankfully, they hadn't taken off all his clothes, but his warm leather jacket was nowhere to be seen. Hoping Jillian had it, he moved into the hallway and looked for the waiting room.

"Hey, where are you going?" a nurse asked in a sharp tone.

"Doc said I was accepted at Trinity. My wife is driving me." He didn't wait for her to respond but followed his instincts and managed to find the waiting area.

Jillian had his leather jacket and was sitting with Ryker. Lizzy was between them. He grabbed the jacket and gestured toward the door. "Let's go."

Ryker didn't hesitate. Jillian helped Lizzy with her coat, then scooped her into his arms. "I'm not happy about this," she muttered.

He ignored her. It wasn't until they were outside and back in the SUV that he relaxed.

"Where to?" Ryker asked as he started the engine.

Good question. "I need to talk to Barton. Where are the Callahans?"

"They're at the cabin motel, working with Barton's men." Ryker glanced at him. "You sure you want to go back there?"

"I think that's the only way we'll put this issue to rest once and for all." He was frustrated that his weakness had sent him to the hospital.

"Ryker, the doctor thinks it's important we get him to Trinity Medical Center as quickly as possible," Jillian said from the back seat.

"Later. Once I've spoken to Barton. I have no doubt I can call him and convince him to return to the cabin motel." Hawk didn't like disappointing Jillian, but she didn't understand what was at stake. Although Yonkers was dead, it didn't mean others weren't involved or weren't already working out a plan to continue selling guns to the insurgents.

"It won't take long to talk to Barton, then we'll head to Milwaukee." Ryker turned onto the highway and glanced back at Jillian. "Trust me, I'll make him go in."

Hawk didn't respond. He respected Ryker enough to know the guy wasn't kidding. He'd hoped to be home with Jillian and Lizzy for Christmas—their first holiday as a family, and maybe that was still a possibility.

A sudden crack echoed through the air. A metallic ping made the SUV jerk as Ryker fought to keep the vehicle on the road. Hawk braced himself with a hand on the dashboard as the scent of gas filled the interior, the fumes adding to his nagging headache.

"What's happening?" Jillian asked in horror.

All Hawk knew was that it wasn't good. Ryker steered the SUV toward the side of the road not far from a densely wooded area, then threw the gearshift into Park.

"Let's go."

Hawk scrambled from the car, then opened the back passenger door for Lizzy, fumbling with the straps to free her from the car seat. Jillian quickly joined him.

They'd barely taken three steps when a spotlight suddenly lit them up brighter than a Christmas tree. Hawk froze, holding Lizzy to his chest and raising a hand against the glare.

"It's been a long time, hasn't it, James?"

He couldn't see but he tried to place the voice. It wasn't familiar, despite the way this guy had addressed him. "Not long enough, obviously," he responded. "Who are you?"

"You don't remember me? I'm crushed." The man stepped forward, but it wasn't until he'd gotten closer that Hawk recognized him.

Former major of the Special Forces unit and current secretary of defense, Todd Hayes.

The man who'd no doubt hired the Blake-Moore group and had been in on the arms deal with Yonkers all along.

Jillian couldn't believe it was happening all over again. She had thought they were safe! That after Yonkers had died, their lives would go back to normal.

But as the man wearing a long winter coat and holding a gun approached casually, she began to realize that they'd never been safe. Not since the moment James had witnessed the gun deal in the Afghan mountains.

"It was you all the time, wasn't it? You were the one Yonkers reported to back in Afghanistan. You knew all about how he was selling guns to the insurgents. In fact, you gave him the order to do so, didn't you?" Hawk subtly shifted Lizzy in his arms. Jillian reached up to take their daughter, who had once again begun to cry in a way that wrenched her heart.

Lizzy had been exposed to far too much danger in the past few days and Jillian wondered how the little girl would manage to cope.

"You should have died in that plane crash." Hayes's voice was laced with annoyance. "If you had, your family would have been safe."

Considering the way her house had been breached by two thugs and her classroom ransacked, Jillian didn't believe him. She was fairly certain that the men with ski masks could have made her death and Lizzy's look like a burglary gone bad, once they had gotten the photos they'd come for.

She wished she'd never made that fateful call to Fort Bragg about the envelope from James.

"Yeah, right." Hawk's sarcastic tone reflected her feelings. "So now what? You're going to kill us all right here at the side of the road?"

"It would have helped if you'd crashed," Hayes drawled. "But we can work with it."

We? She shivered, imagining there were more men dressed

in black, moving through the woods right now. Was it possible that Hayes had brought more members of the Blake-Moore group with him? That this time, they wouldn't have a chance to escape?

"This close to the hospital? Better think again," Hawk shot back.

She realized Hawk was right. Ryker hadn't gotten far from the hospital when the shot had rung out, striking their gas tank. And who'd fired the shot anyway? Not Hayes but one of his minions.

Turning slightly to the right, she verified the lights from the hospital were within view.

So close, yet so far. If anyone at the hospital had heard the gunshot, there was no indication that they'd noticed. Or bothered to do anything about it.

She could feel Ryker coming up on her right side, as if planning to jump in front of her if Hayes started shooting. Sensing his presence didn't make her feel better. She wished he'd found a way to hide in the woods. Unfortunately, the spotlight had made that impossible.

Also, the goons were likely hiding in the woods, waiting for their chance to shoot.

And suddenly she was fed up with everything. "You won't get away with this," she shouted loud enough to startle Lizzy. "Senator Barton knows all about you."

Hayes threw back his head and laughed. Jillian felt her cheeks flush with fury. What was so funny?

"Barton has already been silenced and I've given orders for his men not to go anywhere near the cabin motel where you so rudely took out my main contact, Colin Yonkers." All hint of humor abruptly vacated his voice. "Enough. It's time for you to get back inside the vehicle."

Jillian inwardly reeled at his words. Barton had been silenced? The men hadn't gone to the cabin motel? Where were the Callahans?

She felt Hawk and Ryker go tense on either side of her and knew they were about to make some sort of drastic last-minute move.

Only this time, there was no easy way to get away. Not if there were men hiding in the woods around them.

"Okay, we're getting into the vehicle." Once again she blurted out her thoughts without taking the time to think it through.

"Jilly," Hawk warned in a low voice.

But then the shrill wail of sirens split the air. Jillian couldn't help taking a quick glance down the highway in the direction they'd been headed.

Twin red and blue flashing lights were fast approaching. She stood frozen, wondering if help was on the way or if the secretary of defense had somehow gotten the cops on his side, as well?

# EIGHTEEN

About time, Hawk thought. The wailing sirens indicated the local authorities were on the way. He'd been counting on the fact that the ER doctor had called the police to report his gunshot wound, and likely his recent escape. And here they were, just in the nick of time.

The spotlight went dark, and it took a long moment for his eyes to adjust to the instant darkness. He heard the scrape of footsteps on asphalt.

"We can't let him get away!" Hawk glanced toward Ryker, but the former special ops soldier didn't move.

"We don't know how many men he has with him." Ryker gently brushed past Jillian. "Stay with your family. I'll talk to the cops."

The sound of a car engine rumbling to life made Hawk want to rush after Hayes to stop him. But he wasn't armed. And Ryker was right. They knew for sure Hayes wasn't alone, having more than enough mercenaries at his disposal.

But then there was another SUV coming from the opposite direction from the local deputies. Hawk tensed, fearing the worst.

The oncoming SUV rammed directly into Hayes's vehicle. Two men instantly came out of the car, followed by a K-9.

The Callahans.

"Put your hands where I can see them!" Mike shouted. Even from where they stood, Hawk could hear Duchess growling.

"You don't know who you're messing with, son!" Hawk could hear the undertone of fear in Hayes's voice. "I'm the Secretary of Defense for the United States of America!"

"You're also a lying, gun-selling criminal," Mike retorted. "Keep your hands where I can see them, and your buddy in the driver's seat, too, or I'll shoot first and ask questions later."

"You'll pay for this!" Desperation leached from Hayes. "You can't arrest me! Who do you think you are?"

While Mike held his gun pointed at Hayes, Matt opened the passenger-side door and roughly yanked Hayes out. Duchess continued to growl, encouraging Hayes to comply. Matt turned him face first toward the SUV and slapped cuffs around his wrists.

The driver didn't put up a fight, either, but stood stoic and silent as Matt cuffed him, as well.

Two sheriff's department vehicles pulled to a stop near the group of SUVs. Four armed deputies emerged, holding their guns at the ready.

"Which one of you is Milwaukee County Deputy Mike Callahan?"

"Over here," Mike called, without turning from the two men he still held in the crosshairs of his weapon. "We have two men in custody here, but be on alert, as there could be more."

"He's right. Someone fired at our car, hitting the gas tank," Ryker added. "Had to be from a rifle. If there's no such weapon in the car with them, then someone in the woods has it."

Hawk knew that if there were any mercenaries from the Blake-Moore group still hiding in the woods, they'd be long gone. Mercs were always ready to cut and run in order to save their own skin. It burned to know they wouldn't all be brought to justice.

Although if he had his way, the Blake-Moore group would never be hired by anyone within the US government, ever again.

"Release me this instant!" Hayes shouted. "I'm the secretary of defense! I'm the one who was trying to arrest these men for treason!"

"Save it," one of the deputies replied. "We already heard from the FBI. Special Agent in Charge Dennis Ludwig informed us that they recently caught a man who attempted to kill Senator Barton. Seems he worked for you, Hayes, and spilled his guts to save himself. The Feds contacted us and requested we return to the cabin motel."

Hawk's mind spun at the recent turn of events. It was surreal that events at the highest level of the government had spilled over into small-town Wisconsin.

Because of him.

"I have a photo that shows Colin Yonkers selling weapons to the insurgents in Afghanistan," he offered. "Unfortunately, Yonkers is dead, but he worked for the Blake-Moore mercenary group. I think you'll find Hayes hired them to do his dirty work, including shooting me." He put a hand up to rub his injured shoulder.

"I have the photo and your laptop computer. I've heard parts of the story, but we'll need you to come with us so we can hear it all from the beginning." The deputy who'd called to Mike gestured with his hand. "We'll transport Hayes and his driver to jail, too. The Feds are coming in to pick them up."

"No!" Hayes let out a strangled cry and made a move as if to run. Duchess clamped her jaw around his ankle, preventing him from going anywhere.

"Idiot," Ryker muttered.

"What about us?" Jillian asked, speaking for the first time since her impulsive comments about Barton.

Hawk wanted nothing more than to tell her she could go

home, but her house was a mess and he still didn't feel good about having her out of his sight. "You'll come with us," he assured her. "Hopefully it won't take too long."

"All right," she agreed with a weary sigh.

He was wrong. Upon entering the sheriff's department headquarters, they were taken to separate rooms. Ryker in one, Hawk in another, and Jillian and Lizzy in a third.

Hawk did his best to start the story at the beginning, but Deputy Greg Ashton, the one who apparently knew Mike, kept interrupting.

When his stomach rumbled with hunger, Deputy Ashton brought him something from the vending machine, but Hawk insisted that he provide food and water to Jillian and Lizzy.

"They're being well taken care of," Ashton assured him, plunking a bag of chips and a bottle of water in front of him. "So you and Tillman shot two of Senator Barton's men, but he covered for you?"

"Yes." Hawk picked up the story, and after another hour, finally finished with how their SUV had been fired upon outside the hospital by Hayes and his men. "I'm telling you, the Blake-Moore group is involved in this up to their beady little eyeballs."

"Yeah, I've been thinking the same thing." Ashton looked down at the pages of scribbled notes on the yellow legal pad in front of him. "Anything else?"

"I don't think so." He'd covered everything, starting with the plane crash that had killed his teammates, and Jillian's phone call to Fort Bragg, which had resulted in the break-in at Jillian's house and Brookland Elementary. He hadn't left out a single detail and hoped he wouldn't be held as an accessory to murder as a result of Yonkers's death.

"Okay, stay here for a minute. I need to talk to my team." Deputy Ashton rose to his feet.

"We only shot at Yonkers because he threatened to kill Jillian," Hawk said in a low voice. "It was him or her. She and Lizzy are the true innocents in all of this."

Ashton stopped at the door. "I believe you, but I need to make sure Tillman's story matches yours. If it does, then I think we'll be okay."

After Ashton disappeared from the room, Hawk slumped in his seat, exhaustion weighing him down. He desperately wanted to see Jillian and Lizzy, to make sure they were both okay.

Thinking of the harm he'd brought to them filled him with shame and self-loathing. He never, ever should have mailed those photos to her. He'd dragged his wife and daughter into harm's way, not just once, but over and over again.

Would things have been different if he'd taken the stupid ambulance to Milwaukee? Probably.

He didn't deserve to have a wife and child in his life. Now that the Feds were involved, Hayes was in custody and the Blake-Moore group was under scrutiny, he felt certain the danger was over. For real, this time.

Maybe he'd give Jillian and Lizzy his house to use temporarily, until hers was repaired. He'd need to return to the hospital sooner than later, anyway. He'd pay for the damage to her home, then move on, giving her the freedom and safety she deserved.

Jillian had refused to allow Lizzy to eat a bunch of junk food from the vending machines, so one of the helpful deputies who had a child of his own had run out to get chicken fingers from a local fast-food restaurant. It wasn't great, but slightly better than chips and cookies.

Lizzy was better now that they were inside, surrounded by men wearing uniforms and badges, but she was clearly getting bored.

"Where's Daddy?" she asked for the third time.

"He'll be here soon." Jillian knew her smile was brittle. She was tired of waiting for the deputies to finish with Ryker and Hawk. Especially since she knew Hawk needed to get back to the hospital.

The Callahan brothers had been there for a while but had left when the FBI agents arrived. She assumed they were walking the agents through the various crime scenes.

"I wanna go home," Lizzy whined.

"I know, sweetie. Me, too." Jillian caught sight of Deputy Ashton coming out of the room where she knew Hawk was seated. Her questioning session hadn't taken nearly as long, and she was becoming concerned with the amount of time they'd spent with Hawk and Ryker.

Especially Hawk.

"Mrs. Jacobson?"

She didn't bother to correct the deputy. At this point, she felt like she was Mrs. Jacobson more so than Mrs. Wade. Her life with James was a long time ago,

She was with Hawk now.

"Yes?" She summoned a smile. "Are we free to go?"

"You are. I've validated that Ryker's story mirrors your husband's."

Of course it did. Hawk and Ryker joined her in the office and she looked at her husband with concern. "Hawk? Are you okay?" Jillian shifted Lizzy in her arms, bone-weary from carrying the little girl.

"Fine." He didn't quite meet her eyes. "Let's get out of here."

She was having trouble gauging his mood. "I'm taking you straight to Trinity Medical Center."

To her surprise, he didn't argue. "Ryker, we need a set of wheels."

She blinked, having completely forgotten about the hole in the gas tank.

"Mike Callahan is letting us borrow his vehicle, and he already put Lizzy's car seat inside," Ryker said.

Jillian walked between the men out into the cold December air. "How will Mike and Matt get home?"

"One of the deputies offered them a lift. Besides, they're still talking to the Feds." Ryker opened the door for her and she gratefully set Lizzy inside.

No one spoke during the long trip to Milwaukee. Jillian sensed Hawk was upset about something, but he insisted he was fine.

At the hospital, Hawk dug a key out of his pocket and handed it to her. "Ryker will take you to my place. Yours needs a bit of repair work."

"I'm not leaving," she protested, although Lizzy's eyelids were drooping with exhaustion.

"You are. Lizzy needs to rest." Hawk didn't reach out to touch her or even hug her. "Take care, Jillian."

His words held a note of finality that made her frown. But Hawk was already making his way inside the brightly lit emergency department. She knew he was safe there, but leaving him felt as if she were cutting off her own arm.

She didn't like it, not one bit. If not for Lizzy, she'd stay with him all night.

"Come on," Ryker said. "I'll take you home."

Home was where Hawk was, but she nodded. Lizzy needed a good night's sleep. But first thing in the morning, she'd be back. And no matter what Hawk said, she wasn't going to leave again.

Not until he was able to come home with her, hopefully in time for Christmas.

Hawk felt much better by the following morning, thanks to more fluids and antibiotics. The hospital staff wasn't happy with him, so he tried to be a model patient.

The surgeon, Dr. Cramer, came in early to poke and prod his injured shoulder. "Could be worse. Can't do much until the infection is cleared out."

"So I can get out of here?"

"What, big plans for Christmas?" Dr. Cramer asked.

Hawk belatedly realized today was Christmas Eve. So much had happened over the past five days that he'd lost track of time.

"Something like that." He shifted in the uncomfortable hospital bed. "It's crazy to just sit here for IV antibiotics."

"They saved your life," Dr. Cramer pointed out. "Sorry, but it's not just the antibiotics, but regular dressing changes."

"Come on, it wasn't that bad," Hawk protested.

"Frankly, I expected worse." Cramer logged into the computer and peered thoughtfully at the screen. "You stay until noon to get another dose of antibiotics and you can return home for two days. I'll expect you back on the day after Christmas."

That wasn't exactly part of his plan, but Hawk wasn't about to argue. "Thanks."

"You can thank me by doing regular dressing changes and taking your antibiotics as ordered." Cramer logged off the computer and left the room.

Hawk dozed a bit but woke up when he heard Lizzy's voice. "Daddy? Are you all better now?"

*Daddy?* Hawk opened his eyes to find his beautiful daughter standing beside his bed, looking fresh from a bath and wearing clean clothes. She still had the ragged teddy bear that she'd managed to hold on to from the night he'd pulled her out from beneath her bed. "I'm fine, Lizzy." His gaze lifted to meet Jillian's. She also looked better for having had a good night's sleep, a shower and clean clothes. Her beauty was enough to make his heart squeeze painfully in his chest.

"I heard you're going to be given a few days off for good behavior," Jillian joked.

He nodded and pushed himself upright. "I'm surprised to see you here."

She lifted a brow. "Why? You had to know we'd come visit."

He wasn't sure how to respond. He looked past her at the door leading to the hallway. "Is Ryker with you?"

"He dropped us off," Jillian informed him. "He was up early, working on putting my house back in order."

A flash of jealousy hit hard. If anyone should be helping, it should be him. The destruction of her property was his fault, not Ryker's. "I'll help as soon as we leave."

Jillian rolled her eyes. "Keep saying stuff like that and they won't let you go. You're supposed to be recuperating, not working."

"Here. I think you need teddy more than me." Lizzy shoved her favorite stuffed animal in the crook of his arm. The simple gesture made his eyes sting with tears.

"That's nice of you to share teddy with Daddy," Jillian said with a smile.

"She doesn't have to," he started to say, but Jillian silenced him with a stern look.

"Sharing is a nice trait for children to learn, the earlier the better."

Lizzy found the buttons on the electric bed and made the head begin to rise.

"No, Lizzy," Jillian gently scolded. "Behave or Daddy won't be able to come home with us."

Daddy? Home with them? He tried to think of something to say. "Jilly, there's no reason to rush into anything. We have plenty of time to sort things out."

"What's to sort out?" She pulled the Belle doll out of the purse on her shoulder and offered it to Lizzy. "Why don't you play for a bit, okay?"

"Okay." Lizzy took the doll and went over to the recliner chair in the corner of the room.

"It's her favorite," Jillian offered with a smile. "Because it was a gift from you."

Hawk cleared his throat. "She knows I'm her father?"

"Yes. I blurted it out when you got so sick." Jillian sat on the edge of Hawk's bed. "I was afraid we were going to lose you."

Her words were a balm against his wounded soul. Dredging up every ounce of strength he possessed, he did his best to give her an out. "There's no need to change anything between us, Jillian. The danger is over. You can go back to your place and I'll go to mine."

Her brow furrowed. "Is that your way of telling me you don't care about me, about us, anymore?"

"No!" He couldn't lie, not about this. "You don't understand. I'm trying to set you free. You didn't ask to be mixed up with someone like me."

"Yes, I did," Jillian corrected softly. She placed her hand on the center of his chest, the warmth radiating through his flimsy hospital gown. The modest diamond engagement ring he'd given her five years ago glittered on the third finger of her left hand. "I married you, Hawk. For better or worse. In sickness and in health. Forsaking all others, for as long as we both shall live."

The way she recited their wedding vows while wearing his ring humbled him. And instantly his resolve broke into tiny bits and scattered with the wind.

"I love you, Jillian. I've always loved you."

"I love you, too." She bent down and gave him a long kiss. "You're Hawk to me, now, but the core of you is still James. Crazy as it sounds, I love both of you."

"Does that mean you're willing to become Mrs. Hawk Jacobson?" It was meant to be a joke, but her expression was serious as she nodded.

"Yes, absolutely. But you should know that things are different now. I'm a schoolteacher and love my job. I'm not going to sit home every night waiting for you to get home from work."

"I wouldn't ask you to." Hawk knew that she was right, that things were different now.

Yet somehow, they were also the same.

"Then let me be the first to welcome you home, Hawk." Jillian kissed him again and he held her close, reveling in his good fortune.

Home. Hawk was forced to blink back the sting of tears. He'd never allowed himself to consider the fact that he'd have the chance to return home to be with his family.

"Merry Christmas, Jillian," he whispered.

"Merry Christmas, Hawk," she whispered back.

They wouldn't have gifts or decorations, or presents under the tree, but they'd be together as they celebrated the day Jesus was born.

And that was all that mattered.

\* \* \* \* \*

Dear Reader,

I hope you've enjoyed Hawk and Jillian's story, *Soldier's Christmas Secrets*. Many of you asked for Hawk to find his own happy ending, and frankly, I wasn't quite willing to give up the Callahans, either.

I have the utmost respect for all of those who serve our country, and I hope you give this new miniseries, Justice Seekers, a try.

Please take a moment to leave a review; reviews are very important for authors. Also know I love hearing from my readers. I can be found through my website at *www.laurascottbooks.com*, through Facebook at Laura Scott Author and on Twitter @Laurascottbooks. If you're interested in when Ryker's story will be available, join my newsletter through my website. That's where I announce new releases, and I offer a free novella that is not for sale anywhere else, to all newsletter subscribers.

Until next time,
*Laura Scott*

# Christmas Witness Conspiracy

*Maggie K. Black*

**Maggie K. Black** is an award-winning journalist and romantic suspense author with an insatiable love of traveling the world. She has lived in the American South, Europe and the Middle East. She now makes her home in Canada with her history-teacher husband, their two beautiful girls and a small but mighty dog. Maggie enjoys connecting with her readers at maggiekblack.com.

## Books by Maggie K. Black

### *Protected Identities*

*Christmas Witness Protection*
*Runaway Witness*
*Christmas Witness Conspiracy*

### *True North Heroes*

*Undercover Holiday Fiancée*
*The Littlest Target*
*Rescuing His Secret Child*
*Cold Case Secrets*

### *Amish Witness Protection*

*Amish Hideout*

### *Military K-9 Unit*

*Standing Fast*

Visit the Author Profile page at
millsandboon.com.au for more titles.

Now faith is the substance of things hoped for,
the evidence of things not seen.
*–Hebrews* 11:1

With thanks to all the incredible women
I've had the privilege of teaching self-defense.

And with love to my amazing daughter
who never reads my stories
because she's busy writing her own.

# ONE

Thick snow squalls blew down the Toronto shoreline of Lake Ontario, turning the city's annual winter wonderland into a haze of sparkling lights. The cold hadn't done much to quell the tourists, though, Detective Liam Bearsmith thought as he methodically trailed his hooded target around the skating rink and through the crowd. It was three days until Christmas and a few hours after sunset. Hopefully, the combination of the darkness, heavy flakes and general merriment would keep the jacket-clad criminal he was after from even realizing he was being followed. The "Sparrow" was a hacker. Just a tiny fish in the criminal pond, but a newly reborn and highly dangerous cyberterrorist group had just placed a pretty hefty bounty on the Sparrow's capture in the hopes it would lead them to a master decipher key that could break any code. If Liam didn't bring in the Sparrow now, terrorists could turn that code breaker into a weapon and the Sparrow could be dead, or worse, by Christmas.

Thankfully, his target had finally stopped all that darting-around and doubling-back nonsense he'd been doing when Liam had first picked up his trail. The lone figure hurried up a metal footbridge festooned in white lights. A gust of wind caught the hood of the Sparrow's jacket, tossing it back. Long dark hair flew loose around the Sparrow's slender shoulders.

Liam's world froze as déjà vu flooded his senses. His target was a woman.

What's more, Liam was sure he'd seen her somewhere before. Although in that moment, for some inexplicable reason, his brain had stalled so completely he could only pray God would remind him of where.

It had been almost a year since Liam's secretive team of rogue Royal Canadian Mounted Police detectives had taken down a cyberterrorist duo called the "Imposters" on Christmas Eve, to stop them from auctioning off the RCMP's entire witness-protection database to criminals on the dark web. Two of Liam's colleagues had been reluctantly forced to kill the pair. Their team hadn't realized for months that during the chaos, the Sparrow had somehow slipped her way into the Imposters's criminal auction through a hacked back door and deleted just one witness's file before it could be compromised. That file had belonged to a young woman named Hannah Phillips, whose military contractor husband, Renner, was presumed dead in Afghanistan after having developed a master decipher key that could hack any code in the world.

Now, the Imposters had been reborn, as an all-new group of nameless and faceless hackers had taken up their mantle and hailed the original duo as heroes, vowing revenge on Liam's team. They'd placed a bounty on Liam's target, as well as being so determined to get their hands on Renner's master-key decoding device that they were threatening to cause mass chaos on New Year's Eve by crashing power grids around the world unless someone turned it over to them.

Liam's strategy had been to capture the Sparrow, question her and use the intel gleaned to locate these new Imposters. His brain freezing at the mere sight of her hadn't exactly been part of the plan. The Sparrow reached up, grabbed her hood and yanked it back down again firmly, but not before Liam caught a glimpse of a delicate jaw that was determinedly set and of the thick flakes that clung to her long lashes. She hurried down the other side of the bridge. For a moment Liam just stood there, his hand on the railing and his heart still praying for clarity, as his mind filled with the name and face of a young woman he'd known and loved a very long time ago.

*Kelly Marshall.*

Kelly had been nineteen and he'd been twenty-two when he'd shown up on her college campus, over two decades ago, to break the news that her father had been laundering money for gangsters and she needed to go into witness protection with her mother. Kelly had been defiant, spectacular and beautiful. In the couple weeks they'd been in each other's lives, she'd wrenched open his closed heart, made him question his will to be a cop and left a hole inside him so big he'd never risked loving anyone again.

No. It couldn't be Kelly. Not here. Not now.

She plunged into a crowded Christmas market on the other side of the footbridge and now weaved her way through the mass of shoppers and stalls. Liam strode after her. At six foot five, with the build of a bouncer, he knew it took far more than just hiding his bulletproof vest under a leather jacket to make him look inconspicuous. So, instead, he'd learned how to be invisible—a handy skill for the son of a prominent RCMP officer growing up in a working-class town like Kingston, where over half the kids in his class had a relative in jail. Liam thankfully didn't remember much about his abusive and unstable alcoholic mother, beyond knowing she was the reason he still sometimes flinched when people tried to hug him and why he had always appreciated his late father's focus on calm, rules and self-discipline over emotion and sentiment. Liam moved along the edges of the stalls with the steady gait he'd learned from his father. It was the kind that made people instinctively get out of his way and then forget they'd ever seen him.

His emotions swirled like the snow. He pushed them away

and focused on facts. The rise and fall of military contractor Renner Phillips was fascinating. A low-level computer analyst in Afghanistan, he'd suddenly thwarted a major terrorist attack after breaking a seemingly impenetrable code. Rumor was he'd developed a powerful decryption device. The government ordered him to turn it over. Countless terrorist groups placed him on their target lists, offering Renner bribes and threatening to hurt his young wife, Hannah, as leverage. For a few brief hours he was the world's most sought-after man. Then the SUV he'd been traveling in blew up. Renner was presumed dead, the decipher key was assumed destroyed in the explosion and Hannah had gone into RCMP witness protection.

Everyone had thought it was over, until this woman he was now following—who inexplicably reminded him of Kelly—had nabbed Hannah's RCMP witness-protection file from the original Imposters a year ago, and then these new reborn Imposters had threatened global chaos unless they got their hands on Renner's decoding device.

And Liam, for one, was tired of surprises.

He reached for his cell phone and hit the number of their resident tech genius, Seth Miles. The phone rang in Liam's earpiece. A former criminal hacker himself, Seth had spent most of his adult life trying to be some kind of vigilante, targeting bad guys and exposing their crimes, before he'd gone after the wrong guys and ended up in witness protection. Now, despite Seth's sketchy past and unconventional way of doing things, he was the only noncop on Liam's elite team. Seth didn't answer.

Liam hit Redial. Carolers belted tunes to his right. The smell of hot chocolate tried to yank his attention left. But his eyes stayed locked on the woman ahead, as she slipped from the stalls and attached herself to a small group of people now moving down the docks, as if pretending that she was with them.

Smart move, Liam thought. It was a tactic his father had taught him and that he'd often used himself.

His phone clicked. "Hey, Seth?"

"Yo, Liam." Seth's voice filled his ear. "Tell me you want to split the cost of three toasters."

*Three toasters?* Liam's eyes rolled for a nanosecond before he locked back on the woman ahead. As usual, Liam had no idea what Seth was talking about and limited patience to ferret it out. "Did you know the person who hacked into the file of deceased contractor Renner Phillips's widow, Hannah, was a woman?"

There was a slightly strangled sound on the line.

"Are you sure?" Seth asked.

"That Renner's actually dead?" Liam asked. He and Seth had debated this one more than a few times since the new Imposters had threatened global chaos if they didn't get Renner's decoding device. Despite all evidence, Seth remained doggedly convinced that Renner was still alive. But if so, what kind of man would just abandon his new wife like that and disappear? "Still no. Though I've got no intel to back that up."

"That the Sparrow is a woman," Seth clarified.

"I have eyes on her as we speak." The wood beneath his feet was slippery with ice and damp with melting snow. Now that he'd left the fair behind, all remaining foot traffic seemed to be heading toward a large, three-story cruise ship/party boat. According to the yellow posters taped to metal lampposts around him, it was about to set sail for the Ugly Sweater Holiday Cruise.

"What does she look like?" Seth asked.

*Way too much like a woman named Kelly Marshall I placed in witness protection over twenty years ago.*

"Five foot five," Liam said. "Long dark hair. Athletic legs. About a hundred and forty pounds, but hard to tell in the ski jacket. No clear visual on her face."

"But how do you know that you're following the right person?" Seth wasn't letting it go.

"I got a tip," Liam said.

"From?" Seth asked.

"A contact." Liam kept from pointing out the fact that just

because Seth hadn't been able to get a solid lead on her didn't mean no one could. "I know a lot of people who owe me one."

"How about you get me a picture and I'll run it through the system?" Seth suggested.

"Good idea," Liam said. "Stand by."

A good hard look at his target's face to prove to himself that she wasn't Kelly might not hurt any. Someone had helpfully left a bright pink mitten on the back of a metal bench. He picked it up and rolled it between his fingers, as his footsteps quickened. "Any idea yet which specific power grids these new Imposters are targeting on New Year's Eve?"

"Not yet," Seth said. "Have I told you I think it's a colossal mistake for law enforcement to try to keep news of this threat from getting out?"

"A few times."

But law enforcement tended to avoid leaking news of terrorist threats that could cause mass panic whenever they could help it. And "an anonymous mob of bad guys are threatening to do a really bad thing to unknown locations unless they get their hands on something powerful that might've been destroyed from someone who might be dead" was hardly reassuring. They didn't even know any of these new Imposters's identities. Only that they were young men who were angry, congregated online and had no centralized leader.

"You can't keep something off the internet forever," Seth said. "It's a cyberworld out there, old man."

"Duly noted," Liam said. "Any word yet on who the leaders of the Imposters are?"

"As I've explained, online mobs don't have leaders," Seth said. "They have lots of individuals suggesting chaos and others jumping on the bandwagon, with no one really sure who started it. Even if there was someone on the dark-web message boards posing as the big-bad-boss Imposter, there's no reason to believe he has any more knowledge or leadership than anyone else. Pffft, anyone could randomly call themselves the leader of a group like that and it would be virtually meaningless."

The Sparrow had stopped by a tree a little bit away from the crowd. It looked like she was on the phone.

"So about those toasters?" Seth's voice was back in his ear. "You know we got three weddings in ten days now?"

"Two weddings," Liam corrected. Two of the detectives in their five-person team were getting married over the holidays, both to former witnesses whose files had been compromised by the Imposters. Noah Wilder was marrying Corporal Holly Asher in two days, on Christmas Eve, and Mack Grey was marrying Iris James, a social worker, a week later on New Year's Eve. The team's year of dealing with the auction's fallout had definitely taken some eventful turns.

"Three now," Seth said. "Jess is getting married tomorrow at one."

"What?" Liam faltered a step. Last he'd heard, the final member of their team, Detective Jessica Eddington, was set to marry Travis Tatlow in the spring. "Everything okay?"

"She got offered a contract consulting on a special-victims unit in Florida and decided they and the kids should all go together as a family," Seth said. Travis had recently adopted two small children he'd grown close to while living in witness protection. "I'm really sorry. I just assumed she'd called you before me."

"Don't worry," Liam said. Jess and Seth had gotten close on a previous assignment, and Liam had never viewed his work as a popularity contest. "I'm sure she's got a lot on her mind and a lot of people to contact."

In fact, Liam could see Jess's name popping up on his phone now, but he declined her call, planning to congratulate her later. The Sparrow had ended her call and had started walking again. Her pace quickened, and he sped up to match it.

"So that just leaves us two bachelors standing," Seth said.

"But I'm hoping if marriage is contagious it's only affecting detectives. Not that I think you'd be at risk."

"Uh... Huh?" Liam just grunted in response. What was that supposed to mean?

"You know, I read your file—"

"Don't read people's files—"

"—it's a great read," Seth went on. "Two decades on the force, over a gazillion arrests, but no significant relationships. No brothers or sisters. No family, besides your late dad. Never married. Never dated. Never fallen in love. You're practically one of those clay warriors come to life."

"I think you mean a golem," Liam said.

"Don't think I've ever even seen you hug anyone—"

"I'm not big on hugs." Or on Seth's usual nonsense. The Sparrow slipped her phone into her pocket. Liam was only a few feet behind her now. He readied his cell to snap a picture and then reached out with the mitten, tapping her arm as he did so. "Excuse me, miss? Did you drop this?"

She turned. Kelly Marshall's fierce green eyes locked defiantly on his. The delicate lips he'd once kissed parted in a gasp. Liam felt all the blood drain from his face. Seth had been wrong. Liam had thought himself in love once, with a woman he'd lost his heart, head and almost entire career over.

And now he was going to arrest her.

"Liam?" Kelly felt the name of the man she'd once loved slip from her lips. Shivers cascaded down her limbs as she looked up into the dark eyes she'd never imagined she'd see again. For a moment, she couldn't believe it was really him, or even if she'd said his name out loud, until she saw him nod and heard him say "Hey, Kelly" in that same deep voice that had always rumbled faintly like distant thunder at the edges of her memory.

Faded scars traced the strong lines of Liam's jaw and there were at least two new bends in his nose. Gray brushed the temples of his short dark hair. He looked both weathered and stronger somehow, and maybe a little tired. But despite the outward changes from both past battles and time, the intensity in his gaze was as powerful as it had always been. He lowered his head toward hers. His voice was deep and low in her ear. "Did you hack Renner Phillips's widow's witness-protection file?"

So many questions flooded her mind that for a moment she couldn't find her voice. How did he know? How had he found her? This man who'd once convinced her foolish heart he loved her, and had even asked her to marry him, then had disappeared from her life entirely, leaving her to a life in witness protection, caring for a mother who was having a nervous breakdown, while pregnant with his child—his daughter, Hannah—whom he'd never even acknowledged beyond a terse email telling her to put the baby up for adoption.

"I'll ask you again," Liam said. "Why did you hack and destroy Hannah Phillips's witness-protection file?"

How could he even ask her that? Had he not figured it out?

"To protect her, Liam!" she answered honestly. "Because she's our Hannah! She's our girl."

Yes, the adoption had been closed, but their brilliant, beautiful and incredibly talented twenty-one-year-old daughter had searched for Kelly and found her after her adoptive parents had been killed in a car crash when Hannah was in her first year of college. When Kelly had written to Liam about the birth of their daughter, she'd told him Hannah's first name. Certainly Liam was a smart enough detective to match Hannah's name, birth date and the fact she was an adoptee to the letter Kelly had sent, years ago, telling him their baby had been a girl.

Behind her she could hear someone calling out "final boarding" for the party cruise. She glanced back. The line to board had dwindled down to a handful of stragglers. A thin man with a giant red Santa sweater over his jacket was yelling into a megaphone that anyone left had better hurry up. Hannah and her infant daughter were already on board, waiting for Kelly, so that together they could escape the cruise by motorboat, get into the United States undetected and finally reunite Hannah with her husband, Renner, after over a year apart.

A shiver ran down her spine. Did Liam know that Hannah had been pregnant with Renner's child when he disappeared? Or that Renner was still alive and had spent months in hiding, while working desperately and diligently to find a way to reunite with his wife, so the two young newlyweds could finally be together?

For her part, Kelly had both disliked and doubted the couple's plan from the start. Why not just come forward after the roadside bombing? Why had Renner instead gone into hiding? Hannah had explained that it was because there was no master-key decoding device, and that those who wanted to get their hands on it would never believe that was true, so Renner was doing what he had to in order to keep her safe.

It was clear that Hannah loved her husband and vice versa. The threats against their lives had been real and Kelly knew that Renner was a good man with a good heart. But they were both so young. They weren't thinking through their decisions. And Kelly's attempt to talk them into finding another way had fallen on deaf ears. Now all she could do was go with her daughter, help protect her and ask Renner what he was thinking, face-to-face.

Unless Liam had a better plan? Could Liam be an unexpected ally in talking their strong-willed daughter out of this plan?

"What do you mean she's our girl?" Liam's question drew her eyes back to his face. His tone was baffled, and his face was blank. "Who do you mean by *our*? Some group? Some crew? Are you somehow part of the Imposters or some other criminal gang that's after Renner's master-key decoding device?"

His words hit like a slap.

*She's ours, Liam! Yours and mine. Our secret daughter. The one we gave up for adoption!*

She could feel the words forming on her lips, begging to be spoken. But something in the flat, emotionless look in his eyes made disgust twist in the pit of her stomach. Had he forgotten their daughter's name? The fact they even had a daughter? Or had he never read her letter? Either way, he didn't deserve her trust now. And yet somehow, as she looked up into his face, hope still crashed over her damaged heart, like a fresh wave on the shore. A horn blew behind her. The boat was leaving.

"There's so very much I need to tell you," she said, "and that we need to talk about—"

"And I want to listen," Liam said.

"But I have to go," she said. "Right now. Come with me, please, and I'll explain everything."

"No, Kelly," Liam said. "I'm sorry. You're going to have to come with me." Liam's left hand took her arm. With the right, he pulled back his leather jacket just enough to show her his RCMP badge, gun and handcuffs. He was also wearing a bulletproof vest. "I'm arresting you on suspicion of accessing a criminal dark-web auction site and illegally accessing an RCMP witness-protection file…"

What was wrong with him? What had happened to the thoughtful, logical and caring man she'd loved a long time ago? The boat honked its horn again and the faint sound of party music filled the air.

The cruise ship was about to pull away, taking Hannah and the baby with it.

"Liam!" Her voice rose. "Stop, please, you're making a mistake."

He didn't even blink, let alone pause. "You have the right to retain and instruct legal counsel without delay…"

No, this was not about to happen. She had to go. *Lord, if I'm wrong, please forgive me for what I'm about to do.* Her hand darted to her pocket, yanked out a mini–stun gun and drove it hard into Liam's side, right underneath his bulletproof vest. He groaned and fell back, doubling over in what seemed to be both pain and shock. She shoved him hard, then turned and ran. Her feet pelted down the boardwalk, slipping on the boards.

"Wait!" she shouted. She shoved the stun gun back into her jacket pocket, yanked out a bright yellow ticket and waved it above her head. "Don't leave without me!"

Behind her she could hear Liam calling her faintly, as if forcing her name through pained lungs. The man in the ugly red sweater paused and she nearly crashed into him, barely stopping herself from falling off the dock.

"I have a ticket," she said and pushed the paper into his hand. "I'm sorry I'm late."

The man's eyes darted from her to what she guessed was Liam behind her. "What about him?"

"He's my ex," she said. "I hoped he'd come with me. But instead he tried to stop me... It's complicated."

Twinkling lights shone and music thumped from the triple-deck ship ahead of her. She pressed her lips together and prayed hard. Maybe boarding the boat was a foolish move, but she had no time to come up with a better option. Hannah and the baby were waiting for her, and if she didn't go now she might never see her daughter again. The man nodded, took her ticket and waved his arm toward the boat. "Welcome to the Ugly Sweater Holiday Cruise. This party tour around Lake Ontario is approximately three hours long. The buffet is on the top deck. We return to Toronto at midnight."

And if her last-ditch effort to talk Hannah out of her plan failed, then Kelly, Hannah and the baby would have left the boat long before then.

"Thank you." She scrambled on board. People crowded around the side of the deck, huddled in winter gear and watching as the boat pulled away. She pushed through them and ran up a narrow flight of stairs to the second deck. It was only then she grabbed the railing and glanced back. The boat had pulled away from the dock. Liam stood there shaking his head, still on the shore, a few feet away from where she'd left him.

Had she really just run from the one man she'd waited twenty-two years to see again? How had he just let her go? But there was no sign of a police boat rushing after them or of anyone trying desperately to flag the boat to turn back. A jolly voice came over the speakers and welcomed everyone to the party. A cheer erupted from the deck below her and the music grew louder. What had she been thinking, asking Liam to come with her? Or hoping that he'd step up now after abandoning her and turning his back on her so many years ago?

She'd been a few months shy of twenty and happily pursuing a criminology degree with dreams of a life in law enforcement when Liam had walked up to her in the courtyard outside of class, flashed a badge and quietly told her to pack a bag because her life as she knew it was over. Less than an hour later, she was in the front seat of his truck as he drove her across the country to join her mother in witness protection, all because her greedy father had processed a whole lot of fake bank loans for some very dangerous people.

It had been a white truck, she remembered. Funny which memories had stuck and which ones hadn't. Liam had learned a whole bunch of handy tactics for staying alive from his father, and he'd shared them with her on their journey. One was that white vehicles were most likely to go unnoticed because they got dirty fast. Trucks were best because they were often mistaken for contractors and could handle tough terrain.

She hadn't thought of the introverted detective as her type at first. Liam had been too tall, too quiet and too slow to let her in or even smile. At first, he'd even flinched when she'd touched him. But she'd trusted him. He'd kept her safe when things had gone awry and the men her father had flipped on had ambushed them and nearly killed her. What should've been a two-day drive had instead ended up with them being on the run together for almost two weeks, with only Liam's quick thinking and the survival tactics she'd learned from him keeping her safe.

But more than that, they'd fallen in love. Or at least, she thought they had. Liam had asked her to marry him, she'd said yes and he'd promised he'd find a way for them to be together.

Instead, after he'd kissed her goodbye, he'd never returned, answered his phone or even replied to her letters.

"Mom!" Hannah's hand landed on her arm as her voice snapped Kelly back to the present. She turned to see her daughter's worried eyes. They were the same deep brown as Liam's. "What are you doing out here? Come in where it's warm!"

"I could say the same to you," Kelly said. She looked down at the tiny baby huddled against Hannah's chest, so deeply swathed in a wool hat and coat that Kelly could hardly see her granddaughter. They called her "Pip." It was a placeholder nickname, as Renner came from a military family which had a tradition that a baby wasn't named until both parents had held her. In Alberta, parents had a year to register a baby's birth without penalty and normally that just meant waiting a few days at most. Kelly had no idea what Hannah and Renner would do if they didn't reunite before the year was up. "It's way too cold out here for a baby."

"I'm heading back inside in a second," Hannah said. She ran her hand down Pip's back. The baby was such a sound sleeper Kelly wouldn't be surprised if she slept the whole journey. "I just came looking for you."

Kelly glanced from her daughter back to the shore and suddenly realized how far out they'd gone. They'd already passed Toronto Island and the city's shoreline spread out behind them in a tapestry of shining lights. "Maybe I wanted to say goodbye to Canada."

And goodbye to Liam, too.

Kelly forced a smile she thought would look genuine but it did nothing to change the worry in her daughter's eyes.

"Are you sure you want to come with us?" Hannah asked.

"I'm positive," Kelly said. "As you know, I've got concerns about this plan. But that doesn't mean I won't go with you. I'll talk to Renner. I'll hear from his own mouth why he went into hiding and let people believe a decipher-key device exists if it doesn't. Maybe I'll talk you both out of hiding and into cooperating with the government. But either way, I'll be your mom and Pip's grandma." She'd rebooted her life once before. At least this time she'd be doing it out of love. "So what's the plan?"

Hannah glanced back over her shoulder, even though they were alone.

"In about twenty minutes, when we're closer to American waters, Renner says we need to head to a small motorboat off the port bow," Hannah said. "It'll be very small and pretty undetectable. He says there'll be a big, flashy distraction and that's when we make our move. He has contacts in the United States who've helped arrange for temporary visas if needed through an American contact. But either way he's got a plan to get us out of the US in hours and a new home set up for us somewhere in South America."

"What kind of distraction?" Kelly asked.

"I don't know, but Renner says it'll provide us the cover we need, and I trust him." A smile had crossed Hannah's lips when she'd said her husband's name. Now her daughter frowned as she searched Kelly's face. She was so observant, like her father, and practically impossible to fool. "What aren't you telling me?"

*I just saw your father. He's a cop, he doesn't know you're his daughter and he just tried to arrest me.*

As the words crossed her mind, she bit them back and instead prayed for wisdom. She'd had dozens of both excuses and justifications for not telling Hannah who her father was. None of them rang completely true and all of them came down to some variation of wanting to protect Hannah. She'd tell her when the timing was right—and it still wasn't right.

A tiny plaintive wail arose from below her. Little Pip had woken up. Immediately, Hannah started to sway from side to side on the balls of her feet.

"I've got to get her inside and feed her," Hannah said, her attention diverted. "I'm also going to call Renner and let him know you've boarded safely. There's a very small but quiet room on the lower deck that a kindly member of the crew said

I could use. I've stashed her diaper bag and car seat there. This is supposed to be an adults-only event. Have you eaten?" Hannah searched her face as if to confirm she hadn't. "There's an amazing buffet on the top deck. You should go eat."

It was a good idea. Hannah probably wanted a few minutes alone to talk to Renner, and Kelly really did need to eat. She slipped her arms around Hannah, feeling the warmth of her and the baby between them against the cold air of the night.

"Go," Kelly said. "Get inside. I'll go get something to eat. Where will I meet you?"

"Bottom deck," Hannah said. "Port side. Twenty minutes."

"I'll be there." She followed Hannah inside, then headed up a narrow flight of stairs. Holiday music assailed her ears even before her feet reached the top. She pushed through a door and came into a huge room the width of the boat and the length of a ballroom, with glass windows on all sides. Gold and green decorations festooned the ceiling. Bright red tablecloths were draped over every table and went all the way to the floor. There were about two hundred people, she guessed, all clad in various Christmas sweaters that had everything from billowing trees to smiling elves and even giant bows on them. Hannah hadn't been kidding about the food, though. The spread ran over a dozen long tables covered with turkey, ham, breads and salads. Not to mention more types of cake than Kelly could count. She filled a plate, sat down on a very high chair at a tall table by a window and pushed some cheese around with the tip of her knife.

"Anyone sitting here?" The chipper voice was male and, from what she could see out of her peripheral vision, belonged to a tall man in a blue sweater with grinning jingle-bell-clad puppies on it.

"Actually, I'd rather be alone—"

"Oh, I insist." The voice dropped an octave to a deep rumble that seemed to move over her skin. She looked up, her eyes widening as Liam settled into the chair opposite her. Instinctively, her fingers tightened around her knife, but his hand dropped onto hers in a gesture that was no doubt meant to look friendly, but that kept her hand from rising off the table.

"Now," Liam said. "Let's try this again."

# TWO

Music, chatter and laughter moved like currents around her. She sat there with the warmth of Liam's hand enveloping hers and her body felt momentarily frozen in place.

"Where's the stun gun?" Liam asked.

"Right-hand inside pocket of my jacket," she said. "Let my hand go and I'll pass it to you."

He chuckled. "That's not going to happen."

"Didn't think so." She wondered if he'd been expecting her to act all shocked and surprised by the fact he'd somehow materialized across from her on the boat. If so, she wasn't about to give him the satisfaction. She glanced down at their hands and couldn't help but remember how hesitant and uncertain he'd seemed the first time they'd held hands. The first time she'd hugged this big, strong man, it was like he'd never been hugged before.

"So you're just going to sit there holding my hand?" she asked.

Liam leaned across the table toward her. "I'm sorry, sweetheart, but you know I can't do that as long as you're holding a knife."

"It's a cheese knife that I grabbed off the cutlery table," she said, ignoring the fact he'd just called her "sweetheart," like he had back in the old days. Did he call everyone that now? Had he grown warm and cuddly, for that matter? Or was his brain misfiring at seeing her again, too? "It's pretty blunt."

"Doesn't mean you won't try to stab me with it," Liam said, with a smile. "Of course, if I disarm you of that knife you might throw that plate of food in my face as a distraction and go for the stun gun again. I know it's what I'd advise."

She could feel a smile trying to curl on her own lips and she gritted her teeth to stop it. Instead, she forced her fingers open underneath his and dropped the knife on the table, where it clattered loudly. She waited to see if it would make Liam let go of her hand. Instead, as she turned over her hand, somehow she felt their fingers looping through each other's just like they used to.

Clearly just a standoff tactic for both of them, right?

"I'm really sorry, but I do have to arrest you," he said, his voice barely above a whisper. "I don't want to make a scene and I definitely don't want to whip out my handcuffs. There are a lot of cell phones in this place and my colleague tells me the internet is everything these days. You deserve better than to have videos and pictures of your arrest plastered online."

Because of their past? Because he still cared about her? Or because a quiet arrest suited his purposes? She scanned the room. It was crowded, but she'd intentionally chosen a table for two that was set away from everything else. The noise and chaos around them would mean someone would have to be practically on top of them to catch a word that they were saying. Two people standing alone whispering in a hallway might look suspicious, but stick them at a small table, with their heads bent together, holding hands, and people would instinctively give them space and look away. She'd learned a lot about how to live without being noticed when she'd been on the run during her first two weeks in witness protection. Unfortunately, the person she'd learned it all from was the man now staring her down.

"Believe it or not, this is the first time I've held anyone's hand in decades," she said, convincing herself she was only saying it as a distraction, even though it was true.

"Me, too," Liam said and frowned. "And, no, I don't believe it. Now, here's what's going to happen. You're going to slide your stun gun and any other weapons you're carrying across the table to me underneath a napkin. Then, you and I are going to stand up, nice and slow, and walk hand in hand down to find the captain. I'll ask him to turn the boat around and drop us back on shore. Don't worry, I'll do the talking."

She felt her jaw clench. Sounded like he'd just accused her of lying. Her memory had generously edited out just how confident Liam was in his own abilities—too confident—or how irritating she'd found it even back then. She might not agree with Hannah and Renner's plan, but that didn't mean she was about to let him turn the boat around. Not until she knew Hannah had left safely to reunite with Renner, even if that meant she had to stay behind. As long as she kept Liam sitting here, at this table, talking and holding hands, then the boat was still heading toward American waters.

"What would it take to get you to let me go and walk away?" she asked.

"How about Renner Phillips's decryption device?" Liam asked.

Well, she appreciated the straight answer.

"I'm sorry," she said. "From what I've heard there is no master decipher key."

Liam blinked. "So then how did he decrypt the code?"

"I don't know," she admitted. "Fluke, maybe? He got fortunate and took a wild guess?"

One that had thwarted a terrorist bombing and saved countless lives.

Liam's jaw tightened. "But you believe he's still alive?"

"I do," she said. "But I haven't actually seen him or spoken to him, and I'm not going to lead you to him."

Liam snorted and leaned back so quickly the bells on his

ridiculous Christmas sweater jingled. But his hand never left hers, and for a second she had to remind herself they were only pretending to hold hands.

"That's not quite how it works," Liam said. "He was a government contract worker. He had top-level government security clearance. He cracked a code without telling anyone how and then he disappeared—"

"Because a whole bunch of really bad guys had threatened to kill him and do worse to his wife—"

"Our government would've protected him—"

"He was targeted in a roadside bombing!" Her voice rose, not enough to be overheard, but still Liam's eyebrows rose. The music faded as one song ended. She held her breath and waited as the next song started up. Her eyes glanced to the watch on Liam's wrist. Whatever Renner's big diversion was, it was happening in twelve minutes. Which meant she had about ten left to ditch Liam.

"This isn't a game, sweetheart." Liam leaned forward and something in his eyes darkened. "There's a really bad cyberterrorist group out there threatening to do some pretty bad stuff if they don't get their hands on Renner's decoding device." *Well, that was incredibly vague.* "The idea he took some wild guess on how to decipher some terrorist code and cracked it by a fluke it is frankly insulting. If Renner had turned his decoding device over to the government, law enforcement could've been using it all this time to stop these kinds of threats, instead of it being used as leverage. Renner needs to step up and help us stop these threats. We're not the bad guys here."

"That's twice you've called me 'sweetheart,'" she said. "Don't do it a third. And I wanted to go into criminology, if you remember, before you showed up and told me I had to go into witness protection—"

"Then help me find Renner and talk him into coming to work for us and letting us protect him," Liam said. "I'll pull some strings for you, too, and make sure you never see the in-side of a jail cell."

Now she barely kept herself from snorting. "There's something going on you're not telling me," she said. "How are you even here?"

"How did I find you?" he asked. "Or how did I get onto the boat? A contact in Vice monitoring motels in the area happened to pick up your signal and tipped me off. And another contact in the Toronto Police gave me a stealth ride to catch up with the boat. I know a lot of people in various branches of law enforcement."

"Which contact just happened to have a big blue Christmas sweater with puppies that fit over a bulletproof vest?" she asked.

A laugh slipped from his mouth as if he'd tried and failed to stop it.

"Bought it off a guy on the lower deck for one hundred bucks," he said. "He claimed it was itchy and his wife was try-ing to make him wear it. Told him to take the money and buy his wife something really nice for Christmas." He stood up, holding her hand tightly and keeping the table between them. "Now, enough stalling. Slide over your weapons, otherwise I am going to very publicly arrest you."

She pulled the stun gun from her pocket and slid it across the table, as asked. It was out of juice, anyway, and she was sure Hannah would have a spare in Pip's diaper bag. She watched as he checked it, made sure it was off and then pocketed it.

"Now," he said, "we're going to see the captain."

"Wait!" Her hand tightened on his. Her boots dug into the floor. He stopped, but didn't sit. She'd kick herself later for what she was about to ask, but it would be worth it if it bought Han-nah time. "Just tell me one thing. Why didn't you ever come back for me?"

*Because if you did, if you'd cared or even read my mes-sages, I'd have seen it in your eyes when I mentioned the name* Hannah.

Liam's eyes widened and suddenly something soft pooled in their depths. A warmth? A sadness, even? All she knew was that it reminded her all too much of the man she'd loved a very long time ago.

"I... I tried," he said softly.

"No," she said, "you most definitely didn't."

"But... I did." He stepped closer, until they were just inches apart in the crowded room, and his hand was still locked in hers. "You—you were married."

"Married?" She yelped the word a whole lot louder than she'd intended to. Chatter stopped around them. Faces turned toward them. She didn't know if people thought Liam was in the middle of some kind of disastrous proposal or a shock confession about a previous relationship. But either way, they'd just lost the anonymity they'd enjoyed. Liam had noticed it, too.

"Come on," Liam said. He led her through a doorway and into a narrow hallway. Then he stopped, and for a long moment, they both just looked at each other without saying anything. She could feel her heart pounding so hard it ached. As she watched Liam's chest rapidly rise and fall, she guessed his heart was probably thumping, too.

"Yeah, you got married," he said. "I may be many things, but a gentleman is one of them. When I returned to the office and was debriefed after dropping you off, I was immediately pulled into a new undercover assignment that involved total radio silence and kept me from contacting you. The moment I was out, three months later, I got hit with the news you'd married some man you met undercover."

"Married," she repeated. *What fresh nonsense is this?* "You think I married some man I knew less than three months?"

"We'd known each other two weeks when I asked if I could marry you," Liam said.

Yeah, and when she'd said yes she'd thought it meant something. Her heart was still knocking wildly. Did this mean he'd never gotten any of her messages? Did this mean he had no idea she'd been pregnant and they had a daughter?

"I never got married," she said.

He rolled his eyes, but more like he was in pain than frustrated. "And you never had four sons?"

"What?" She shook her head. "No!"

"Kelly!" Liam said. "Look, I'm not proud of this but I used to check your official RCMP witness-protection file."

"Then I'm telling you my official RCMP witness-protection file is wrong!" she said. "I never got married. I never had a son. Let alone four. And I wrote to you, a lot, in those first few weeks. Letters you clearly never got."

His nostrils flared. He let out a hard breath. Liam didn't believe her. He believed his own files and sources in the RCMP. A faint buzzing sound came from his jacket pocket. He yanked out his phone and answered.

"Hey, Seth," he said. "Yeah, sorry—before you say whatever it is you're going to say, I need you to pull an RCMP witness-protection file for me. Kelly Marshall. Placed in protection a couple of decades ago. I need to know her family status. Specifically spouse and kids. Yes, it's urgent. Yes, super urgent. No, I'm not going to tell you why."

He paused as if waiting for him to pull the file.

"Who's Seth?" Kelly asked.

"Seth Miles," Liam said. "He's a member of my team."

"Seth Miles," she repeated. "The criminal hacker?"

Seth Miles was either famous or notorious in online circles depending on one's opinion of vigilante Robin Hood figures who tried to do the right thing outside of the law. Did Liam have any idea how many laws Seth had broken? And yet he judged Renner for going outside the law?

"Yes, the formerly criminal hacker," Liam said. He turned back to the phone. "Okay... Okay..." She watched as he nodded and then nodded again. Then his face paled. "All right, call you back in a moment."

Liam hung up. His eyes locked on her face.

"Well, sweetheart, according to your official RCMP file, you got married three months after entering witness protection to a man named Robbie, and had four sons with him, named Robert, Gordon, Frank and Bill—"

"Well, that's obviously not true—"

He held up a hand as if to stop her. "It also said you died in a car crash four and a half years ago."

Liam watched as her face paled and her eyes widened. The fact that she was still so beautiful it knocked him sideways whenever he looked at her wasn't doing much to help his focus. Then she laughed. It was a mildly hysterical giggle that meant she found his information more unsettling than funny. Yeah, so did he.

"I can't believe I'm saying this," Kelly said, "but I'm not dead and I really did not get married to a man named Robbie. You can go find him and ask him yourself."

"I know you didn't." Liam ran his hand over his face. "And, no, I can't ask him, because apparently Robbie's dead, too. Your whole fictional family is. You all died in the same car accident."

Her hand rose to her lips. This whole situation was like a sick joke. One that his gut actually felt queasy over. He'd built his entire life around the integrity of the RCMP. The idea that someone could've deliberately falsified Kelly's file was unthinkable. A burst of cold air rushed in to their right, as a small mob of happy partygoers ran down the narrow hallway. Kelly pressed her back against the wall and he braced his hand on the wall beside her, placing his body protectively between her and the people pushing past.

As tempted as he was to get the captain to turn the boat around, this was also the second time in one night he'd been knocked sideways when he'd discovered what he thought he knew was wrong. Just how much didn't he know? The new Imposters had placed a bounty on Kelly's head in the hopes she'd lead them to Renner and help them get his decoding device, not that there was any indication they knew who she was in real life. *Thank You, God.* In fact, these new Imposters were so gung ho on committing the kind of major crimes they'd be able to do with a master key that could open any online door that they were willing to crash power grids worldwide on New Year's Eve.

And Kelly had just informed him that she was sure Renner was alive and there was no master decipher key. Hearing it from Seth was one thing. Seth had all sorts of crazy ideas. But Kelly?

What Liam needed most right now was information—information Kelly had—and he'd learned in his line of work that sometimes it was better to keep a subject of an investigation talking for a while before arresting them. After all, some people tended to get pretty upset at being arrested and would stop cooperating, and he was fairly sure she'd be one of them.

More chattering came from the other direction now as a fresh group of people came down the hall, then more cold air rushed in. Then suddenly another fact hit him—Kelly hadn't actually tried to escape from him. That in itself was pretty interesting.

"I'm sorry I called you 'sweetheart,'" he said finally. "I won't do it again."

And he didn't know why it kept happening.

"Well, I just assumed you called everyone 'sweetheart,'" she said, as if trying to lighten the moment.

"No," he admitted. "Just you." He took a deep breath and prayed for wisdom. "Come on," he added. "You and I are going to go back to the party. Just for another quick minute."

Was it his imagination or had she barely managed to keep herself from sighing in relief?

His fingers looped through hers and they walked back into the party holding hands. He wasn't exactly sure which one of them had grabbed the other's hand first or why they'd decided to do it. But here they were now, and he was going with it. A couple of guys were sitting at their table, but without a word, they got up and vacated it when Liam nodded at them. Liam pulled the table closer to the wall and positioned the chairs to block people from seeing them.

"Sit, please," he said quietly. He let go of her hand and she dropped into the chair. He grabbed a clean red-and-green cloth napkin from a nearby table, spread it open and then slowly slipped his handcuffs underneath it, making sure she could see them.

"If I didn't know any better I'd think you were about to do a magic trick with those," she said.

"And if I didn't know any better, I'd say you've been trying to stall me," he said. He sat so close her shoulder was almost touching his. "And I'd like to know why. Now, I don't want to take you out of here in handcuffs. I really don't. But you clearly aren't in a hurry to get off this boat, which is very interesting to me. So how about we play a game of twenty questions. You can sit here and keep enjoying the atmosphere, handcuff-free, as long as you keep answering. Fair?"

"Fair." Her eyes—strong, determined and full of grit—met his. She leaned her arms on the table and he did likewise. "So what aren't you telling me, Liam?"

A laugh erupted in his throat. Had she always been like this? He'd remembered her as tenacious and someone who challenged and pushed him. If she'd also been this irritating, he'd forgotten.

"The person with the badge asks the questions," he said. "Starting with, how do you know Renner Phillips?"

"I met him through Hannah."

"Okay," he said, "and how do you know Hannah?"

Her shoulders rose and fell. "Pass."

"Why did you call her your girl?" he persisted.

"I called her 'our' girl," she said. "And the answer is pass."

"You don't get to pass." He clenched his jaw to keep his voice from rising an octave and his hands inched toward the handcuffs. Then he frowned. It was hard to tell with the darkness outside the window, but it felt like the boat had stopped moving. Was that part of the party cruise? "Who falsified your witness-protection file?"

Worry flickered in her eyes. "I have no idea."

And that he believed.

"Do you know why the boat's stopped?" he asked.

"No, I didn't realize it had." Her gaze darted to his hands. "Did you really not get any of my letters or messages? Not even one?"

"No," he said, "I really didn't—"

"And you honestly thought I was married?" she asked.

"Yes, but—"

She grabbed his hands. "And if you hadn't thought I was married, you'd have done what?"

"I have no idea." He heard the faint sound of a baby crying somewhere in the crowd to his right. Not wailing, but just the small cry of a tiny infant trying to be noticed. Odd, he thought this was a child-free event. But between the question and the fact that Kelly's hands were on his, he didn't turn and look. He couldn't even remember ever having a woman suddenly try to grab on to his hand before and him not flinching or jerking away like he'd been electrocuted. "But it doesn't matter now, does it?"

*Help me, Lord. I don't know what to ask.*

He tried again.

"If you hacked the dark-web auction last year on Christmas Eve to prevent the sale of Hannah's file, then you've clearly heard of the Imposters," he said and watched as she nodded. "You probably don't know that three detective friends and I, along with a hacker, are the ones who took them down." At this revelation, her eyes widened. "As you probably know, the original Imposters are dead. Did you know a new group of Imposters have risen up to take their place? There's dozens of them, spread across the country. No known leader. They're threatening to crash international power grids unless someone hands them Renner's master decipher key. They also put a bounty on the Sparrow's head in the hopes you'd lead them to Renner."

"No," she said, softly. "I had no idea."

He searched her eyes. "I believe you."

"Do they know I'm the Sparrow?" she asked.

"I don't think so," he said. "I'm praying they won't find out."

"What are they planning?" she asked.

He left the question dangling for a moment without an answer. The baby cried again. This time he turned. A woman was heading out the door and onto the deck. Long dark hair fell over her face and her head bowed over a tiny little baby that couldn't be more than a couple of months old. Then she glanced up. Their eyes met. They both froze.

It was Hannah Phillips.

And then it dawned on him. *Oh, I've been a fool!* The party cruise would be crossing into American waters. As long as he stayed on the boat, he retained his full authority. But if either Hannah or Kelly slipped off the boat and made it to American soil, he'd lose jurisdiction to arrest them without an international warrant. He leaped to his feet only to feel something cold click against his wrist. He spun back in disbelief. Kelly had handcuffed her wrist to his...with his own handcuffs.

"No," Liam said, holding up a finger on his free hand. "I've been more than patient, but now you've gone too far. Hannah Phillips is not supposed to be outside Alberta without RCMP authority or have any contact with criminal activity. So being on a Toronto party cruise with the same woman who deleted her file is definitely suspicious. Not to mention she's supposed to report any significant relationship to her local RCMP contact, so if that's her child she's holding she's kept that tidbit about her life hidden, as well. I have no clue what's going on here. But I'm arresting you and detaining her for questioning."

He reached around in his inside pocket for his keys.

"Please, Liam, listen to me." Kelly tried to grab his other hand. "Let me explain."

Yeah, like that was going to happen.

His phone was ringing again. He stopped fishing for his keys long enough to decline the call only to have Seth's voice unexpectedly sound in his ear, letting him know he'd just accidentally done the opposite. "Hey, Liam?"

"Hey, Seth, I'm sorry, I really don't have time—"

"Just got online chatter the new Imposters are planning some kind of major stunt in your area tonight—"

"What do you mean by 'my area'?" Liam said. "I'm on a boat."

"I know!"

Suddenly the doors on both sides of the ballroom flew open. Five young men in blue jeans, Christmas sweaters, black ski masks and colored eye patches stormed in. Four waved an array of semiautomatic weapons. One held a video camera.

*Oh, Lord, please, help me now.*

"Everybody down!" a masked man yelled. "We're the Imposter cyberpirates and we're taking over this ship!"

# THREE

For an instant Kelly just stood there, her body almost paralyzed with fear. The world was a tableau of disbelief and confusion around her, as partygoers were momentarily too shocked to even scream, think or move. Then she felt Liam's handcuffed hand grab on to hers and squeeze tightly. And something, like the memory of once feeling strong and empowered, swept over her. Liam had protected her before. Not only that, but he'd also made her feel capable of protecting herself. He would again.

His free hand grabbed the table they'd been sitting at and hurled it at the men. Before it could even land, Liam had pulled her down to the ground and rolled with her underneath the closest banquet table. The thick red tablecloth fell like a curtain, sheltering them. She lay there for a moment listening as chaos erupted on the other side. A cacophony of voices shouting, screaming and barking orders clashed with the sound of more furniture throwing and things crashing. But, thankfully, there was no gunfire. She closed her eyes and prayed.

*Please, Lord, end this before anyone gets hurt. Please keep Hannah and the baby safe. Help them escape this boat, even if it's without me.*

"We don't have long," Liam whispered. "It'll take them a

few moments to secure the ballroom and right now they'll be focusing their attention on anyone trying to fight back. Once they think they've secured everyone they can see, they'll start searching around for more. We wait for the right moment, then we run." She opened her eyes to find his gaze was locked on her face every bit as firmly as his hand held hers. "You with me?"

She forced her head to nod and a word to cross her lips. "Yes."

"Okay."

"Also, I'm—I'm sorry about the handcuffs."

"Don't worry," he whispered. "They're only number four on my list of problems right now. I can't reach the key from this position, but I'll get them off soon enough." Then he tapped his earpiece and spoke into what she now realized was a tiny button-sized microphone on his jacket.

"Seth? Can you hear me?" Liam's voice was low, urgent, and even right next to him she could barely make it out over the chaos filling the room outside their hiding spot. "Yeah, we've got a situation. Top deck. Five of these new Imposters at least. In pirate getup. Upward of a hundred and fifty civilians."

This was who the new Imposters were? A group of heavily armed men in pirate patches? While they were masked, something about their voices and builds made her think none were much older than college students.

Liam turned back to her. She noticed he hadn't mentioned her or Hannah.

"Seth's watching the live feed now," Liam said. "It's all over the internet apparently. The Imposters say that they're cutting off cell-phone and internet access to everyone on this boat in six minutes, so everyone on board should get their final calls, texts and social-media posts in now. Law enforcement will take down their cell blockers eventually. Tactically it's a brilliant move. If everyone's staring at their phones nobody's fighting back, plus it's great publicity."

*Oh, Lord, please don't let them find Hannah and the baby...*

"Thankfully, I wasn't relying on the internet to get out of this," Liam said. "I always prefer going old school."

Old school. Like tossing furniture and hiding under tables? "Who's behind all this?" she asked. "Who are they working for?"

"They're like a swarm without a leader," Liam said. "According to Seth, even if someone did claim leadership it wouldn't necessarily mean anything." He peeked through the curtain. His voice was low, quick and blunt, like he was giving a briefing. "No clear goal beyond getting attention and hurting those they think have wronged them. Imagine an ugly internet chat group come to life, in masks and colored eye patches."

He let the curtain fall and turned back to her.

"Our best guess is there are a couple hundred of them worldwide," he added. "Dozens signed the online pledge to take out their local power grids on New Year's. Maybe some of them thought this would be good publicity for that. Or maybe a splinter group decided to go do their own thing. Now come on." Liam tugged her hand. "We're getting out of here and finding you a better place to hide while I try to sort out this mess."

But her fingers dug into his.

"We have to get to Hannah and the baby," she said. "We can't let the Imposters get to them. If they wanted to use me to get to Renner, imagine what they'll do if they get ahold of his wife and child."

Liam's face paled as if his brain was suddenly recalibrating. "So the baby is Renner's child?"

"Yeah," Kelly said. She prayed hard for wisdom. "Renner and Hannah are still very much in love and a couple. He arranged for there to be a motorboat docked alongside this party cruise that Hannah, the baby and I could take to join him. Yes, I know the plan sounds stupid. Believe me, I tried to talk them into trusting law enforcement. But they're very young, very much in love, still seem to think they know everything and that it's them against the world." Liam, of all people, should remember what that'd felt like. "Renner doesn't trust law enforcement to protect Hannah and is convinced going into hiding is the only way to keep Hannah and the baby safe."

And the fact that her own RCMP file had been falsified was quickly eroding her faith in law enforcement's ability to keep Hannah and the baby safe, too. If her own file could be corrupted that way by someone inside the RCMP, who's to say Renner and Hannah were wrong to go it alone?

"If you get Hannah, the baby and I to the boat," Kelly added, "I'll personally beg Renner to contact you, explain everything and help you stop these new Imposters in any way he can. He loves his wife. He just wants to know she's safe."

The noise of voices and chaos was growing quieter on the other side of the tablecloth now. It wasn't a good sign.

"No deal," Liam said. "I'll keep you, Hannah and the baby safe. But I'm detaining you all unless Renner turns over his decipher key."

"There is no decipher key!" Her whisper rose.

"Then how did he decrypt the code?" Liam demanded. "And don't say he took a wild guess."

"I told you, I don't know!"

"My intel said—"

"Your intel also thinks I'm dead!" she interrupted. Was Liam really trying to negotiate a deal in the middle of an armed standoff? Just how many deals with criminals had he negotiated under fire? More than he could count, she guessed, just as she imagined a lot of cases had been solved as a result. But this wasn't any other case. "I need to explain about Hannah."

There was a loud crash and more people screamed. By the sound of things, the new Imposters had started searching the room.

"No time," Liam said. "Just tell me where she is."

She glanced at her phone screen, thanking God to see a message from Hannah. "Bottom deck. Stern. Small office room."

"Got it. Let's go."

He grabbed her hand, which was still handcuffed to his, and they slid out of the relative shelter of their hiding space. They crawled side by side, keeping their stomachs flat against the floor. Liam pushed through a swinging door and into a narrow and empty galley kitchen. Instantly, he stood, pulled her up after him and shoved a food cart against the door, wedging it under the handle. "We've got about thirty seconds before someone's brain registers the fact they just saw the door move and they send someone after us."

They ran through the galley into what looked like another food-prep room, then Liam rapped on the door of what she suspected was a supply cupboard. "Detective Liam Bearsmith, RCMP—everyone all right in there?"

Even hushed, his voice rang with an authority that seemed to crack the air like a whip.

There was a pause. Then she heard an older male voice. "Yes."

"How many of you in there?" he asked.

"Six," the voice replied.

"Anyone hurt?"

"No."

"Good," Liam said. "Stay there. Keep the door locked and don't open it until law enforcement tells you it's safe. Don't panic if the cell signal goes down. Rescue is on its way."

He led Kelly to another door, checked the hallway behind it and then turned to her. "Keys are inside my jacket, right-side chest pocket. I need you to grab them for me."

A large bang sounded somewhere behind them. Someone was trying to break through the first door. She looked back.

"Focus," Liam said sharply. Yet his hand was almost tender as it touched her face. Then he reached for his weapon. "I can get us out of here, but I need your help first."

She reached inside his jacket and her fingers looped through the keys. "Got them."

Another bang. Then the door behind them flew open and a

masked man rushed through. The keys fell from her fingers. Liam spun around, placing his body between Kelly and the criminal, raised his weapon and fired. The criminal fell back behind the door. Liam scooped up the keys, grabbed Kelly's hand and pulled her into the hallway. They raced down it, reached the stairs, waited while Liam glanced to see if the coast was clear and then ran down. He paused on the second landing and his hand moved over hers—she didn't even realize he'd unlocked the handcuffs until they fell from her wrist. They kept running.

"Hey, Liam?" A faint voice crackled from Liam's earpiece and she realized it'd fallen into his scarf.

"Seth," Liam said. "Hey. Can't talk. Running. Update?"

"Law enforcement from both sides of the border are on their way," Seth said. "Helicopters and boats. They're currently in a holding pattern. It's all over international news. Internet's lighting up. It's quite the spectacle." Which she guessed was the point. "We're losing phone and internet in sixty seconds. You?"

"I'm with Kelly Marshall," Liam said. "Turns out she's not dead. Trying to locate Hannah Phillips, who's on this boat, and Renner's baby."

Seth choked out a cough. "You're telling me all this now?"

"It was need-to-know." Liam ended the call.

They reached the bottom deck, and after another spot check, stepped outside. Cold wind assailed them. Both the sky and water were pitch-black, dotted with the bright lights of police boats and helicopters that were keeping their distance for now. She followed him down the deck, but it wasn't until he stopped at a nondescript door that she realized he'd probably memorized the boat's blueprints before boarding. He grabbed the door handle. It was locked.

"Let me." She leaned past him and knocked rhythmically.

"Secret knock or not," Liam said, "she's got thirty seconds or I'm breaking the door down."

The door flew open. There stood Hannah, holding Pip in one hand and a handgun in the other.

"That's an illegal handgun," Liam said under his breath as if adding to the charges he could detain her for.

Hannah's eyes cut to Liam and narrowed.

"And if you make one wrong move," Hannah said, "I'll shoot you with it."

"Hannah," Kelly said. "This is Liam. He helped me escape from the party room upstairs. Liam, this is Hannah."

Kelly's voice was soft, firm and urgent, and Liam couldn't help but notice she'd left out that he was a cop. His gaze rose from the handgun to the woman holding it. Nothing about Hannah Phillips matched the person her file had led him to believe she was. It wasn't just that she seemed younger in person. Since he'd passed forty and kept going, it seemed increasingly clear that people in their early twenties were half his age. But her file had identified her as overwhelmed, nervous and weak. One glimpse into her eyes showed a fierceness and determination that was anything but.

She reminded him of Kelly.

Hannah turned away as if she knew she was being analyzed and didn't like it. She slid the gun in her pocket. He took in the room. It was small with a short love seat, an infant car seat on the floor, a desk with a huge diaper bag on it and a chair that seemed way too big for the room. He watched as Kelly and Hannah hugged. Then Hannah eased the tiny little baby into Kelly's arms, and after a hug Kelly buckled the baby into the car seat.

*Okay, and what is going on here?*

"The internet and phones are completely down," Hannah said, "but I've hacked into the Imposters's feed."

"Excuse me?" Liam almost stuttered. She'd done what? Hacking skills had also been missing from his intel. Yes, Hannah's file had indicated she'd tested as gifted when she was young, but she'd also struggled through school and started a computer-related degree in college that she'd never completed.

It was theoretically possible Hannah had taught herself to hack, but more likely Renner had taught her.

Hannah ran around to the other side of the desk and dropped the diaper bag onto the floor, and suddenly he saw the slim laptop she'd apparently been hiding behind it. Her fingers flew over the keyboard with a speed that rivaled Seth's.

"All crew and guests have been escorted to the third-floor ballroom," Hannah said with her eyes locked on the screen. "It seems the Imposters are gathering them all there. It's a slapdash operation. The call for volunteers went out on the Imposters's message board thirty minutes ago. 'Wear your own Christmas sweater and ski mask. Pirate eye patches will be provided.' They boarded the boat after the cruise passed Toronto Island, from a handful of motorboats they've now got all docked off the cruise ship. Now we've got eight hostiles total taking about two hundred people hostage. It's a complete logistical mess."

Hannah sounded like a cop. No, she sounded like him.

"Trust me, the boss Imposter isn't happy with it," she added.

"The Imposters have a boss?" Liam asked. Seth was sure they didn't.

"Not really." Hannah shrugged. "Someone stepped up as a theoretical figurehead a few days ago, but he seemed out of the loop on this one."

She spun the laptop around. Video of the room he and Kelly had just escaped from filled the screen. The camera scanned over the dozens of people sitting on the floor, then back repeatedly to an extreme close-up of a masked Imposter who seemed to be yelling directly at the camera. No volume.

"Any casualties?" he asked.

"No," Hannah said quickly, "or major injuries that I can see." He thanked God for that. She turned the laptop back toward herself and glanced at Kelly. "You do know he's an undercover cop, right? He practically reeks of it."

*No, I don't!* He bristled. *Look, kid, I've been fooling criminals into believing I was one of them since before you were alive.*

Kelly didn't answer. Instead, her gaze just ping-ponged back and forth between them and she had an inscrutable look on her face. The baby began to fuss. Kelly rocked the car seat gently and the baby stopped.

"And if your husband had stepped up and been there for you last year," Liam said sharply, "instead of disappearing into the ether with his decipher key, or told the truth about how he'd hacked the code, then maybe none of this would've happened."

Any worry he'd pushed the young woman too far evaporated as he saw the fire flash in her dark eyes.

"My husband did what he did to protect me," Hannah said. "If he'd come forward after that bombing, my daughter and I probably wouldn't even be alive right now."

She couldn't possibly know that. But something pinged loudly before he could answer. She spun the laptop toward him.

"And apparently you're not above working with criminals," Hannah said. "You've got an incoming call from hacker Seth Miles."

Liam had no idea how Seth had breached the Imposters's cyberbubble and located Hannah's laptop. But he'd long stopped being surprised by what Seth could do.

"He's reformed," Liam said. He crossed the floor in three strides and Hannah moved out of the way to let him take her place behind the desk. He glanced at the screen. Seth's surprised face looked up at him.

"Seth, you're a genius," Liam said.

"I know," Seth said. The hacker looked every bit as confused as Liam had been feeling. The two women seemed to be fussing over the baby. Liam dropped into a chair and rolled it into the far corner of the room holding the laptop in one hand. "So you found Hannah Phillips?"

"Yup." Though she wasn't anything like what he'd expected and he still hadn't gotten to the bottom of Kelly's connection to all of this. "What's new?"

"No casualties or major injuries that we know of," Seth said.

"Law enforcement's still trying to figure out who's even negotiating for the Imposters. What I want to know is how you managed to call me on a dark-web channel when I thought all connections in and out of the boat were down."

Liam froze.

Seth hadn't called Liam on Hannah's computer?

Hannah had called him?

A gust of cold air swept in to his right. Liam leaped to his feet. But it was too late. The women were gone. No, this wasn't happening. He hadn't been played. Not by such a basic distraction. He yanked back the door, but it caught after an inch. Seemed one of them had tied it shut with a baby blanket. His late father's tactical tip that everything was a potential weapon flickered unhelpfully in his mind. Dad had also been big on strategic distractions. Was Kelly going to use everything he'd taught her against him? He gritted his teeth and pulled harder. He could hear Seth's voice yelling behind him.

"Call you back!" Liam shouted. The fabric ripped and the door flew open. He ran out onto the deck and saw them. Hannah had climbed over the ledge and was lowering herself down by a ladder into a small speedboat below, which he guessed was one of the boats the Imposters had used to board the cruise ship. Kelly stood at the top of the ladder with the diaper bag over one shoulder and the car seat over the other.

Liam yanked his gun from its holster.

"Kelly!" he shouted as he ran to her side. "Step away from the ladder."

Kelly turned. He looked over the ledge. Hannah had reached the boat and her weapon was pointed right at him. He raised the weapon toward her. "Please, don't make me shoot you!"

"Liam! Stop!" Kelly shouted. She dropped the diaper bag and threw her arm between him and the boat. "Hannah is your daughter!"

*My daughter?*

His head swam, and he suddenly felt worse than he'd felt

with any concussion he'd ever had. He had a daughter? Hannah Phillips was his daughter? The baby Kelly held was his granddaughter?

"She's your daughter," Kelly said again. "Our daughter. Our girl. I was pregnant when you dropped me off. I wrote and told you. I thought you knew. I always thought you knew."

He turned to her. His mouth opened but no words came out.

"Please, Liam." Pleading filled her gorgeous green eyes. "Come with us. Meet Renner and talk to him yourself. Consider it an undercover mission to meet a source. I don't care. Just, please, get on this boat and we can all leave together."

His heart stopped beating.

*Help me, Lord. Please. Tell me what to do.*

Gunfire sounded beneath them, mingled with the sound of Hannah screaming. He looked down to see two masked men, who it seemed had been hiding in the boat to ambush her, now holding Hannah at gunpoint.

"It's not Renner's boat!" Hannah cried in a panic. "They're Imposters!"

# FOUR

Liam didn't have time to think. Maybe if he had, everything would've gone differently. But as the speedboat motor roared, he knew that within seconds Hannah would be kidnapped. Taken. Gone. And sometimes a person only got one chance do the right thing.

He leaped, launching himself overboard, then yanked out his weapon and fired on the way down. A bullet struck the controls. So far the goal was to stop them, nothing more. A man on the boat returned fire. Liam hit the boat and landed on the balls of his feet, just in time to note one of the Imposters throwing a fist toward his head. He blocked the blow and knocked the man back with one of his own.

The motorboat gunned beneath him, throwing him off balance.

"Don't move!" The man at the helm yanked Hannah against his chest and pressed a gun against her head. "Down on your knees, now! Or I'm shooting her!"

Liam paused a moment and prayed, as he analyzed the situation before him like an athlete would choreograph an upcoming play. First, he'd take out the man who was trying to punch him.

Then, he'd turn the man's weapon on the criminal at the helm who was holding Hannah. Then, he'd turn the speedboat around.

But as he ran the plan through his head, the sound of angry shouting floated over the waters from the cruise ship behind him. Then he heard a plaintive and terrified sound fill the air. The baby was crying. He glanced back. The Imposters had captured Kelly.

"Save them!" Hannah begged, her voice rising above the noise of the boat's motor and the voices shouting. He turned to her. Panic flooded her face. "Please, Liam! If you're really who my mother says you are, go rescue my mother and daughter! Please!"

And leave her to be kidnapped?

But before he could move, he heard a gunshot crack from the boat behind him and felt a bullet smack against the small of his back, wedging itself in his bulletproof vest and knocking him off balance. The engine gunned. He stumbled and fell, pitching against the side of the tiny boat as it swerved hard to the right. Then he fell overboard and into the dark waters below. Instantly the freezing water yanked him under, knocking his breath from his lungs. *Help me, God!* Inky blackness surrounded him on all sides. His gun had fallen from his grasp and he was sinking fast. He gritted his teeth and shed his jacket and sweater, then freed himself from the weight of his bulletproof vest, letting it sink down into the waters beneath him. Then he grabbed his jacket in one hand and forced his body to swim, the cold numbness in his limbs battling the burning pain in his lungs. He broke through the surface and gasped a breath. Chaos reigned around him.

The tiny speedboat was gone, taking Hannah with it and leaving nothing but the faint sound of a motor in its wake. On the cruise ship, masked Imposters surrounded Kelly. The lights of distant helicopters and rescue boats still hovered on the horizon, no doubt waiting for the signal from whoever was heading up the operation to board, and that person was probably waiting for some assurance of being able to keep the hostages safe.

And somehow, through it all, one sound seemed to rise above it all. The tiny baby was crying out in fear.

*And I will save her, so help me, God.*

Still clenching his jacket in his freezing fingers, he swam, his aching body cutting through the dark waters toward the anchored boat. Thankfully, whoever had fired at him from the boat had stopped. He reached the rope ladder, forced his arms back through the sleeves of his sopping leather jacket and then began to climb, rung after rung, until he reached the top. Then he heard Kelly gasp his name. He surveyed the scene, his numb fingers still clutching the ladder's rungs. Four Imposter pirates greeted him. One with a yellow eye patch had his weapon pointed at Kelly. Green- and blue-eye-patched ones pointed their weapons at him. A red-eye-patched one held a camera phone. Looked like the new Imposters were filming the hijacking from multiple locations.

Out of all the bad options he had, his gut and his experience said the least bad one was to let himself get taken hostage. That way he could get back inside, warm up, dry off and catch his breath, and most importantly not start a firefight around a baby. Yet, as his eyes glanced at Kelly's face, he knew if she hadn't been there in the line of fire, and holding a child—*my grandchild*—that even battered, bruised and freezing numb, he'd have fought back, relying on the fact he knew how to fire, evade and disarm weapons like these better than these complete amateurs did.

He might've even won.

Instead, he slid his body over the edge. His knees hit the deck and stayed there, as the man in the green eye patch pressed his weapon against Liam's forehead.

"I'm detective Liam Bearsmith, RCMP," he said, "and I'm surrendering."

Kelly clutched the handle of Pip's car seat and she watched as Liam kneeled on the cruise boat's deck in the darkness with the barrel of a gun between his eyes. Maybe it was the cold, the darkness or the fact he was shivering, but the lines of his rugged jawline seemed even deeper than they had before. He'd gotten older, just like she had, and was no longer the seemingly indestructible young man he once was. And for the first time since he'd accosted her back on shore, she had the overwhelming urge to just throw her arms around him and keep him safe.

And maybe, if it hadn't been for little Pip, she would've.

Instead, she held her breath and prayed, for the baby beside her, the man at her feet and the daughter now being abducted by people willing to hurt her to get their hands on something that didn't even exist.

*Help me, Lord. Tell me what to say. Show me what to do.*
Liam wasn't fighting back—he was surrendering. And somehow she knew it was because he wanted to keep her and Pip safe. *Is it my fault he's in danger?*

Maybe. Either way, she didn't just have to save Liam, she also had to get herself and the baby out of there. The Imposters were discussing what to do with Liam, debating whether or not to kill him. Apparently getting revenge on Liam's team for taking out the original Imposters was big on their to-do list. But that didn't mean they were in agreement about how to go about it. At least two of them thought they should just shoot Liam on the spot.

Despite slight variations in height and weight, there was something ubiquitous about them. As if these Imposters weren't individuals, but were just parts of an anonymous swarm. Maybe the anonymity emboldened them. Maybe it made this bunch of insecure, angry and violent young men feel important. The thought of begging, pleading and even bargaining with her own life to save Liam's crossed her mind. But two of Liam's tactical tips appeared in her memory as if with one voice. The first: know the enemy's weakness and use it against them. And the second: when facing the barrel of a gun, do whatever it takes to buy time.

"Are you a bunch of total amateurs?" she snapped, straightening to her full height like a mother scolding a group of rowdy teens. "You don't want to shoot him here! First of all, you're all about publicity and the lighting is terrible. Nobody will be able to see anything. Secondly, nobody will be able to hear anything properly with a baby crying. At least let me take the baby inside. Unless you want to sabotage your image by having every internet chat board discussing whether or not you're monsters for terrorizing a baby! Is that really the publicity you want?"

An odd strangled noise slipped from Liam's throat.

All four masked men turned to face her. She glanced past them to the rescue vehicles on the horizon, silently urging them to hurry up. Then she glanced back at the masked men.

"Thirdly, you guys are all in this for the attention, right?" she said. Her chin rose. "Well, you've got Canada's most significant, prolific and successful RCMP officer in your grasp, and you're debating whether or not to shoot him right here, right now? What's that going to accomplish? At least use him as a bargaining chip to get those helicopters and rescue boats out there to give you what you want. So get him back inside. Somewhere lit, where he can warm up and dry off enough to look threatening. Because right now he looks like a poor and feeble old man. With how bad the video will be out here, nobody will ever believe you four actually managed to capture the one and only Detective Liam Bearsmith."

A ripple seemed to move through the men as if each was imagining how it would look if they got the credit for ending Liam's life.

Then the man with the green eye patch ordered Liam to stand. Blue eye patch took Liam's cell phone, wallet and phone. Yellow eye patch hesitated for a moment, as if wondering what to do, and then took Kelly's diaper bag. The one with the red eye patch told them to move. They walked single file back inside the boat, with two men leading the way and two taking up the rear. Pip's cries fell silent, probably from a combination of movement and warmth. Kelly could feel Liam, just one step behind her. His hand brushed hers for a nanosecond, filling her with reassurance and strength. They walked down a hallway, climbed stairs, went down another hallway to another flight of stairs and then reached the third-level ballroom again. A man in a purple eye patch escorted them inside.

A couple hundred people sat on the floor in the large room, huddled together in clumps and talking to each other in whispers, while armed and masked men guarded them. She couldn't help but notice several passengers were recording video on their cell phones, although presumably none of them were online.

"Sit," the man with the red eye patch barked in her ear, so she did.

"I'll need my diaper bag back," she said, fixing her eyes on the man in the yellow eye patch and realizing he no longer had it. "So wherever you dropped it you'd better go get it."

His whole body flinched, as if he wasn't expecting a hostage to talk to him that way. He slipped out the door, as another one of the Imposters practically shoved Liam to sit.

For a moment Liam didn't even budge. Then he slowly sat down beside her. Liam waited until the guards moved back, then he leaned in and whispered, "Poor and feeble old man? Really?"

"Well, it worked, didn't it?" she whispered back.

He didn't answer and instead scanned the room. "Approximately a hundred and ninety hostages, give or take, and only four guards. Which puts them at a definite numbers disadvantage if it wasn't for how many rounds one of those weapons can get off in a minute."

"How's your back?" she asked. "Looked like you took a direct hit."

"Fine," he said. "Bit bruised but vest absorbed most of the impact. I've seen worse."

Somehow she suspected "I've seen worse" was his answer to a lot of things.

He glanced at her sideways. "Exactly what were you trying to accomplish with that speech?"

Seemed he wasn't about to let that go. "I was trying to buy you time, get us inside and use their obvious weaknesses against them."

"I had the situation under control."

Had he now? She felt her eyes roll and turned away to hide it. The baby cried softly. Not a full-out wail, just the kind of whimpering that meant she was looking for attention. Kelly rocked the car seat gently and prayed that rescue was imminent. Then she leaned down, brushed her lips over the soft top of the baby's head and prayed.

"To be honest, my biggest worry was something happening to you and the baby," he said. "When you've faced down as many evil amateurs with weapons as I have, you get a fairly good sense of how to get out of a situation like that with the minimum number of bullet holes. Turns out it's a whole different situation when you've got someone else to worry about." His hand reached out as if wanting to brush Pip's face and then stopped, like he was worried of accidentally breaking her. "Sorry, you never told me her name."

"We call her Pip."

"Seriously?" He quirked an eyebrow. "Pip Phillips?"

"It's a nickname," Kelly explained. "Renner's family tradition is you don't name a baby until both her parents have held her and Renner hasn't seen her yet. In Alberta, they have a year to register her name before it becomes a problem."

Liam nodded slowly and for a long moment he didn't say anything.

"I'm sorry I couldn't save Hannah," he said softly. "But we'll find her. I promise." Then his dark and soulful eyes turned back to her face. "So Hannah's our daughter?"

He whispered the last word so quietly it almost moved silently over his lips.

"Yeah." She nodded and something in his gaze was so intense she couldn't hold it any longer and instead looked down at the baby. "And this is really your granddaughter."

She looked around at the room again with its huddled groups of whispering and terrified people intent on recording every moment until their phone batteries died, even though their internet had been cut off. The jittery guards seemed to be growing more agitated and nervous by the second. "Although this really isn't how I wanted to tell you."

"Okay," Liam said softly.

It was amazing how a single word could carry so much weight.

"How old was Hannah when you, when they…" His words trailed off.

"When she was adopted?" Kelly asked. "A couple of hours. Her parents were there in the delivery room. They let me hold her. They were really good people. I owe them everything. They died a few years ago. Hannah found me then."

And Kelly had known, somehow, that it was right to entrust them with Hannah, let them raise her and be her parents. She'd known then and never doubted it was right. Even though giving them her baby girl had felt like tearing off a piece of her own heart.

"You never had kids?" she asked.

"I've got no family." He shook his head and chuckled softly, as if the sound was coming from somewhere very deep inside him. "I've never even kissed anyone who wasn't you."

A door slammed open behind her. She glanced back to see the man with the yellow eye patch stride through, her diaper bag under his arm.

"You!" He pointed at her with the butt of his gun. "Lady with the baby. Stand up. You're coming with me."

# FIVE

But as Kelly got to her feet, she felt Liam's hand grab hold of hers.

"I'm going with her!" Liam's voice rose and seemed to boom around the room. "They're not going anywhere without me."

As if on cue, the masked men focused their weapons on Liam, filling the air with shouts, swearing and threats. Pip's cries grew into a full-throated wail. She needed to get the baby out of there. Unless the Imposters had thoroughly searched the diaper bag and found each hidden compartment, there might still be an encrypted burner phone and mini–stun gun inside it, along with other helpful tools. She couldn't miss her opportunity to get her hands on them.

"Please, lady," the man in the yellow eye patch said. "You've got to come with me. Now."

There was a slight waver in his voice, almost like he was pleading with her. Did Liam hear it, too? Or was he too focused on the cacophony around them? She didn't know. But another of his tactics filled her mind. *Nobody's fully evil.* Every enemy has the potential to do the right thing. Was the man in the yellow eye patch trying to do the right thing now?

"It's okay," she said, glancing at Liam. "I've got to get Pip out of here and to somewhere quieter. We'll be okay. And if not, you'll find us."

His jaw set, and something hardened like flint behind his eyes. "You're sure right I will."

She swallowed hard and the man with the yellow eye patch practically pushed the diaper bag into her hand. She prayed that everything she needed was still inside. The Imposter led her out of the room and down a hallway, until they reached a door in the wall. He opened it and she looked inside. It seemed to be a cross between a security office and a supply room. A clunky monitor in the corner flickered black-and-white security camera footage of the chaos she'd left behind in the ballroom, but the rest of the space was crammed tightly with spare linens, decorations and chairs for the events. But, thankfully, it had a table she could change Pip on.

"I'm not a bad person," the anonymous man with the yellow eye patch said. "Just so you know. I just believe the wrong people are running the world, the system is rigged against the little guy and someone needs to teach them a lesson."

So had how many other people across the world throughout history? The mother's heart inside her found itself praying for him. And that he'd live long enough to both repent and grow.

She took the diaper bag from his hand and walked into the room, planning out her next steps as she did so. She would set down Pip, pretend to search the bag for a diaper and then get the mini–stun gun. She'd get close enough to zap him, then tie him up with some of the brightly colored decorative cord on the shelf. And then, what? *Help me, Lord.*

"I'll just be one moment," she said. She took the diaper bag from him and put it on the table, wishing she didn't have to turn her back on him even if it was only for a moment.

"Stay here," he said. "You'll be safe if you stay in here."

The door slammed shut. Something clicked.

"Wait!" She turned quickly. "Stop!"

She set down Pip, crossed the floor and grabbed the handle. It turned but the door didn't budge. Instead, as she pulled she just heard the thump of metal against the frame. Her heart leaped into her throat. For a second it pounded so hard she could barely breathe. They were locked in.

Pip's cries rose again. Kelly ran back to her, unclipped her from the car seat and held her to her chest. "Shh. It's okay. Don't worry. It's all going to be okay."

She rocked back and forth, shifting her weight from one foot to the other. Her gaze ran to the security camera, trying to seek out Liam's form on the small screen. But whether it was the angle, the crowd or something else that had happened to him, she couldn't see him anywhere.

*Lord, keep him safe. Keep Hannah safe. Keep Pip and I safe. We all need You now.*

Liam was right. It was different when there was somebody else to care for. When she and Liam had been on the run when they were younger, it had just been a matter of fight, run, hide and survive. But how could she do that with a baby? Somehow the true weight of being a mother hadn't really hit her until the moment Hannah had told her she'd be taking the Ugly Sweater Holiday Cruise as a cover to escape Canada and rejoin Renner. And now the weight of her love for Hannah and Pip seemed heavy enough to crush her heart.

"You see, Pip," she told the tiny baby, as she rocked her back and forth, "the thing with being a mom is sometimes you've got to let your children make their own decisions. Your mommy loves your daddy so much, was so determined to be with him and so convinced he was right, that my choices were either to rat them out to law enforcement, let her go on her own or agree to go with her, to take care of you and try to keep her safe. She said once we met up with your daddy, he'd explain everything and I would understand. But now we're locked in a closet on a hijacked boat. And I've gotta figure out how to get out of here while keeping you safe."

The baby's cries stopped. She waltzed Pip over to the table, opened the diaper bag, put down a change mat and laid Pip on top of it. Pip looked at her, with wide eyes, and kicked and waved her limbs.

"Now, listen to me," Kelly said as she emptied the bag onto the table. "You and I are not going to fall apart. We're made of tougher stuff than that, little Pip. You and I are going to hold it together, and figure our way out of this one step at a time."

Her fingers brushed a pacifier. It was pink and had a duck on it. She popped it into Pip's mouth. The baby sucked on it thoughtfully. Kelly kept searching. *Thank You, God!* The mini–stun gun was still there, along with a backup roll of both Canadian and American cash, an old-fashioned compass and the encrypted cell phone. No handgun or computer, though. She turned on the phone. It had a little bit of battery left but no cell signal. No phone charger, either. She let out a long breath.

"Well, it's literally a mixed bag," she told Pip. "But the good news is we've got enough formula to last twenty-four hours. It might be lukewarm and we're just going to have to make do with that. One way or another, we're getting out of this. Your grandfather's a really good guy and the strongest man I've ever met. If anyone can find us, it's him. And if not, we'll find our way out of here and go find him."

A lump caught in her throat. She ignored it. Pip needed her to be strong right now and that's what she was going to do. That and pray.

Sudden movement on the monitor drew her eyes back. Seemed the Imposters had ordered everyone to their feet. She watched as the hostages stood, quaking and holding their hands in the air, some still clutching their phones. What was this? What was happening? Then through the crowd, she saw Liam. His eyes were locked on the camera, defiant and unflinching.

A faint haze moved across the top of the screen, like a distortion or smoke moving across the top of the room. Liam's nose twitched and his gaze rose as if sensing something.

Then as she watched, people began to fall, collapsing and dropping to the ground like marionettes whose strings had just been cut.

Liam held his breath. Whatever it was they were piping in through the air vents, it felt thick, smelled sickly sweet and had the people around him dropping like flies. No doubt it looked pretty impressive on camera. But was it deadly? Hopefully not. Screams rose around him. People were panicking, collapsing and fainting. For a moment, he couldn't even see their Imposter captors in the mayhem. He quickly crouched beside an elderly woman to his right and checked her pulse. Seemed like she'd fainted.

Whatever the toxin or illness, the very old and very young were invariably the most at risk. He prayed hard that Kelly and the baby were okay. But first, he had to take care of the hostages. *Help me, God.* He yanked the neckline of his shirt up over his nose and mouth and focused on moderating his breathing to inhale as little toxin as possible.

He fought the urge to raise his voice and shout at everyone to stay calm. He'd need every breath right now.

Every gas he knew that knocked a person out tended to take a different amount of time for different people, depending on all sorts of factors, from age, to build, to even how much they'd eaten. Thanks to his build, metabolism and his ability to moderate his breathing, he'd probably be the last man standing. But it was only a matter of time before he, too, fell.

He scanned the room, pushing his way through the panic. Then his eyes locked on the Imposters. Three remained, standing between him and the doors leading out to the fresh air on deck. All of them looked wobbly and unsteady, even like they were shaking.

Huh. Guess none of their friends warned them about the gas. But that matched what he knew about the criminals. Seemed it really was every Imposter for himself.

So three woozy, probably panicked and confused gun-wielding men stood between him and breathable air. Liam didn't even hesitate. He charged, lowering his head, and plowed his body right into the chest of the nearest man, praying he'd catch him off guard before he had the chance to try and pull the trigger. Bull's-eye. He caught him in a football tackle and planted his shoulder into the man's sternum while one hand wrenched the weapon from his grasp. The Imposter went sprawling. Liam glanced at the gun and almost growled. It wasn't even loaded. Again, not surprising considering an ad hoc online mob would likely have some problems arming themselves.

Hopefully, the other two masked men's weapons were equally ineffective. Either way, it was a risk he was about to take.

"Drop your weapons!" Liam bellowed, swinging the useless weapon around and aiming it at the two Imposters on the other side of the room. "Now!"

They dropped their weapons so quickly it was like their arms had collapsed. Good. *Thank You, God.* One problem down. A bunch more to go.

His experienced eyes quickly scanned the room, looking for anyone in the chaos who still potentially had their head on straight.

"You!" He gestured first to an athletic-looking middle-aged couple near the middle of the room and then to two fit young women in matching sweaters at the far end. "Secure those weapons. Throw them overboard if you need to. Just don't let anyone else get a hold of them."

People throwing semiautomatic weapons overboard would be as good a sign as any to those law-enforcement people in hovering helicopters and rescue boats that it was time to swoop in and make their move despite whatever story the designated Imposter hostage negotiator they were talking to was feeding them.

"All right, everyone!" His voice rose above the chaos. "If you can crawl, get outside. If you can walk, drag someone who can't with you."

"The doors are locked!" a woman shouted.

Yeah, but not for long.

"Everybody get back!" Liam grabbed one of the tall tables with his free hand, swung it around like a club and smashed it through the window. Glass shattered and cold, clean, pure night air rushed in. Liam dove through the window, hit the deck and rolled to his feet. Sure enough, someone had looped what looked like bicycle locks around the door handles. Cheap and effective, and he was about to break them off. The table he'd bashed through the window had seen better days, but all it took him was one of the legs to break through the lock and tear the door handle off. The door flew open and people rushed through.

He quickly glanced at the rescue helicopters circling in the sky and waved both hands above his head. He'd been behind the scenes of enough hostage situations to know not to judge when rescuers made their move. It was possible the Imposters were feeding them all sorts of nonsense and stringing them on with all kinds of false threats and negotiation points. And he had no idea what signal they were waiting for that it was go-time.

Well, he was now giving them a pretty big one.

He glanced both ways down the deck and didn't see a single Imposter. He wasn't sure if that meant they'd run or just pulled off their masks and mingled with the crowd. He ran down the deck to the next door and the next lock. This one was heavy-duty, so this time he wedged his piece of broken table leg into the door frame and, with the help of a couple of partygoers, bent it back until the door broke free of its hinges. More people poured past him. Some led or carried loved ones and strangers along with them. Others pushed and shoved as they stampeded for the door. And his job was to save them all. One whiff of the air that accompanied them and he could tell the toxin was growing thicker. The dizziness in his head warned him if he inhaled any more, he was at risk of passing out.

He ran back in, feeling his body being buffeted by those

streaming out. He prayed with every breath that Kelly and Pip had fresh air to breathe. Either way, he'd give his final breath for them. The room was emptying fast. He ran across the polished floor toward the door that the man with the yellow eye patch had led Kelly and the baby through. Then he saw another young woman passed out on the floor. She was waif thin and barely four feet, but, thankfully, she was breathing. He dropped his piece of broken table and bulletless gun, scooped her up into his arms and ran back toward the deck. He spotted a broad-shouldered man, at least six foot seven, Liam guessed, helping a couple of other men get the last few remaining partygoers out the door.

"Officer!" Liam shouted. It was an educated guess given the young man's bearing and one that proved correct when he turned. Liam locked eyes with him. "You—I need you to come and take her."

Without missing a beat, the young man did a swift check of those around him, made sure they were okay without his help and then jogged toward Liam.

"Up-to-date on CPR accreditation?" Liam asked. The man nodded, looking baffled. Liam eased the tiny woman into the man's arms. Her eyes fluttered and Liam was thankful she was conscious. "Police division?"

"I'm from York Region," he replied. "But I haven't passed the academy yet. I'm not actually a cop."

Not yet, but he would be.

"I'm Detective Liam Bearsmith, RCMP," he said. "Come find me when you graduate."

He allowed himself one more gasp of fresh air, then he ran back through the ballroom. It was empty now, but he still yanked back tablecloths and looked underneath to make sure no one was left. The air seemed to thicken around him. He pushed his body deeper and deeper into the sickly sweet and pungent smoke. The walls and floor undulated around him, as if he was underwater. Somehow he'd lost sight of where he'd dropped the bulletless gun and his makeshift weapon, but thankfully another broken table leg wasn't hard to find. Or was it the same one? He couldn't tell. He leaned on it like a crutch and pushed through, inhaling more and more knockout gas into his lungs with every breath. He had to find her. He had to make sure she was safe, even as he could feel the heaviness of the toxin filling his body like quicksand dragging him down.

He reached a door, yanked the handle and found it locked. He swung back with the broken table leg, then smashed the handle over and over again until the door broke free of the frame. He fell through it, back into the same kitchen he'd been in before, and immediately the air felt lighter. He stumbled through, thankful to see the door to the pantry where he'd once found hostages was now open and the room was empty. Hopefully they'd made it to where the air was clean.

As for him, he now stayed upright by sheer willpower alone.

"Kelly!" He stumbled down the hall, forcing her name through his burning lungs, yanking open doors and almost tumbling through, as the ship seemed to move like it was being tossed in an ever-worsening storm.

Then he saw a bicycle lock looped around a doorknob ahead and on his right. He blinked, as his vision focused on the black-and-gold object sitting on the floor, propped up against the frame as if someone had left it there waiting just for him. He bent down and reached for it, stumbling and falling against the door. No, it couldn't be, he had to be hallucinating. His fingers clamped on to the object, feeling its old, familiar form.

It was his police badge.

But who had left it there? And why?

"Liam?" The sound of Kelly's voice calling his name cut through his foggy brain. The door shook in front of him as if someone was trying to jar it loose from the frame.

"Kelly…" He forced her name over his heavy tongue.

"Liam!" Her voice rose, full of strength and joy. "We're in here! Pip and I are okay. But the door is locked!" *Not for long.*

"Is everything okay? There's a monitor in here. I saw people fainting and you helping break them out."

"The Imposters pumped some kind of knockout gas into the air vents," he said. "Big snazzy finale. But now law enforcement will move in and secure the boat." In moments it would all be over. Liam would make sure Kelly and Pip were taken to a safe house, where someone he trusted would watch over them. And he could talk to his team and figure out how they were going to find Hannah. "Step back and take cover. I'm going to break the door down. Not much gas in the air out here, but you'll want to inhale as little as possible and help shield the baby until we're outside."

The lock was lighter than the other ones, flimsy even, but his swings felt slower, heavier and sluggish. The door fell open and there stood Kelly.

His heart caught in his throat.

Had she always been this beautiful? Dark hair fell around her face in waves. Her green eyes sparkled with a warmth that made him think of happiness and home. Her gorgeous lips parted slightly in the smile that had never once, in over twenty years, left the edges of his heart.

"Liam!" Her voice was sharp, almost worried. Her hand brushed his face. "Are you okay? You look dazed."

He was fine. He was just sleepy, his head was woozy and things weren't quite looking right.

She slung the diaper bag determinedly over her shoulder and picked up the car seat. There was a small baby in a pink knit hat inside.

*Oh, right... Pip. I—I have a granddaughter.*

Kelly's other hand grabbed his and squeezed it so tightly he almost winced.

"Come on," she said. "We're getting you out of here before you pass out."

She ran down the hallway, carrying the baby's car seat in one hand and pulling him after her with the other. Stairs seemed to rise and fall beneath him as he stumbled down them like he was in a fun house. They pushed through a door and stepped out onto the deck. Cold winter night air filled his lungs. Noise and lights assailed his senses. Law enforcement had arrived, and the boat was being evacuated.

"This way." Kelly grabbed his arm and pulled him down the deck, away from the rescue operations. "We have to try and get Hannah's laptop. I'm sure she wiped it clean but maybe we can find a way to use it to track her. I just hope it's still there."

"Stop!" a voice barked. Liam turned to see a young man in a black-blue Toronto police uniform. "Police! Drop your weapon!"

*What? What weapon?*

It was only then Liam realized he was still clutching the piece of broken table leg he'd used to break open the doors. He let it fall to the deck with a clatter, yanked his badge and held it up.

"De Tec'ive Leeyam Bears-s-smith," he called, his words slurring. "Rrrr. Cee. Em'p."

The cop swore at him. "Get down!" he barked. "Now!"

Who was the cop talking to? Liam turned and looked behind him, feeling the world spin out of focus. There was no one there.

"Duuuuude," Liam shouted. "Chilllll!"

But it was like the cop didn't even hear him.

"Ma'am!" he shouted. "Step away from the suspect."

What suspect? What was going on?

"Get down!" The cop's voice rose. "Now!"

Liam didn't understand. None of this was making sense. "Look, kid, I'm detective Liam Bearsmith…"

His words felt thick and mushy on his tongue.

"Stop lying!" the cop shouted. "You keep that name out of your filthy mouth. You hear me? You don't get to lie about something like that. It's disrespecting the uniform and everyone who wears it." The cop was definitely getting heated.

"Hey, buddy," Liam said, as firmly as he could muster. "Cool it."

"You get down and stop talking," the cop said. "Now, or I'll shoot!"

Shoot him? For what? For saying his own name? For holding his badge?

Was this really happening? Was he hallucinating all this?

The cop rushed toward him with his weapon raised. Liam's knees began to buckle beneath him. Then he felt Kelly pull away from his grasp. Liam stumbled. His knees hit the deck.

"I'm arresting you on suspicion of murder and impersonating a police officer—"

He felt a hand on the back of his head shoving him against the deck. His hands were wrenched behind his back. Pain shot through his injured back. A handcuff clicked over his right wrist. The cop struggled to secure the second.

*Help me, Lord! What's happening to me?*

Something crackled loudly by his face and flashed like bright blue lightning. Something thudded to the deck beside him. A hand grabbed his and pulled him up.

"Come on!" Kelly's voice swam somewhere around the edges of his mind. "You can still run, right?"

He didn't know if he could. He didn't know if he could even walk, or how long he'd be able to outrun the unconsciousness threatening to pull him under. He'd inhaled so much gas that he should be out cold by now. His feet stumbled beneath him, and he was barely able to complete each step he took. Lights and noise seemed to screech at the corners of his barely conscious mind. Then it was like the sky above him was exploding in a bright, wild and inexplicable array of popping sounds and dazzling color. Fireworks? How? He felt something bash into his stomach so hard it winded him. He pitched forward.

And the last thing Liam Bearsmith knew was that he was falling.

# SIX

Air rushed past him. He was tumbling and falling into darkness. Something cold and hard smacked against his body. Pain shot through him. Unconsciousness swept over him. He tried to fight it, willing himself to move, only to feel his body collapse beneath him. Then he felt the vibrations of an engine seemingly rumbling around him and heard Kelly's reassuring voice promising him that everything was going to be okay. Something warm fell over his body. And then there was nothing but sleep.

He had no idea how long he'd been out when he felt something jolt him back to consciousness. He opened his eyes. The sky was still dark, but now the world had fallen silent. He was lying on the floor of a small motorboat. Stars peeked through the moving clouds above. Water lapped gently against ice. A blanket was over his body, and what looked like an empty water bottle and empty bag of animal crackers were on the floor by his face.

A light flickered on ahead of him, shining over his face.

He sat up, his hands shielding his face from the light, and he felt the weight of a handcuff dangling from one wrist.

"I'm—"

"Detective Liam Bearsmith," Kelly said. "I know. You say

that a lot. But this is one problem just shouting your name won't solve."

*Oh, ha ha.* The light moved from his face down to his feet. He was sitting in the back of a small speedboat that was docked at what looked like a tiny island no bigger than the size of one of those large backyards in the suburbs. Kelly was standing on the shore. A small cabin, not much more than a shack, sat behind her. Dim light flickered in a window.

"Welcome back," she said. "You finally going to stay awake on me this time?"

Yeah, he had the vague sense he'd woken up before, but couldn't really remember it.

"Where's Pip?" he asked.

"Safe in the cabin." She swung her light to the building only a few feet behind her. "I built a little nest out of blankets and pillows for her on the floor. She's excited to wriggle and move. But she'll start crying for me if I'm gone more than two minutes. No electricity, but there is well water coming out of the tap. I was able to light a lamp and there's a gas heater I can use to heat Pip's bottle. She was getting tired of drinking it cold."

"You broke into a cottage?" he asked.

"The key was on a hook under a welcome sign beside the front door," she said. "It wasn't exactly hidden."

And that wasn't exactly a denial.

"How did we get here?" he asked. "How did we even get off the boat?"

"Renner's original plan was to dock a small and undetectable motorboat off the port side of the cruise ship," she said. "Hannah and I were supposed to wait for a big distraction and take off during the confusion. I was steering you, trying to find Renner's boat, when a whole lot of fireworks went off at once. It was utter chaos. You fell and landed in the boat. We took off. Sure enough, the fireworks and general mayhem provided enough distraction for us to escape without being caught. No one was chasing after one tiny speedboat in all that. Plus, I kept the lights completely off until we cleared Lake Ontario, so we'd have been pretty hard to spot, especially when people had their hands full of a boat full of Imposters and rescued hostages."

He frowned.

"That whole explanation is ridiculous," he said. "If Renner set up fireworks to help Hannah escape wouldn't they have gone off earlier? Wouldn't it make more sense for the Imposters to have set them off to make a giant spectacle or give them cover for escaping? And driving off in a speedboat like that with the lights off was risky. You had no way of knowing you'd evade detection."

She crossed her arms. "Well apparently it worked because we weren't captured and we're here now."

"Where are we anyway?" he asked.

"On one of the Thousand Islands in the St. Lawrence River," she said. She swung the light up a flagpole by the cottage to where an American flag hung limp. "We're on US soil," she added. "So you've got no jurisdiction to arrest me."

He snorted. The Thousand Islands were a stretch of small islands in the St. Lawrence River between Canada and the United States. Some had houses on them and others had cabins or cottages. Many were nothing more than a rock. There was often no way to tell which side of the border each one was on if it wasn't for the flags, and some even spanned the border.

It wasn't a half-bad place to hide. Not that she hadn't been completely wrong to run from the authorities.

"We've had this exact same conversation before," she added. "But you kept falling back asleep. We don't have a lot of gas left in the tank, Renner still hasn't responded to any of my messages and my phone is almost dead. This seemed like a good place to stop and regroup."

Maybe, but they shouldn't have to stop and regroup. She should be back in Toronto, fast asleep in a well-guarded safe house or hotel room, while he figured out this whole thing with the police.

"I only have a few minutes of battery left on my phone," she said, "but is there anyone you need to contact? Any family or friends who'll be worried about you or wonder why you didn't come home?"

"Told you, I have no family," Liam said. There'd just been Dad and he'd died four years ago. "Or friends like that, really. What I need to do is contact my team and come up with a strategy to handle this."

She pressed her lips together. "Then let me talk to Renner first. The phone is very close to dying and I need to tell him what happened to Hannah. Then you can have it to call whoever you need."

"If the Imposters have Hannah they'll have posted about it on the dark web," Liam said. "Whether they'll be bragging about it or just putting out feelers trying to attract Renner's attention, either way, they definitely won't keep quiet about it. That means Seth will spot it, know what's happened immediately and alert my team. Law enforcement will already be looking for her. They won't hurt her, I'm sure of it. Based on my experience and what we've seen, they like chaos, not cruelty."

At least for now. It had only been a few hours, but who knew what would happen if the situation dragged on.

"You told me all that before, too," Kelly said, "and hearing it helped keep me sane. So, thank you. Also, we need to get online as soon as possible."

"I really don't think surfing the web is a priority," he said.

"Anything could have happened while we were off-line," she said. "The whole world could be different."

Not that different. She turned to go back to the cabin.

"We shouldn't even be here," he said. "Just because your plan apparently worked doesn't mean it wasn't completely wrong, risky and ridiculous. We shouldn't have left the boat. We should have gone with the police."

She stopped and turned back. Her hands snapped to her hips, sending the light to her feet. "One, we've already talked about this, every single time you've woken up, even if you keep forgetting. Two, I saved your life. And three, that police offer wanted to arrest you for murder."

Yeah, but that was the part that hadn't made any sense.

"Look, that was obviously a misunderstanding that would've been cleared up immediately," he said.

"And I think that you're wrong and I made the right call," she said. "But I don't really care if you believe me right now. I've got to get back to Pip and keep trying to reach Renner."

Before he could splutter another word, she turned and walked back to the cabin, taking the light with her. Frustration burned in the back of his throat. Who did this woman think she was? If she'd been anyone else, he might've actually thought she'd kidnapped him. That idea was almost enough to make him chuckle. But, no, this whole situation was not happening this way.

*Lord, help me handle this mess the right way. And help her listen to me.*

He glanced around the boat. Thankfully, he couldn't see any form of tracking device and the boat wasn't fancy enough for an onboard computer. So she was probably right no one had tracked them. The keys weren't in the ignition, but it would be easy enough to hot-wire if he needed to. He couldn't tell how low they were on gas. But the river was narrow enough that he could probably make it to shore on fumes. If need be, he could swim back to Canada.

He headed for the cottage, knocked twice on the door and then pushed it open. Warmth swept around him. Kelly looked up from where she sat cross-legged on a blanket on the floor. Pip was lying on her back, with her eyes seemingly locked on Kelly's face. She was waving all four limbs at once and making this cute little cooing sound Liam had never heard before. It was like Pip was trying to talk. A light filled Kelly's face as she looked down at the tiny child, and as frustrated as he was with her, something about it still took his breath away. When he'd been a much younger man he'd thought Kelly Marshall was the most attractive woman he'd ever seen. But now, two decades later, there was something so much deeper and richer to her beauty that defied description.

She looked up at him.

"I know it's not much," she said. "But I figured it was safer that we stop somewhere and get warm than just keep going in below-freezing temperatures until the gas ran out."

It was only then he looked away, long enough to look around. The cabin was one large room. There was a couch with a mattress wedged upright behind it, a small table with two chairs and a kitchen counter with a bucket sitting under the open pipe of the sink. A small array of candles of different sizes and shapes flickered from various surfaces. The gas heater was at least fifty years old and the small fire burning within it was warming a battered pot of water she'd placed on top of it.

"Don't worry," she said. "I'll lock the door before I leave and leave more than enough cash to cover what I used. I have a couple thousand dollars in emergency money in the diaper bag. Hannah and I emptied our bank accounts."

Defiance rumbled in her voice. The flames around them reflected in her eyes. He opened a drawer and rooted around until he found a paper clip. Then he picked the handcuff lock and took it off.

"You've gotten better at picking handcuffs," she said. "Used to take you a lot longer than that."

"I've gotten a lot of practice," he said. He noticed her phone was sitting beside her on the floor. "Have you heard from Renner?"

"No," she said.

Worry washed over her features, wiping the smile from her face. Should he feel guilty about that? She was the one who'd made wrong call after wrong call.

"We're not staying here," Liam said and sat down on the carpet opposite her.

"Do whatever you want," she said. "But I'm going to wait

for a message from Renner and figure out how I'm going to find my daughter."

Considering the depth of pain and worry in her eyes, he decided not to read anything into the fact she'd said "my" instead of "ours."

"Look," Liam said, "as romantic as it might be to paint Hannah and Renner as just two foolish kids in love, who were trying to run off into the sunset together, law enforcement exists for a reason."

"Says the man who—"

"Who broke all the rules and was willing to throw his entire career away to be with you some twenty years ago?" Liam interrupted her, completing the sentence. "I know, foolish kids in love don't always make the best decisions, Kelly. Believe me, I get the irony."

Her mouth set in a thin line.

"Actually," she said, "I was going to say 'the man who is willing to have a criminal hacker like Seth Miles on his team.' I know Seth's reputation. I know what he's done. He broke the law, repeatedly, which is more than you can say for Renner or Hannah."

Yes, but Seth had turned his life around and had believed he was doing the right thing at the time when he'd hacked criminals and worked outside the law to bring down bad guys. But if Liam pointed that out, Kelly would only counter that Hannah and Renner thought they were doing the right thing, too. Liam had perused Seth's file enough to know that unlike Liam's father—who'd done his best in his own faulty way to protect him—Seth's high-ranking military father had been downright abusive, which had instilled in him a deep distrust of anything law enforcement. The steps Seth had made to help his team in the past year had been a series of huge steps of personal growth.

Seth's past choices weren't right, but they were forgivable.

Pip squealed loudly. Liam looked down. She seemed to be

trying to figure out how to twist and turn her body around to face him.

"She wants you to pick her up," Kelly said.

He'd take her word for it. He didn't pick up the baby, but he did shift his body around the carpet so that she could look up at him. Pip smiled, and he found himself smiling back.

"Believe me," Kelly said, "I argued against Hannah and Renner's plan until I was blue in the face. But at the end of the day, my options were to let her go alone or agree to go with her. I figured at least if I went with her I could keep Pip safe and try to talk some sense into them. Despite what you might think, Renner and Hannah aren't criminals. Renner was working as a military contractor, decoded a terrorist's online code and stopped a major bombing—"

"And within hours the internet was reporting he'd done so by creating a master-key decryption device," Liam added. "One which by rights would've belonged to the Canadian government."

And which, to be fair, was one that a lot of terrorist groups were suddenly ready to kidnap and kill Renner's young family to get their hands on. Liam could give Renner that much.

"Yup," she agreed, "and then he nearly died in a targeted bomb strike. So he went underground until he could find a way to reunite safely with his secretly pregnant wife. Are you saying that's any different than what you would've done?"

Liam gritted his teeth. Maybe not, but he wasn't twenty-two anymore.

"It's not illegal to walk out of witness protection," Kelly said. "I get you had the right to detain Hannah for questioning. But how exactly is it a crime to steal a decryption key that doesn't exist? Or to aid and abet someone accused of stealing a non-existent thing?"

"How did a low-level engineer in Afghanistan decode a code that complex without the assistance of a decryption key?" Liam asked, and he'd keep on asking until he got an answer.

"How does my witness-protection file say I married a man named Robbie, had four sons and died?" she challenged. "How did the Imposters track us to the boat?"

"Obviously they had a tail on you or Hannah," Liam said.

"Or they had a tail on you," she countered, "and it was a fluke they saw Hannah. Or maybe Seth is an Imposter."

"That's not possible." He could feel the scowl on his face. "We're wasting time and you're being just as foolish as Hannah and Renner. I need to call my team, get them to relocate you and Pip somewhere safe and ensure they're focusing the full might of law enforcement on finding Hannah."

"So you're just going to ignore the fact that a cop tried to arrest you for murder," she said. "He had one handcuff on you and a knee in your back before I rescued you."

The memory of the zapping sound and flash of light filled his mind. Zapping a police officer with a mini–stun gun and then running off with his suspect was most definitely a crime.

"I didn't want or need to be rescued," he said.

"He called you a liar," she said. "Look, I don't know who he thinks you killed. If only we could get online, we could figure that out. But he was really steamed up about it."

"He was just a bad cop!" Liam's voice rose. "There are a few bad cops out there. But a whole lot more who are good ones."

"My gut says he was looking for any excuse to shoot you for resisting arrest."

"Your gut is wrong."

Pip whimpered. He glanced down. The baby's chin was quivering.

"She can tell you're angry," Kelly said.

"I'm not angry," Liam said. He scooped up Pip onto his lap, turned her to face him and made himself smile. "See, Pip?" His voice rose an octave. "It's all good. Nothing to cry about. I'm not angry. I just think your grandma did something very silly."

Pip stopped crying but she didn't smile. Instead she looked

at him skeptically, as if to say "yeah, sure." He hadn't known someone so tiny could call him out so thoroughly.

Kelly chuckled softly under her breath. And suddenly it hit him: she could've just taken off with the baby and left him behind to be arrested. Probably would've made her life a whole lot simpler.

"Look," he said, trying another tack. "I get that I was practically unconscious, that cop's behavior was bizarre, it probably seemed safer to make a quick escape and that considering the freezing temperatures, taking shelter indoors made sense." He bounced the baby and kept his voice upbeat and cheerful. Pip latched her tiny fingers around his. "But I fundamentally disagree with every call you've made."

And yet defiance still filled her eyes. She was just so convinced that she was right and he was wrong. In a world full of people, how was this woman the only one he'd ever thought himself in love with? Two of his teammates were getting married in the next forty-eight hours and a third was getting married on New Year's Eve. Somehow those couplings had always made sense. His gut told him that Mack the detective and Iris the social worker just belonged together, as did Detective Jess with former detective Travis and Detective Noah with Corporal Holly. So how was it the only woman for him had been someone this obstinate, difficult, challenging and impossible?

Kelly shrugged. "All I can do is tell you what happened," she said. "If I made the wrong call, I'm sorry. But at least I made it trying to save your life."

She stretched her hand out toward him. For a moment his eyes lingered on her face, then he looked down at her hand. She was offering him her burner phone.

"It's secure," she said, "according to Hannah. But it's also down to less than five percent battery power. It could die at any moment. It was only supposed to be used to send encrypted messages to Renner. But he's not responding. You might not trust me, but I still trust you."

She placed the phone into his palm and their fingers brushed. Then she stood up, walked over to the small stove and pulled the pot of water off the heat. She put the pot in the sink and set a bottle of formula inside it to warm up.

Liam dialed Seth's number.

"Hello, you've reached Seth Miles..." The hacker's voice was oddly formal. Despite the fact it was the middle of the night, he'd answered on the first ring. "How can I help you?"

"Hey, it's me," he said. "It's Liam. Good news—I'm still alive. I can't tell you how thankful I am to hear your voice—"

"Sorry, sir," Seth interrupted quickly. "I think you got the wrong number."

Liam's eyes rolled. Did Seth think he was being funny?

"Seth, don't start with me," Liam said. "I've been through way too much in one night for jokes right now."

"And I'm saying, you dialed the wrong number," Seth said.

The phone went dead. Liam blinked. Seth had hung up on him.

He looked at Kelly. She'd barely let the bottle sit in the water a few moments and already she was tapping out a few drops of formula milk on the inside of her elbow. She frowned and set the bottle back in the water.

"Why did he just hang up on me?" he asked. "What do I need to know about this number?"

"I don't know," she said. "All I know is it's encrypted. Should be impossible to trace. Of course, that doesn't mean someone isn't tracing Seth's phone from the other end."

The phone began to ring in his hand. Call display said the line was blocked. Was it Renner for her? Was it Seth for him? He hesitated, then offered her the phone.

She leaned over and pushed the button for the speakerphone. He answered the call. "Hello?"

"Don't talk—just listen." It was Seth. "This call is probably being traced. I mean it's as hidden as I can make it. But we're up against a couple hundred hackers here. Strength in numbers and all that. And I don't have much time before they figure it out—"

Liam's heart rate rose. "Hannah Phillips was kidnapped by Imposters—"

"I know and I told you not to talk." Seth's voice grew urgent. "Go dark. Okay? Really, really dark. No internet. No phones. No people. Definitely no cops. They might shoot you on sight. Assume you're putting anyone you contact in mortal danger just by talking to them. Also, don't let yourself get arrested. I've got no time to explain and don't even know how I would, honestly. Just stay where you are until we figure this out. You're wanted for murder."

The phone went dead. The sound of a dial tone filled the tiny cabin. Kelly watched as the color drained from Liam's face. He stood slowly, still holding Pip. And despite everything that had happened between them, suddenly all she wanted to do was wrap her arms around him and hug him tightly. Instead, she checked the bottle's temperature again and found it was still too cold.

All sorts of words filled her mind, most of which—well, maybe all of which—she knew would be unhelpful. In all the time she'd spent with Liam, she'd almost never seen him thrown off balance or at a loss for words, let alone like things were out of his control. But if she'd remembered anything it was that he needed to be alone inside his own brain to think. For a long moment, neither of them said anything as the wind howled, snow buffeted against the window and Liam jiggled baby Pip in his arms.

"I'll give Pip her bottle," he said. "You lie down and try to get some sleep. I promise I'll wake you up the instant Renner calls or anything happens."

"So we're just going to ignore what Seth said about going dark?" she asked.

"I'm going to take it under advisement," Liam said and his jaw set. "But Seth's not a cop and tends toward exaggeration."

In other words, Liam thought he knew better.

"Now please, get some rest while you can," he said. "You'll need your energy for whatever happens next. You also haven't slept all night and you probably let yourself freeze piloting a speedboat through subzero temperatures, while keeping me and Pip covered by blankets. You apparently kept letting me fall back asleep—"

"You said you needed to sleep it off—" she began.

"You took care of me," Liam said. "Please, let me take care of you and Pip. I promise I won't ditch the phone."

And even as she felt the temptation to be independent and not accept his help, she saw something else in his eyes. He needed this. He needed to take care of her. He needed to do something useful and productive.

*Lord, help Liam right now. He looks even more lost than I feel.*

"Okay," she said softly. She walked over to him and brushed a kiss over Pip's head, then her hand lingered on his arm. "You'll know the formula is at the right temperature when you don't feel it inside your elbow. She'll complain if it's too cold. I'm pretty sure I won't fall asleep, but I appreciate the chance to lie down."

"Thank you." He nodded. "I've never been the best at knowing the right words to say. But maybe you did make the right call when you took me off that boat. I don't know. But thank you for trying to have my back." Then he broke her gaze and looked down at the baby, but somehow the fingers of Liam's other hand found Kelly's and held them. "And thank you for trusting me with Pip."

She swallowed hard. Her fingers lingered on his for a moment. Then she pulled away and walked over to the couch. It wasn't until she lay down that she realized just how much her entire body ached. She curled onto her side and watched as Liam paced, bouncing Pip gently in his arm and singing something to her softly under his breath. It reminded her of an athlete trying to psych himself up to run onto the field or leap into the ring. For a long moment she just lay there and prayed, not even knowing how to put words to what she was thinking.

To her surprise, sleep swept over her. It was fitful at first, as she went in and out of consciousness like waves lapping on the shore. She was vaguely aware of Pip crying softly and then stopping as Liam fed her. There was the muted sound of Liam's voice as he talked to Pip, to someone on the phone and then to Pip some more, but she couldn't make out the words. Then she heard the sound of Liam singing, his voice a deep and raspy baritone rumble, as he sang a couple of Christmas carols and classic rock-and-roll tunes. It was somewhere during his rendition of "Let Me Call You Sweetheart," mingled with "Baby Love," that she finally fell into a peaceful sleep.

She awoke when she felt the couch shift and opened her eyes to see Liam sitting beside her. The cold blanket that he'd been sleeping under in the boat was now toasty warm, as if he'd laid it over the heater, and was wrapped around her shoulders. The snow had stopped and the sky was dark gray outside the window.

"Hey." His voice was a husky whisper. "Sorry to wake you."

"It's okay." She pulled herself up to sitting. He sat back, but they were so close on the couch their arms brushed and it would've taken nothing for her to lean right into his chest. "Where's Pip?"

"Playing on the floor," he said. She turned. Pip was lying on her back with a pacifier in both hands. "She drank her whole bottle, and I changed her. But she didn't seem to want to go back to sleep."

"She's an incredibly deep sleeper," Kelly said. "Hannah says she can sleep through anything. But on the flip side, when Pip's awake she's wide-awake for a long while. It's like she has an on-off switch." Kelly's arms wrapped around her body and her fingertips brushed his arm. She looked at where her hand sat, barley an inch away from his. "How long was I asleep?"

"Couple of hours," Liam said. "A little less."

"Did Renner call?" she asked.

"No." Liam shook his head. Worry darkened his eyes. "Nor my team. We're no closer to getting any answers and I'm sorry but the phone's battery died." He pressed his hands onto his knees and stood. "It's time we move on. There's no food for us here, we need a phone charger, we'll run out of gas soon and I don't want us to freeze in a shack on an island."

"Me, neither." She also needed more diapers and formula for Pip.

"Thankfully, I was able to get through to a contact of mine before the battery died," Liam went on. "He owns a waterside BBQ restaurant, gas station and motel about half an hour by boat from here. Nothing fancy, but we'll be able to warm up, eat something and charge the phone. Trust me, nobody will find us there. I'm not trying to trap you. I'm just trying to keep you and the baby safe until we sort this out."

She swung her legs over the edge of the couch and ran her fingers through her hair.

"I thought Seth warned you to stay off-the-grid and away from cops," she said.

"He did," Liam said. "My contact isn't a cop. He's a criminal. In a career as long as mine you meet a whole lot of people and sometimes they owe you a favor."

"You're joking," she said.

He wasn't—in fact, he was incredibly serious. His jaw was set, and he was in that focused mode now where he was convinced he'd made the right decision and arguing with him about it wasn't going to work. Her mind might've conveniently edited out those memories about just how big and stubborn a pain in her neck Liam could be, but they were returning to her now.

*But you still said yes when he asked you to marry him.*

How had she handled this side of him when they were young

and in love? She'd let him be focused and do his thing, and then try to talk to him. He'd always listened once he'd completed whatever task was at the top of his mind, and more than half the time he'd agreed with her. And besides, they were short on options. They needed heat, they needed food and she needed to charge her phone. She could always take Pip and go it alone once they got to shore if she didn't like how things were playing out.

But just because something wasn't the worst possible option didn't make it a good one.

They cleaned the cottage, left some money under one of the candles and changed Pip one last time before they left. Both the snow and wind had died down. The sky was a lighter shade of gray now, with just the smallest wisps of pink brushing the very edges. She wrapped Pip up in a cocoon-type sleeping bag that all but engulfed her and buckled her into her car seat.

It took them over half an hour to slowly maneuver the motor-boat down the St. Lawrence River, traveling east. The river was so deep and wide it usually didn't freeze over until the very end of January, and even then icebreakers were usually deployed to keep parts of it open. Still, the air was so cold it seemed to nip at her skin and thick ice was already building around the island shorelines. Between the intense cold, the sound of the motor and the rushing wind, she gave up trying to discuss Liam's plan further until he pulled the boat to a stop in a small marina on the Canadian mainland.

She looked around. A sprawling waterside restaurant stretched along the shoreline with a huge snow-covered deck overhanging the water. There were four docks, with space for twenty-five to thirty motorboats, a gas station for both vehicles and boats and a small convenience store that advertised ice, Popsicles and worms. According to a sign, there were motel rooms over the restaurant as well as cabins and camping space. Several signs that read Sorry, Closed for the Season dotted the windows. According to huge red-and-blue lettering, the whole place was straightforwardly named Bill's BBQ, Motel and Gas.

Liam docked the boat, climbed out and reached back for her. She slung the diaper bag over her shoulder, took hold of the car seat and climbed out onto the dock. Pip had just fallen asleep in the last fifteen minutes and hopefully she'd sleep for a while. The wood was slippery. Dark water rushed beneath them.

"So I take it your contact's name is Bill?" she asked.

"That's one of his names, yeah," Liam said. "Bill Leckie is what I think he's going by now. Before that it was William Hancock, Stephen Griggs, Harlow Daly and Gilbert Petticrew, among others." Liam shrugged. "He's been around a long time."

None of this was filling her with confidence. He turned slightly, like he was ready to head to the restaurant. But when she instead stood there on the dock and stretched, he stayed put.

"You said he was a criminal?" she asked. "What kind of criminal?"

"He...moves things," Liam said. "Or at least he used to. He acquires things and transports them, often across borders."

"Like weapons?" she asked.

"Nah," Liam said. "Pills and medications. There's a huge black market for cheap pharmaceuticals, especially considering different things are legal in Canada and the States. Convinced himself he was helping people. By the third time I'd arrested him, he'd gotten smart and realized it was easiest to plead guilty, take a lesser punishment and point me toward someone worse than him. He eventually started keeping his work low-key and doing more informant work for me. He claims he's gone completely legit and is in retirement."

Again, he turned to walk up toward the building, and once again she didn't budge. It was hardly her fault he hadn't felt things were up for discussion and that they hadn't been able to talk on the boat due to the wind and noise. Fact was, now that she and Pip were here, there really wasn't any reason why she couldn't just leave Liam to sort things out on his own while she and Pip tried to make their own way, somehow. The sun would be up soon. And sure, she didn't have a phone charger, a cell signal or a plan, and she was down to one final diaper change and meal for Pip. But she still had some cash, not to mention her wits.

"At the risk of sounding like a cliché," she said, "I've got a really bad feeling about this. The place looks abandoned and something about it is giving me the jitters."

"I don't blame you," Liam said. "But it's okay. Bill owes me a favor."

"What kind of favor could a former pharmaceutical drug smuggler owe you?" she asked.

"A big one," Liam said.

He turned for a third time to step off the frozen dock and head toward the building. But this time her hand darted out and grabbed his.

"Not good enough," she said.

He turned back, his eyes met hers and then he looked down at her hand holding his.

"Bill has a daughter," he said slowly. "Her name is Emily. She's six. She's his whole entire life and the reason he retired. Bill made a lot of mistakes in his life and then when he thought his life was over he was suddenly surprised to have some precious little person who needed him and loved him. A few months ago some people with an ax to grind kidnapped her. They threatened to hurt her. Bill called me. I had her back to him, unharmed and safe, by dinnertime."

He looked at the sleeping baby for a long moment. Then he looked back up at Kelly and his dark eyes met hers.

"The guys who kidnapped her are in jail now and will be for a very long time," he added. "My dad always told me that when you dedicated yourself to a rough life, surrounded by bad people, any kind of close relationship was a risk. It could throw you off your game and put the people you love in danger."

"I remember," she said.

Somehow she suspected it was the only one of his father's

tactical tips Liam had ever gotten close to breaking. He stepped back and his hand slowly, almost reluctantly, fell from hers.

"Anyway, Bill owes me a favor," Liam said. A wry smile turned at the corner of one lip on one side of his mouth. "So I told him that my former old lady was back, with a grandkid she said was mine, and we needed a place to hide."

She took in a sharp and icy breath.

"He knows I like to keep my life private," Liam said, "and that I've got a reputation within the RCMP that doesn't include having a secret grandchild due to an ill-advised, against-protocol relationship I had with someone I placed in witness protection. I might've even been kicked off the force. My career would've tanked then if news of what had happened between us had gotten out. Even now, despite whatever else is going on here, I could still face a disciplinary hearing over my past relationship with you or some kind of negative consequences to my reputation and career. But, Bill will have my back. Like I said, he owes me. Now come on, he's probably in there waiting for us."

He turned and walked toward the restaurant, so quickly and firmly she couldn't have grabbed his hand again if she'd wanted to. She followed him up the stairs and across the deck— the empty deck with its picnic tables inches deep in snow. He reached for the door, found it unlocked and pushed it open. They stepped into the restaurant. It was empty and dark. Chairs were stacked upside down on empty tables.

As the door clicked shut behind them, a young man in a thick beard stepped out from behind it and pressed the barrel of a gun to the side of Liam's head.

"Down on your knees." The voice was low and mean. His face was lost in shadows and the click of the gun was unmistakable. "You're about to learn what happens to someone who tries to lie to Bill Leckie, and it ain't going to be pretty."

# SEVEN

"You tell Bill, I didn't cross him," Liam said calmly, raising his hands, "and I await his apology when he figures that out. Now, tell me, what exactly does Bill think I've done?"

Then, before the man could even formulate an answer, Liam struck, apparently more interested in distracting his attacker long enough to get the upper hand than hearing what he had to say. Kelly watched as Liam spun toward the gun-wielding man, grabbing the weapon before he could even fire and slamming him into the wall. She felt a gust of wind and heard the door slam and click shut again. She blinked. Liam had disarmed his attacker, thrown him out and locked the door behind him, without even breaking a sweat. Then she felt Liam's strong hand on her shoulder, guiding her and the still-sleeping baby underneath a table, sheltering them with his body.

"Stay here," Liam whispered, his voice urgent. His face was just inches from hers. Worry flooded his eyes. "It's an ambush. That guy won't be alone and just because I was able to catch him off guard doesn't mean the others won't put up more of a fight." Not to mention the guy he just locked outside would be trying to get back in, no doubt. "There are other doors to this place, but we'd have to go through the kitchen or down the hallway, both of which are risky. This is an easier place to defend. Whatever Bill thinks I've done, he won't want his goons hurting you or the baby. He's got way too much honor than to allow a woman or child to get hurt on his watch, and has probably already told his attack dogs to leave you alone. I'm the one they're after. I'll get you out of here. Just promise me, if you get a clear path to escape, just take Pip and go, okay? Don't wait for me and don't look back."

Before she could answer, his hand slid to the side of her face. His lips brushed over her forehead. Then he rolled back out into the room and leaped to his feet, knocking a table in front of Kelly and Pip's hiding space as he did so, further shielding and protecting them.

"Like I told Bill, I have a woman and baby with me!" he shouted to the seemingly empty room. He tucked the gun he'd lifted into his belt. "If you're Bill's men you'll know full well that hurting innocent women and children is against his code. Whatever his problem is, it's with me, not them. And no weapon fire, please. The kid's asleep and Bill won't want you making things loud and scaring her awake."

He sounded so calm and in control, as if he was the only person there who really understood what was going on. Kelly slid Pip's car seat into the corner against the wall, sheltering it with her body and praying God would protect Pip from realizing they were in danger. Then Kelly crouched up onto the balls of her feet and looked out through gaps in the chairs and fallen table that barricaded her from view. As she watched, two more men, of varying heights, wearing plaid jackets and with full-length beards, stepped out of the shadows. Liam had been so convinced that Bill would protect them and he'd been wrong.

*Lord, please keep us safe.*

She watched as Liam raised his badge high.

"I'm Liam Bearsmith!" he shouted at the approaching men. "RCMP. Stand down! Now! Or I'll arrest you for assaulting an officer."

The taller of the two men chuckled. The other swore and told Liam in colorful language he was about to hurt him.

"Well," Liam said, "it was worth a shot."

And then, it was as if everything was happening at once. He dove and rolled behind a table on the far side of the room, disappearing from view and drawing the men away from her hiding spot. The men charged toward him. He leaped up and tossed a chair high in the air toward them. Somebody fired and the chair exploded, sending splinters raining down around them. Pip whimpered in her sleep. But Liam was already on the move, somehow coming up from behind the man who'd fired. He wrenched the weapon from his grasp and delivered a blow to his jaw that sent him to the ground. A gust of cold wind dragged her attention toward the kitchen. The man whom Liam had tossed outside had apparently run around the building, come in the front and was back to join the fray. Did that mean the coast was now clear outside again?

If she grabbed Pip and made a run for it, out the back door, would she make it? Did she really want to run without Liam? No. Somehow, she knew she didn't.

*Please, Lord, get Liam and I out of this together.*

The second man charged toward Liam now with his weapon raised. But Liam got to this one before he could even fire, catching him around the middle, and tossed him to the ground. Just one attacker left, and this one seemed determined to take Liam, dead or alive. He roared in anger, raising his weapon and firing, again and again, as Liam dodged and rolled out of the line of fire as if somehow his body knew just where every bullet was about to land. Windows shattered. Pictures cracked. Pip awoke with a howl. The weapon clicked. Liam's attacker was out of bullets and Liam was on him, sweeping out his legs with a roundhouse kick before he could even reload.

"When Bill comes groveling for this, I'm telling him you're the one who woke my grandkid," Liam said. He bent down and grabbed something from the man's pocket. Then he turned and ran for Kelly. He slid to a stop beside her hiding place, bent down on one knee and reached for her hand.

"Come on," he said. "This is when we run."

Kelly felt him grab her hand. With his other hand, Liam grabbed Pip's car seat, and almost immediately the baby's tears faded.

"Sorry, girl," Liam told Pip. "We're getting you somewhere quiet right now."

Kelly glanced toward Liam's attackers, who were now groaning on the floor, but Liam tugged her hand.

"Trust me," he said. "They'll be okay. Let's go."

They ran outside, leaving the shambles of the diner behind. They raced from the diner, past the convenience store and into a parking lot.

"Stay close!" Liam shouted. He dropped her hand and reached into his pocket, and then she realized what he'd taken from the third attacker. It was a set of car keys. He pointed them at the closest car and clicked the remote key fob. Nothing happened. Just as swiftly, he yanked the gun from his waist and shot out one of the vehicle's tires.

"Not that one," he said, as if to himself.

Two more cars and a truck lay ahead. He clicked the fob at each of them. No response. He shot out one of each of their tires, as well. Then the lights flashed on a black four-door truck ahead on their right. It was sturdy, with four-wheel drive and snow tires. Liam whispered a prayer of thanks under his breath. "That's our ride."

They ran for it. He yanked open the back door and she tumbled in with Pip.

He leaped in the front and waited as she buckled Pip's car seat in and then climbed in the front. The moment her seat belt was buckled, he hit the gas. The vehicle shot forward, swerved out of the parking lot and onto the road. She glanced back. Men were stumbling out of the restaurant into the parking lot after them, and Pip was already falling back asleep.

"I'm so sorry about that," Liam said. "I have no clue what that was about, but I promise you I'll find out." He glanced over his shoulder at Pip and then back to Kelly. His right hand reached for hers and took it, linking her fingers through his. "Are you okay? Is she okay? You weren't hit by splinters or anything?"

"We're okay," Kelly said softly. "We're both okay."

"Are you sure?" His voice was oddly husky. Something tender rumbled in its depths. And despite everything that had happened back at the restaurant, something made her suspect what upset him the most was the fact he'd put her and Pip in danger.

"I'm sure," she said. She squeezed his hand, letting her fingers run over his, and something tightened in her chest. "We're okay. Shaken up but not injured."

He whispered a prayer of thanks to God. Then he stared straight ahead down the empty road as the sun rose higher over the snowy tree line. His hand hadn't left hers and neither of them pulled away.

"Is your favorite getaway vehicle still a white truck?" Kelly asked.

His eyebrows rose. "White because it gets dirty fast and so is often overlooked," he said, almost to himself, "and a truck for maneuverability, yeah... I'm surprised you remembered."

"I remember a lot," she said.

"Yeah, so do I."

Then he pulled away his hand and something inside her missed the feel of it. Deep lines furrowed his brow. She glanced over her shoulder. So far, it looked like they weren't being followed. Then again, Liam had shot a few tires.

"Okay, so let's recap," Liam said. "Now Bill thinks I'm lying to him about something. He sends his guys after me. But doesn't come personally. So he expected they'd be able to handle me without much trouble."

There was something routine about the way he said it, as if being ambushed and having his life threatened was something he was used to. It was a little bit impressive and incredibly sad. His jaw was set so tightly it was almost clenched.

"And again," he added. "I have no idea why. But I'm going to find out."

"How?" she asked.

"I don't know yet."

Liam fell silent. The icy road spread out white ahead of them. Snow-covered trees were tinged with shadows and gray in the early morning light. For a long time he didn't say anything, and neither did she, and when she glanced at Pip she saw the baby had fallen asleep. Questions, worries and fears cascaded through her mind. Why hadn't Renner messaged her before her phone died? Was Hannah okay? Why had the cop on the boat tried to arrest Liam and why had Liam's contact, Bill, sent criminals after him? Why had both called Liam a liar?

Who'd doctored her witness-protection file and kept them apart?

Why had God allowed the man she'd once loved to crash back into her life now?

The sun rose higher, lightening the gray around them. They passed a tiny town and then a second, both barely more than a handful of buildings and a momentary speed-limit change. Tension was building inside her. She needed a phone charger. They needed food. They'd eventually need gas for the vehicle they were in, which was most definitely stolen, or a new set of wheels. More than anything, she needed information. But getting anything out of Liam was like chipping at a stone.

"So let me try the recap thing," she said. Worked for him, so she might as well try it. "Seth told you not to trust police, and after what happened with the cop on the boat, that makes sense. But based on what happened with Bill, maybe you can't trust criminal contacts, either. Renner hasn't contacted me, Hannah's been kidnapped by the Imposters and neither of us have been able to get online for almost twelve hours, so we have no actual idea what's going on in the outside world. We need food, diapers, a phone charger and a quiet, warm and safe place to lay low. Am I missing anything?"

"I'm supposed to be at a wedding sometime today," Liam said dryly, "and another one tomorrow."

"Two weddings in two days?" Kelly asked.

"Three weddings in eight." Liam cast her a sideways glance. "Every detective on the team but me is getting married over the holidays."

He nodded at something on the empty road ahead and even as she followed his gaze it took her a moment to see it. Parked ahead, half-hidden in the trees, was an Ontario Provincial Police car, its white doors dingy with snow.

She watched his lips move as if taking stock for himself.

"Speed trap," he said. "One cop. OPP. Routine traffic duty. Likely a rookie. Here we go."

"What does that mean?" she asked.

"I'm going to get myself arrested."

*He was what?* But before she could even argue, Liam gunned the engine, revving it so quickly she felt the vehicle lurch beneath her. He began to accelerate, pushing the vehicle faster and faster as they sped past the police car.

Its lights flashed and its sirens blared. She glanced back as the cop pulled onto the road and came after them.

Liam's eyes cut to the mirror.

"Okay," Liam said. "He'll sit behind us in his car for a moment and run the plates. He probably won't call for backup. Considering this truck belongs to one of Bill's men, he's unlikely to report it stolen, because Bill's never been one to get the police involved when he can avoid it. He'd rather write the vehicle off. At least my hope is that's the case and that this truck isn't linked to a crime. If all goes well, the cop will walk over here and ticket me."

Liam pulled over to the side of the long, empty highway. The cop pulled over behind him. Liam turned to Kelly.

"You've got money, right?" Liam asked, his eyes intense and

intent on hers. "Stun gun? A way to contact Renner once you charge your phone?"

"Yes." She nodded. She had all of that. But what about Liam?

"Here's what's going to happen," Liam said. "I'm going to draw him away from the car. He's going to arrest me and I'm going to let it happen. No, don't argue. I know the inner workings of law enforcement better than anyone, I know how to get answers and the name 'Detective Liam Bearsmith' still counts for something, despite what Seth might think I should do. There's only one of him so he can't detain us both and I'll be sure to tell him that you had nothing to do with this. You're going to wait until you see him handcuffing me, then go find a safe place to hide and lay low. Get rid of the car. Get a phone charger and contact Renner. I know you can do it. And I will find a way to get in touch as soon as I can. And maybe, we can meet up."

*But, maybe not?*

He glanced back. The cop had gotten out of his vehicle and was walking toward them. There was no time to argue. No time to find another plan.

Liam looked at her. "Goodbye, sweethea—" he began, but his voice caught on the last syllable like he'd just realized what he'd said. "I'm sorry."

"Don't be," she said. "You can call me that whenever you want."

And then, she kissed him.

It wasn't the first time someone had unexpectedly tried to kiss Liam Bearsmith. When he'd told Kelly the day before she'd been the only woman he'd ever kissed, that had been completely and entirely true. He hadn't so much as held another woman in his arms or even held her hand. But during his myriad undercover assignments, pretending to be a bodyguard or thug, people he was either targeting or rescuing had occasionally tried and failed to embrace him, which had always been awkward and uncomfortable, and not the slightest bit pleasant or welcomed. But this was definitely the one and only time, in over twenty years, that he'd ever kissed a woman back.

Time froze. Logically, he knew the fleeting kiss must've only lasted seconds. But there was something almost indescribable about feeling Kelly's lips brush his. It was warm and comforting. It was like coming home to a place he'd missed, or finding something he'd lost far too long ago.

No, it was like he was the one who was being found, when he hadn't even known he'd been lost.

They broke the kiss, he got out of the car and started toward the cop now walking toward him and for the first time in a long time, Liam felt an unfamiliar feeling grinding inside him. *Doubt.* Something about this whole plan he'd just concocted felt wrong. Really wrong. Yes, Seth had warned him off contacting anyone in law enforcement. But considering Liam's complete and total lack of a phone right now, getting taken in was a very effective way for him to pull rank, flex his muscles and take charge of the situation. It just made sense.

So then why did it feel like his heart was getting chewed up inside a set of invisible gears? The cop drew closer. He couldn't leave Kelly and Pip. Not without making sure they were safe. And while he was mostly sure that everything would be okay if Kelly and Pip were taken into custody by law enforcement, the number of unusual things that had happened in the past few hours gnawed at him. What if they thought Kelly had committed a crime and arrested her? What if they took Pip away from Kelly? How long would it take to get Kelly and her granddaughter reunited? Sure, he'd given Kelly his word the night before that he'd be able to make sure everything went smoothly for her and she was taken care of, but now after everything, how could he really be sure?

*Help me, Lord. What's this thing inside me? What's it trying to tell me?*

He'd failed Kelly once. He couldn't fail her again.

"Good morning, sir," the cop called. "I'm going to have to ask you to get back in your truck."

Which was protocol to avoid anyone getting hit by a passing car. Liam respected him for that. Not that every officer would worry about it on a road this desolate. Liam eyed the man, taking in all the information he could with a glance. He was young, maybe twenty-five, with a polite and professional voice and the kind of build that implied his strength wasn't just a temporary side effect of youth. He was someone who'd either volunteered for an incredibly boring, bone-chillingly cold side-of-the-road duty in the early morning that most cops would do anything to avoid, or he didn't have enough seniority to avoid it. He wasn't much older than Hannah, so was young enough to be his son.

"Get back in your car, sir," the officer repeated. "And if you'd be so kind to get your license and registration out for me."

Liam glanced back over his shoulder at Kelly. And a prayer filled his heart as his eyes met hers. *Help me, Lord. What do I do?* He could put Kelly in danger by getting her arrested, or leave her to fend on her own, or make this cop's life a whole lot harder. And he never liked making a good cop's life difficult.

He turned back to the cop. The young man's hand reached for his weapon, but his tone remained both firm and polite.

"I said, get back in your truck."

*Lord, forgive me for what I'm about to do.*

Liam turned and ran.

"Hey!" the cop yelled. "Stop!"

Oh, he would, Liam thought, as soon as he figured out what his game plan was. For now, he was buying himself all the time he could. Liam raised his hands high, showing the cop pursuing him that he was unarmed. Liam passed the car, putting as much distance between himself and it as possible. The idea that he could evade this cop, give Kelly a chance to drive off and then double back and find her again crossed his mind. Then another realization hit him. The young man was actually gaining on him. This man could possibly outrun him. For the first time in his life, the great Liam Bearsmith was actually about to be outrun and taken down by a younger, fitter cop. Huh. Well, that narrowed his options. There was only one thing left—he had to put his trust in the training, dedication and innate goodness of the men and women in blue he'd served alongside his entire career and pray the man behind him now was no exception.

"Sorry, change of plan!" Liam called. "I'm surrendering!"

Before he could turn, the cop launched into him, tackling Liam hard from behind and forcing him down on the ground. The two men tumbled and Liam rolled clumsily, clutching the other man as if to steady himself in a move he hoped looked more accidental than intentional.

"I'm sorry!" Liam said. His hand brushed the cop's shoulder. "I'm really, really sorry."

And he was, especially for everything that was about to happen next.

The young man leaped to his feet, instinctively checking that his gun was secure, but missing the fact Liam had just disabled his radio.

The man stepped back, pulled his weapon and aimed it at Liam with both hands.

"Stay down!" The cop's voice rose. "Hands up!"

Textbook, Liam thought admiringly. He crouched on the balls of his feet and raised his hands.

"I'm sorry," Liam said again, "but you would not believe the night I had. People keep trying to either kill me, drug me, shoot at me or arrest me. It's been crazy. I know I should've stayed in the vehicle, but there's an innocent woman and infant in there, and I wanted to get them as far away from me and my mess as possible. I really don't want anyone getting hurt because of me."

"Nobody's going to get hurt," the cop replied and while his weapon didn't waver an inch, Liam could tell the young man was actually listening. Yeah, Liam was definitely going to recommend him for a promotion when this whole mess was cleared. "Now, again, I need to see your license and registration."

"I don't have it!" Liam called. "I was robbed at gunpoint a few hours ago by masked criminals who took it. They took everything, except my police badge. Run the number, I'm Detective Liam Bearsmith, RCMP. And you're OPP, right?"

Something flickered behind the young man's eyes, but all he said was, "Constable Jake Marlie, Ontario Provincial Police, Thousand Islands Detachment."

Liam snorted. "Marley, like the Christmas ghost?"

"No, Marlie like the Toronto hockey team."

"Can I call you Jake?" Liam asked.

"No." Constable Marlie shook his head. "Now, tell me again, what's your name?"

"I already told you," Liam said. "But clearly you don't believe me! Which isn't new. So how about you tell me why nobody believes I'm who I say I am?"

Constable Marlie didn't answer. Instead he turned his head toward his radio and called for backup, shooting off police codes rapid-fire. There was 10-33, 10-35, 10-62, 10-26 and 10-64—which basically summed up as "come help me quick, there's a major crime alert about a possible suspect who needs to be detained quickly—proceed with caution." Marlie added 10-93—calling for a roadblock. Then Marlie's brow furrowed. He'd realized his radio wasn't working.

*Lord, help me de-escalate this before it gets out of hand.*

"Get down!" Constable Marlie yelled. "On the ground. Hands behind your head."

There was a click and Liam watched as the truck door opened behind him and Kelly stepped out. The early morning light caught her features, illuminating her form in an almost ethereal glow.

"Get back in the truck!" Liam called.

But she ignored him and instead focused on the officer.

"Hey, Constable!" Kelly yelled. "Mind telling me why nobody believes him when he tells them who he is?"

Constable Marlie spun.

"Ma'am," he shouted and his voice rose. "Get back in the vehicle! Now!"

"I can't do that," Kelly shouted. "Not until somebody explains what's going on. You're going to have to arrest me first."

And something snapped inside Liam like a rubber band that had been stretched too far returning back to its normal length. He leaped, catching Constable Marlie's arm, and then wrestled the weapon from his hands. Then he marched Marlie back to the truck and pushed him against the hood of the truck, as if he was the uniformed cop and Marlie was the suspect.

"Don't worry," Liam said. "I'm not going to hurt you. I promise. You're a good cop and I respect that. I'm just going to cuff you with your own handcuffs long enough for us to talk and sort this out. And then I'm going to let you go."

He wrenched the cop's hands behind his back and cuffed them.

"I feel really bad about this," Liam added. "Don't take it personally. Because as one cop to another, I can tell you that you did everything by the book. I've just got like two decades experience on you and an encyclopedic knowledge of how you do our job. That's all."

Then he turned the constable around and stepped back.

"When this mess is all cleared up and I file my police report about this," Liam added, "I'll make sure it reflects your professionalism and recommends you for promotion. I'm genuinely impressed."

Although, it was clear by the look in the cop's eyes he wasn't much impressed with Liam and didn't believe a word he was saying.

"Now, please, tell me why people keep trying to kill me and don't believe me when I tell them who I am?" Liam asked.

"Liam Bearsmith is dead," Constable Marlie said bluntly. Then despite all obvious evidence to the contrary, he added, "And you're under arrest for his murder."

# EIGHT

She watched as Liam startled, like his whole being was shaken by the news. Then he stepped back and offered his own hand to help the cuffed constable stand. Liam opened his mouth but no words came out, and he closed it again. He looked up to the sky in what she guessed was either silent prayer, processing or both. Then finally he turned back to the officer.

"Well, that's a new one," Liam said. "First of all, Constable Marlie, total respect for trying to tell me that I was under arrest when you were the one in handcuffs. You remind me of myself at your age, and I mean that as a compliment. Secondly, and I can't believe I'm saying this, but I'm not dead and I'm not my own murderer. So why would you possibly think I was?"

Constable Marlie didn't even blink—instead, his chin rose.

"Let's start with the fact it's all over the news," Marlie said. "The cruise ship had security cameras, plus people posted videos online. There's clear footage of your...of Bearsmith's death, including you shooting him—"

"Me?" Liam interrupted.

"A man who looks similar enough to Bearsmith to pass for him," Constable Marlie explained as he turned to Kelly, "but who clearly isn't the same man if you look closely enough.

This man not only killed the RCMP officer, he stole his identity. There's a nationwide warrant out for his arrest. Divers are searching Lake Ontario for his body. So I don't know when the actual funeral will be. But there's going to be a candlelight vigil for the real Liam Bearsmith in Ottawa tonight at seven. Police officers are coming from across Canada to attend."

Then Constable Marlie's eyes cut back to Liam and something hardened in their depths.

"This man's name is Steve Parker," he said. "He looks similar enough to Bearsmith, but if you put pictures of him and Bearsmith side by side it's easy enough to tell them apart. This man's a bit shorter, heavier set and the shape of his face and nose are different."

Kelly felt her eyebrows rise. Liam rocked back on his heels and let out a long breath.

"Steve Parker is one of my deep covers," he said. A rumble almost like a roar was building in the back of his throat. "Last used him about eighteen months ago."

He ran both hands over his face as if trying to wipe away his former cover. Then he turned to Kelly.

"You know I'm really me, right?" he asked her. And she was surprised to see how much doubt filled his eyes. "I know I look different than I used to. I mean, I know it's been over twenty years and I probably don't look anything like you remember. I'm a lot older and battle-worn. I've got a few more scars, I'm nowhere near as fit as I used to be and my nose has been literally bent out of shape."

"Stop it," Kelly said firmly. "Of course I know who you are. You're you, and you're perfect at it."

His eyes widened. Okay, she wasn't sure why *perfect* was the word she'd blurted out. Her hand brushed his jaw and she felt him shiver slightly under her touch.

"I know you, Liam," she went on. "You're the same stubborn, driven, too-independent-for-your-own-good, cop-through-and-through man that you've always been."

Suddenly she remembered how natural it had felt when she'd spontaneously kissed him. And how he'd kissed her back.

She stepped back and looked at Constable Marlie.

"Obviously heard of the Imposters?" she demanded. "You know, the slew of young men in masks and eye patches who took over the boat?" The look on Constable Marlie's face didn't confirm much of an answer one way or the other. She pressed on. "The Imposters are cybercriminals. The original two died last year after stealing the RCMP's witness-protection database and trying to auction it off to criminals online. Now this new bunch have sprung up. Can you imagine how impossible it is to take out an organization with no leader or set goals? I can't. They're threatening global chaos." *They kidnapped our daughter!* "They're behind this. And we have to stop them. That's all that matters."

She heard the sound of a vehicle rumbling softly up the empty and desolate road toward them. Instinctively, it seemed, Liam stepped between them and the passing car to shield them from view.

"Come on," Liam said, his voice thick with an emotion she couldn't place. "Let's see what we can find out, quickly, and then get out of Constable Marlie's hair and let him go on his way. Thankfully, several sectors of law enforcement have implemented an automated fingerprint-identification system. All I've got to do is run my fingerprints through it and it'll prove who I am."

It was such an incredibly simple and almost anticlimactic solution that there was something comforting about it. Less than five minutes later, Kelly was sitting in the back of Constable Marlie's patrol car with the door wide open, to allay her fear of getting locked in, and baby Pip reluctantly awake again and bouncing on her lap.

Liam sat in the driver's seat, with the still-handcuffed Constable Marlie in the passenger seat. She was frankly amazed at how Marlie had been mostly listening and observing. Had she been in the constable's shoes, she would have been alternating between shouting the place down and asking nonstop questions. But Marlie seemed focused on listening and taking in as much information as possible. She suspected Liam would've done the same.

She held her breath as Liam scanned his own fingerprints and ran them through the police's automated fingerprint-identification system, comparing them to the ones on file for Liam Bearsmith. Then she watched as the color drained from his face.

"They're not a match," Liam said. He looked back at her over his shoulder. "They changed my fingerprints. Somebody actually hacked into my official RCMP police file and changed my fingerprints." He scanned the laptop screen and his scowl deepened. "My height, my age, my weight, even my official photo—they've all been tweaked. Somebody actually hacked into my official file and tried to get rid of me."

He let out a hard breath and stuttered some unintelligible syllables under his breath, like he was trying to make words but his tongue was failing.

"Somebody changed my official witness-protection file, too," she reminded him.

*To make it look like I was married to drive us apart. And then that I was dead.*

Liam turned to the constable.

"How do I find this video footage that apparently shows a version of me killing me?" he asked. "Where exactly is it?"

"The internet," the cop said dryly, with just the slightest tinge of sarcasm in his voice, as if he'd just stopped himself from calling Liam "Grandpa." "It's literally all over the internet. You just need to put your name in a search engine and it will come up."

*Your name,* Kelly noted.

Liam did so, found an entire page's worth of videos and clicked the first one. A shaky video appeared, with bad audio and low-res graphics. There was a younger, fitter and stronger version of Liam Bearsmith kneeling on the deck of the boat with his hands raised, looking so movie-star impressive he might as well have been airbrushed. There was a tired, older, shivering, wet and exhausted-looking Liam, who looked a lot more like the man now sitting in front of her, taking Superstar Liam's wallet and badge before holding a gun to his head and shooting him. Superstar Liam collapsed in a pool of blood. Tired Liam turned and looked directly at the camera.

"Well...that..." Liam shook his head. She glanced at him in the rearview mirror. Any remaining vestiges of blood fled his face, leaving his skin as ashen as the dirty snow outside. "That...is... I... Wow..."

"It's what's called a deep fake," Kelly said quickly. "They use computer-generated images and digitally altered existing footage to create this. It's not real."

Then a stray and disconcerting thought crossed her mind. She'd never asked Hannah how she knew for sure Renner was alive and that it was him communicating with her. Could that have been faked, as well? Could he really have created a master-key decryption device and been killed for it, and it had been somebody else pretending to be him to lure Hannah into danger?

"If I didn't know any better I'd think a younger and stronger version of myself traveled through time and I killed him," Liam said wearily.

"Yeah, that's the point," Kelly said, forcing her worrying thoughts aside for a moment. "Judging by the time stamp, it was posted online minutes before that cop tried to arrest you on the boat. Which might explain why he was so off his game, if he'd just gotten word you had a murderous doppelgänger on the loose. I'm guessing that's also why Seth told you to go dark and a man whose daughter you saved sent goons to kill you. Guess the downside of being famous and beloved is that everyone wants to help avenge your murder."

"I'm neither of those things," Liam muttered. He turned to Constable Marlie. "And this is all over the internet?"

"And television," Marlie said. "It's the top trending story on all the major social-media sites. It's international news."

Liam pressed his lips together and nodded slowly.

"Well, Kelly," he said. "Seems you were right about thinking we should've gotten online as soon as possible." He really was waking up to a whole new world. One where he was both dead and wanted for murder. "How do we get this off the internet and prove that I'm not dead and not an evil double who murdered the real me, before the next person we run into isn't as professional as Constable Jake Marlie here and instead has a shoot-first, ask-questions-second mentality?"

"With a lot of difficulty," she admitted, "and a lot of help."

She watched as Liam closed his eyes and a silent prayer crossed his lips. Then he turned to Constable Marlie.

"You're a great cop from what I've seen and I don't want to do anything to hurt your career," Liam said. "If I give you the key, do you know how to get your hands free from the cuffs?" Marlie shook his head. "Well, it's a good skill to learn, and I'll cuff one hand to the steering wheel instead to make it easier. Then I'll leave you with the key, let the air out of your tires and go. By the time you radio for help and they get here, we'll be gone."

"Look," Constable Marlie began, "I don't know what's going on and I'm not saying I'm convinced you're Liam Bearsmith but—"

Liam held up a hand to silence him.

"No," he said. "I'm Steve Parker, or whoever. That's all you know. You stick with that. Because if I was Liam Bearsmith, the last thing I'd want or need right now is for whoever's behind this to think that I have a clue what's going on. I'd want them to think I'm clueless. And I also wouldn't want a good cop taking collateral damage over this, either. Got it?"

The constable nodded.

Liam turned to Kelly. "Take Pip back to the truck and get her buckled in. I'll meet you there in five."

She did as he asked, saying a quick goodbye to Constable Marlie because it felt wrong to just walk away without saying something. True to his word, Liam met her back at the truck four minutes later.

"Thanks to the constable's computer, I've confirmed that law enforcement have mounted a full-scale operation to locate and rescue Hannah," he said as he slid back into the driver's seat. He closed the door and did up his seat belt. "The good news is that she appears to be safe and unharmed for now. The Imposters have been posting about her online, offering to trade her safe return for Renner's decryption key."

"But Renner hasn't responded, has he?" she asked.

Liam shook his head. "No, why?"

"Because almost all of Hannah's communication with Renner has been typing," she said. "They've only had a few quick video calls. What if you were right? What if Renner is dead and it was all faked? What if no one was ever going to message me back?"

Liam reached for her hand and squeezed it. "She's alive, and we're going to find her. That's all that matters right now." He glanced over his shoulder at the baby in the back in her car seat.

"Restless," Kelly said. "Along with needing food and a steady supply of fresh diapers, I'm worried she's not getting enough time to stretch and move. She's very wriggly. Even babies this little need time to play."

"Understood," Liam said. He pulled out onto the road and started driving.

Her eyes glanced to the clock. It was almost eight in the morning and had been less than eleven hours since she'd bumped into Liam back on the Toronto docks.

"I feel bad for Constable Marlie," Liam said after a long moment.

"He knew it was you," Kelly said. "Not at first, but by the end you'd convinced him."

"Maybe," Liam said. "When this is all sorted I'll make sure his career doesn't take a hit for this."

"For arresting the incomparable Liam Bearsmith when he was on the run under false charges?" Kelly asked. "Or for the fact a suspected criminal overpowered him and handcuffed him?"

"A bit of both," Liam said. "Maybe more A than B."

He was quiet for a long moment. Her eyes gazed over at the impossibly incredible and handsome man, whom she felt closer to than she'd ever felt to anyone else, and yet in some ways who still felt like a stranger. His brow was furrowed. He'd been willing to throw away a career in law enforcement for her, and now his dedication to it was so strong he was worried about the junior-level officer who'd tried to arrest him.

Maybe it had been right he'd ended up in the RCMP instead of with her.

Liam turned toward her, as if sensing her eyes on his face. "Do you want to go to a wedding?"

Detective Jessica Eddington stood alone in the tiny study of the apartment on the second floor of Tatlow's Used Books in the small town of Kilpatrick, Ontario. Jess looked somewhat like a fairy-tale princess, Liam thought as he cautiously stepped foot onto the freezing second-floor fire-escape platform and continued to watch her through the window, to ensure she was actually alone. Her long blond hair was somehow both piled on top of her head and falling in loose waves around her shoulders, and the white cape that draped over her white wedding dress seemed to fall in glittery waves all the way to the floor. Jess spun toward the window, yanked her weapon from somewhere inside the shimmering fabric and aimed it straight between his eyes.

Liam's hands rose.

"Jess!" He hissed. "It's me! Liam! I'm—I'm not dead."

But he'd barely gotten a handful of words into his rambling explanation when the bride dropped the weapon back into some hidden pocket in her dress, ran across the study and yanked open the window.

"Liam!" A delighted smile burst across her face, like a little sister welcoming her brother home from college. "Come in! Get in!"

Despite being half his size, pretty much, she practically yanked him through the window.

"I'm not dead," he said again.

"I know!" She laughed. "Now get in before anyone sees you."

"Did Seth fill you in on the situation?" he asked.

Jess's eyes widened. "I haven't heard from Seth in hours. He was supposed to be one of our witnesses, but then he sent a text to both Travis and I in the middle of the night saying he wouldn't make it to the wedding. According to Travis, Willow isn't that happy with him over it."

No, Liam didn't think she would be. Six-year-old Willow definitely had strong opinions about things and was a force to be reckoned with. Seth had grown close to former detective Travis Tatlow, his adopted daughter, Willow, and her baby brother, Dominic, when Seth and Jess had gone undercover to help them escape deadly criminals from Travis's past last June.

What could possibly be serious enough to make Seth miss Travis and Jess's wedding?

"Mack, Noah and I did touch base about you briefly this morning," Jess added, referring to the other two detectives on their team, Mack Grey and Noah Wilder. "We agreed that if any of us heard anything, we'd tell the other two right away."

And Liam had a lot to fill them in on. He glanced down at the truck, now with altered plates, he'd parked in the alley below. "I've got people with me. A friend of mine and a baby. My..." He swallowed hard and forced the words over his lips. "My granddaughter. Turns out I have a baby granddaughter. They need a place to hide."

Jess's blue eyes went wide.

But all she said was "Well, they're safe here. I've still got one of Dominic's old cribs and playpens here. I'm pretty sure we have formula. There are a few diapers in the bathroom. I don't know if we'd have any the baby's size, but we might. Check in the back of the cupboard. Either way, there's a drugstore just down the street."

Travis had become like a father figure to little Willow and Dominic while in witness protection and he'd eventually adopted them when they became orphaned. The love that Jess felt for Travis and the kids practically radiated through her. Gratitude overwhelmed him.

"Thank you," he said. "But we can't stay."

"Of course you can stay." Jess's arms crossed.

"But, it's your wedding day," Liam said.

"Yeah, I know it's my wedding day." She laughed. "I'm the one in the big white dress. And you're not going to miss it. How many years have we worked together? Five? Six? And how many times did you save my life or have my back?"

He wasn't sure. He didn't keep count. It wasn't the kind of thing a person did in a job like this.

"Travis, the kids and I might not even be alive today without your backup," Jess said. "So you're coming to my wedding and that's final. The church has a small balcony that's never used. We'll close it off and you can hide there. We'll find somebody both you and I trust to watch the baby. Then after the wedding, we'll sit down with the rest of the team and figure this all out."

He almost laughed. "But. It's. Your. Wedding. Day."

"I know!" She laughed. "And don't worry. I'm heading to church soon and getting married in about an hour. I'll still catch a flight to Florida with my new husband for our honeymoon tonight. Noah and Holly will still be getting married tomorrow and Mack and Iris will still be getting married on New Year's Eve. But we can still be there for you, too."

Jess's smile was gentle, but her blue eyes were strong.

"Go get your friend and your granddaughter," Jess insisted. "We'll get them sorted, and I'll fill the team in. Just let me have the wedding and get married, then we'll carve out a little bit of time to meet back here and hash things out before the reception. It'll give Travis and I a nice little interlude between doing all the fancy, formal wedding things. Considering the fact we have a one-year-old and a six-year-old in the wedding party, we planned a pretty short ceremony, and the reception's a potluck at the volunteer fire hall." Her eyes glanced to the clock. "I should have the team back here in two and a half hours. Maybe three. Don't worry. It'll be fine."

"Thank you," Liam said, suddenly finding it hard to speak words as something welled in his throat.

Sure, he'd been there to help rescue her, Travis and the children from violent criminals, and to assist her out of a few tight spots. But that was the job. That was what he did. Maybe even, on some level, what God had put him on the planet to do. What Jess was doing now somehow felt like so much more.

"Now again, hurry up and get your people," Jess said. "I can't wait to meet them."

His people. Huh. He'd never thought of himself as having people before.

"Kelly," he said. "My friend's name is Kelly. She's...the grandmother of my grandchild. We haven't seen each other in a very long time. I didn't even know we had a child. The baby's name is Pip. It's a nickname. They haven't named her yet." He ran his hand over the back of his neck. "Sorry, I don't even know what to say about this situation yet. It's all very complicated and confusing."

Jess nodded. "Family often is."

And there was something about the simplicity of her answer that helped.

"Not sure how to say this, but you look really nice, by the way," Liam added, partly to change the subject, but mostly because it was true. "Like a princess only not cheesy."

"Thank you," Jess said. "Willow helped pick it out. She has a matching dress in navy and silver. According to Travis, she was running around in the cape all last night and he barely talked her out of sleeping in it. Considering she's six, my getup could've been much more sparkly. I barely talked her out of tiaras."

Liam chuckled. "Travis was really blessed to find you."

"We're blessed to have found each other."

Liam turned to go, then paused as a question he'd forgotten to ask crossed his mind. "Why do you have your service weapon—a gun—in your wedding dress?"

"Because for some reason the world thinks Liam Bearsmith is dead," Jess said. "And while I didn't know why or what that meant, I was pretty sure he couldn't be."

He could still hear her laughing as he climbed back down the fire escape to get Kelly and Pip, and then he hid the truck.

There was something peaceful, almost homelike, about how the next hour passed. Jess let them in through the closed bookstore instead of making them climb the fire escape with the baby. It turned out there was indeed a diaper Pip's size hiding in the back of the closet, and before Jess left to join her bridesmaids and get ready for her wedding, she had a friend drop by with a fresh box of diapers, two different types of formula and a bag of donated baby clothes. Then Liam and Kelly camped out on the living-room floor and spread out a Noah's Arc play mat for Pip to stretch and wriggle on, along with fuzzy animal toys that squeaked, crinkled and rattled. They leaned against pillows, played with the baby and ate a simple meal of ham-and-cheese sandwiches and fruit, thanks to Jess's insistence they help clear out what was left in the fridge.

A small television was on in the corner and they watched the twenty-four-hour news station, with the sound off, for news about the Imposters. Kelly's phone charged and Liam used one of Travis's tablet computers to scan the internet in vain for more information about the new Imposters, Hannah's kidnapping and his supposed death.

Despite the tension and fear, a comfortable silence fell between them, while hundreds of words tumbled silently through

Liam's brain that he left unsaid. He glanced over to where Kelly was kneeling, her long dark hair falling around her face as she played with Pip.

Something ached like a deep wound buried by scar tissue inside his chest.

*Lord, I'd have given anything for this beautiful, amazing woman to be my family. Why were we torn apart? Who can we be to each other now?*

She glanced up, as if sensing his gaze. Their eyes met. Emotions crashed like waves over his heart.

*I wish I hadn't believed you'd moved on without me. I wish I'd been brave enough to show up at your door and find out myself. I wish I hadn't let my father talk me into forgetting you and moving on, for the sake of my career. I wish I'd had the courage to have my heart broken to my face. I should've come back for you.*

Her lips parted slowly. He watched as silent words formed there. But before she could speak them, a buzz sounded behind her. She spun.

"It's the phone!" she yelped. She snatched it from the cord. "It's Renner. I've got a message from Renner!"

She squeezed the phone in both hands for a moment and clutched it to her chest. Then she typed a quick response and set it back down.

"It's all good news," she said. "Renner has found Hannah. He'll be rescuing her later today and then coming to pick up Pip and I. We'll all be reunited and leaving Canada by tonight."

The warmth and joy that flushed her cheeks did nothing to temper the cold dread that spread over Liam's limbs. Something about this was wrong. Very wrong. But for once his mind was too murky to figure out what.

Then she frowned. "Renner's telling me to turn on the news."

He turned to the television and froze as he stared in disbelief at the face filling the screen.

"A warrant has been issued for hacker Seth Miles's arrest," he said, reading out loud, "on suspicion of being the Imposter mastermind behind the holiday party boat hijacking."

# NINE

"Don't believe it!" Liam said quickly. "Just because the news says that Seth's an Imposter doesn't make it true. I don't know why the news is saying that, but there has to be a reason."

"The Imposters are exactly the kind of group he'd have teamed up with in the past," Kelly said.

"I know," Liam said. "But he's changed."

Footsteps sounded on the stairs.

"Get behind me!" he ordered. In an instant, he leaped in front of Pip and Kelly, sheltering them with his body, just as two figures appeared at the top of the stairs.

Tall and lanky, Detective Mack Grey had an intensity that had allowed him to move through countless criminal hotbeds undetected, while his fiancée, social worker Iris James, had a light and airy smile that lit up a room, which was coupled with an endless drive to help those in need. They'd fallen in love when Mack had been undercover and he'd risked everything to be with Iris. And yet, it was nothing compared to what Liam would've faced if his relationship with Kelly had become public.

Notably, despite the fact that Jess's wedding was probably minutes away, they were both in blue jeans and sweatshirts.

"Whoa, hey! What are you guys doing here?" Tension fled

Liam's shoulders as he stepped sideways and reached for Kelly's hand to help her up. "Kelly, this is Mack, one of the detectives on my team, and Iris, who runs a homeless drop-in center in downtown Toronto. Two of the best people I know."

"Nice to meet you!" Kelly said, and as she stepped beside him, Liam found himself brushing Kelly's back right between her shoulder blades. Her hand reached out and shook theirs in turn. Then she glanced down. "This is Pip."

Liam gestured to the television screen. "Tell me you know something about this."

"Yeah." Mack nodded. "A friend gave me a heads-up about the warrant. I don't know where they're getting the intel and I don't believe it for a moment." Then the detective looked down at Pip. Liam watched as a question hovered in Mack's eyes. He suspected his colleague had heard the rumor and wanted to hear from Liam's own mouth if it was true. "Now, please tell me this isn't what I think it is."

"Pip is...her... My... Our...granddaughter," Liam said. As awkward as the words felt leaving his lips, somehow they felt just a little bit easier every time he said them. "Kelly and I met a very long time ago, when I was placing her in witness protection. She's the hacker who kept Hannah Phillips's file out of the Imposters's hands last year. Hannah is our daughter... I—I didn't know about Hannah or Pip until yesterday."

Mack didn't say anything at first. Instead, he just stood there, his eyes on Liam's face. It was like two gunslingers waiting to see if the other would flinch as an uncomfortable pause spread around the room.

"Mack tried to place me in witness protection, too," Iris said to Kelly, as the two women sat on the play mat and turned their attention to Pip.

But there was far more to the story than that. And Liam understood, or at least he thought he did, the conflicting emotions behind Mack's gaze.

Mack had been suspended and had faced a significant knock

Christmas Witness Conspiracy

to his career after it was suspected he and Iris had gotten too close when he was on an undercover assignment. This was despite the fact Mack had never even acted on his romantic attraction to Iris. Mack had risked absolutely everything for the woman he was about to marry. He'd paid a hefty price for falling in love on assignment. But Liam had broken the rules on a much bigger scale, kept it pretty much a secret and then had gone on to have a stellar career afterward with people being none the wiser.

"I didn't know," Liam told Mack quietly, stepping away from the women and lowering his voice. "Someone covered it up. I'm guessing to protect me. I was immediately sent on a long undercover assignment. None of Kelly's messages got to me and her RCMP witness-protection file was doctored. I will always regret I didn't do more to fight for her back then."

It was an admission that had been building for a long time, like steam wanting to escape from the top of his heart. And considering everything Mack had been through to be with Iris, he was the right person to admit it to.

"But what happens now?" Mack asked. "If word gets out that you fathered a child with a witness—even if it was twenty years ago—there will be consequences. You'll be investigated. You could be suspended or demoted. You might even be fired."

*Or nobody ever has to know.* Liam felt something inside him push back. Kelly was still planning on leaving the country with Hannah, Renner and Pip. He'd only confided anything about the relationship to a tiny handful of people, all of whom he trusted. There was no reason why the news would need to come out. Not unless Kelly wanted to stay in his life in some kind of present and visible way, and there was no proof or evidence she wanted to do that.

"In case you haven't heard, I'm dead," Liam said with a laugh that even sounded hollow to himself.

"So you'd actually keep it a secret?" Mack asked, and again, there was an edge to his voice. No, it was more like a knife, peeling away at something Liam didn't want touched. And even though he knew Mack was a good man who meant well and wanted what was best for him, Liam felt his jaw tighten.

"Don't worry," Liam said. "I'll do the right thing." *As soon as I figure out what that is and where we go from here.* "Shouldn't you be heading to the wedding?"

"We're actually here to babysit," Mack said, raising his voice to include Kelly and Iris, as well. "We're going to watch Pip for an hour while you and Kelly go to the wedding. Jess said she's got the balcony closed off, so you guys can sit there."

Liam watched as his friend's arms crossed over his strong chest. His tone, while warm, implied it wasn't up for debate. No wonder they'd both shown up in jeans.

"You should go to the wedding," Liam stated.

"And so should you," Mack countered. "You've worked with Jess even more than I have. Iris and I don't even know Travis. Jess and Travis wouldn't even be getting married if you hadn't helped save their lives." Then he glanced at Iris and something softened in his eyes. "Iris and I wouldn't be getting married on New Year's Eve if you hadn't helped save our lives, either. Liam, we owe our lives to you. I know I do."

Liam's head shook. "I'm not going to let you—"

"Stop." Mack held up a hand. "Let me do this. You've done so very much for me. For all of us. Besides, it'll give me a chance to just hang out with Iris and relax. Between everything going on at the drop-in center over Christmas, two weddings this weekend and our own wedding next week, we haven't had a quiet hour to just sit around and do nothing in forever. I can also use the time to read up on your so-called death, the warrant out against Seth, the Imposters and Hannah and Renner Phillips for when we all meet up and plan our way forward between the wedding and reception." Then he grinned. "And we'll still be going to the reception. I'm not missing barbecued ribs and cake."

Liam chuckled softly. If he stood here and argued with Mack

much longer, none of them would be making it to the wedding. Besides, Mack was already sitting on the play mat.

"I give you my word your granddaughter will be safe," Mack said. "I will guard her with my life."

Liam knew he would. He turned to Kelly and as she started to stand, he found himself reaching for her hand.

"What do you think?" he asked as her fingers lingered for a moment in his. "Mack is an incredible officer, and I'd trust him with my life and yours and Pip's. The church is only a few minutes' walk from here. But I'm not going anywhere without you. I want to be there if Renner calls or if you get an update on Hannah. Whatever we decide, I think we should stick together."

He didn't know how to explain it to her, let alone to himself, but something inside him couldn't bear the thought of not having Kelly there by his side.

Kelly looked up at him and bit her lip. And he realized she still hadn't pulled her hand away from his.

"Pip will be safe here," he added. "Travis installed a state-of-the-art security system in this apartment when he was first placed in witness protection, and then Seth upgraded it even more."

He felt himself frown as he said Seth's name. Where was he? Why had he decided to skip Jess and Travis's wedding? Why was the world now convinced he was an Imposter? True, Seth had made some dubious decisions. But still.

"Iris runs both teen-mom and high-risk parenting groups at the drop-in," Mack added. Pride gleamed in his eyes as he looked at his fiancée. "I promise you we'll keep Pip safe."

"But it's up to you," Liam said. "If you want to stay, we stay."

"And where I go, you go," Kelly said, softly. She nodded slightly, as if coming to a decision, then pulled her hand from his and turned to Mack. "Thank you. I don't know how much Pip is able to pick up of what we're feeling. But maybe it will be good for Pip to have a break from us to play with a friendly new face. I think I need to take a walk, breathe and pray, too. And right now a church feels like the right place to be."

Yeah, he understood that feeling, too. Pip cooed and waved her arms at him as Liam bent down to kiss the top of the tiny baby's head goodbye. He was surprised just how much it tugged at his heartstrings to leave her, even if it was only for an hour and with someone he trusted implicitly. How hard would it be when Kelly and Pip left his life for good?

Kelly declined Iris's kind offer to lend her something fancy, but accepted her follow-up offer of a spare T-shirt and change of sweater. She'd freshened up and done something else to her appearance before they left, too, but Liam wasn't sure what. Changed her hair, maybe? Added lip gloss? He wasn't sure. All he knew as they walked in comfortable silence to the small church was that Kelly somehow looked even more beautiful than ever in a way he couldn't put a finger on.

The small church sat alone on a small rural road surrounded by fields. It was already full—the service was about to start and nobody seemed to notice them—as they snuck in a side door and up into the empty balcony. There they sat, on battered folding chairs, and watched as the wedding unfolded beneath them. Travis stood at the front of the church, holding baby Dominic in his arms—they wore matching tuxedos with dark blue bow ties. Willow practically twirled with joy as she walked Jess down the aisle, their smiles shining more than the dazzling beads on their dresses and the winter light shimmering through the window ever could.

Liam felt Kelly's thumb run over his and he looked down at their hands. Their fingers were linked. And he couldn't even remember when they'd started holding hands or which one of them had initiated it.

Noah Wilder, the fourth and final detective on his team, and his fiancée, Corporal Holly Asher, stepped up to the lectern and began to read a passage from Song of Solomon together. "'Set me as a seal upon thine heart, as a seal upon thine arm, for love is strong as death..."'

"They're the couple getting married tomorrow," Liam whispered. "They're also the two that stopped the witness-protection auction and were there when the initial Imposters were killed. If these Imposters are out for revenge, these two are probably in the line of fire, too."

Kelly nodded.

"'Many waters cannot quench love, neither can the floods drown it,'" Noah and Holly continued. "'If a man would give all the substance of his house for love, it would be utterly contemned.'"

*Contemned,* Liam thought. In other words, it was contemptible to trade worldly possessions for love. And what had he traded for love? A career? A job? His father had spent his childhood drilling into him that close relationships and a career taking out bad guys just didn't mix. But during the past year, Liam had watched the other three detectives on his team, and the people they were now marrying, give up so much for each other. And Liam hadn't even been willing to drive to Kelly's door and see for himself that she'd moved on for someone else.

"Have you ever wished for all that?" Kelly whispered. "A marriage, a family, kids?"

"Never," Liam admitted. "Not even once. To be honest, once I was told you'd moved on without me, and we disappeared from each other's lives, the thought of marriage and kids never crossed my mind again."

"Because of your job?" she asked.

"Because of you," Liam said. "Because losing you hurt so much I didn't even know if my stupid broken heart was even capable of beating again."

He watched as her lips parted, then he looked down at their hands.

"I've been shot," he said. "Too many times. I've been stabbed, punched and kicked. My nose has been broken. I've had a concussion and been in a medically induced coma. I've faced down way too many rooms full of killers. And somehow, none of that ever scared me off going right back into another undercover case. I never even hesitated. I guess I was just wired that way."

Then he pulled his hand away from hers, feeling their fingers brush against each other as they parted.

"But losing you was a one-and-done thing for me," he admitted. "It was the worst thing I'd ever gone through and I never wanted to feel it again."

Everyone stood and the room burst into song. The service was ending. He touched Kelly's arm, guiding her to follow him as he dropped to the floor so that anyone looking up while leaving wouldn't spot them. She sat cross-legged and he sat with his back to the wedding, facing her.

"I told myself and anyone else who would listen that I was married to my job," Liam said. "But maybe, if I'm honest, it was always you."

"It was always you for me, too," she said.

Below them he could hear people shuffling out of the church. Kelly leaned forward and her hand brushed his jaw. He couldn't imagine ever trusting anyone else to touch his face like that. His fingers ran up into her hair.

Then he kissed her. Despite the fact he was still in no place for a relationship, their lives were uncertain and she'd be leaving his life as soon as Renner texted her back, he let his lips linger on hers and his hand reach for hers. Here alone in the church balcony, surrounded by the smells of wood and candles, old books and flowers, it was just him and Kelly. And he wasn't about to miss what could be his last chance to hold her the way his foolish heart had longed to since he'd first laid eyes on her back on the docks.

They broke the kiss, but didn't pull away. Instead they stayed there, with Kelly's head on Liam's shoulder and his arms around her as they listened to the final person leave, and then the lights switched off. Only then did they both end the hug and stand.

They walked down the staircase in silence, as if both their hearts were heavy with words neither of them knew how to speak, then stepped out the side door, into the cold. The door clicked shut behind them. Pale, barren fields covered in snow spread out ahead of them.

"Ready to head back to the apartment, meet up with my team and plan our way out of this?" Liam asked.

But before Kelly could answer, he heard the sound of someone running. Instinctively, Liam turned back toward the church. Kelly's hand was already on the handle of the door they'd just gone through. Her eyes met his. "It's locked!"

"Liam!" A figure dashed around the corner. And Liam blinked. It was Seth. The hacker's form was swamped in a puffy, hooded coat, and a ski hat was pulled down over his shaggy head.

"Seth!" Liam said. "Hey, what are you doing here? Why does the television think you're an Imposter?"

"Long story." Seth was panting so hard he had to bend over to catch his breath. "I've got a car. It's parked down the street. You guys have to come with me. Now."

"No!" Kelly said, saying the word before Liam could. "We've got to go back to the apartment and get Pip."

"You can't." Seth shook his head. His eyes were pained and he was still gasping for breath. "You've got to come with me. Now. No time to explain."

"Why?" Liam asked. He reached out and put a hand on Seth's shoulder. The hacker flinched under the touch. "Stop, take a deep breath, calm down and tell me what's going on."

"I'm not going anywhere with you," Kelly said. Her arms crossed. "Not without a real good explanation."

He heard the cars before he saw them, two expensive-looking black sedans—they pulled up on either side, blocking them in. Armed and masked men stepped out of both sides, wearing not only the same black Imposter masks, but also, incongruously, the same colored eye patches they had when taking people hostage on the boat. Kelly's hand grabbed his. The door was locked, their backs were against the wall, they were outnumbered and surrounded on both sides. There was nothing for Kelly to hide behind. Not this time. If shooting broke out there was no way to keep her out of the line of fire.

*Help me, Lord! What do I do? How do I get her out of here safely?*

But it was the look of guilt in Seth's eyes that scared him most of all.

"Liam, I'm sorry," Seth gasped. "They—they were waiting in the alley beside the bookstore."

Horror rose up inside Liam. "What did you do?"

Then as he watched, Seth turned and faced the masked men.

"Well, I did it!" Seth called, almost theatrically, despite the fact he was still rasping from being out of breath. "I led you to them. Now where's my money? I told you, if you want the credit for this one, I'm not letting you have it for free."

"You led them to us?" Anger radiated through Kelly's voice as it rose to a hiss and Liam suspected that despite being surrounded by weapons, it was only the slight pressure of Liam's own hand on her wrist that kept her from lunging at Seth.

"Yeah, let's go with that." Seth stepped forward, glancing at the masked men flanking them on either side. His chin rose. "No hard feelings, but you know I was never a true part of your team. You never respected me like you did the others or let me forget my past. And now with everyone going off to their own thing, what was going to happen to me? I'm just supposed to go back to a life of witness protection? I had nothing before I joined your team. Law enforcement had even banned me from using a computer or going online, until you and your buddies came along and convinced me to help you solve crime."

Liam remembered all too well. Seth's life had been not much more than glorified house arrest when they'd invited him to join their team. And while his heart told him there was no way Seth would betray them and there had to be a good explanation for everything, he could still hear the tremor of truth moving through Seth's words.

"Besides," Seth added, "these guys pooled together and are offering me ten thousand dollars for letting them get the credit and video footage of your kidnapping. I mean, what's the point of a mob if people aren't vying to climb over others to rise to the top?" Seth raised his cell phone and aimed it at the masked men and away from Liam and Kelly. "Chop, chop. Hurry up. Otherwise I'll stream this whole conversation on the dark web, and everyone will know you not only bribed me to get credit for my hostages, you don't pay your debts."

For a moment, nobody moved. Then a masked man with a green eye patch tapped some buttons on his phone and Seth's phone beeped. The hacker glanced at his screen and grinned like someone had painted a smile on his pale face. *What are you doing, Seth? What is the game plan?* Liam could feel Kelly's pulse racing under his fingertips. *Was I wrong to trust him?*

"Congratulations, gentlemen," the hacker said. "Now everyone will know you mean business."

The Imposters moved in toward them on either side.

"I mean, sure, I've got a pretty big target on my head, too." Seth leaned forward and clasped Liam in an awkward hug as if wishing him luck. "But I've disappeared before. I can do it again. I'm just sorry you're going to miss your candlelight vigil."

Then Kelly screamed in fury as masked Imposters yanked her from his grasp.

Imposters gagged her mouth and handcuffed her hands behind her back, then picked her up and tossed her into the huge trunk of one of the black and very expensive-looking cars. Her heart pounded in her chest. Panic welled up inside her, sending hot tears to the corners of her eyes. Then she heard the sounds of a struggle and saw the light disappear as Liam's handcuffed body tumbled in beside her. The trunk slammed shut with a bang that seemed to shake the darkness around them. She felt the sound of the engine rumbling beneath them and cold air seeping in as the car began to drive. The fabric of the gag tasted stale in her mouth. The sickly smell of a freshly shampooed car interior filled her nostrils. Then she felt Liam's strong form roll beside her. She leaned into him and, slowly, felt the warmth of his core. He couldn't speak, he couldn't hold her and she couldn't see his face in the darkness. And yet something about just knowing he was there seemed to push back against the panic threatening to overtake her.

The road grew bumpy beneath them. The trunk rattled, rumbled and jolted. Liam rolled away from her and for a moment, she was all alone in the darkness. Then she heard him roll back, his legs bumped hers and she felt his breath on her face.

"Don't worry," he said softly and she wondered how Liam had freed his mouth from the gag. "Pip will be okay. No matter what's going on with Seth, I guarantee Mack and Iris won't let anything happen to her. With what's on the news, Mack won't even let Seth near her. He's the most protective man I know."

Fear pounded through her heart. How could he possibly know that? She'd told him that she didn't trust Seth. He'd argued with her that the hacker should be trusted. And look where it had gotten her? Bound. Gagged. Tossed into the trunk of a car. Kidnapped by the same criminals who'd kidnapped her daughter, Hannah. She just prayed that Renner had managed to rescue Hannah and that someone would find them.

"Hey," Liam said softly. "It's okay. It's all going to be okay. I promise."

And she wondered if he could somehow feel or sense her racing heartbeat.

"Now, I need you to stay as still as you can," Liam said. "I'm going to get your gag off and it might hurt a little bit. Now, don't move. I'm fairly hopeful this will work."

She felt him lean closer, his mouth brushed just behind her ear, a shiver ran through her skin and then she felt a swift tug as the fabric tore. For a brief instant pain shot though her skull, then it stopped as she felt the gag fall from her face.

She gasped a breath, thankful to feel air fill her lungs. "How did you get the gag off?"

"My gag?" Liam asked. "Old trick. Clench your jaw when they put it on, then relax it when you're alone. Gives you a tiny bit of wiggle room. Then use the friction of your shoulder to ease it off your mouth. Like I said, I've been doing this job a really long time."

Okay, but while this might not be the first time he'd been bound, gagged and thrown into the trunk of a car, something in his tone implied a silent *but* hovering in the darkness.

"Then how did you get mine off?" she asked, suspecting she knew the answer.

"Tore it off," Liam said. "Well, bit and ripped. Just behind your ear so as not to hurt your face. You can rip most fabrics off your wrists that way if you know how to tear against the grain."

"Including gags?" she asked.

"Apparently," Liam said. "That was a first for me. Everything is a first with you."

For a moment they lay there side by side in the darkness.

"I haven't quite figured out how to get my arms free yet," he admitted. "With rope, fabric, duct tape or even zip ties, your best option is to find something sharp to tear them off with. Although sometimes it takes a long time, it's doable eventually. But handcuffs are trickier. Have you got anything in your pocket?"

"No, I don't," she said and rolled from side to side to double-check. "Actually, no wait. I still have my burner cell."

Even in the darkness she could tell that Liam jolted.

"They didn't take it?" he asked.

"They patted me down quickly," she said. "But the phone's tucked inside my jacket and I guess they didn't feel it or find it."

"Mmm-hmm." Liam made a noncommittal sound. "That's an interesting mistake for them to make."

"You think they did it on purpose?" she asked.

"I think, I don't know," Liam said. "Maybe. Clearly they're after Renner. Maybe they're hoping he'll call and they can use you as bait. But it's also likely the person who patted you down was an amateur who'd never kidnapped anyone before. These new Imposters are basically an online mob, following whatever loud idea floats to the top of their message board."

"And maybe Seth's one of them," Kelly countered.

"I doubt it," Liam said.

"Then why did he lead them to us?" she demanded.

"I don't know," Liam said.

"The news said he was the head of the Imposters." She could hear the bitter and angry bite in her voice and didn't try to hide it. "And don't tell me the Imposters are a swarm without a leader, because those men clearly thought he was on their side. They didn't shoot him or kidnap him. They bribed him. Why do you think that is?"

"I don't know," Liam said again. His voice was oddly neutral in the darkness. She didn't need neutral. Not now. She needed anger, or reassurance, or something. She needed emotion. "I don't know what to think."

"How can you not know what to think?" Her voice rose.

"I don't have enough information!" Liam's voice rose, too, but not like he was upset at her, more like he was trapped. "I don't know why Seth did what he did. I know that he used to hack bad guys. He'd convinced himself he was doing the right thing and that the only way to do that was off-the-grid. He didn't trust law enforcement. For a long time, Seth didn't know if he could trust me. We bumped heads over his methods more times that I could count and our personalities never really clicked. But..." His voice trailed off and for a long moment he didn't say anything. "But...oh, wow, I just realized he hugged me goodbye."

"So?" Kelly asked.

"So neither Seth or I are huggy people," Liam said. "Seth is the last person I'd expect to hug me like that. If I roll over, can you check my jacket? He might've slipped something in my pocket."

"Sure," she said, even though it sounded like he was grasping at straws. But they shuffled and jostled, turning this way and that in the shaking trunk, until finally her fingers brushed his jacket pocket.

"Do you feel anything?" he asked.

"Not yet," she said. She felt around the corner of his pocket, then her fingers brushed something thin and plastic. "Wait, yes." She pulled it out. "I think it's a twist tie. You know, the kind you use to close a bag of bread?"

Liam let out a long breath. "Okay, we got something. Let me take it from you and I'll go to work."

She felt him pry it from her fingertips and roll away.

"You think Seth slipped a twist tie into your jacket pocket?" she asked. "Because he knew you could use it to pick handcuffs that are behind your back?"

"I don't know," Liam said again. "But I'm going to get your handcuffs off first. Now, please, lie as still as you can."

She did as he asked. His fingers moved against hers for a while, then there was a clink and her handcuffs fell from her wrists. *Thank You, God!*

"Thank you," she said. Her freed arms hugged his shoulders quickly. Then she pulled out her phone. No cell signal. "But I don't know how to do the same for you."

"It's okay." Liam let out a long and weary breath. "I can do it. I just need to get my hands in front of me. Which if I was twenty years younger would be as simple as sliding my legs through my arms almost like a somersault. As it is, I'm going to have to dislocate my shoulder."

She gasped.

"You don't happen to remember how to put my shoulder back in its socket?" he asked.

He'd dislocated it two decades ago while fighting for their lives when they'd been under attack from the men sent to kidnap her. They'd escaped together with her driving getaway and Liam's shoulder still out of its socket. Then he'd talked her through popping it back in for him when they'd been safe and alone. It had been pretty emotionally intense for her, seeing how much pain he'd been in.

It had been the first time they'd kissed.

"I think I remember," she said. "If not, I'm sure you can talk me through it."

She hated the thought of him being in that much pain again. But what choice did they have? They were still locked in a trunk, the car was still speeding somewhere to their unknown destination and they had no way to contact the outside world. She gave Liam's shoulders another quick hug. Then she waited in the darkness and prayed, as she heard a pained shout leave Liam's throat as he wrenched his shoulder from its socket and then maneuvered his hands around in front of him. Then carefully, deliberately and at his direction, she helped him pop his shoulder back into place.

"It's going to be okay." Liam's voice was ragged as he picked his own handcuffs, aided by the light of her cell phone. She couldn't imagine the pain he was in. "Sometimes you've got to go old school. And this is pretty much as old school as it gets."

The handcuffs clinked.

"You get them open?" she asked.

But before Liam could answer, she felt the world yanked out from under her, as she found herself tossed hard against the hood of the trunk. Pain shot through her body. Then the world around her flipped again, gravity suddenly losing all meaning as she felt her body fly into the back of the trunk. The car was flipping, end over end, flying out of control.

They were crashing.

# TEN

The car was rolling and tumbling down an incline. How steep was the hill? How long would they fall? What would they hit at the bottom? She didn't know. For a moment, all she could do was shield her head and pray as she was violently tossed around, terrified. Then she felt Liam throw his arms around her and clutch her to his chest, cradling her with his body, praying over her and keeping her safe, as they fell together into the darkness.

Then, just as suddenly as it had started, the vehicle stopped rolling with a jolt and everything went still. Odd shapes of light seeped through the edges of the bent and smashed trunk hood, and it took her a moment to realize the car was upright again.

"Still alive?" Liam asked, his voice low and deep in her ear.

"Yeah."

"Injured?"

"No…"

"Hurt?" he persisted, and she almost smiled.

"Probably," she said. "But nothing major."

"Thank You, God," he said. Then slowly he let her go, easing her from his arms as carefully and gently as if she was made of glass. Then he began to kick hard with both legs, repeatedly and rhythmically stomping against the dented trunk hood until it flew open. Winter sunlight streamed in.

"One second," he said. He climbed out and disappeared from view. Moments later he was back. He reached in for her hands—she let him take them and leaped out into knee-deep snow.

"It's just us," he said. "They're gone. I'm guessing they bailed out when the car spun out of control."

Blue sky stretched above snow-capped trees. A long steep hill was to her right, picturesque in unbroken snow, except for the harsh slashes, littered with broken glass and bumpers, where the car had tumbled down it. A road was empty above them. Then, finally, she steeled herself to look at the car they'd just escaped. It was a flattened wreck, like a child's toy that someone had stomped on.

"By the looks of things, the computer went haywire," Liam added. "If I had to guess, somebody hacked the car's computer. I've seen Seth do it before. But I don't know if it was him. Or if whoever did it was trying to kill them or rescue us. All I know is they're gone and we're alone. This apparently wasn't planned because nobody stuck around to film it."

A quick scan of the vehicle found nothing worth taking. They trudged up the hill, following the path of destruction.

"Yeah, yeah, I know shouting 'Detective Liam Bearsmith, RCMP' isn't going to be much help right now," he said as they reached the road, and an unexpected giggle burst through her lips, thankfully breaking the tension in her chest. "But old-school detective work, like looking at tire tracks and footprints, tells me the car swerved out of control here." He pointed at a mess of tire tracks. "The driver didn't even have the opportunity to try and regain control. He and his passengers just leaped out...there." He followed the path of their footprints. "A second car was traveling so close behind the first it had to swerve to avoid it. They all hopped in the back seat, turned around and kept driving. If I had to guess, none of them saw this coming, and when they saw how the car crashed they assumed we were dead. Again..."

His words trailed off as his hands rose in frustration.

"We're dealing with a mob, not an organized group," she concluded. "Setting aside for one moment whatever's going on with Seth."

"Right," Liam said. "Don't ask me how we take them down, because I don't know. They're too big and unwieldy. We'd have to not only shut down the entire Imposters online operation, but track every single person who logged into their site. And who knows how many people that is? We'd need not only an entire online team, but then a full-scale operation to coordinate people on the ground to find and arrest these people." Liam glanced back down the hill at the wrecked car and shook his head. "Gotta say, two presumed deaths in twenty-four hours is a couple more than I'm used to."

Kelly patted his arm. "Welcome to the club."

He chuckled. "Well," he said, "we're alive and we've got Renner's phone, a twist tie and each other."

"I think this is where you tell me that you've survived worse," she said.

"I have," he agreed. "And with much worse company."

His hands slid onto her shoulders and she stepped toward his chest, and as she tilted her face up to look at him he bent his down toward hers. Their lips almost met. But this time neither of them seemed willing to move that extra inch. She wasn't quite sure why. But something inside her was holding her back and it seemed to be holding him back, too.

"So what do we do now?" she asked.

Liam's features set into a picture of determination. He stepped back and as their bodies parted, he crossed his arms over his chest.

"All right," he said. "For now, we walk. We'll follow the road and wherever possible head south because that's usually the fastest way to find civilization in Ontario. I'm guessing there's still no message from Renner, and the fact that Seth asked you not to use the phone is now giving me a weird feeling about it. We need allies, we need answers and Seth's comment about attending my own memorial vigil keeps rattling around in my head. Judging by the sky, it's somewhere between two and three. The candlelight vigil is in Ottawa, which is four hours from where the wedding was in Kilpatrick, and happens at seven. That gives us about five hours to figure out where we are and get there." He sighed. "Old-school detective work takes a whole lot of thinking."

"Or hopefully," she said, "Renner will call any moment to let us know Hannah is safe, he'll come pick us up and we'll go get Pip."

But her phone stayed stubbornly quiet as the afternoon spread out long, slow and empty, like all the afternoons they'd spent together back when they'd been on the run. They walked for over forty minutes and turned down several hitchhiking offers from people Liam apparently didn't like the look of before Liam accepted a ride from a young man, who looked to be barely more than a teenager, with a beat-up car that had a car seat in the back that smelled like it had recently been wiped down with sanitizing wipes. Liam sat in the front, where he and the driver made small talk about the weather and didn't exchange names. Then, when he dropped them off in a small town, Liam slipped him fifty dollars.

"Why him?" Kelly asked as he drove away.

"That's a good kid with a criminal record, consisting of a minor offence or two," Liam said, nodding at the departing car. "My hunch is minor drug possession or drunk driving. He's no longer with his baby's mother but is trying to do right by his kid. Didn't get many breaks in life and doesn't want trouble. Just wants to keep his head down."

"You got all that from a quick glance?" Kelly asked.

"Yup." Liam nodded. "My old-school skills haven't gotten totally rusty. Like I said, I've survived this job a long time."

He led them past both a coffee shop and a restaurant before they finally stopped at a diner that had a pay phone out front. It took buying a map from a nearby gas station to get correct change. But Liam finally had it and they stood outside in the snow while he stared at the phone as if trying to decide what number to call. Then he punched in a number and stood back. The phone rang. It clicked through to the answering machine and then a few bars of "Be My Baby" by the Ronettes played, followed immediately by a couple of lines from an even older song from Bobby Darin about a shark's pearly teeth.

Liam hung up and his hand shook as he set the receiver back. "Thank You, God."

Her hand brushed his back. "'Mack the Knife'?" she asked. "What does that mean?"

He turned toward her, relief filling his eyes. "It means Mack and Iris still have Pip and she's safe."

And suddenly it hit her. He'd been even more worried about Pip's safety than she'd been. Because when he'd promised her that Pip was safe, she'd believed him.

"Who did you call?" she asked.

"A very long time ago, when I was training to be a cop, I was friends with a guy named Trent," Liam explained. "An excellent cop, now an RCMP detective, who went on to marry an exceptional OPP detective named Chloe. Back when we were teenagers, cell phones weren't that big a thing, or if they were we couldn't afford them, so we'd call each other's answering machines directly and leave messages. Trent and I agreed to keep one open as an emergency messaging device. It's the closest thing we could get to an untraceable number. An unused twenty-five-year-old phone number is the last thing anyone's going to be tapping. Like me, Trent used to go undercover in a lot of very rough assignments, sometimes for months at a time with really bad people."

"Very old school," Kelly said. "How many times have you used the number?"

"In over twentysomething years?" Liam asked. "He's used it maybe twice."

"And you?" she asked.

"This is the first time I've called it," Liam said, and there was a weight to his words she didn't quite understand.

"How did he even know you'd call that number?" she asked.

"He didn't." They kept walking. "He probably followed a hunch and took a shot in the dark because he heard something from someone he trusts. It was an act of faith and hope."

"So these new Imposters aren't the only ones with a network," she said. "You seem to have a lot of people looking out for you, wanting to help you."

He didn't look at her. He just kept walking. "Cops look out for each other."

"Jess offered to help you on her wedding day," she countered. "Mack and Iris are taking care of Pip. An old buddy called a secret number you set up over twenty years ago. That's way more than cops looking out for each other."

He didn't answer and she wasn't sure why. It was like there was something inside Liam blocking him from seeing how much he mattered to people. Just like he apparently hadn't seen just how much he'd mattered to her.

"Come on," he said. "We should eat something and figure out our next ride."

They reached a diner and Liam scanned it for lines of sight. Their conversation dropped to low and innocuous small talk, as they went inside, hid in a corner booth and bought greasy burgers that they paid cash for. A television mounted in the corner ran the twenty-four-hour news channel. Every now and then the younger, stronger, more classically handsome, de-aged Liam without all the scars and wounds of his life flashed on the screen. It was almost impossible to believe he was the same tired, drained, exhausted, battered and bruised man sitting in front of her. It wasn't surprising that no one recognized him.

The gas-station map told them they were a little over three

hours from Ottawa. The burgers arrived and Kelly watched as Liam created a pool of ketchup on the corner of his plate and dipped his burger in it as he ate. "You know, you're the only person I've ever known who does that."

Liam's eyebrows rose slightly. "Well, maybe other people do, but you haven't had burgers with them."

She smiled. "Yeah, probably."

He paused, then dipped his burger into the ketchup and took another bite.

"Did you ever get a cat?" he asked.

"I fostered some kittens for a while," she said. "I also had some birds. Do you still dislike cats?"

He laughed—it was a deep and warm chuckle that seemed to cut through space and time, back to when they'd sat in similar diners and had similar conversations all those years ago.

"Cats dislike me," he said. "Because they're sneaky and I see through them."

She laughed, too, and for a long moment neither of them said anything, they just ate from their shared basket of fries, their hands lightly bumping as they reached for them.

"I wanted to call when I heard your mom had passed away," Liam said. He looked down at the table. "I just didn't know what to say."

"She never really recovered from the shock of my dad laundering money and us being forced into witness protection," she said. "Didn't help my dad ran away with someone else. You said your dad passed?"

"Four years ago," Liam said. "It was cancer, pretty fast, but he had a few months in a hospice to tie up loose ends and say goodbyes."

Her hand reached for his across the table and linked through his fingers. "I'm sorry."

"Thanks." Liam nodded. "Me, too."

"He must've been proud of all you've accomplished," she said.

"He was," Liam said. "This was all he ever wanted for me."

A silence fell between them again that was both comfortable and awkward at the same time, like a cross between a first date and catching up with an old friend. They left the diner ten minutes later, keeping their heads down and moving quickly. At first it seemed a choice between hitchhiking again or taking a bus. But then they spotted a beat-up car in front of someone's house with a for-sale sign on its windshield. The owner wanted fifteen hundred dollars for it, but Liam talked him down to nine hundred cash, and off they drove. They were down to their last few hundred dollars now, hardly enough for a few days' worth of food and a motel room each for them to sleep in when night fell. The car's summer tires were threadbare, the heater was broken and the right back-seat window was cracked. But it moved and it got them to Ottawa in time for the vigil.

And still her phone stayed silent. Had something happened to Renner? Had he been able to rescue Hannah? Worry permeated every beat of her heart, just like it had back in the day when she and Liam had first been on the run together. And yet, despite the pain, fear and uncertainty, she also knew there was no one else she'd rather have by her side.

A long, sprawling park ran along Ottawa's water's edge. Liam parked in a mostly empty lot and they walked, following a winding bike path. The faint sound of singing and gentle glow of lights rose ahead of them.

"Considering it's almost Christmas, there are probably several events going on in this park right now," Liam said. "I don't know how easy it's going to be to find this vigil, or even how many people are going to be there. I'm guessing no more than a dozen or so. Maybe less, considering the weather. But hopefully at least one member of my team will be there, or someone else I trust, and I'll be able to signal them." He frowned. "Although with Jess gone on her honeymoon, Noah getting married tomorrow and Mack hunkered down somewhere protecting Pip, there might not be."

They crested a hill as the sound of music seemed to swell and rise to meet them—the final verse of "Amazing Grace." Liam's footsteps faltered. Hundreds—no, thousands of candles were spread out in a rich tapestry of lights beneath them.

"This can't be it," Liam said. "This must be some kind of Christmas event and the vigil moved."

He turned as if to go. But Kelly's fingers grabbed hold of his and held fast.

"This is it," she said. "This is your candlelight vigil. All these people are here to celebrate you."

His head was shaking, but something in the slight quiver of his jaw as it set told her that he knew it was true.

"But they don't know me," he said. "They don't know anything about me. I'm a name on a police report or a tip sent their way."

"I know." Her hand tightened on his. He had no idea how honored she was that she got to know him and that out of all the lives he'd touched, she was the one person he'd opened up to, been vulnerable with and decided to love, no matter how fleeting their time together. "But you changed their lives and for some, they're only alive today because of you."

The music gave way to talking, as cop after cop spoke into a megaphone about Liam Bearsmith. And sure, it was clear most of them only knew of his uncanny knack for finding the right piece of evidence, pulling the right strings, finding the right source and showing up in the right place at the right time. They didn't know anything about his sense of humor, his insecurities or his heart. But the fact he'd existed, done his job and been dedicated to his work mattered to all of them.

*And he was willing to give all this up for me.*

Between the distance and the snow it was hard to get a good look at who was speaking as the megaphone was passed around. But there was something about the tone of the strong woman's voice when it took over the air that made Liam's back straighten.

"I'm detective Chloe Brant-Henry, OPP," she said.

"Wife of the man who left the message," Liam whispered.

"Liam and I worked a lot of cases together," Chloe said. "Some of them were incredible, hair-curling stuff, which you'll never get to hear about because they're above your pay grades." A ripple of laughter moved through the crowd. "When you grow up in a dysfunctional family, like my sister and I did, you learn to appreciate the family you find. As some of you know, when I married Trent I inherited three new brothers. What you probably don't know is that Liam has always been like an honorary brother to us. He's been there, without question, without hesitating, whenever we needed him. So wherever you are, Liam, I hope you know that you're our brother and we're here for you."

Liam pulled his fingers from hers and rubbed his hand across his eyes.

Her phone pinged, she pulled it out and glanced at the screen.

Hey, it's Renner. Got Hannah. She's safe.
Locked onto your GPS in Ottawa now. On our way.
There in fifteen minutes. It's time to go.

"Renner has Hannah," Kelly said, glancing up at Liam from her phone. "She's safe and he's on his way to pick me up. He'll be here in fifteen minutes."

*Renner was here? In Ottawa?*

Liam felt himself blink. "What do you mean, he's on his way?"

"Apparently he can track my phone on GPS," Kelly said.

Since when? All this time he'd thought the phone was completely untraceable.

As he looked down at Kelly he could see the palpable relief and joy washing over her. He couldn't blame her. But something didn't sit right in Liam's core. Something felt off.

*Help me, Lord. I've always been able to trust my gut. But right now I don't know what this thing is I'm feeling and it's clouding my vision.*

"Come with me," Kelly said suddenly, as she pocketed her phone and then grabbed both of his hands in hers.

"What do you mean?" he asked.

"I mean…come with me." She said the words slowly. Her beautiful eyes locked on his face. "Come with Renner, Hannah, Pip and I. We'll all go hunker down together somewhere and sort out how to stop the Imposters and prove you're alive. You can get to know Renner and Hannah. We can figure this out together. Please, Liam, we've found each other again and I don't want to go without you."

Go with her? Leave his work? Just run away with Kelly and start a new life? She had no idea how much he'd been willing to throw everything away for her before. But now?

"I—I can't…" he said.

"You can." Something firm moved through her voice and for a moment he almost believed her. "Why not, Liam? Why not come with us?"

He wasn't even sure. He just knew whatever it was came from somewhere deep inside him he'd never tapped into before. "I have a life here. I have a team…"

"You *had* a life here," she said. "You had a team. But now your team is disbanding and everyone else thinks you're dead." She waved her hand toward the array of dazzling lights. "I'm not saying you shouldn't clear your name, prove you're alive and stop the Imposters. But why can't you do that with us? We can be your new team. We can go off-the-grid and find a way to do it together. For all your dedication to law enforcement, clearly somewhere along the line law enforcement let you down. Someone changed my file to keep us apart. Why not do what you wanted to do all those years ago—walk away from all this, and start again with me?"

*I don't know!* The words moved through him and he didn't know how to speak them. Kelly would never know how much he'd wanted a life with her then and was tempted to leave everything behind to start a new life with her now.

But he had no identification and no passport. His fingerprints matched a man who was wanted for murder. The only way to start anew with her was to go on the run and break the law.

"Because that's not the kind of man I am," he said, the words crossing his lips the same moment they did his heart and mind. "Maybe it was never meant to be, as much as I wanted to give everything up to run away and be with you. This is my home, and this is my fight."

Her head was shaking and as he watched, a light dimmed in her eyes. Couldn't she see?

"You deserved a far better man than who I was when I asked you to marry me twenty-two years ago," he said. "You deserved a husband who didn't sneak around, break the rules and run from his responsibilities. You deserved a man who stepped up."

She pulled away, and as her eyes searched his face, they were filled with a look he couldn't quite decipher.

"And so, how are you going to be the kind of man who steps up now?" she asked.

*That's just it. I don't know!*

Before he could speak, her phone began to ring. Kelly pulled it out and held it between them. "Hello?"

"Mom?" Hannah's voice floated into the night and suddenly Liam realized Kelly had put it on Speakerphone.

"Hannah?" Kelly's voice broke as her eyes flooded with tears. Immediately, Liam pressed his arm around the small of her back, supporting her weight as her limbs began to shake. "Is it really you?"

Silence fell on the other end of the line. A sob escaped Kelly's lips. Liam glanced around and spotted a snow-covered bench sitting in a pool of light under a lamppost. He led Kelly toward it, wiped it off and helped her sit. She clutched his arm.

"She's gone." Kelly looked up into his eyes. "It was Hannah. She was here and now she's gone."

"It's okay," Liam said. "She'll call back. The line must just be bad."

He glanced around and then he saw him. A lone figure standing by the road, not moving, not signaling him in any way, just staring at him. And even without seeing the man's face, he recognized his form in an instant.

It was Seth.

Liam stood. "I... Give me a second."

Her phone rang again.

"Hello?" Kelly answered it. "Hannah! Hi! Can you hear me? I can barely hear you."

She put it on Speakerphone so Liam could listen in.

"I'm here," Hannah said. "Stay where you are. We're driving your way."

Out of his peripheral vision, Liam could see Seth turn and walk toward the parking lot. He glanced from Kelly to Seth's disappearing form. *Help me, Lord! What do I do?*

"I'm here," Kelly told Hannah. "I can't wait to see you."

Seth was rapidly disappearing, but if Liam ran after him now he'd reach the other man in seconds.

"Stay here," Liam told Kelly. His hand landed on her shoulder and his eyes locked on hers. "Right here. On this bench. Don't move. Don't go anywhere. And if anyone approaches you, scream. Okay?" She nodded. He glanced back—Seth had disappeared from sight. He turned back to Kelly. "I need you to promise me, if anyone approaches you, you'll scream for me and fight them off with all your might."

Kelly nodded. "I promise. Unless it's Hannah."

"Deal," he said, "unless it's Hannah. I'll be back in a second."

He brushed a kiss over the top of her head and bolted after Seth. For a moment he thought he'd lost him altogether. Then he spotted the hacker walking between the vehicles in a half-empty parking lot.

"Seth!" Liam shouted. "Stop!"

The hacker turned, his hood fell back and Seth's eyes widened. Then Seth began to run. *No!* Whatever was going on, Seth was not getting away now. Liam pressed his body forward, his feet pounding on the icy ground as he ran after his former teammate. Within moments Liam had caught him—he grabbed Seth's coat at the back of his neck and spun him around.

"I'm sorry," Seth said, his eyes wide. "I really am. I can explain."

"Not good enough," Liam growled. He let Seth go and watched as the hacker's knees buckled. "I thought we were on the same team."

"We are!" Guilt flooded Seth's face. "It's just, a buddy asked me for help and I had to help him."

"Who?" Liam demanded. "Who are you helping?"

Too late, he felt the prick of a mini–stun gun against the back of his neck. Seth was bait. The real threat was standing behind him.

"He's helping me." A voice—male, young and unfamiliar— filled his ear as electricity shot through Liam, bringing him to his knees.

# ELEVEN

"Hello?" Kelly called into the phone. "Hello?"

She glanced around the empty winter night. The music from the vigil had surged. Hannah's voice had been there a moment ago and now she was gone again. And Kelly couldn't see Liam anywhere.

"I'm almost there." Hannah's voice was back in her ear. "Can you walk down the road and we'll meet you there?"

"I…" She swallowed hard. If she left now she might never see Liam again. That was more than she was willing to risk. "I'm sorry, I can't. I need to wait for Liam. He—he did a really great job of taking care of Pip."

No answer. Just more crackling came down the line. She sighed. Kelly wasn't sure what to make of the fact Hannah hadn't asked about her daughter yet. But it was possible she was worried the call was being hacked somehow. Not to mention the signal kept cutting out and they'd barely exchanged a handful of sentences. Her phone had almost no bars. If only she hadn't promised Liam she'd stay on the bench, she'd go wander for a better signal. She glanced to the streetlamp behind her. Then again, she hadn't agreed to anything about how she'd stay on the bench. She stood up, bracing her feet on the slippery metal seat, and leaned against the lamppost. Bingo. She now had another bar. Not to mention a better view. She could now see the road on one side, cold and white, and the glittering candlelight vigil on the other. But she still couldn't see Liam anywhere.

"Okay, we'll come find you," Hannah said. "Just driving down the road toward your GPS signal now."

Okay, but where was Liam? Even if he didn't come with her, even if this was the last time they saw each other again, she wasn't about to let him leave her life without saying goodbye. And asking him to please find a way for them to stay in each other's lives. She closed her eyes and prayed.

*I lost him once, Lord. I can't lose him again.*

"I need a minute," Kelly said. "Liam just needed to sort something, and I promised I wouldn't go anywhere without telling him."

"We don't have a minute," Hannah said.

A horn honked and Kelly turned to see a black SUV with tinted windows pulling up on the road. Faint snow blew between her and the van, catching the light like glitter. The driver was a dark and featureless shape. Then the van's back door slid open, and she saw the young woman sitting in the back seat, her figure silhouetted in the van's interior seat. And even though she couldn't see clearly from the distance, snow and combination of darkness and shadows, Kelly's heart leaped.

It was her daughter. It was Hannah. Safe, alive and in one piece.

She leaped off the bench and jogged toward her, across the snowy ground.

"We've got to go." Hannah's voice came through the cell phone and Kelly wondered if she was intentionally keeping her voice low instead of yelling out.

*Come on, Liam. Where are you?*

"I don't want to leave without Liam," she admitted.

"Where is he?" Hannah's voice came through the phone.

"I don't know," Kelly said. "Somewhere close. It's a long story."

"Just get in the van and we'll drive around and look for him."

Her eyes glanced to the falling snow and to the sky above. *Help me, Lord. If I leave now, will I ever find him again?*

"Let's go!" Hannah called.

Kelly's footsteps faltered. Something was wrong. Her daughter's tone was off and now that she was closer she could tell her daughter's body had barely flinched. She stopped. "What's wrong?"

"Nothing's wrong," her daughter's calm voice said on the phone.

Yet, as she watched, Hannah's body moved, and she was tossing her head violently and jerking toward Kelly as if forcing her unwilling limbs to move. And then Kelly saw it.

Hannah's mouth was gagged.

The voice on the phone had been a deep fake, just like the video of Liam. Hannah wasn't safe. She wasn't with Renner. The Imposters still had her. Hannah's desperate eyes met Kelly's, as if silently begging her to run.

*I will. I'll find your father. And then I'll find you again.*

Kelly turned and ran, her feet crunching over the snow. Behind her she could hear van doors opening and people pounding after her.

"Liam!" she screamed, feeling his name rip from her throat. "Help me!"

She had to find him. She had to reach him before it was too late.

A sudden body blow came from behind as one of the Imposters tackled her. It was too late. She fell forward, her body hitting hard against the snowy ground. She thrashed hard, trying desperately to fight. But there were too many of them. One Imposter was pushing her down. A second was tying a gag around her mouth, silencing her screams and barely giving her time to clench her jaw the way Liam had told her about. A third tied her hands behind her back. Then she felt her body yanked backward, half-carried and half-dragged through the snow. Her body was flung into a seat beside Hannah. The SUV doors closed. Kelly met her daughter's eyes. Their shoulders leaned into each other, as mother and daughter silently passed each other faith, strength and hope.

The van drove off into the night.

*Please, Lord, may someone find us before it's too late.*

Of all the problems Liam had envisioned when Seth had joined their team, finding himself stunned and dragged into the back of a freezing van by some unseen accomplice hadn't exactly been at the top of the list. But now, as Liam's head was beginning to clear and he could feel the cold metal beneath his knees and hear the wind whistling through a cracked door, he suddenly realized that he cared a whole lot less about the identity of the unknown man behind him, who had one gloved hand clamped on Liam's shoulder and the other holding a knife to his throat, than he did about the hacker now crouched on the van floor in front of him. The man behind him, whoever he was, was just one more threat and menace in a long line of people who'd tried to take Liam's life over the years.

But Seth was something far more important.

"Believe it or not, Seth," Liam said, "I cared about you and I respected you. I considered you a friend. So whatever this is, it's low. Even for you."

Seth rocked back on his heels and his face paled so suddenly it was like Liam's words had actually winded him. "You've never called me a friend before."

"And you've never kidnapped me!" Liam's voice rose. "Now are you going to tell your buddy here to let me go and explain why you joined forces with the Imposters and what it is you think you're doing? Or do I have to break his arm, risk getting myself stabbed and fight my way out of here?"

Seth cast a glance at whoever was still holding Liam hostage at knifepoint. The figure was a man, judging by both the grip and the voice he'd previously heard. There appeared to just be the three of them.

"Let him go," Seth told the man.

"Not yet," the man behind Liam said. "Not until we've talked things out and know for sure whose side he's on."

"You want to know what side I'm on?" Liam snapped. "I'm on the side of both following the law and taking care of the people I care about."

He had to get back to Kelly. It had only been a few minutes since he'd left her alone on the bench. But a lot could happen in a few minutes. He gritted his teeth. Then again, it always amazed him how much intel he could get out of someone who was threatening his life. He prayed for wisdom and listened to his instincts. Maybe he didn't need to be told what was going on.

Maybe there was only one answer that explained everything. But was he right?

"Fine, I'll listen," Liam said. "But not while Kelly's in danger. Because I left her, out there on a bench, talking to Hannah on the phone and waiting for Renner to pick her up."

There was a sharp intake of breath from the man behind him and the knife flinched half an inch away from his throat. But it wasn't enough. Not yet.

"Actually, I owe you an apology, Seth," Liam said. "I haven't been fully honest with you. I'm not the clean-nosed, by-the-book guy everyone thinks I am. I made a major mistake years ago, one that by rights should've derailed my career if someone hadn't altered Kelly's witness-protection files to cover it up. Kelly and I were romantically involved. I asked her to marry me. I thought she moved on without me. What I didn't know is we had a daughter. Her name was Hannah Phillips. I'm Hannah's biological father. Her daughter, Pip, is my granddaughter, and Kelly is the only woman I ever fell for. And no matter what ridiculous story you're about to tell me, I'm not about to let anything happen to them."

This time the knife fell ever farther from his neck. The hand gripping his shoulder began to shake. There, now that was the signal he was waiting for.

Liam struck, grabbed the knife with both hands and spun hard to the side. He slammed the offending arm against the side of the van wall, forcing the knife to fall from the man's grasp. Then he glanced at his kidnapper. The man was of average height, average build and masked. Also seemed he wasn't about to give up that easily. The man swung. Liam rolled out of the way and almost made it, absorbing the glancing blow in his shoulder.

Liam almost sighed. He was getting too old for this.

"Stop!" Liam shouted, crouching up on his feet and holding up his hands. "I get that you're scared, desperate or whatever it is that's motivating you right now. But you really think three grown men throwing punches in the back of a van is going to solve anything?"

"Hey, *I* wasn't about to punch anyone," Seth muttered.

Maybe not, but the masked man was about to try to. Liam ducked his blow, shoved him back against the van wall and yanked off the man's mask.

"Renner Phillips, right?" Liam said. Renner nodded without answering. "Rumor has it you're dead. But that seems to be catching right now."

"Where's my daughter?" Renner demanded.

"Safe." Liam sat back without letting Renner up fully. The curly-haired young man looked younger than Liam expected and every bit as desperate as Liam had felt when he'd first realized, so long ago, that he was falling in love with a woman whose life was in danger.

"I get why you're an emotional, irrational wreck," Liam added. "If what you feel for my daughter is half what I felt for her mama then your brain is a mess right now. And that's not even considering Pip. The woman and baby you love are in danger. I feel that. So, I understand why you're being dumb."

Liam let out a long breath. Then he glanced at Seth. "You, on the other hand, should've known better."

Seth opened his mouth, like some big explanation was hovering on his tongue, then wisely thought twice and shut it again.

"Now, if I didn't need your help, I'd arrest you both," Liam said. "Even without a badge and presumed dead." He looked at Renner. "Please tell me that you've been texting Kelly, you rescued Hannah and she's filling Kelly in on everything right now."

Renner shook his head. "I haven't been texting Kelly. Her phone was compromised and I had to go dark. I don't know where Hannah is. The Imposters have her."

That was what Liam had been afraid of.

"I tried to tell you not to use that phone," Seth said.

Liam leaped out of the van.

"I'm getting Kelly," Liam called, turning his back on the men his brain wanted to interrogate and instead following his heart. "I left her on that bench talking to who-knows-who. Join me if you want or run off and keep up with whatever foolish thing you think you're doing. I don't have time to try and stop you. Not while she's out there alone."

He sprinted across the snowy ground, back toward where he'd left Kelly.

*Lord, please help me get there in time. Please keep Kelly safe.*

He pushed through the snow, hearing the other two men running behind him. A motor sounded in the distance. He reached the bench and sank to his knees.

Kelly was gone, leaving nothing but the signs of a struggle spreading out like ugly gashes in the snow where Kelly had fought for her life.

He looked up as Renner and Seth reached his side.

"You're going to tell me how to find her."

# TWELVE

A few minutes later, the three men sat in a diner. It was the kind with stained mugs, cracked saltshakers and faded vinyl tablecloths that looked like they hadn't been changed in so long they were now melded to the table. It also was the type of place where nobody looked at another person twice and the waitstaff ignored you unless called. Liam had met with dozens of informants in this exact place and countless others like it, while wearing all number of different personas. But not once had he done so with his heart burning like a furnace inside him, threatening to consume his rational mind.

He glanced from Renner to Seth and back.

"So," Liam said. "The Imposters still have Hannah and presumably now have Kelly, too. Her supposedly secure phone was compromised this whole time and Renner was never messaging Kelly."

He thanked God the phone's battery was dead for as long as it was.

"The world thinks you're dead and took your special master-key decryption device to the grave," he continued. "The Imposters don't believe that, though, and are willing to cause chaos to get their hands on it." He reminded himself Kelly said there was no decipher key. "And the world still thinks I'm dead," he added. "Now you two are going to help me fill in the gaps."

"Are you sure my daughter is safe?" Renner asked.

It wasn't the first time he'd asked the question, but it was about time Liam did more than give him an answer.

"Yes," Liam said. But before he put Renner's heart at ease, he had to ask Seth something. He turned to the hacker. "Please tell me you're not a criminal, you had a really good reason for letting the Imposters kidnap Kelly and I and that you're about to convince me to trust you."

Seth nodded. "Yes. I promise."

Liam believed him. "Then text Mack and tell him where we are and who's with us."

He turned back to Renner. "Now, fill me in."

"What makes you think you're Hannah's father?" Renner asked. His voice was so stretched thin with stress Liam was surprised it hadn't snapped.

Fair question, Liam thought. It's not every day a man accidentally kidnapped and tried to fight his father-in-law.

"Kelly said I was," Liam said, "and that's all the proof I needed."

She was the first person he'd ever trusted implicitly. He glanced from Seth to the twenty-four-hour television screen now showing his own vigil. Kelly had been the first. But maybe not the only one.

"Seth," Liam said. The hacker glanced up from his phone. "Like I told you, I had an inappropriate and secret relationship with Kelly when I was a rookie. If word had gotten out, I'd have faced even more severe consequences than Mack did and my career would've taken a major hit. I might've even been fired. Instead, someone blocked her attempts to contact me and her RCMP file was changed. I trust you can figure out how and why."

Although he suspected he didn't want to know the answer.

Liam turned back to Renner. "I care about Kelly. I've risked my life to protect her, Hannah and Pip, and I will do everything in my power to ensure they're safe. Now talk." As much as he was dying to ask Renner how he'd broken the code, his gut told him Renner wasn't about to tell him that yet. "You hacked an unbreakable code. Then what happened?"

"My life changed instantly," Renner said. His face paled at the memory. "My email, phone and social media were flooded with job offers and people trying to buy my method, which was overwhelming. Some were really pushy. But what was far worse were the threats. All these anonymous accounts and criminal groups were threatening to find my wife and do terrible things to her if I didn't give them the master key."

"And you didn't trust the government to keep you safe?"

"My vehicle blew up!" Renner barely caught himself from raising his voice. "If someone could do that to me, who's to say they couldn't do worse to Hannah. She was only a few weeks pregnant with Pip."

So Hannah had gone into RCMP witness protection and Renner had gone underground.

"Then when the original Imposters stole the RCMP witness-protection database a few weeks later, you knew people would be looking for Hannah's identity," Liam said, "so you got Kelly to get to her file first. Someone had to talk her through how to do it. She couldn't have done it herself. Was it you?"

Renner shook his head. Liam glanced at Seth.

The hacker raised his hands. "It wasn't me."

Okay, that he believed, too. So who was left then?

"So," Liam continued, "then the original two Imposters died in a shoot-out with our friends Noah and Holly. Everything dies down. You decide instead of coming forward, you're going to try to set up a new life somewhere, off-the-grid, with Hannah and Pip, where you'll all be safe. Then a bunch of copycat Imposters emerged, and they decided they wanted your nonexistent decipher key. Got all that right?"

Renner sat there stone-faced. Liam took that as a yes.

He rested his elbows on the table and leaned in toward Seth. "Now, where did you two meet?" he asked.

"Online," Seth said. "I've been curious about Renner for a while, found him online, told him about my own background and offered to give him a hand if he needed it. We have similar backgrounds and I figured we were like-minded individuals."

Liam ran his hand over his face and wished he was more surprised by this. "So, you've been talking to a wanted man online?"

"Our team wasn't investigating him," Seth said. His chin rose. "And considering my own past, I really related to his decision to drop off-the-grid. I thought maybe I could talk him into trusting us. Besides, I didn't know where in the world he was and we never met in person or had a real conversation until Hannah was kidnapped and he asked me for my help."

Renner nodded, confirming Seth's account. Liam didn't like it. But he believed it.

Then again, if Liam himself hadn't been so stubbornly independent, would Seth have trusted him with this earlier?

"Okay, and why do people think you're an Imposter?" Liam asked.

To his surprise, Seth blushed slightly. "Because I am. Sort of."

"You're what?" Liam felt his voice rise to a roar. Of all the possible answers, he hadn't been expecting that one. Other patrons swiveled their eyes their way for an instant, and then back to their own business. Liam forced his voice to drop. "Care to explain?"

"I went undercover," Seth said. "Without authorization. But I'm a hacker, right? Not a cop. I told you these new Imposters are decentralized. They have no leader. Nobody is in charge. I was monitoring their group, saw the opportunity and I took it. But that still doesn't mean I know what's going on more than any other person on that site. I found out about the attack on the boat about two minutes before it went down. It's all splinter cells."

Liam ran his hand over the back of his neck. "Does this mean you can shut them down?"

"Hypothetically," Seth said. "But it would take some serious computer power, a way to get into the code behind their main system and at least three of me."

So that would be a no.

"Why did you sell Kelly and I out at the church?" Liam asked.

"Because somebody tracked you to Tatlow's Used Books when Kelly's phone came online," Seth said. "I was in the area. I wanted to catch a glimpse of the family from afar, even if I couldn't be there. I saw you leave a baby in the apartment with Mack and Iris. Then I saw the Imposters show up. They were going to storm the building and put the kid in danger. More importantly, there was no indication the Imposters even knew about the baby. It seemed like the smartest way to rescue her. I figured there wouldn't be that many of them, I could lure them to the church, get there first and then you'd do your thing and take them down. When we were outnumbered, I improvised, did what I had to do to maintain my cover and then took the car you were in out remotely. Which, unfortunately, took a lot longer than I expected."

"Which is why people shouldn't go off-the-grid and try to take the law into their own hands," Liam said. He felt his eyes narrow. "They paid you off."

"You think I cared about the money?" Seth said. "I wanted the electronic transfer to back-channel into the cell phone of whoever took the money. I've managed to pinpoint it down to a general geographic area near Lake Simcoe, which tells us practically nothing."

"Which tells us a lot," Liam said. "Because Noah and Holly, who fired the shots that took down the original Imposters, are getting married in that area tomorrow. Might give these new Imposters a nice opportunity to achieve both their goals of getting Renner to hand over the nonexistent decryption key and get revenge on my team on Christmas Eve."

So Seth had slid backward and foolishly tried to solve crime his old, independent and vigilante way. And Renner was so focused on protecting the woman and child he loved he went off-the-grid and let his emotion overwhelm his judgment.

But there was still one piece of the picture he didn't have.

Liam leaned his elbows on the table and fixed his eyes on Renner.

"I believe you love my daughter and my granddaughter," Liam said. "I believe you'd do anything to protect them. So I'll ask you, one more time, man to man—if there was never a master-key decoding device, how did you break that code?"

Something hardened in Renner's face, like an invisible steel trap dropping over his eyes, locking Liam out.

Something jangled behind him. Liam turned and glanced down the back hallway. There stood Iris, half-hidden in the shadows and yet with an unmistakable smile on her face.

"Come on," Liam said softly, gesturing for Renner to follow him. "There's someone you need to meet."

The three of them stood and walked through the diner and out into the back hallway. There by the open back door stood Mack, with baby Pip in his arms.

Her little eyes opened wide. Her arms stretched out toward them as a happy squeal slipped from her lips. He heard a sob escape from the back of Renner's throat and for the first time since they'd met, Liam watched all bravado fall from Renner's eyes.

"Is that…" Two words were all Renner got out before emotion swallowed up the rest.

"Your daughter?" Liam said softly, feeling something well up in his own voice. "Yeah, that's your little girl."

He watched as Renner ran down the hallway, swept the baby up into his arms and cradled her to his chest. Prayers of thanks poured from the man's lips as he held his baby girl for the very first time.

Liam turned away, feeling tears brush the corners of his own eyes.

He looked at Seth, Mack and Iris.

"Renner's telling the truth when he says he doesn't have a master-key decryption device," Liam said. "I wasn't sure what I believed about that. But that man would give absolutely anything for his wife and baby."

"What does that mean?" Seth asked.

"We have to get creative if we want to get Hannah and Kelly back alive." Liam stretched out his hand for Seth's cell phone, and when the hacker gave it to him, Liam opened a new message and typed.

It's me, Liam. I'm alive. I need your help. I need a team.

He needed a family.

Kelly was lying on the cold concrete floor in the darkness, surrounded by the smell of hay and earth, feeling the warmth of Hannah leaning against her back. She had no idea how many hours it had been since she'd been kidnapped in the park. They'd been in the car for at least four, she guessed, before the vehicle had pulled up outside what appeared to be large abandoned stables in the middle of nowhere, surrounded by nothing but snow and trees.

Then they'd been shoved into a narrow stall where they were lying on the floor, napping in fits and starts, slowly working their gags away from their mouths and pulling at the bonds holding each other's hands whenever whatever Imposter was on sentry duty walked out of view. Although clenching her jaw had helped Kelly some, it'd still taken her a long time to work it free enough to speak, especially as they were being watched.

Mostly she'd prayed. She prayed for her and Hannah's safety, and for Renner and Pip. She prayed that every single Imposter would be stopped and caught, no matter where they were in the world.

And she prayed for Liam, asking God to clear his name, guard his life and give him an amazing future.

"I'm sorry, Mom," Hannah's muffled voice behind her let her know her daughter was awake. "This is all my fault."

"Stop saying that," Kelly whispered firmly. Hannah had been trying to apologize ever since she'd been able to speak. But between the gag still in her mouth and the tiny windows of time they had to talk, Kelly still didn't know why. "None of this is your fault."

Footsteps drew nearer as their latest guard grew closer. Kelly was still. Her fingers squeezed Hannah's. The guard passed. The women went back to trying to loosen each other's bonds. She'd searched the floor the best she could for anything sharp she could loop the bonds around to rip them free but hadn't found anything yet. When Liam had told her how to break free from gags and bonds, he hadn't explained just how long it could take.

"Listen, I'm sorry I never told you that Liam was your father," Kelly said. "He's a good man. He took care of Pip and me. He would've loved you."

"Did he love you?" Hannah asked.

Kelly swallowed hard and sudden tears rushed to her eyes, as she finally let her heart acknowledge the truth she hadn't for far too long. "He did. The very best he could."

*And I loved him.* Liam had been the love of her life.

Voices rose from elsewhere in the stables. Footsteps stomped down the floor toward them. Something crashed. She looked up. Three masked Imposters stood in front of them. Two held guns. The third grabbed them each by an arm and yanked them up.

"Come on." The voice was male and young. "Time for a show."

They were marched down the hall into a large room with a huge double door. In the middle of the room sat a folding table with a couple of chairs and multiple laptops. She counted about a dozen masked and armed men standing around it, but it wasn't until the crowd parted that she saw the one unmasked man standing in their midst.

It was Seth.

"Hey." Seth waved nervously in their direction. There was a small bright red and cylindrical memory drive in his hand. "So, funny story. I managed to track Renner down and get my hands on Renner's supersecret master-key decryption device. Figured out where these guys were holding you, based on some pretty savvy old-school detective work, came here and offered to trade your lives for the decipher key. Turns out this disorganized gang isn't big on making deals or loyalty. Mob rule, eh?"

*Old-school detective work.* The words jolted Kelly's heart, sending hope beating through it. Did that mean Liam had helped him? Was Liam there?

One man ordered Seth into a chair. Another held a gun to the back of his head. Voices rose as Imposters argued amongst themselves. It sounded as if they'd agreed on forcing Seth to hack into the Bank of Canada to prove his decipher key was legit and would shoot Kelly, Hannah and Seth himself if he couldn't. Specifically, they wanted him to go after the $888 million that the bank had collected from closed and unclaimed bank accounts across the country and was now holding in reserve as it awaited the rightful heirs and owners of that money to come claim it. Although, the Imposters couldn't quite agree on how much of those millions he should steal or how many accounts that money should be transferred into. Seth looked down at the laptop and sighed. A weary look crossed his face.

"Believe it or not," he said, "this is not the first or even fourth time I've been stuck in a chair, in front of a laptop, at gunpoint. Twice, I've even had a bomb strapped to me." The hacker's eyes closed. "God, this has gotta be the last time I go through this," he prayed out loud. "I'm sorry for all the stupid choices that led me here. So if You're there, and I get out of this alive, please help me make whatever changes I need to to make sure this never happens to me again."

The honesty and simplicity of his prayer made something catch in her throat.

"You have fifteen minutes to break in," an Imposter said, jabbing his finger at the screen. "After that, I start shooting hostages."

Kelly's eyes scanned the barn, looking at one Imposter after another, hoping against hope to spot Liam's strong form under one of the masks. She couldn't see him anywhere. And yet somehow she knew, with every beat of her heart, that Liam was close, and one way or another he would find her.

*Help us, Lord! Please get us out of this alive!*

Then she saw the rough metal hook behind her on the wall, bent and rusty with age. She backed up toward it. Seth stuck the memory drive into one of the laptops and started typing. His hands shook and his face was pale, and suddenly she realized Seth didn't actually have the decoding device. The hacker had been faking it and now he was going to die for it. Kelly's bound hands snagged on the hook. Desperate prayers poured through her.

"No! It was me!" The muffled words ripped through Hannah's gag in a panicked cry. "It was me! It was me!"

What was she doing? Instinctively Kelly started toward her daughter, but her snagged hands held her back. A masked Imposter grabbed Hannah with one hand and yanked the gag from her mouth.

"It was me!" Hannah shouted. "It was me. There was no master-key decryption device. There never was. I hacked the code."

Hannah gasped a panicked breath. The Imposters's voices moved in a babble of confusion around her.

"Stop this now," Hannah said. "Please. Let him go. There was no decipher key. It was only me." Hannah spun back and her eyes met Kelly's. "I've been hacking codes for Renner for a long time, even though I didn't have security clearance. I didn't want to have to work a high-pressure government-contractor job like that. I saw what it did to Renner. So I thought he could sneak me codes every now and then and I'd decode them, and no one would have to know. But then it got too big and things went wrong. I'm so sorry, Mom. Renner was trying to protect me."

Hannah's chin rose. Pride mingled with the fear in her gaze. And Kelly saw what her heart had been hiding from her all this time. Liam's voice floated in the back of her mind.

*Foolish kids in love don't always make the best decisions.*

"Stop!" Kelly called through her gag. "Please!"

But it was too late. The masked men were already forcing Hannah into another chair and turning another laptop toward her. Arguments rose among the masked men about their new plan. Some decided they'd shoot whichever one didn't break into the Bank of Canada first. Others thought they should both be shot if they didn't start the online heist within fifteen minutes.

The metal hook pressed against Kelly's fingers. Absolutely no one was looking at her and again Liam's voice hovered in the back of her mind, reminding her to never miss an opportunity to use distraction.

She gritted her teeth and prayed that she was physically and emotionally strong enough to do what she was about to do. Then she lunged forward, pain shooting through her arms as she felt the already weakened bonds rip away from her wrists. Her hands fell free. She turned and ran, bolting back down the hallway.

A doorway loomed ahead, showing a glimmer of pale gray morning light. Shouting sounded behind her. She didn't let herself look back. Instead, she burst through the barn door and out into the snow, and ran up the hill in front of her.

Fields of white filled her vision on all sides. There was no Liam, no rescue, no buildings, nothing but endless snow with a fringe of trees on the horizon. She was all alone. Liam wasn't there. He hadn't come to save her.

Then she saw the truck, white and dingy with snow, sitting at the crest of the hill, half-hidden in the trees. She ran for it.

# THIRTEEN

"I think maybe we've got a runner," Renner said. He leaned on the steering wheel with one hand and peered through the binoculars. Seth had pointed out that the same kind of electronic tracking methods he'd used to locate the stables could be used against them in reverse. So they hadn't so much as used a cell phone since reaching the location, let alone any high-tech tracking devices. It had been ten long hours since Kelly had been kidnapped and Liam still wasn't sure what he thought of his newfound son-in-law. Renner was reckless, selfish and stubborn. When Liam had finally gotten Renner to confess that Hannah had broken the code, that he'd been secretly passing her codes for months and he'd let rumors of some magical decoding device proliferate to keep from putting a target on her back, Liam suddenly felt the desire to knock Renner and Hannah's heads together for being so reckless, along with the competing urge to hug them and tell them that he understood. Maybe that was what being a father was like. Also, Liam kind of liked him.

"Maybe?" Liam asked.

"Definitely," Renner said. "Headed straight at us."

"Let me see." Liam stuck out his hand, Renner passed him

the binoculars and in a single glance, Liam knew what he was looking at. "It's Kelly!"

He tossed the binoculars at Renner and leaped out. "Cover me!"

"Cover you?" Renner shouted. "You're out in the open running through an open field! If someone comes after you, you're a sitting duck!"

Yeah, but so was Kelly. And he was going to be her cover and protection.

Liam raced down the hill, running toward Kelly with all his might. Yes, he knew that running right into danger was breaking one of his father's most important rules of staying alive. But for the first time since he'd first kissed Kelly's lips and asked her to marry him, over twenty years ago, Liam knew he was heading in the right direction with nothing holding him back. He raced through the snow, pushing his body toward her, as he watched her run for him.

"Liam!" Her voice called for him, the sound muffled—he could see she was gagged.

"Kelly!" He felt her name explode through his core, like it was coming from somewhere deeper than the breath in his lungs. "I'm coming!"

They pressed closer. His heart ached with each step. Then he reached her and swept her up into his arms. He ripped the gag free from her mouth and kissed her, feeling her arms lock around his neck.

"I love you." The words flew from Liam's lips the moment their kiss ended. "I'm in love with you, Kelly, and I have been forever."

"I know," Kelly said. "Because I love you, too."

"Incoming!" Renner shouted.

Liam swung Kelly behind him, positioning himself between her and the approaching Imposter. Liam fired, catching the man in the arm and robbing his ability to aim and fire back. The Imposter fell into the snow.

Then Liam wrapped one arm around her shoulders and ran with her back to the truck.

"Hannah's in the barn," she shouted to Renner as Liam yanked open the door and they tumbled into the passenger seat, and he pulled Kelly onto his lap. "She and Seth are both hacking." She glanced at Liam. "Did you know?"

"That she's the hacker and there was no decipher key?" Liam asked. "Yeah, Renner told me, eventually."

"Well, Hannah told the Imposters," she said.

Renner took in a sharp breath. Kelly spun her head toward him.

"If I was the kind of person who hit people I'd have a hard time not smacking you right now!" she said. "You violated security clearance and broke the law by letting Hannah even see high-security codes, let alone crack one for you. You put Hannah and Pip in danger. You kept the truth from me!"

Her words tapered off as Renner's face went pale.

"I love your daughter," he said. "I did what I thought I needed to do to protect her."

She let out a long breath.

"I know," she said. "And I forgive you. Now, we've got to focus on saving her."

She brushed her lips across Liam's cheek in a fleeting kiss and then she climbed in the back seat.

"We've got to get in there," she said. "They told Hannah and Seth if they don't break into the Bank of Canada and rob it in fifteen minutes they're going to start shooting people, and we're down to like six minutes now. What's the old-school way of stopping killer hackers in a barn?"

Liam and Renner exchanged a glance. Then Liam nodded and Renner revved his engine.

"Buckle your seat belt," Liam said.

Kelly did so. Then she felt Liam reach back and squeeze her hand.

"How far away are Hannah and Seth from the barn door?" Renner asked.

"Maybe thirty feet?" she said. "They're seated at a table."

"Anyone want to get out before we do this?" Liam asked. "Not going to pretend crashing a truck through a barn door isn't dangerous."

"I definitely won't be any safer running down the hill without cover than staying in here," Kelly said, "especially if they open fire on us. Hannah's in there, and I'm the only one who knows what the layout is. I'm not staying behind."

"Neither am I," Renner said. "Hannah's your daughter, but she's also my wife."

"Stay low," Liam said, "and brace for impact."

Renner hit the gas. Liam's hand tightened on hers for a fleeting moment, then let go, and she braced herself against the back of his seat. The truck flew down the hill, plowing through the snow and picking up speed as it went. Her prayers mingled with Liam's as the barn grew closer.

Forty feet. Thirty feet. Twenty feet. Ten.

Then Renner hit the brakes and the truck spun sideways in a controlled skid as it crashed through the barn doors. Instinctively, she unbuckled her seat belt and ducked low beneath the seat as the sounds of shouting, crashing, banging and gunfire surrounded her.

"Try to rescue Hannah and Seth if you can," Liam shouted. "Renner and I will take out the Imposters."

Doors slammed, she looked up and found herself alone in the truck. She scrambled into the driver's seat and watched the scene unfolding around her in the stables, like something out of a dance choreography, as both Liam and Renner moved in tandem to take cover, surge forward, fire and then fall back, taking out one Imposter after another with a skill and precision that took her breath away. Liam was clearly leading, with Renner following close behind, as if the men had known each other for years instead of hours.

*Thank You, God, that Liam didn't give up law enforcement for me. This is who he is. This is where he belongs.*

Kelly scanned the room and spotted Hannah and Seth, crouched side by side, underneath the table. They were both still typing madly. The truck's keys hung from the ignition. Kelly started the engine and inched through the chaos toward them, placing the truck between the hackers and the battle, even as she heard the sound of bullets pinging off the other side of the truck. She shoved open the back door.

"Get in!" she shouted.

They crawled toward her, staying low and dragging their laptops with them.

"Everybody good?" Kelly called.

"Yeah," Hannah said.

The clacking of keys grew louder. She glanced back. Seth and Hannah were both still typing, sitting on the floor behind the seats.

"What are you doing?" Kelly called.

"We've hacked inside the Imposters's online system," Hannah said, without looking up.

"I knew if they made us hack they'd accidentally let us in," Seth said. His eyes were equally locked on the screen. "This is the opportunity we've been waiting for."

"You're able to stop their threat to take down power grids on New Year's Eve?" Kelly asked.

A smile curved on Hannah's lips.

"We're able to take down everything," Hannah said. "Every single thing is going down and for good."

"Everything?" Kelly asked.

"We're in their membership database right now," Seth said. "Back-channeling Imposters from their online signatures to find their real names, locations and addresses. Basically, everything the police will need to find each and every one of them, and take down their organization."

Hannah laughed under her breath. Despite the chaos around them, the light in Hannah's eyes was pure determination and joy. After all their months apart, had Hannah and Renner even seen each other in the chaos, let alone managed to say anything? She didn't know. But here her daughter was, taking out criminals online while her husband was outside doing the same in his own way. This was who her daughter was. This was the woman she and Liam had made, and who'd been raised by the incredible and loving couple who'd adopted her. This was who she was meant to be.

"When we get out of here, I want you and Renner to come forward," Kelly said. Hannah looked up and met her eyes. "I know it'll be hard and scary, there might be ramifications and it'll change your lives. But look at you. You're amazing. You're happy. You're incredible. You love this, don't you? I don't want you to hide from who you are."

Hannah nodded slightly, then she looked back to the screen.

Too late, Kelly heard the truck door wrenched open to her left. She looked up to see one of the Imposters, hulking, huge and masked, looming over her. She screamed, yelling to Hannah and Seth to stay down and safe, as she felt the masked Imposter cuffing her hard against her temple and yanking her from the truck. She fell and her body smacked hard against the cold stable floor, knocking the breath from her lungs. Then she felt the Imposter dragging her across the floor, toward the stable's stalls. Kelly kicked and screamed, thrashing and fighting against her attacker with every ounce of strength in her body. Her eyes searched in vain for Liam in the chaos. She couldn't see him anywhere. Desperate tears filled her eyes.

Then she heard Liam's voice, like a deep and guttural roar. "Get your hands off her!"

And it was like her attacker was literally lifted off the ground, as Liam yanked the man off her and tossed him to the side. The Imposter scrambled away and disappeared back into the chaos.

She looked up and there Liam stood, protecting her and shielding her, placing himself between her and those who wanted to hurt her.

"Are you okay?" Liam asked. She nodded, as he pulled her

up into his chest, placing one strong hand at the small of her back and keeping his weapon at the ready with the other. He led her backward into one of the stalls.

"How did you find me?" she asked. "How did you even know I was in danger?"

He looked down at her and something deepened in his gaze.

"Sweetheart, I'm always going to be looking out for you."

A shiver ran through her body that seemed to seep deep into her core.

She glanced past him. Renner was pinned down in a corner fighting off several Imposters at once. Others were now advancing on the truck, where Seth and Hannah were still hunkered down in the back.

"We have to help them!" she said. "They're sitting ducks!"

But even as she spoke, she heard a chorus of shouts and watched as Liam's team members Jess and Noah, along with almost a dozen other men and women, stormed through the entrances like a precision team and quickly moved to secure the scene. For a moment they just watched as the team moved in, covering Renner's back, protecting the truck and arresting Imposters. Then she felt a long sigh move through Liam. He holstered his weapon.

"I texted a few friends last night," Liam said. He wrapped both arms around her, and nestled her into his chest. "They've got this."

"Who are they?" Wonder filled her voice. "What is this?"

"The three other detectives helping Jess and Noah round up and cuff suspects are Chloe and Trent Henry and Trent's brother, Jacob," he said "Chloe's provincial and the other two are federal."

"I thought Jess left for her honeymoon," she said.

"So did I," Liam said. "And Noah's getting married this morning. Then again, that's his bride, Holly, helping Seth and Hannah."

"So they're skipping the tradition of not seeing each other the day of the wedding?" she asked.

His laugh was husky with emotion. "Looks like it."

It looked like the threat was over as one by one, Imposters were disarmed, unmasked and handcuffed.

"Hannah and Seth are taking down the Imposter network online," Kelly said. "They're gathering data of who each Imposter is in real life, so local law enforcement can round them up."

Liam breathed a prayer of thanks. "Well, we've got some of the best law-enforcement people I know in the room to help with that. Wouldn't be surprised if warrants are issued before they even leave the barn."

"I encouraged Hannah that she and Renner should come forward, face the consequences and admit she's the one who hacked the code," Kelly said.

"Considering Holly's history with the military, as a former whistleblower, she's the right person to help them with that." Liam watched the scene unfolding for a few more moments. Then he gestured to a young man kneeling over some of the wounded Imposters, joined by a second who was helping carry the Imposter that Liam had shot outside in the snow.

"That's Trent's brother Nick, who's also a corporal, and his other brother, Max. He's a paramedic," Liam said. "I'm glad they're here. I always try very hard at making sure nobody dies on my watch."

Liam continued pointing out people in the small and efficient tactical team, as they moved through the room, booking criminals, securing weapons and even tending to the Imposters's wounds. Then Kelly's heart caught in her throat as Renner broke through the crowd and ran for Hannah, and she remembered that despite all that had just happened, they probably still hadn't greeted each other. Renner swept his wife up into his arms and kissed her deeply. Hannah clutched her husband, his arms enveloped her and they held each other as Liam's friends in law enforcement moved around them, swiftly locking down the scene.

Then the small but mighty cry of a little voice seemed to pierce through the din, and Kelly watched as Hannah and Renner turned together in unison and ran toward Mack as he carried baby Pip through the doorway.

Liam's arm tightened around Kelly and they watched as the small family cried and hugged each other in the middle of the stable.

*Thank You, God. For bringing mother, father and child back together.* She leaned against Liam's chest, feeling his heart beat against her cheek. *And thank You for bringing Liam back to me.*

"Come with me," Liam said. He stepped back and grabbed her hand. "Just for a moment, please. Unless you want to stay with Renner and Hannah?"

She looked over at the small and elated family.

"Nah, I think they're good without me, right now," she said. "I'll talk to them later."

Hannah and Renner were going to have to make some difficult decisions about their future. While Kelly would love and support them whatever they decided, right now, the young couple needed to rely on each other and make their own path. Liam tugged lightly on her hand. She hesitated.

"But don't they need you to coordinate this?" she asked.

"Coordinate what?" He chuckled. "Sweetheart, I'm dead and I was never here. Clearly a bunch of random somebodies got an anonymous tip. Probably from an untraceable cell phone, I'm guessing." He looked around the room again and his head shook in amazement, as if finally taking in the scope of all that had happened. "I don't even know how to begin to explain a random group of federal, provincial and local cops, plus some military, a paramedic and even a handful of civilians all showing up for a joint operation."

She did, and looking at the unshed tears that glinted in the corners of his eyes, she knew he did, too.

For a man with no family, he certainly had a big one.

She followed him out of the stables, watching as he greeted person after person on the way out, with subtle nods and gestures that spoke volumes. They stepped outside and bright sunshine streamed down the snow toward them.

"One of them will eventually step up, take charge of how the cover story gets told, follow up on all the arrests and sort this whole thing out," Liam said. "Probably Chloe. Normally it would be someone on my team, but Jess still has her honeymoon and both Noah and Mack have weddings to worry about. I'm not actually sure how long Noah and Holly have until they're supposed to get hitched. Hopefully, we'll make sure they make it to the church on time." His voice trailed off and he looked down at her hand holding his.

"I still need a date for two weddings," he added. "With Noah and Holly's later this morning, it'll probably be a matter of sneaking in to watch from the shadows again. But Mack and Iris are getting married on New Year's Eve..."

His voice trailed off. It was a silence that seemed to spread, thick and deep like a wave of warmth through the cold, empty morning air. Somehow she knew it wasn't a silence he wanted her to speak into, so she waited.

"I don't want you to go," Liam said eventually. "I want you to stay here, by my side, with me, as I fight my way out of whatever burlap sack has descended around me and figure out how to prove to the world I'm alive. But, if you want to go, with Hannah and Renner, I will go with you and stay by your side however long it takes to figure this out. Don't get me wrong, if it was up to me I'd stay here while the Imposter network is taken down, trust Seth to untangle what they did to my online profile and work with my friends in law enforcement to figure out how best to prove the video is fake and confirm the fact I'm actually alive. That would be my first choice of what to do." He took a deep breath, took her other hand in his and raised both up to his lips. He looked at her over their knuckles. "But I don't ever want to lose you again, Kelly. No matter what happens next, that's nonnegotiable."

"You won't lose me," she said.

A grin brushed his lips. "Promise?"

"Promise, promise."

His smile spread to his eyes until it seemed to illuminate his entire face.

"You have no idea how much I love you," he said.

"I love you, too," she said. She pulled her hands from his, reached up and wrapped them around his neck. "And I'm not going anywhere. As much as I love Hannah and Renner, this is their fight to figure out together. But for me, I belong with you. It's as simple as that."

She kissed his smiling mouth, for a long moment reveling in the warmth, the strength of his arms and the security of having him there. Then suddenly, he stepped back and a look crossed his face that she'd come to think of as his detective brain activating.

"Some things are actually simple, aren't they?" he said. He closed his eyes and whispered a prayer for wisdom and courage. Then he took her hand in his. "Come on, it's time I did this the easy way."

Baffled but trusting him, too, she followed him back into the stables. All the Imposters had been carted away and the crowd had reduced to just a small handful of people standing around talking, including Hannah and Renner and the members of Liam's team.

"Hey, Seth!" Liam pointed his finger at the hacker. "How long will it take to do your thing online to prove that I'm really me, I'm not dead and the video was a deep fake?"

"Anywhere between twenty-four hours to a few days," Seth said. "The fact Hannah and I hacked the Imposter network will certainly make it easier. She unraveled the whole system and tracked every single Imposter's real identity and location." He cast their daughter an admiring glance filled with respect.

"Honestly, she did like seventy percent of the work. I know I told you it would take at least three of me to take their network down, but your daughter seriously hacked circles around me. Maybe I'm getting old, too."

Hannah pressed her lips together to hide a smile that perfectly mirrored the one on Liam's face. Kelly suspected Liam had never heard Seth give anyone such high praise before.

"Now, I wasn't planning on working through Christmas," Seth went on. "But if it'll help you get your life back on track faster, I'll be on it around the clock."

Liam's Adam's apple bobbed. "I trust you to do your thing," he said finally. "In the meantime, can I assume there's something in this place that will record a video?"

"Many somethings," Seth said and yanked a cell phone from his pocket. "Will this do?"

"You're the tech guy," Liam said. "Again, I trust you to make it work. Just point at where you want me to stand. All I care is that there's nobody else in the frame and the light's good enough to see me clearly."

Seth nodded and then pointed to a patch of wall. Liam brushed a kiss over Kelly's cheek, then he let go of her hand and stepped to where Seth had pointed. Seth waved at him like a man directing traffic and Liam took a few steps in one direction and then another, until Seth held up his hand to show him he'd reached whatever specific square inch of floor the hacker apparently thought had the best light.

"Okay," Liam said. "Do your thing."

Seth held up his phone. "It's going."

A deep breath rose and fell in Liam's chest. He whispered a silent prayer.

"Hey, so I'm Liam Bearsmith, RCMP," he said. "If you know me, you know I'm not much for words, I don't like the spotlight and I'm not big on being noticed. I prefer to just quietly go about serving my country, with a lot of very amazing women and men in uniform."

He took another deep breath and glanced around the room like he was at risk of losing his words for a moment. She flashed him a thumbs-up. He smiled and looked back at the camera.

"Two things." Liam's chest rose. "Number one, clearly I'm not dead. I certainly wasn't killed by a younger, stronger and better-looking version of me. That's a deep-fake video thing that the Imposters rigged up to wreck my life. So now, I've got to clear my name, of my own murder, and prove I'm me, which is probably going to be a bit tricky. Secondly, I'm incredibly thankful to everyone who came out and said nice things about me after you thought I died. That meant a lot and I hope nobody feels weird about it now that I'm not actually dead.

"But I don't want anyone putting me on a pedestal. Or ever thinking you have to be perfect to be a good cop. On one of my first assignments, I fell in love with a witness, had an inappropriate romantic relationship and fathered a child I didn't even know about. I'm sure now that I've just blurted it out, there'll be a lot of questions I'll have to answer about that, too. But, bottom line, I'm done hiding. From my past and from this trumped-up murder charge. I'm going to go out living my life now and we'll see how things work themselves out. Okay, thanks and bye."

He nodded to Seth. "You can put that online?"

Seth nodded. "Yeah, I can even make you sound good."

"Thanks," Liam said and blew out a long breath. Then he glanced around the room at his friends. "I figure after the wedding we can sit around and strategize something. Except for you, Jess. I appreciate you being here but expect you to hurry up and get to your honeymoon. Same to you, too, Noah and Holly. Go put on your fancy clothes and get married. I'll see you there." He looked around. "Oh, and Chloe, there's a really great provincial officer in the St. Lawrence River district named Jake Marlie, like the hockey team, who deserves the opportunity for advancement." Liam yawned suddenly and then chuckled. "Also, I might need a nap. I haven't really slept in a couple of days."

Kelly walked over and slipped one arm around his waist. Liam leaned down and rested his head on her shoulder and she brushed a kiss over the top of his head.

"You okay?" she asked.

"Better than okay," Liam said.

"What happens now?" she asked.

He tilted his head and looked at her. "No idea, sweetheart, but whatever it is we're facing it together."

# FOURTEEN

"Five, four, three, two, one—happy New Year!"

A chorus of celebratory voices shouted around Kelly and Liam. Streamers and balloons cascaded down from the ceiling of the downtown Toronto community center. The lights flickered briefly.

She cast a glance at the tall and handsome man in the black tuxedo and bow tie who sat beside her on the fabric-draped chairs at the back of Mack and Iris's wedding-reception party. His eyebrows rose. The lights stayed on. He chuckled under his breath, then reached over, grabbed her hand and squeezed it.

"It's all over," he said softly. "There won't be any blackouts, the Imposters were all arrested and their network is gone. We're safe."

"I know." She smiled.

The last week had been incredible. After all those months she'd spent stuck alongside Hannah in the quagmire of uncertainty, it was like everything had happened at once. Over three hundred Imposters had been arrested by local law enforcement all over the world, thanks to information Hannah and Seth had gleaned from the internet. Some had just been detained and questioned, but others, like those who'd hijacked the boat and kidnapped her, Hannah and Liam, were now behind bars awaiting their trials. Despite Liam's reassurances that Seth didn't need to work over Christmas, thanks to Seth and Hannah's combined computer power, it had taken less than seventy-two hours to prove Liam's death had been faked and restore his fingerprints to file. His welcome-back email from a superior officer had added that Liam would be facing a disciplinary panel regarding his initial relationship with Kelly, all those years ago. Rumor had it that the worst Liam was facing was a slap on the wrist. But he'd assured her that whatever the consequences, it was worth it to be able go through life with Kelly and their family by his side.

More importantly, Hannah and Renner had decided to stay in Canada and come clean to the military about the true circumstances surrounding how the code was cracked, and how Hannah was the person who'd really done the decoding. Nerve-racking, Kelly knew, and the young couple were still facing a lot of uncertainty about what they'd be doing next. But they'd both been considering finding ways to use their skills to serve their country, and it seemed Liam's friends would be helping them find their way.

And Liam, Kelly, Hannah, Renner and baby Pip had been able to spend their first Christmas as a family together.

Kelly glanced down at the little baby girl, clad in a black-and-white polka-dot dress with a big red bow, now curled up asleep in the crook of Liam's left arm.

"I can't believe she's sleeping through this," Liam said.

"I can't believe they've finally agreed on her name," Kelly said. She rolled it around on her tongue. "Alexandra Maria Katrina Phillips."

"That's a lot of name for a tiny baby." Her grandfather smiled softly. "I reckon I'll still just call her Pip."

"I think I will, too."

She looked out over the dance floor at where Renner and Hannah stood, with their arms wrapped around each other and lost in each other's eyes. Whatever consequences they were facing for their actions didn't begin to dim their joy at being reunited.

"Were we ever that young, foolish and recklessly in love?" she wondered out loud.

"I know I still am," Liam said.

He leaned forward and she thought for a moment he was about to kiss her. But then his eyes darted to the side as if spotting something in his peripheral vision. He pulled back.

"Stop hovering, Seth," Liam said. "I can tell you're antsy to say something."

She turned and sure enough Seth was standing a few feet away, half looking at them and partly looking at his feet. "I—I didn't want to interrupt..."

"Just spit it out," Liam said. But his smile was warm.

Seth looked at Kelly. "I was just wondering if you'd told him your news yet, because I want to tell him my news and..."

His voice trailed off as Liam's keen eyes narrowed, looking from Seth to Kelly and back again, before finally fixing on Kelly. "What did you do?"

"I enrolled in university to finally finish my criminology degree," she said.

"Really?" Liam's eyes widened. "I'm so proud of you and happy for you."

She felt a flush rise to her cheeks. "Well, I figured it's never too late to have a fresh start at life."

His gaze lingered on hers a long moment. Then his smile quirked at the edges and he glanced at Seth. Liam's eyes widened. "Don't tell me you're looking for a career in some kind of crime fighting or law enforcement, too?"

"I'm trying to," Seth admitted, shuffling from one foot to the other. "It'll mean getting a pardon for my hacking past. But it's time for me to go legit and actually use my skills to make a difference in the world. I mean, after all, the great Liam Bearsmith called me his friend."

Liam laughed, then he let go of Kelly's hand long enough to reach for Seth's and shake it. "Well, I'm proud of you, too, and I'll have your back, whatever you need."

Somewhere out in the crowd he heard Iris's voice announcing she was about to throw the wedding bouquet.

"Go on," Liam said, shooing Seth. "You don't want to miss this."

The hacker hesitated, then he frowned slightly. "You asked me to look into who changed Kelly's witness-protection file—"

"It was my father, wasn't it?" Liam asked, cutting him off.

Seth nodded. "I'm sorry."

"No, thank you," Liam said. "Now go enjoy the party, friend."

She had the distinct impression Seth was about to say something mushy or goofy. Then he turned and disappeared into the crowd.

Liam's hand found Kelly's again. He ran his fingers over hers gently.

"How long have you known?" Kelly asked.

"Since the moment I actually let myself think about it," Liam said. "He knew how deeply I loved you and that I'd asked you to marry me, because I told him. I don't know what strings he pulled to keep us apart or how he convinced himself he was doing the right thing. I know he was very badly wounded by his relationship with my mother and wanted to protect me. He loved me, but he was wrong. He wanted the very best for me. But he was wrong." He leaned forward—so did she—and his lips brushed lightly against hers. "I've found what's best for me. Twice."

"We both did," she said.

His free hand slipped to the side of her face and he kissed her with a confidence and strength that blew away whatever they'd felt for each other all those years ago. The sound of people chanting and cheering swept around them.

Suddenly she felt Liam's shoulders straighten as if sensing danger. He let go of her. His hand shot up protectively and snatched a projectile flying toward them out of the air, before it could threaten her and the baby.

A ripple of laughter filled the room. She watched Liam's face as he looked down at what he'd just caught.

It was a dazzling bouquet of white and purple flowers. For the first time in her life, Kelly saw the strong and mighty Liam blush and she felt a matching heat fill her cheeks. He raised the huge array of flowers like a shield between them and the crowd of people now looking their way.

Kelly giggled. "You just caught Iris's wedding bouquet."

Liam laughed. "Yeah, looks like I did."

"You think she threw it to you on purpose?" Kelly whispered.

"Wouldn't put it past her," he said softly. "But I didn't know she had the aim."

They paused another moment. Neither of them spoke. She risked a quick glance around. The entire room had turned to look at them.

"You think I should tell them I'm already engaged?" Liam asked.

"Are you now?"

"Well, I seem to remember asking you to marry me two decades ago," Liam said. "And you did say yes."

"Well, maybe you should ask me again," she said.

The smile that she felt curling on her lips seemed to match the curve of his own.

"Kelly Marshall," Liam said, "mother of my unbelievably brilliant daughter, grandmother of my insanely cute granddaughter, love of my life and the only woman I've ever wanted to spend my life with, you are going to marry me, right?"

She laughed. "Yes, Liam, of course I'll marry you."

Then their lips met in a kiss and the flowers fell to the side, as they heard the room explode in applause around them.

\* \* \* \* \*

Dear Reader,

Thank you so much for joining me for my twentieth Love Inspired Suspense! Huge thanks goes to my incredible editor Emily Rodmell, who guided, encouraged, pushed, refined and helped me through every book and along every step of the way.

I had so much fun finding a partner for Liam Bearsmith. I fell in love with Liam when he appeared on the train in *Rescuing His Secret Child* and he was such a fun character to write. By my count this is both Liam and Seth's sixth book, tying them for book appearances with both Chloe and Trent Henry.

Some of you asked why I haven't written Seth a romance yet. To be honest, I didn't think Seth's ready to be anyone's husband or father yet. He appeared as a dubious character in two books before joining Liam's team, and while I love Seth deeply, I want to make sure that when he does find love, he's ready to step up.

Thank you as always to all of you for all your letters and for sharing this journey with me,

*Maggie*

# Subscribe and fall in love with a Mills & Boon series today!

You'll be among the first to read stories delivered to your door monthly and enjoy great savings.

WE SIMPLY LOVE ROMANCE

# MILLS & BOON